Tails in

the West

FOR LITERARY HEAT

www.BarbarianSpy.com

BarbarianSpy
Jindalee St
Toronto, NSW 2283
Australia

Tails in the West

by habu

Table of Contents

Introduction

With *Tails in the West*, habu's series of gay male "Tails" anthologies moves to the area encompassing what is thought of as the Old West of the United States. Although the traditional American West is broader than this, the twenty-one stories in this collection are set in a north-to-south band of U.S. states stretching down from Idaho and Wyoming (with an eastern jaunt into Nebraska), down through Utah and Colorado (with an eastern jaunt into Kansas), to Nevada, Arizona, and New Mexico. The characters in these stories predominantly are cowboys, or the modern equivalent, and the themes center on male-male relationships. Although the stories are presented in alphabetical order by title, they fall into two categories: The Old West of the traditional cowboy in the late nineteenth and early twentieth centuries and the West of the modern day.

A theme running through many of the stories is the concept of the male brothel, often set at a ranch or a town saloon. The reader will find both Old West and current West stories including these settings. These arise from a phenomenon of the Old West that has continued to today. There weren't many women in the Old West, particularly on the range where cowboys worked. It was a lonely life, though, and one where fit and sexually prime men found only other men around to satisfy their natural needs. Therefore the homosexual lifestyle, although always kept below the surface, was not unknown. Male brothel ranches can be found throughout this region even today if one knows where to look for them. Habu has conjured up some to entertain you with in his stories.

Readers will also find several of the stories centering on a valley in the middle of the Rockies in Colorado, running down from the Wyoming border from the towns of Baggs and Dixon to Hayden, Colorado. This is a favorite setting of habu both in short stories and in books, as he has deep connections with this valley and with the legends of the Old West arising from this area.

Seven of the stories are set in the Old West in the latter quarter of the nineteenth century. "3 Shot Jealousy" and "Bad Neighbors" are separate stories connected to a male brothel on the Platte River in Nebraska on the cattle drive route from Colorado to the Omaha stockyards. "Retreat to Eremenos" is set at a male brothel ranch in Idaho, across the Teton mountains from what is now Yellowstone Park. The saloon brothel of "Snowy, Snowy Nights" is set in Hayden, Colorado, at the south end of the Slater Creek Valley through the Rocky Mountains. The goal of the young man assaulted by Indians in "Western Tail" is the original fort at Hayden. "Fort Bent" (Bent is an actual old fort town in New Mexico) also has an Indian assault theme. "Last Rodeo" follows an Old West rodeo down from Wyoming into New Mexico.

The fourteen current-day stories in the collection broaden out in themes. "Ride 'Em Cowboy" and the twin "The Photograph: John and Jamie" stories not only are set in Slater Creek Valley, but they also hone in close to what is familiar to habu. There are male brothel bar, hotel, and ranch stories in this set as well, including "9:30 Bus from Abilene," "Hey, Good Buddy," "Mascot," "Night Ride in Old Albuquerque," and "Porn War." Each of these has a different story plot and theme, though. The remaining stories are eclectic in both setting and theme. "Body Snatcher" is about kidnapping, defilement, and revenge. "Desserts" is a fun ditty inspired by a visit habu made to Mesa Verde. "Road Romeo" is also a humorous story of a gifted "initiator" who rides both the truck route across Wyoming and young men who seek out the special something he has. "Roswell's Frontier Motel" is an alien Sci-Fi story of a special-service motel, and "Shark" is also an "other-world" story, which is set in western Kansas, in what few think of as the Old West but, as the location of Cimarron and Dodge City, most certainly was the setting for many Old West legends. "Who's Jeff," which concludes the collection, is an excerpt, set in Santa Fe, New Mexico, from habu's novel *Journey to Mirage*.

3-Shot Jealousy

"Maybe you best take it easy on the rotgut," Skinner said as the man at the bar raised his empty glass again. "That's your third shot in less than ten minutes. The ass isn't gonna be ready for you any sooner than it is. It's a busy night. Friday nights are always busy at the Buckhead ranch, and this was a payday here abouts. At this rate you gonna be well past ready before your number comes up."

"Maybe you're right," Jess said, with a sigh. "Rustle me up a cup of coffee then, and you might as well fill the shot glass too for a chaser. How long do you think it will be?"

"You're waitin' for Ned, ain't you? At least two ahead of you. Now if it was one of the other three . . ." He left that open. He couldn't quite catch up to why the guy wanted Ned. He was a looker himself. Good condition, especially for his age. Didn't look like he'd hit forty yet. Closer to thirty-five, Skinner thought. The hair was blond or reddish depending on how you looked at it, and he'd cleaned up before coming in. What you'd call a downright handsome face. He looked more like a guy who controlled on top rather than one who wanted it. Clothes were pretty expensive for a cowpoke. Skinner saw him in here maybe twice a year. The timing was like stopping here coming and going to the stockyards in Omaha, Nebraska, from, maybe, an eastern Wyoming ranch. Cattle driver maybe. But probably the rancher himself, not just a cowpoke.

"No, it'll have to be Ned or nothin'. I'll wait some more, but I don't have all night."

"Comin' or going to the cattle yards in Omaha?" Skinner asked. He liked to know who was using his male bordello. It was getting so that folks couldn't do what they damn well pleased on the banks of the Platte anymore. Getting too civilized for him in Nebraska of late. People were starting to look around. Those Holy Rollers were beginning to get their noses in other people's business. He could take the Holy Rollers one on one—some of his best customers were Holy Rollers—but when they got together and decided to start telling others what to do . . .

"Goin'," Jess answered. But then he tightened up. He stopped here to keep his business off of other people's tongues in Sterling, Colorado, where his ranch was. He had a family and a reputation there. "But how did you—?"

"You have cattleman writ all over you, and you come here twice a year, not far apart. In the season of the cattle drives. I'm just curious. Don't mean much by it. You can let it down in here. That's what we're all about. Gettin' here what you can't be seen gettin' where you come from. Wyoming? Laramie area maybe?"

"Somewhere close to there, yes," Jess said, tossing off the shot glass, his coffee still unfinished.

This wasn't what he wanted. Not at all. He stopped here outside North Platte not only because he knew about the place but also because he wasn't known here. Nobody knew anything about him here. He had this itch. Couldn't do anything about that. But his business was his business.

"Maybe I don't have the time to wait," he said, standing up and pushing away from the bar. "Maybe it's best if you just take my marker off the board. Hadn't tried a Friday night before. I didn't realize how busy it would be."

"Not just a Friday night. A payday Friday night," Skinner reminded him, as he stared down at the glass he was drying. He'd been too nosy.

It was true that Jess didn't really have the time for this. He'd left James and John and the hired men out on the range, on the eastern side of North Platte, and had ridden back for the evening. He figured they knew what he was doing while they camped out with the herd. They just didn't have a clue

14

where he was doing it and who he was doing it with. His sons, James and John, didn't seem to have a problem with it—at least in thinking it would be some woman. James, nineteen, and John, eighteen, would be doing something like this soon—if they weren't already sneaking off with girls from the neighboring ranches. He had been married and had both of them in the house before he was their ages. They were both fine, strapping young men. They respected their mama, but they knew what men were prone to do. They just didn't know exactly what it was that their father wanted. And he didn't want them to know either.

"Sorry. I didn't mean to pry. There's no harm from knowing where a man's from."

Skinner could have shot himself. The man's money was good and he never caused trouble when he was in here. And he was a good looker—something for the other men to look at and dream about while they were waiting for their turn upstairs. And that he took cock—which all knew as soon as he asked for Ned—rather than was looking for male pussy like nearly all the rest in here, made him good business interest while men waited. Skinner had half a notion to make an offer to him that he take up some of Ned's slack tonight, and then he'd be getting what he wanted for nothing.

"No, no. Nothin' to it. It's just getting' late and we need to push off early in the morning."

"Catch you when you're coming back through in a week or so?"

"Yeah, maybe. Yeah, sure. I'll try not to make it a Friday night."

"That'a be good. Ned's off Sundays and Mondays."

"Good to know, thanks." Jess pulled his hat down over his eyes and headed for the door. The barkeep had mentioned Ned in a pretty loud voice and it had started a buzz again in the room. Anybody talking about Ned knew that he gave cock; he didn't take it. The mention of his name in relationship to this good-looking, nicely dressed, blond guy with a good body caused many in the room to start sniffing the air. They all were waiting longer than usual for their turn upstairs on a Friday night.

One guy, standing at the other end of the bar from where Skinner and Jess were talking, had been listening in for some time. He was taller and more muscular than Jess was. He was maybe ten years younger and several rungs down the economic scale from Jess. His drinks were being husbanded. He'd barely come in with enough money for his turn up the stairs. His clothes, a plaid shirt and jeans, with cowboy boots, were worn and a bit tight on his muscular body. This only accentuated how muscular he was, though. At closer to seven feet than six feet tall, he towered over Jess. His hands and feet were huge. The hands were calloused from hard work— probably in the fields rather than on a ranch. He was dark and swarthy, but also sultry in a sensual way.

When Skinner had looked at him and assessed him, his first thought was to wonder why he was in here at all. He didn't look like he could spare the money, but he also looked like he didn't need to come in here at all—that he could get poontang of whatever variety he wanted just by walking down the center of the street. Although maybe, from the bulge at his crotch, he scared some men off.

As Jess walked out of the barroom, Skinner started to move down the bar, thinking it was time to push another drink on the tall, dark stranger. But the man was tipping his hat, pushing his glass away from him, and turned to leave in Jess' wake.

Jess was starting to unhitch his horse at the rail, when he heard the voice, a low, smooth bass.

"Hold up a minute."

He turned to see a tall, muscular, dark-haired man walking across the porch toward him. He shivered at the sensual look of the man—the hugeness of him. His eyes focused on the man's crotch. It might not have done so if he hadn't been thinking all day on the hot and dusty trail about his planned session with Ned tonight. But he was keyed up, and disappointed he wasn't going to be getting his rocks off from Ned fucking him.

"Yes?" he said, realizing that his voice was wavering a bit.

"You wanted Ned in there. Did I hear right?"

16

"Yes. So?"

"So, I got tired of waitin' too. Seems we could both get off without the wait or either of us spendin' the money. You're a good-lookin' guy. I could fuck you for nothin'. Could do you right good too, I imagine. And we wouldn't be on anyone clock. I'm a double-load kind'a guy."

"I . . . I don't . . ."

The man had reached his side, put an arm around him, grabbed Jess' other arm, and pressed Jess' hand into his crotch. "Feel what you could have? There's a nice cottonwood grove over there by the Platte. I can give you a real good ride, and neither of us would have to pay for it."

* * * *

"Hold steady there," the man commanded. Jess was on all fours on the soft ground next to the riverbank. The man was crouched over him, one booted foot on the ground next to Jess' knee and the other on top of a rock next to Jess' hip. Both men were still wearing their shirts, although they were unbuttoned and flapping open. Neither was wearing britches. The man had a heavily muscled arm under Jess' heaving belly, holding him steady and his other hand wrapped around Jess' throat, arching Jess' torso back. The bulb of the man's cock was already lodged inside the rim of Jess' hole.

"Here we go," the man growled. "Gonna ride you hard."

Jess whimpered. He'd been whimpering and apprehensive ever since he'd seen the size of the man's cock and had gotten the measure of it in his mouth. "Be good to me; go slow," he pleaded.

But though, in the long run, Jess had to agree that the man was good to him, he didn't go slow.

"Oh shit! Oh, fuck!" Jess cried out as the man plunged his cock into him and started to piston hard and fast.

Afterward, Jess lay on his back, on top of an encasing arm of the man stretched beside him, moaning and babbling on about his life and what a release this was for him from the Tharp ranch east of Sterling, while the man stroked his cock.

17

When Jess had ejaculated again, for his second time that night, the big man rolled over on top of him, lifted one of Jess' ankles to his shoulder with one hand, covered Jess' mouth tightly with the other to cover any outcries—the two having heard the men starting to leave the Buckhead ranch bar over the past twenty minutes—and thrust his cock home again.

Lying on his back and looking up at the towering figure standing over him, legs spread, feet planted on either side of Jess' thighs, Jess' eyes were arrested by the size of the cock dangling down from the man's groin. He had had this in his throat. He had had a larger measure of it up inside his ass. The man was buttoning up his shirt. He saw Jess looking up at him and laughed.

"You have a sweet channel for a man your age," he said. "I could just about go again. You get what you came for? You feel fucked?"

"Yes." Jess was still panting from the second fucking. He raised a hand and placed it on the meat of the man's calf, above the boot top. He moaned. He was exhausted, but still . . .

"You'd like me to fuck you again?"

"Yes." It came out as a moan.

The man laughed. "Maybe someday. Maybe someday I'll get to that Tharp ranch you talked about. Where? Sterling, Colorado, was it? Yeah, maybe. You were a good lay. Better than they got upstairs there at Buckhead. Can you imagine what it would have cost both of us for the time we been at it?"

A chill went up Jess' spine. Had he really told this man—this magnificently built man—where he lived? And was what he said about maybe seeing him there sounding more like a threat than a fantasy? Danger signals were buzzing in his head.

"Couldn't fuck you again unless I was hard," the man said.

It was humiliating, but Jess couldn't help himself. He grabbed the man's other calf with his other hand, and, with a groan, raised his torso so that he could open his lips over the bulb of the man's cock and sucked.

Laughing, the man grabbed Jess by the forearms, pushed him away, and lowered his torso back to the grass. "I think you've had enough," he said. "Any more and you'd need to be paying me for it."

"I would. I will—pay you for it," Jess said, his voice coming out in a whine.

The man just laughed again, stepped away from Jess' body, scooped up his jeans, and faded into the blackness of the night.

* * * *

Jess didn't remember much from the rest of the cattle drive. His thinking was consumed with the man who had fucked him on the banks of the Platte. They did camp again near North Platte on the way back to Colorado, and Jess returned to the Buckhead ranch—this time on a Wednesday evening. The visit wasn't all that satisfying, however. The session with Ned this time seemed seedy and unfulfilling in relationship to the cocking he'd gotten from the tall, dark stranger. Jess wondered if a visit to the Buckhead ranch would ever be the same again.

So preoccupied was he with both the humiliation and glory of the night on the banks of the Platte that Jess almost missed what was happening in a field at the back of the ranch house, a field his wife had been after him for a couple of years to have planted to vegetables and fruit to augment their needs, as they approached their ranch. It was James who keyed him in.

"My god, who is that? Look at how big and muscular he is, father."

Jess looked up to see the field half plowed—by a tall, muscular man guiding a plow behind two horses. The man was stripped to the waist. His torso muscles rippled and bulged from the effort. He was dark-headed and his torso and forearms were matted with curly black hair. So hard-bodied was he and so much was the exertion of his work that the veins running through his torso and arms popped out on his tanned skin.

19

The man looked up; it was the man. The man who had fucked Jess on the banks of the Platte. He stopped plowing momentarily and turned and gave a nod to the owner of the ranch, his two sons, and the three cowboys returning from the Omaha stockyards. Then he returned to the plowing.

Jess hoped that his gasp wasn't audible.

James was just staring hard at him. John asked his father, "Who is he, Father?"

"I have no idea. He ain't from around here."

"Perhaps Mama will know," John said.

"Indeed, maybe she will," the father answered. But he had the sinking feeling that it was his own babbling in the postcoital cooling off from sex that had led the man here. Panic set in—but so did the reaction of Jess' body. His skin was crawling with the memory of the touch of the man's strong hands on him, and his ass was twitching—also with the memory of a special touch of another kind.

* * * *

"I told you we needed to get a field plowed to vegetables and fruit," Mary told Jess over final preparations in the kitchen for dinner. "I grew weary of telling you and the man showed up looking for work. And he obviously can do the work. He has most of the field plowed already. That's more than you've gotten done for us out there in the last three years."

"Careful woman," Jess said, "You forget yourself on who makes decisions around here. The man looks like trouble. I will not—"

"Shhh, he will hear you, Jess. And the man has a name. He is Damon. Damon Smith, he told me."

"How so will he hear me, Wife?"

"He is in the dining room with the children. He has come for dinner."

"Come for dinner? Eating with the family?"

"Yes, and I have given him our old homestead cabin to live in. He's a farmer, not a cowboy, Jess. He will not mix well with the other men. And just you wait, what he produces for us will be far more useful and valuable for the family than any one of your other hired men."

Jess bit his tongue from saying that there was only danger to the family unit from this man's presence here, but he said nothing. To say anything would be to say too much. And she had a point about the man. Putting him in the bunkhouse with the cowboys would be like putting a rooster in the hen coup. And beyond that, in the back of his mind, he was thinking that having him bunking alone in the old homestead cabin had possibilities. But then he shook his head. He couldn't possibly be thinking that. The man had to go.

Dinner was covered with a veneer of comfort and conviviality, but under that was a deep layer of tension—at least for Jess, although he fancied he could feel it in others as well, except, perhaps in the man, Damon, himself and the younger son, John, who obviously saw nothing wrong in another man than his father putting his feet under the family table. James seemed drawn to the man and asked him all sorts of questions about farming. It didn't help the level of tension in the room that James' interest in farming rather than cattle ranching had a history of battle lines drawn in the family—not just between father and son but also between husband and wife, as Mary supported James in his interest.

Perhaps, Jess thought, this was the source of the tension underneath the surface of the conversation at the dinner table. Perhaps, though, it was because he had told Mary that this would be the last dinner the man took in the family dining room.

He brought the subject up near the end of the meal, saying, "We asked you to dinner as a welcome, Damon. But henceforth you will be eating in your cabin—unless you wish to eat with the other men in the bunkhouse dining room. Your meals will be brought to you unless you have said you wanted to fix a meal for yourself."

Damon took the command well—in fact he was taking the subservient roll of a field hand well at the dining room table. This didn't lessen the tension inside Jess, though, and he only hoped that when he spoke he didn't reveal how nervous—and aroused he was.

Late that evening Jess closed the Bible on his lap and spoke up. "I forgot to put out the feed for the cattle in the north pasture, Mary. I will go do that now. I may be late in getting it done. You need not sit up for me."

She looked up from the stitching she was doing, looked over her glasses at her husband, and smiled. She said nothing—not even about the tremble Jess seemed to have acquired in his hands on the just-completed cattle drive.

The path to the north pasture passed by the old homestead cabin, which was beyond the line of sight from either the ranch house or the bunk house.

A light was glowing in the cabin, and Damon was standing in the doorway, naked to the waist, An arm flung up the frame of the doorway, and his opposite hip thrust out at a provocative angle. A smile was fixed on his face as he watched Jess approach on his way to the field. He had a stalk of wheat in his mouth that he was chewing on, all casual like.

It wasn't long at all before Jess was standing at the side of the bunk beds in the cabin's second room, grasping the side slat of the upper bunk, his buttocks rearing out into the room behind him, and his feet planted firmly on the worn wood floor. Damon stood behind him, an arm wrapped around Jess' waist with a broad hand palming Jess' naked belly and the other hand around Jess' throat, arching the older man's chest back, as Damon's cock pounded hard and deep up into Jess' channel.

Jess was whimpering and moaning. Damon was laughing. He was still chewing on the stalk of wheat.

* * * *

"We must move away from the kitchen window," Mary murmured. "If he returns from the north pasture early, he might be able to see your head beside mine if he goes into the barnyard."

"Whatever you say, sweet lady," Damon whispered. He lifted her with strong, calloused hands at the waist from where he was bent over her at the kitchen sink, turned her, and, taking two steps, bent her over the kitchen table. He managed all of this without dislodging his cock from her ass channel. He moved one hand back to covering a breast in her unbuttoned dress top and the other one from her crotch, where he had a thumb on her clit and fingers buried in her cunt. He was moving the fingers, but otherwise he was standing, steady, and letting her fuck her ass on his cock.

"Please, can we go to the bedroom and do it proper—like we did before Jess got home from the cattle drive?" she whispered through pants and moans. "Jess and the boys never come into the house this time of day."

"I wouldn't want—"

"Jess lies with me frequently. If it happens, I'll have yet another magnificent boy. Jess will never know."

Damon thought rather that Jess *would* know. There was a hell of a difference between a normal-stature blond and a tall, husky brunette. But this would be the woman's worry. He had done her originally to get the job and was doing her now mostly to keep her on his side. He picked her up and carried her into the bedroom, laid her down on her back, lowered himself between her spread legs, and thrust his cock up into her cunt. She arched her back and moaned and began to move with the stroking.

"You're so big," she moaned. "Bigger than he is." Damon thought Jess was plenty big enough, but it was still flattering to hear her say so.

He remained holding her, inside her, and was stroking her hair and kissing her on the nipples when they were finished.

"My dinner."

"I'm sorry about that, Damon. I think Jess would be suspicious if—"

"That is not it. I want James to deliver my dinners to me, if you please. I sense his father doesn't want him talking about farming, and it would give us some time to converse. I think, if I'm not wrong, that you support James in his wish to become a farmer."

"Yes, yes, of course," Mary answered. In the back of her mind there was a bit of question there, but his cock had regained its hardness, and his resumed stroking took all other thoughts from her mind.

Later that night, when Jess approached the old homestead cabin en route to putting out the cattle feed in the north pasture, the cabin door was open and lights were on, but Damon was not waiting for him at the door.

Jess heard the moaning as he entered the cabin and moved silently over to the door into the second room. He could see James' bare legs, bent, and the young man's heels caressing the backs of Damon's calves, and James' arms around Damon's neck. James was on his back on the lower bunk, and a naked Damon was lying between James' thighs. James was moaning and Damon's body was straight as a board, risen off of James' body, his long thick cock pounding James' ass in long, deep strokes that clearly showed several inches of cock coming out and then reentering James' channel with each thrust.

Jess turned and fled the cabin.

For the next several days, whenever Damon wasn't plowing the field, looking so sexy as he worked, Jess came upon him fucking James. On a haystack in the barn, behind a haystack in the field, twice more in the old homestead cabin bunk, and while they were cavorting naked in the creek. Damon didn't seem to making any effort to hide what he was doing with James from Jesse.

James took Damon on an overnight ride up into the mountains, looking for stray cattle. Jess followed them at a distance and watched Damon fuck James bent over a saddle next to the camp fire for an hour or more.

They were young and virile. Jess no longer was. But, after that first night, Damon hadn't come for Jess again. He spent his time fucking James—at least as far as Jess knew.

This couldn't continue. Jess knew he had to put a stop to it. The situation came to a head one Sunday morning when Jess and Mary had gone to church. Mary forgot the pies she'd made for the church picnic afterward, and Jess came back to the house for them—and found Damon fucking James in Jess and Mary's bed. Damon was lying flat on the bed, his beefy hands encasing James' waist, as James rode his cock.

Jess went crazy.

* * * *

"I keep telling you that it was an accident," Jess said wearily to the sheriff.

"I understand the grief of a man losing his son, Mr. Tharp," the sheriff said as the men sat in the ranch house parlor, Mary so taken with grief that she was in another room being consoled by women from neighboring ranches

"But you have readily admitted that it's your rifle and that you fired the shots."

"But it was an accident."

"A man doesn't get off three shots that hit home by accident, Mr. Tharp. It's not an accident when a man shoots his son dead with three shots in the back."

"Don't be afraid, Jess. We will manage."

Jess looked in the direction the voice came from. His eyes were having difficulty adjusting through his tears and the dull ache behind his eyes. He knew the voice, though. Damon had somehow managed to dress again and cover the blood that must be on his chest and thighs before any of the men in the bunkhouse had reached the house. No one had suggested that Damon was even in the house when James got shot. The dull ache moved—to more than one place. It moved to Jess' heart but also, in humiliation and frustration, it moved to his groin as well. Now, even now, he wanted Damon.

His eyes focused enough to see that his younger son, John, was sitting beside Damon. Damon's arm was around his shoulders and he had a hand on the young man's thigh.

"We'll manage," Damon answered, a look on his face that Jess couldn't understand escaped the scrutiny of the sheriff—although Jess didn't want the sheriff to suspect Damon of anything. There had to be a way, somehow a way, for he and Damon to be together again.

"I'll take good care of John," Damon said, "And Mary has already said it would comfort her if I moved into the house while you were away facing this trial."

9:30 Bus from Abilene

Sometimes I think I was born with a "fuck me" sign painted on my butt. But then, I seem to have been born with that young and vulnerable look that turns some men on, and I'll have to admit that I love being touched—especially in one particular sensitive spot below and to the left of my navel, where I have a blue rosebud tattooed. Ever since I started having sex, if a man touched me there, I hardened right up and softened to anything he might suggest. I'd just lay down and open my legs to him and let him do whatever he wanted. It didn't help that, no matter how much I fought it, I loved being cocked. And so I had the spot marked with a tattoo for reference. If I really, really liked the guy I'd move his hand there myself to short-circuit any early indecision on his part.

I was trying to fight my impulses just to lay down for whatever man who wanted me that morning I caught the 9:30 bus from Abilene headed up to Denver. Dave didn't want me to go. He agreed to drive me down to the bus station, but up to the very last minute I'm sure he didn't think I really was going. However, I'd pole danced in Dave's men's clubs for a couple of months now, which was as long as I'd stuck around anywhere since I'd gotten old enough to hit the road. And as nice as Dave's cocking was and as good as the tips for the extra service to the men in the club were, I had gotten myself in an old familiar rut, and I had started to tell myself that there must be something else out there for me to do other what whoring in sleazy little bars.

And something got into my head that if only I could get to Denver, I could start a whole new life and that this weakness in me—these urges, this vulnerability to the wants of other men—would just go away.

Just before I got on the bus in Abilene, Dave tried his last ploy. He pulled me around to the side of the station and pulled me in close to his chest. A hand sneaked up under the hem of my athletic T, and he pressed a thumb into that blue rosebud tattoo. His lips clamped down on mine, and I involuntarily danced on his pole for a few moments. First one leg went up around his hip and then another, and then he was dry humping me up against the wall—and I was loving it.

I was saved by the loudspeaker calling the "all aboard" for the 9:30 bus from Abilene, though, and I managed to break away and head for the bus without a look back. Instead, I looked up along the windows in the bus and saw that two cowboys were eyeing me real close. I wondered what they could have seen in the shadows at the side of the station house.

I climbed up into the bus and found a seat near the back on the side away from the platform. I didn't want to see Dave out there. I was fighting with myself, telling myself that life with Dave and in his sleazy little clubs wasn't what I wanted. That I wanted something more from life. But I was afraid if I saw Dave out there, looking oh so forlorn, as Dave was so good at when he wanted something from me, I'd lose my resolve to leave Abilene.

The bus started out, and I felt a sudden sense of freedom. It was going to work. I knew it was.

As the bus moved out into the dusty countryside outside of Abilene and headed north, I looked around to see what there was in the way of travel companions. An Hispanic family, a man and his wife and three children, the oldest a sullen-looking teenage boy of fifteen or sixteen, was sitting near the front. From the way they were dressed, I thought maybe they were field workers moving north to start the harvest up there and to work their way back to Abilene again over the season. A couple of elderly ladies, all dressed out in their Sunday best—off on an adventure. A young woman who always seemed to be huddled close to the window and asleep.

And the two cowboys I'd seen in the bus window from the station platform. They must have been together, because they were sitting side by side on a row about two thirds of the way back until the bus got started and then one moved to the window seat in the same row on the opposite side of the bus. One was older than the other, wiry with ropy muscles. Clean shaven, graying at the temples, with startling pale blue eyes in a deeply tanned and weather-lined face. Piercing eyes when he stared at you—eyes that told you you'd better do what he asked if he told you to do something. The other, younger one, was dark-complexioned, probably half Hispanic, equally tanned, but chunkier than the older one. Not fat by any means, but heavily muscled. Both were in checked shirts and jeans, with fancy leather cowboy boots and big fancy silver belt buckles. Both had tattoos running up their arms and the hint at the neckline of more on their chests. And both were looking back at where I was sitting occasionally and then whispering to each other.

Buses weren't popular anymore as a means to move long distances, but what with the cost of gas and the overall economic conditions in the States at the moment, I thought they'd probably come into their own again. I had chosen the bus because I'd never owned a car, couldn't afford the plane fare, and there were no rail connections between Abilene and Denver that didn't go hundreds of miles out of the way and that didn't, in the long run, take longer—and cost more—than the bus.

I don't know why I picked Denver. I just had seen posters of it sitting right there next to the snow-capped Rocky Mountains and it looked so prosperous and clean and open that it had become somewhat of a Holy Grail to me, the symbol of a new, cleaner, less-complicated life.

We stopped at a gas station–convenience store just off the highway in the middle of nowhere for a lunch break. There was a small dining room off the lunch counter with only three tables. The young woman didn't leave the bus, but the elderly ladies took one table and the Hispanic family another, and I sat down at the third after I'd gotten my burger and fries.

The two cowboys sat down at my table.

29

"Hi, I'm Tex," the older one said as he sat down. "This here's Dusty." They were both wearing the traditional ten-gallon cowboy's hat, and Dusty just tipped his hat at me without saying anything. But he had a big grin on his face.

"Hi, I'm Glade," I answered.

"Glade. That's an unusual name," Tex said.

"Yeah. I sorta picked it out myself," I said. "Didn't much care for what I'd been called before that." I didn't tell them that it was my stage name. All of us pole dancers picked out names that the customers would find intriguing and easy to remember. Most picked out suggestive or downright explicit names. I had wanted to be a bit more subtle with mine.

"Goin' far?" Tex asked.

"All the way to Denver," I answered.

"Dusty and me are gettin' off in Durango. We work a cattle ranch west of there. Been down in Abilene to see the sights. Were you in Abilene long or just passing through from somewheres else?"

"I was there a couple of months," I answered. I was feeling a little disconcerted. Dusty wasn't saying anything, but his leg was touching mine, and I felt those old yearnings building up inside me. Dusty was a real hunk. The strong silent type. And he was touching me. Any man who touched me set me going.

"Found something to do in Abilene, did you?" Tex asked. He was eyeing me with those piercing blues of his. It made me scared to lie.

"Oh, this and that," I answered.

"You look kinda familiar, like we've seen you before. Dusty was remarking on that when we saw you climb into the bus. Spent any time around the tenderloin district? That's mostly where Dusty and me sat drinkin' our beers. Place called Rapier mostly. Any chance we'd have seen you there?"

"I've heard of it," I answered in a rather tight voice. More than heard of it, it was one of three clubs Dave owned. I'd pole danced there. I wondered if Tex was establishing something with me—not just about me, but about him and Dusty too. You didn't go into the Rapier looking for women.

Tex started to say something else, but the bus driver was tooting his horn, and it was time for all of us to make that last rest stop and to return to the bus.

When we climbed back into the bus, Dusty returned to his seat, but Tex followed me back to where I'd been sitting and sat down in the aisle seat right next to me.

The driver started up the bus and got back onto the road. I tried to settle my nerves. Tex's leg was right up against mine, as was his upper arm. I could feel the hardness of his lean body through his checkered shirt. I was wearing an athletic T, so my biceps were bare. Just a thin layer of shirting between me and Tex's hard, warm skin.

"Born and raised in Texas?" Tex asked.

"No," I responded. "Lived here and there before that—mostly in the Midwest."

"Family in Texas or in Denver? Going to Denver to visit family?" Tex asked.

"No. No family," I answered. "No family anywhere."

"None at all?" Tex asked. His face was turned to me and his pale blue eyes were full of sympathy.

"No. I was an orphan. Floated around a lot. A couple of foster families, but not anything I'd want to talk much about." I certainly didn't want to talk about those foster families. If I'd gone down a bent path, it could all be traced back to that part of my life. The first man who'd ever found that erogenous spot of mine. I'd had a pretty rough life up to now; it looked like the only way I could go from here was up. I turned my head toward the window. My eyes had suddenly gotten a little watery, and I didn't want Tex to see that.

"No one at all waitin' for you in Denver, either?" Tex asked. His voice was soft, full of concern.

"No. No one at all," I answered. "Just startin' out again. I do that a lot. I start out again a lot."

I was still looking out the window, but I could see the reflection of Tex's face in the window, as I thought he could see mine.

He had a hand on my thigh, just above the knee now, and I'm sure he could feel me trembling.

"Just relax, Glade," he was whispering to me. "You're so tense. I can help you with that."

His voice had gotten low and guttural and his hand had moved up my thigh and was gripping me hard.

"Nice name, Glade," he was murmuring. "An unusual name. I think I saw that on a poster at the Rapier. Not a name you'd forget too fast. Not a body, either. Some even had distinctive markings. Dusty and me like tattoos. We've got 'em all over our bodies. Would like to show them to you. Would you like that?"

My trembling increased. He had fingers at my waistband now, very near my belly, with the grip of that other hand still on my upper thigh.

"Tex . . ." I said in a choked voice.

"Shush, it'll be fine. I lied about the poster. It was more than that. I know you. I was set to pay for you one night—to go into the back rooms at Rapier beyond the door, through the beaded curtain. But another dude got there first. You went along with him real friendly like. No one can see us back here." Tex stripped off his shirt to reveal full-body tattooing in a riot of colors and patterns against a rock-hard muscled chest. "Do you like my tattoos, Glade? If I remember rightly, you have a very nice one yourself. Somewhere near here, wasn't it? That's what I remember of you on that pole, dancin' away. That nice little tattoo. A rosebud, isn't it? I remember how that dude you went with touched you there, and you suddenly were wrapped around him. A little sex pot, you were after he'd touched you there."

He was pulling the T out of my shorts and a finger was moving across my belly and his thumb was on the rosebud tattoo. He was rubbing it and his other hand was on my basket, and I was falling apart. My leg involuntarily moved over his lap, my basket pushing against his, with his hand in between, and I gave a little shudder.

"Happy day. You're just aching for it, ain't you?" Tex muttered through his heavy breathing. "Hot damn, you harden up fast." His hand snaked under the waistband of my gym shorts and he was pulling them down below my balls. My dick was standing straight up, betraying my arousal from his thumbing on my rosebud tattoo.

"Tex . . ."

"So tense. We must do somethin' about that," Tex was whispering. He pushed my leg back around to where I was sitting in the seat again, facing forward. His ten-gallon hat came off and he dropped it onto my lap, fisted my cock under it, and started to slow pump me. I turned my face to him and he could tell from the look in my eyes that I was lost to him. He leaned over and gave me a kiss and then he just pulled away and we sat there, staring into each other's eyes from six inches away, our cheeks resting on the nubby material of the seat backs, and he slowly beat me off, enjoying the look in my eyes as I was transported by his hand job.

"You can touch my tattoos, Glade. Go ahead."

I tentatively, involuntarily reached out with my fingers and ran than over the markings on his hard chest. His nipples were taut—ready for me. He could feel the trembling of my fingers as I got lost in the sensuousness of his tattooing.

When I had jacked off up into his hat, he gave a little laugh, leaned over, and kissed me again. Then he stood up in the aisle and rummaged around in the overhead compartment. He opened a duffle bag he had up there and took something out and then reached up and pulled down a blanket.

"Time for a little nap, don't ya think?" he said, and then he winked at me.

What he'd gotten out of his bag was a condom packet and a small tube of lubricant. When he sat back down, he leaned over and pulled down on the waistband of my gym shorts and, out of instinct, I raised my hips for him so that he could strip them off.

I knew what was happening, but still I made some effort to resist. I was trying my best to get beyond Abilene. "Tex . . . No, I don't think . . ."

"Shush," he whispered. "I wanted to do this back in the Rapier. But you'd gone off with that other customer before I could get to you. Come on. You know you want it. Look at what I got for you." He unbuttoned his jeans and fished out a nice plump cock, already hard. Tattooing wound down around that too, and I moaned.

But still I fought the cravings. "Here? Now?" I asked incredulously. "There isn't much room . . ."

"Hush. We'll manage. Just don't do much yelling. They always yelp for me. Just try to keep it quiet like. Too bad it's dark in here and we have to use the blanket. They always like to see the designs on my pecker disappearing into their holes. You know you can see them through the rubbers. I buy ones that you can do that with."

"Tex . . ."

But he just kept going. I watched as he opened the condom packet and rolled the transparent condom on his cock. Then he slathered himself with lube. He covered us with the blanket and turned me toward the window onto my hip and I felt the cold lubricant at my hole and searching and stretching fingers. The palm of his other hand was on my belly and his thumb was on my tattoo and he was rubbing it. All of the resistance drained out of me. It was almost as though he knew that that was the key to my ass channel.

"Oh, god, fuck me," I murmured, all of my senses focused on that thumb on my tattoo.

I shuddered as he worked his hips under mine, both of us turned toward the window. And then he was entering me, slowly, but relentlessly—showing me that indeed we could do it in bus seats. I moved a hand back there, holding the base of his cock steady, as he penetrated me. He slowly pumped up into me. His thumb was stroking my rosebud tattoo, and I was moaning and sighing softly for him. My head was against the cool window, and I watched the desert landscape drift by, as in another dimension I could also see the reflection of Tex's face and see how deeply he was enjoying the fuck.

This was my element. As much as I had tried to resist, I knew that this was what I was meant for. I pretty much cleared my mind, enjoying the fuck myself, but being frustrated at the same time that I was doing so. Why was it so hard to leave Abilene and all that was Abilene so far behind, I wondered.

After he was finished with me, Tex left me under the blanket with no more than a kiss on the neck and a pat on my naked butt cheek. He pulled his shirt back on and buttoned up and went back up and sat down with Dusty, and the two of them whispered in low tones and laughed.

Near dusk we stopped for dinner and a change in drivers at a stop almost identical to the lunch stop, and I got my burger and fries from the fast food counter and took it out and ate it standing up by the gas pumps. Neither Tex nor Dusty made any effort to approach me. As I ate, the young woman stumbled out of the bus, looking dazed and her eyes all puffed up. She came back moments later with a sack of food and climbed back up in the bus. I wondered what her story was and whether it was any rougher than mine. It made me feel a little better, if a little guilty, that there may be folks in the world worse off than I was.

In my case, I enjoyed the cocking. Couldn't get enough of it really. What I was having trouble with was the guilt of enjoying it and wanting more of it. Even knowing that it degraded me, like now, when Tex and Dusty were so friendly before Tex had me and now they stood off from me, like I was below them—the somewhat downtrodden feeling that I was being taken advantage of all of the time. What I really needed and wanted was just one guy. An older man, maybe. One with a good income who would stick by me and give me a somewhat normal life. I'd want him to be virile and have a nice cock, though. I knew myself enough to know I didn't want to stop the cocking. Maybe in Denver. Surely in Denver that's what I'd find.

When we got back on the bus, I waited until Tex and Dusty had gotten on and settled themselves before I climbed into the bus. I wasn't in the mood for Tex to visit me again—at least not this soon. He cocked real well, though, and those tattoos of his were a real turn on, so I wouldn't mind having him again at some point.

Dusk turned into night, and I managed to go to sleep, huddled under the blanket that Tex had covered us with earlier in the day.

It was quite dark when I felt a nudge on my shoulder and swam up from a groggy, unsatisfying sleep into the grinning face of Dusty.

"Come on," he whispered. "Want to show you something in the back of the bus." He'd already stripped off his shirt and he was almost as tattooed as Tex was. He was covered in a swirled design, some of which curved under the bulge of his pecs and made them stand out and emphasize how well-defined he was there.

I was groggy and didn't react quickly. "Come on," he whispered. "You want it, don't you?"

I struggled up, knowing full well what he wanted to show me, but he was already reaching down and palming my belly under my T, and the touch was enough for me to want what he was going to give me. My hands snaked up to grip his biceps and I pressed my check into his chest.

He laughed a low laughed. "Hot damn. Tex told me about this, but I didn't half believe him. Come on back with me. I got a big one for you."

He followed behind me to the backseat of the bus, a bench seat that stretched the width of the bus carriage, with the palm of his hand on my belly and his forefinger rubbing that rosebud tattoo. My knees were going to jelly, and I was whimpering, my dick hardening and forming precum, the rim of my hole already puckering.

When we reached the back of the bus, Dusty scooted into the seat all the way into the corner; pulled me down onto the center of the seat, a good two and a half feet from him; unbuttoned the fly of his jeans; and pulled a thick, stubby cock out. He reached for one of my wrists and pressed my palm to his chest so I could feel how hard his nipples were for me and he moved my other hand to the root of his cock. Then he wrapped a hand around my neck and brought my face down to his cock and I gave him head. I was good at it.

He didn't say anything. He just sat there and moaned and sighed softly, with his hand on the back of my head guiding me, and his hips slowly rolling up as I deepthroated him and his stubby cock slowly became not in the least bit stubby.

After I'd gotten him all hot and bothered, he turned me, full length on my belly on the backseat, one of my legs hanging down, the ball of my foot leveraging on the floor of

36

the bus to keep me steady in the tossing and turning motion of the bus, which was pronounced at the back. Then he pulled my gym shorts off my legs, crowned his cock with a condom, straddled my hips, and fucked down in me to his ejaculation. He had both of my arms pinned behind my back, holding my wrists together with one strong hand, holding me quite immobile and giving me the feeling of being taken almost against my will in a dark, enclosed corner of the world, which gave me a little thrill.

We were both breathing hard when he was done, but I knew he wasn't finished. I knew these young, virile cowboys with their hard and hard-worked bodies. I'd had them by the hundreds, it seemed, in Abilene on their one night a month off and coming into town to get their rocks off. He'd shot off, I could tell, but he was still hard. I'd known of guys like him who could recharge and fountain off three times before they went soft. Just one night of relief a month that wasn't self-initiated for a young cowboy can build up a whole lot of cum.

And, sure enough, He was pulling me up. Not dislodging his cock, which had lengthened out to gigantic proportions. He struggled up into a sitting position, with me lapped, his lips and teeth working my shoulder blades and the hollow of my neck, his hands wrapped around my belly, a finger pressing into that rosebud tattoo. Almost in a frenzy myself again, not least at watching the muscle roll on those tattooed arms encasing me, I started fucking myself on his impaling cock in long strokes. One of his hands snaked around and fisted my cock, and we came almost simultaneously, all the time softly moaning and groaning, careful not to project the sounds of sex toward the front of the bus.

I looked up as we climaxed—and into Tex's eyes and then down to his naked, tattooed chest. He'd come back to watch the second fucking and was leaning over the seat, knees in the seat bottom, and face almost touching mine. His pale blue eyes were alight with lust and he leaned in and took my lips with his as I spouted off onto the back of the bus seat in front of us.

Dusty pulled out from underneath me and, after a little whispering session with Tex, moved back up the aisle. When he got to my seat, he picked up the blanket and brought it back and draped it over the aisle between two seats a couple of rows up from the back. Now, in the darkness anyone from the front of the bus couldn't see what was happening in the aisle beyond that blanket, and the interior of the bus was so dark they couldn't even have told the aisle was blocked unless they were coming back to use the bathroom in the rear corner.

Tex pulled me over and planted my butt in the center of the backseat, lifted my ankles to the tops of the separated aisle seats in front of the backseat, crouched between my thighs, and fucked me long and deep. Dusty sat there, turned around in an aisle seat in front of the backseat, and watched the action. And when Tex was done, Dusty replaced him again, turning me and pressing my head and chest into the center seat of the backseat, my rump pointed up the aisle, and doggy fucked me.

They left me wondering if maybe they hadn't had any success in getting their rocks off while they were in Abilene. And leave me they did, to stumble back to my seat on my own, exhausted and stretched and sore—but well-fucked and happy. This wasn't anything I hadn't endured on any given night in Dave's clubs.

The next morning, after breakfast at a small way station where there was another change in drivers and the two elderly ladies got off—in the middle of nowhere, as far as I could tell—Tex followed me back to my seat and sat with me and jacked me off again while murmuring in my ear about how nice I was—and how really sweet I'd been the night before.

"We'll be in Durango this afternoon," he said when we were finished and I was laying back in the seat, mellow and satisfied.

"Will we?" I murmured.

"It's pretty expensive in Denver, you know," he said from out of the blue.

"Is it?" I asked.

"Sure you got enough to get started there?"

"There's never enough, I've found."

"Could you make good use of, say, two hundred more?" he asked.

"Who couldn't?" I responded. I was just making small talk. Tex gave great hand jobs.

But Tex wasn't just making small talk. "You know you can stop off in Durango and get on the bus later on the same ticket?"

"Can you?" I said.

"Yes you can. You know, I've been thinkin'. Dusty and me had promised to bring something back to the boys at the ranch from Abilene and we plumb forgot to do that."

"Did you?"

"Yep. We got a pole in the middle of our bunk house. You could stop over for a day or two and give them guys a pole dance. I'm sure I could collect at least $200 for that. What do ya say to that?"

What I was thinking was that no matter how far down the road this bus had taken me, I was still in Abilene. But what I said was, "Sure, why not?" As I said, Tex gave the best of hand jobs and there he was, hand on my belly, stroking my rosebud tattoo with his thumb while he was making his proposition.

The ranch was a good hundred miles out of Durango in the direction of nowhere, but the bunk house did, indeed, have a wooden pole holding up the center of it. There were six interested cowboys out there in nowhere in addition to Tex and Dusty. I danced for them to a scratchy record on an old-fashioned record player, wearing one of the sparkly gold G-strings I'd brought with me from the Rapier. I wowed them and then they fucked me—all eight of them in succession over a three-hour period. A few had seconds.

I heard Tex telling them how turned on I got when my rosebud tattoo was rubbed, and they all made sure to give it attention, and thus they all got enthusiastic fucks.

They may have gone another exhausting round, but the foreman broke up the party and extracted me and helped me hobble out of the bunkhouse and into his cabin—where he bent me over a chair and satisfied his own need.

I made $350 off that afternoon of work, and Tex suggested that I stay on for a while—that the cowboys worked harder with a daily fuck and that there was plenty of money from where the $350 had come from.

But I really, really wanted to get out of Abilene.

Tex was good for his promise; he drove me back to the bus station in time to catch the next bus rambling through from Abilene to Denver. We left early, though, because he stopped behind a rock formation before dropping down into Durango and fucked me again in the backseat of the ranch's station wagon. He gave me another fifty for that, though.

The bus between Durango and Denver was more crowded than it had been on its initial leg into Durango. We were getting closer to big towns. And there was much more of a variety of people getting on and off as we rumbled along.

In Colorado Springs, a middle-aged guy in a business suit got on. He caught my attention, because he looked like someone who should be driving a Mercedes rather than riding in a Greyhound bus. He was smartly dressed; was in good, and obviously pampered condition; and was flashing a big diamond ring. It struck me that this looked like just the sort of guy I was looking for in Denver.

He looked around the bus as he got on. It was half full, although most of the passengers were in the front half. His eyes caught mine, and thinking what I had been thinking about how he was the type that filled my Denver bill, I probably gave him a more welcome smile than was absolutely necessary. I thought I saw his eyes sparkle up and he returned my smile, and then he was moving toward me. I was surprised when he came all of the way back to where I was sitting and sat down in the aisle seat next to me. There were lots of vacant seats back here, but he was sitting next to me. He'd taken his suit coat off and slung it into the overhead bin before he sat down. His warm arm was rubbing up against mine, and his thigh was touching mine, and I felt like I was going to hyperventilate. I looked down and was somewhat distressed that if he looked in my lap too, he'd see that I was tenting up.

But he wasn't looking at my lap, or so I thought. He came on with a briefcase and had taken some papers out of it and was sifting through those, looking for something.

The bus was out on the highway now.

"Wouldn't you know it?" he was muttered.

"What?" I asked more out of politeness than curiosity.

"They gave me a receipt back there at the garage, and now I can't find it. It had their telephone number on it. I'll need that to find out when the car will be fixed."

"The car?" I asked. He was on a bus.

"Yeah. My Merc broke down back there in Colorado Springs. God, I haven't had to ride a bus in years. But I needed to get back to Denver by this evening and the bus station was right there by the garage. It would have been more complicated to get a rental car. You come from far away?"

"From Abilene," I answered.

"Working there, were you?"

"Yeah, a place called the Rapier." I have no idea why I told him that. Being disconcerted by him touching me put me off center, I guess. That and assuming he'd have no idea what the Rapier was.

"Ah, I see," he said.

And, for a moment, it seemed like he did, indeed, see. He had turned to me and was looking at me real hard.

To try to cover, I asked him about where he lived and what he did for a living.

"I'm a few miles out of Denver. Out toward the mountains. Run a specialty service of sorts."

I didn't pursue the question further.

I did, though, ask him if he'd ever been to Abilene and he answered that, yes, he went there on business. But then he settled back in his seat and started talking to me about his family.

"Adolescent girls," he snorted as his monologue moved along. "Daughters are such a challenge. You have any girlfriends with tattoos?"

"No girlfriends," I answered. I was trying to keep my answers short. I was sure that he was able to hear my arousal in my voice if I said too much.

"Well then, boyfriends perhaps?" He'd let it come out straight, as if there was nothing behind it. But I saw him eyeing my tented lap now, and I was beginning to figure out he was building up to something. I said nothing, but I know he could feel the intake of my breath and how tense I'd gotten.

"Tattoos aren't so bad," I said after a pause.

"Oh, you got any?" he asked.

"One," I answered.

"Somewhere I can see it?"

"Just here, near my navel," I said, and I raised the hem of my T-shirt to show him my blue rosebud tattoo. And he touched it with his finger, and I fell apart and my gym shorts tented up even further—and noticeably. And he was looking now. No doubt.

He looked into my eyes for a moment and then said, "Go back to the restroom at the back of the bus, and enter, but don't latch it. If I'm wrong just stay here and I'll move to another seat. But I don't think I'm wrong. I've been to Rapier."

Dumbly, knowing already what would happen, I stood up and walked by his legs as he swung them into the aisle and unsteadily—not only from the rolling gait of the moving bus— walked back to the compact bathroom at the back corner of the bus and entered it.

Shortly afterward, the door opened, and he was inside with me. He'd rolled a condom on before coming back and he merely unzipped himself again, reached down and pulled my gym shorts and briefs off my legs and pulled my T-shirt over my head. I was naked. He wasn't but he unbuttoned his shirt so that our chests would be my bare skin against his hairy chest.

"Fifty dollars enough?" he asked.

"Yes," I answered, and that was that. I climbed his hips with my legs and he was holding me there against the back paneling of the bus restroom, his legs straddling the toilet basin, and he fucked me hard and deep by pulling me up and down on his cock with a broad hands palming and spreading my butt cheeks, giving him deeper, wider access in my channel. He had obviously done this before, and he was good at it.

I turned my face toward the mirror over the basin and watched his other thumb strumming my rosebud tattoo, and I ejaculated up his belly.

I returned to my seat first, leaving him to try to clean up the damage to his shirt. I looked around the bus as I moved up the aisle, but no one was showing any interest. No one had noticed.

Soon thereafter, he plopped back down into the seat next to me and reached into my gym shorts and pulled out my cock and slowly stroked me.

"That was nice," he said. "You know what you're doing. You mentioned the Rapier in Abilene. A professional, are you?"

"A dancer. A professional dancer, yes," I answered between sighs brought about by what he was doing with my cock.

"And other things too?"

"Yes . . . OK . . . yes. I've done other things too. But you know that. We've just—"

"I like to be clear about things like this—when I'm thinking possibilities. A professional rent-boy too? Not just in the back rooms of the club, but take out, as well? For weekends and such?"

I didn't answer.

"Any limits to what you'll give?"

I didn't answer that one either.

"You're good. You're really good. Good enough for an all nighter or a weekend. I like that little thing you have going of turning on quickly when your tattoo is touched. Genuine is that, or an act?"

"It's what happens," I said.

As if he was rechecking, he reached over and pressed a finger from the hand not working my cock into the tattoo, and I shuddered and collapsed into myself and moaned for him.

"Sweet. How well can you give head? I'll give you a twenty for a blow job." He was unzipping himself and pulling my head down to his cock, and I showed him that I was an expert in that.

"Very nice," he said when I was done and had pulled out a twenty that I pocketed up against the fifty he'd given me in the bathroom.

"That special service I said I operated in the hills above Denver. It's a men's club. A special men's club. Would you be interested in working for me up there. At, let's say, $1,000 a week plus any tips you get, for starters? If I took you for a weekend, I'd throw in another $500."

As far away from Abilene as I traveled, I still never could leave Abilene, it seemed.

But now I had a goal, even if it was, in some ways, a lot shorter goal than I had thought I would have.

Bad Neighbors

"You just come in for a drink and a look see, or you want something more, Oskar?"

"Just the drink today, Skinner, thanks. A shot and a chaser, please."

"Been some time since you got any, hasn't it?" the bartender at the Buckhead Ranch said as he set up two shot glasses for the big Swede bellied up to the bar. "You're still in fine shape, Oskar. You should be usin' it."

"And payin' you well to use it?" the big-boned Scandinavian with the fine head of blond hair said, towering a good foot above the barkeep as he leaned over the bar. His beefy arms, matted with curly blond hair, spread out dramatically on the surface of the wooden bar top that was marred with the carvings of hundreds of customers. He was smiling through his full mustache and trimmed beard, though, so he wasn't taken as trying to be critical.

"If you think I'm in such tip-top shape, why are you thinkin' I need to come here and pay for it?"

"You passed three tame bars to get to mine," Oscar. "Don't shit me why you chose mine. When you pay me for it, you get quality. Doubt you're spiking any of those grizzled old cowpokes you've got out there at that ranch of yours."

"Got that right."

"We got a new guy here who might appeal and get you out of your funk. Over there, the well-built guy with the dark hair and the sulky look. Just your type, I think."

The muscular giant turned to look in the direction the barkeep, and house pimp, directed his attention. Skinner had a moment of panic, though. He might have gone too far. The funk the Swede was in had lasted a good ten years. And the new man, a really fine piece in his mid twenties, really did look like Pete had at that age. Still, Skinner thought it was time for Oskar to move on. The man did occasionally take a guy upstairs and Skinner had reports that he was horse hung and a good fucker. He really did need to use it more while he still could. He had to be, what? forty-five or so. He didn't have too many more years of getting it up easily and getting pleasure out of it.

"I don't know," the Swede said. "Really good-lookin' and a fine body, but I don't know. He don't look like one to lie under a man."

One of Oskar's arms had slid off the table and was stretched down in front of him between his belly and the bar. Skinner knew when a man was feeling himself up. So, he knew Oskar was interested in Frank.

"His name's Frank. He goes both ways, depending on what's wanted. And I'm told he's a real firecracker and has a sweet ass. Course he's given some say here. If he don't like the look of a man, he don't have to go with him. You want to take him upstairs and go for a ride, Oskar? I reckon you're overdue."

"Yeah, yeah, I guess."

"A real sexy piece. Go for an hour with him?"

"Now you're pushin' it, Skinner. A half hour should do."

"Already hard just lookin' at him?"

"Yeah, guess you got that right."

"OK. Half hour, one shot, paid now. You don't come down after that, though, you can pay for the rest later." Skinner turned and called out. "Frank, over here, please."

As Frank walked over to the bar, his eyes latched onto the big Swede. There wasn't much else to look at in the room when the Swede was there, he was so tall, broad of shoulders, and barrel chested. Frank wasn't a small guy himself, but Oskar towered over him. And Frank was well-muscled, but he didn't have the bulging musculature of this rancher, who obviously was a hands-on worker. And hairy. The first impression Frank got was of the hair. Not just the unruly blond, curly pile on his head—some of it going gray—that curled around his ears and went down to his shirt collar, but the matting on his forearms and the tuft showing over the V of the plaid shirt he wore, material distressed across the bulging chest, above worn jeans and scruffed cowboy boots.

Frank gave Oskar a big smile as he came up to the bar, the Swede turned to him, leaning on the bar, and Frank looked him up and down, his eyes lingering at the crotch. When his hazel eyes under thick, long black lashes flickered back up to the man's face, Frank's smile was even broader. He preferred big-dicked men, and this guy looked like he was ready for it already.

"Frank, this is Mr. Swenson. You like what you see, you can take him to room three, please, and show him a good time."

"Gladly," Frank said.

This brought out a big grin from Oskar. He obviously was happy he'd passed muster, even if Frank was nothing more than a male whore.

Oskar didn't waste any time, and Frank didn't hold him off. He gathered Frank into him with a beefy arm around his waist and was working the buttons on Frank's shirt, with Frank doing the same with his, as soon as the door to room three slammed shut behind them. It was much like all of the rooms upstairs: a small room with all the essentials—a three-quarters bed, a small bureau, a straight chair, a wooden clothes horse for the client's clothes, and a porcelain bowl with water and a towel for cleanup afterward. They were standing in the middle of the room, swaying against each other, their mouths plastered together in a long, deep kiss.

Each were pulling arms back at the same time to shrug shirts off, and then they were back in a clutch, Oskar grabbed and squeezed Frank's buttocks through his jeans and Frank buried his face into the curly hair of Oskar's chest and searched for nipples with his mouth, while his hands worked between them, unbuckling Oskar's belt, unbuttoning his jeans, and pushing them and his under linen down to the floor. Oskar kicked those across the room and out of the way with the toe of his boot. No niceties of folded clothes on the clothes horse here.

Frank two-handed Oskar's cock and started working it, as Oskar grabbed his head in two hands and pulled his lips back up to Oskar's mouth. This didn't last long before Frank sank to his knees and was gagging on the big guy's cock.

Oskar held Frank's head to his crotch, reared his head back, and roared, his thoughts obsessed with the word "firecracker" that Skinner had mentioned downstairs. Got that right, he thought. The honey was all over him. Wanted it as much as he did—or was a real good actor in pretending he did. He felt the juices rise. He wouldn't be long at this.

Frank had taken care of getting his own jeans down his legs while he was on his knees, and bounded back up and was climbing Oskar's hips with his legs. Oskar went into a crouch, holding Frank's torso cantilevered away from him. Oskar's thick, hard cock had no trouble locating Frank's slack hole and sliding into him, while Frank grabbed gobs of hair on Oskar's pecs with his hands, locked his ankles behind the small of the big man's back, arched his back away from Oskar, and moved his hips in the rhythm of Oskar's deep thrusts inside him.

It was all over for Oskar in less than five minutes of pounding.

He hobbled over to the bed, with Frank still draped on his front, and laid the younger man down on the end of the bed, with his butt on the edge. He dropped down on his knees on the floor between Frank's thighs, grabbed for both of Frank's wrists, and started giving the smaller man head. Frank arched his shoulder blades back onto the surface of the bed and moaned. They were right on the thirty-minute mark when Oskar had come for his second time, crouched over Frank, between his thighs, where he had been placed by Oskar on the bed. Oskar had held Frank's waist and Frank had spread and raised his own legs and, when tired of that, had run them up Oskar's hairy torso, while Oskar was pounding his ass again to a second ejaculation.

"That's it, I guess," Oskar said, as he stood up from Frank's prone body. "Sorry for gettin' in two. Guess I was more anxious for it than I thought. Only a half hour I see, but Skinner will charge me for two—for a full hour."

"We could make it three in an hour with you only having to pay for the two you already owe," Frank said.

"You'd do that for me?"

"Yes. For return business. You fuck real good."

That deflated Oscar just a bit. He'd hoped the answer was that he was just too sexy to resist. That's what most johns wanted to hear. Of course, that's the line most prostitutes gave their johns. Oscar guessed he should be happy that this one was giving him a more honest answer, and still was complimenting him on his fucking. This one certainly had been into the fuck.

"I don't usually fire off that fast. I don't know if—"

"Come, lay on the bed with me. I'll make sure you want to go again inside the hour and can."

They lay on the bed, Oskar on his back and Frank half draped on top of him, stretching his full length. Frank had one hand stroking Oskar's cock back to life and the other playing in Oskar's chest hair.

"I'm too hairy for some men," Oskar whispered.

"Not for me," Frank whispered back.

Oskar felt a lump in his throat. That's what Pete always said. And this young hunk was so much like Pete had been when they left it off.

"I'd like to see you again—and again," he murmured. "But I ain't that rich."

"It could be cheaper if I came to you on my off days," Frank said.

"You'd do that? You want me to fuck you regular?"

"Again and again," Frank whispered. "You're a rancher, right? Tell me how to get to your ranch."

Oskar couldn't figure out what this guy's angle on this would be other than liking the cocking he gave him. He gave up trying to see the bad side of this. He barely was able to get through the directions before his was panting heavily again, and his cock was at full staff.

49

With a low laugh, Frank rolled fully on top of him, sat up on his pelvis, lowered his channel, on the cock, and fucked himself, moving up and down and back and forth and in revolution, with the palms of his hands buried in the hair of Oskar's chest, while Oskar moaned and groaned and grunted—and did what he could to thrust up into Frank's channel in rhythm.

Frank lowered his mouth to Oskar's chest and slicked up the man's chest hair with his tongue, making little noises to indicate pleasure that Oskar was so hairy. When he nipped one of Oskar's nipples, the man jerked and fired off again.

When he hit the bottom of the stairs, Skinner leaned over the bar and winked. "Really somethin' special, ain't he?"

"Oh, shit yes. If you could bottle poontang like that, you'd be a rich man. That ain't your usual whore house lay. Really gets the jizm pumping, that one does."

* * * *

Sunday was the first of two days off for Frank, and he rode out along the dirt road paralleling the Platte River away from the town of North Platte and the Buckhead Ranch male brothel. Oskar had given him directions to his ranch, and Frank was almost there when he came upon some sort of community gathering. At first he thought it was a church service, but it was mid afternoon already, and he quickly was able to see that, though the women and children appeared to be wearing what they would to church, they were gathered around tables, packing up what looked to have been a picnic, and the men were dressed in work clothes, some stripped to the waist, and were raising a small barn. The log cabin beyond it looked derelict enough that this might have been a deserted homestead. But not, Frank thought, if they were having a barn raising.

It was more of a big shed than a barn, but, nonetheless, it looked like they were working hard to get it up by nightfall— and were falling behind in the task.

Frank had been raised to be neighborly and he'd been to many a barn raising. The barns on his family's spread in

50

Pennsylvania had always been raised this way, so he turned his horse into the yard, rode up to the house, dismounted, and tied his horse's reins to the porch railing. He was stripping off his shirt, preparing to go help on the barn when a man, in his mid thirties, came out of the house.

Frank took his breath it. The man was the spitting image of his own father, but a bit younger, somewhere between his father's age if he had still been alive and his own. His father had died at thirty-six, though, so, here, standing in front of Frank, was the image of his father when he'd lost him—and when the family had been forced into the poverty that eventually led to Frank doing what he was doing.

"Yes, may I help you?" the man asked. It wasn't lost on Frank that the man was looking at his bare chest rather than in his eyes. The man looked weary, but his eyes narrowed when he looked at Frank.

"Saw there was a barn raising as I passed, and I was taught never to pass one by without helping."

"Thank you, but it's almost over. There's no more food laid out anymore, and the families are beginning to pack up to leave."

"The barn's not all up yet, though," Frank said. "It looks like there's a few more hours of light up there. And it looks like it might rain tomorrow. Best to get the roof over it before the day ends."

"It doesn't look like that's going to happen," the man said, a sadness in his voice. He was fully dressed and not out helping on the barn. It made Frank wonder if he was crippled or something. But then he heard a voice, couched in pain, coming from inside the cabin.

"Pete? You out there? 'Fraid I made a mess in here. Need your help."

"On the porch, Sven. Be there in a minute," the man, whose name evidently was Pete, called back into the house. He turned to Frank. "Sorry. Have a dying man in here. It's hard to get away. Been hard for a while. I thank you kindly, but . . ."

"I'll just go over and see what I can do to help on the barn," Frank said gently. "You go in there and do what you have to do."

51

Pete gave Frank a grateful look. "Thank you kindly again, then. There's no food from the barn raising, but maybe, if you have the time, you'll tarry afterward and I'll feed you some supper before you're on your way again."

It was almost a hungry look the man was giving Frank, and Frank could imagine how isolating and difficult it was for a man to care for a dying man—probably his father—alone. And from the looks of the condition of the homestead, the man had been a long time dying and needing constant attention.

"Sounds good to me," Frank answered. "I'll be going over to the barn now."

While he was nailing planks of wood on the barn roof to get it closed up, with another man nailing at the other end who he was chatting with, Frank asked, "Who is this Oskar men have been talking about who didn't come to the barn raising?"

"That would be Oskar Swenson, just the next ranch over. This is the first barn raisin' hereabouts where he wasn't front and center and doin' the work of three men. We'd got this one up well before dark if he'd been here. Looks like we'll still make it—get it under cover at least—thanks to you comin' along."

"Is this Swenson man sick today?" Frank wondered whether he should go on to Oskar's place.

"Naw. Guess it's about him and Sven and Pete. Bad blood there. Not something we talk about if we can help it. It's probably good he didn't come. There'd be too much tension in the air."

"Sven?" Frank asked.

"The man dying in that cabin there. Don't know if this work is all for nothin'. Don't know what Pete plans to do with this ranch when Sven goes. It was Sven who did the ranchin'. But not much use to talk about it. You got any extra nails over there I can use?"

Frank got the "we don't talk about it" message.

Pete was shy and nervous throughout a very good dinner despite his need to run back and forth between the two rooms. There were only two rooms in the cabin, the bedroom the dying man was in and the main "everything else" room, other than the outhouse, which, as with nearly every ranch in the West in 1915 was "out there."

At first Frank hadn't understood why the man was so nervous, but it began to dawn on him when he'd looked into the bedroom and had seen that the man in the bed wasn't old and decrepit; he was maybe in his mid forties. Another one of those big Scandinavians whose families had immigrated to this part of the States to farm or ranch. The man was probably only second generation, and now that Frank thought about it, when he heard him call for Pete, there had been a distinct accent in his voice.

He wasn't Pete's father and he wasn't his brother either, Frank, didn't think, unless the mother had really been messing around.

"So, how did you come to this?" he said over some sort of delicious peach cobbler they were eating for dessert and a cup of coffee. Pete could cook for him any day of the week, as far as he was concerned.

"To this?"

"Taking care of another man full time like this. He isn't your father or your brother, is he? It looks like you're devoting your whole life to him. Is he paying for you to do this? If so, why you rather than some housekeeper who could nurse him as women can better than most men?"

"I nurse him quite well," Pete said, flaring up a bit.

"I'm sure you do. You certainly feed him well if he'll take it. But you obviously are tied to him full time. What happened to the old barn?"

"It fell over—and then burned."

"This cabin looks like it would do so too if these weren't solid logs it's built with. The question remains."

"He's more to me than a father or brother," Pete answered in a small voice.

"Now, I knew that, but I think you needed to get it out and say it. And if you think that matters to me in some judging way, you're wrong. I understand."

"You understand?"

"Completely. How long has it been since you two have made love?"

53

"Made love?"

"Had sex. With each other." Frank wasn't going to let him avoid this.

The small voice again, without being able to look at Frank. "Almost a year. No, maybe already a year."

"Any other man taking care of you now?"

"No."

"Do you really think Sven in there would have it that way—would make you deny yourself if he couldn't give it to you?"

Pete didn't respond.

"Look at me, Pete. I said, look at me. There. Why are you being so shy with me? Is it because I repulse you or you fear me? Or because you fear that you could want me."

Pete was making a gurgling sound, but he eventually managed to whisper, "Because I could want you. Because . . . because I do want you."

"Come here," Frank said, pushing his straight chair back from the table and against the wall and opening his arms. "I said, come here. You need something. I have it to give."

Pete rose and took a couple of steps toward Frank, who leaned forward, grabbed the man's wrists, and pulled him to where he was standing between Frank's spread thighs.

Pete let out a low moan as Frank pushed the older man's shirt up from his trousers and exposed his flat belly. Frank kissed the man's navel and laid his cheek on the bare skin of the belly, which was trembling at his touch, while he unbuckled and unbuttoned the trousers and pushed them and the under linen down to the floor. Pete already was barefooted.

"Step out of them. You won't need them for a while."

"Why?" Pete asked nonsensically.

"Because we're going to fuck. I'm going to give you what you need."

With a groan, Pete did as bade and Frank lowered his mouth to Pete's cock. The table, and the butter on the table, was within reach. Pete gasped as the greased fingers found and entered his passage. He came quickly on Frank's face.

"I can't . . . sorry . . . I can't remain standing." His legs were wobbly and he was only being held up by the strength of Frank's hands grasping his waist.

Frank chuckled. "I don't intended for you to stand up." He had managed to unbutton himself, expose his cock, and work it up while he was giving Pete head. So it wasn't a long trip for him to lift Pete by the waist and settle his greased channel down on his cock. He pushed Pete's shirt up to his armpits and attached his lips to a nipple and started raising Pete's pelvis up and down on the cock with the strength of the arms embracing the man's chest.

Pete gasped and threw his own arms around Frank's head. Completely into the fuck, Pete raised his legs and pressed his feet against the logs of the wall on either side of Frank's chair. Using his feet for leverage, he took over the stroking. Rising and falling on the cock, faster and faster, forcing the cock deeper and deeper.

"God, god, you're good at this," Pete babbled.

"I do this for a living," Frank answered matter-of-factly. "You're pretty good at it too. Some things you don't forget to do, right?"

They both let out a small cry as they came almost simultaneously.

This must have been enough to wake the man in the other room.

"Pete? What is it? Pete."

Pete lifted his face from the kiss he and Frank had been locked in as they both flowed for each other. "It's nothing, Sven. I'll be in there in just a minute."

"I have to go to him," he whispered to Frank, his voice full of regret. "Thank you for this. I will be a bit. I know you need to be on your way. You can go ahead and go. But . . . thank you . . . You were right. I needed this. What do I? . . . I don't know what men pay for this. You said you do this as a job."

"Not you. I don't do you for a job. I did you because I wanted to fuck you. Don't sell yourself short. And because you needed it."

When Pete returned to the main room, Frank was stretched out naked on a rug in front of the fire in the fireplace.

Pete moaned.

"Didn't I tell you I wasn't finished fucking you? Maybe all night long."

Frank fucked him on the rug-covered dirt floor in front of the fire, with Frank kneeling, his knees under Pete's buttocks, holding Pete's waist, and Pete's torso arched back to the ground, his weight on his shoulder blades and his arms stretched out, with his fists opening and closing to the rhythm of the fuck.

They slept in each other's arms for an hour or more. And then Frank mounted Pete's buttocks as the older man lay on his belly, in a drowsy state, and rode his ass to another ejaculation.

Pete woke at dawn, on his back, with Frank reversed on top of him and closing his mouth over Pete's cock. Frank's cock was pressing at Pete's cheek and he just opened his lips and Frank filled his mouth cavity.

Breakfast was just as good as supper had been, and before leaving, when Sven had called for Pete again and, with a look of gratitude Pete went into the other room, Frank took one more look around the room. It wasn't much, but what was here was tidy and kept up well. A contrast to the ranch grounds. Pete was no rancher, but he was the perfect companion for one.

* * * *

It took a half hour to ride to Oskar Swenson's ranch. Frank could see that there was a bustle of activity going on at the ranch as he rode up under the arch broadcasting the ranch's name and could barely see the central compound ahead down a long, dusty trail. The place looked quite prosperous and well kept, and the ranch hands were already up and moving about on their chores even though it wasn't much beyond dawn.

He saw Oskar climbing the porch of the substantial ranch house from some early-morning chore of his own. Oskar turned and saw him and grinned. He continued on into the house, though, leaving the front door open.

He was naked by the time Frank entered the house, slamming the door behind Frank, and pushing him up against the wall beside the door. In a flurry of shared activity, Frank was naked too and, his back against the wall, had his legs crossed behind Oskar's back, the ankles hooked there, his arms around Oskar's neck, his face buried in the Swede's furry chest, and his pelvis bouncing on a big cock as Oskar fucked him against the wall.

"I haven't had breakfast yet. We'll have it together," Oskar said only a few seconds after he'd ejaculated and while he still had Frank pinned to the wall. One of his muscular arms was raised over Frank's head and Frank's face was in the armpit, licking the profuse patch of hair there.

"I can't get over that you like the body hair," he whispered. "Only one other . . . well, it makes me hard that you like it. We might have to fuck again before breakfast."

"I've had breakfast."

"Where? This ranch is a long way from anywhere."

"On the road. It wasn't much. I can have another one." Frank didn't want to reveal where he had spent the night. He had gathered enough information to know that the two neighbors didn't get along.

But he was to regret that he had said he was hungry. Oskar was a shitty cook.

"There's a housekeeper most days of the week. Housekeeper had illness in the family today." Oskar said in his defense. "Sunday's the best time for you to come."

"A housekeeper?" Frank said, looking around the great room—which was a whole lot greater than Pete's main room was. The place was a mess. More like a man's workshop than a house.

"She's not much of a housekeeper. But she's a good cook. Have you had enough grub? I have. I want to fuck you again."

"Don't you have chores to do?"

"Not many. Nothing that can't hold till tomorrow. The men can handle what has to be done today."

"I can't stay long. It will take me all afternoon to ride back to the Buckhead Ranch."

"Do you have to go back at all? I can hire you here."

"You know I do."

"Then . . ." without saying more, he rose from his chair at the table, where they had both been sitting, naked; pulled Frank's chair, with him in it, from the table; and was crouched in front of the sitting Frank. Frank put his ankles on Oskar's shoulders and his hands on Oskar's sides and rolled his pelvis up, as Oskar slid his dick inside him and began to pump again.

"Let's go into the bedroom," he whispered after he was done and they had been nuzzling for a few minutes.

"Already?" Frank asked, with a laugh.

"You say you have to leave this afternoon."

Taking a panting break between fucks in the bedroom, Frank took a chance. "They were raising a barn on your neighbor's ranch when I passed. Thought I'd see you there."

"Raising a barn in the night?"

"I thought I'd see you there. Don't you get along with your neighbor?"

"No, I can't say that I do."

"Nice looking guy on the porch who seemed to be living there. Heard him talk about a man in the house dying."

"A man was dying in the house?"

"Yeah. The place really looked run down. I think the younger guy really has his hands full."

"His name is Pete. Older guy's probably Sven. You say he's dying? That this Sven is dying?"

"That's what I was told. The younger man was sticking close to him in the house."

"He once lived with me. Pete did. He was mine once. Sven took him away."

"Ah," Frank said. And "ah" is what he felt too. "It's Sven who's dying, I'm sure, not the younger guy."

"You don't say." Frank could tell that Oskar was thinking about more than he was saying.

"The younger man looked like a real nice guy. In good shape. Wonder what he'll do after the other man dies. It don't look like he's gonna be able to handle that ranch on his own."

"I'll tell you what *I'm* going to do now," Oskar said, as he rolled over on top of Frank, and Frank spread and bent his legs, raised his pelvis for the angle he'd come to know Oskar liked, and pressed his feet into the sheets on the bed, ready to meet the big Swede's thrusts with counterthrusts.

He cried out as Oskar slid up into him. He would always cry out for Oskar's entrances, no matter how many men he took like this in a day. Oskar had a cock to shame all the rest. What amused Frank, though, was that Oskar never took his boots off when he fucked him. He said he never knew when he'd have to take off in the middle of something, and keeping them on gave him the extra arousal of doing something illicit, something that should put him on the run quickly.

As he was fucking Frank this time, Frank whispered a question in his ear. "Would you ever want to do a threesome? I could arrange that at Buckhead some evening." The intake of breath and Oskar's increase in the vigorous strokes gave Frank his answer.

"You'll come next Sunday?"

"Probably several times."

"I can't wait that long. I'll be there, at Buckhead, sometime during the week too."

"Good. Skinner deserves a cut. Feel kinda guilty steppin' out on him." Frank also named a date and time he'd try to set up a threesome at Buckhead.

Later in the afternoon, Frank stumbled out onto the porch, bowlegged and not walking a straight line, but humming to himself.

* * * *

Frank made it back to Oskar's ranch the following Sunday and had another romping day in bed with the big Swede, but he didn't stop at Pete's ranch on the way back to Buckhead on Monday, as he had planned to do. Instead, he rode into North Platte, where he joined in the funeral of Sven at the town's burying ground.

Pete was too distraught for any sort of mixing with anyone that day, including Frank, but Frank managed to get him to agree to come to the Buckhead Ranch that Friday evening at a specified time.

"Sven would want you to jump right back in," Frank had said when Pete said he couldn't go back home with Frank after the funeral. "You took care of him for so long and denied yourself. If Sven loved you, he'd want you to move on—maybe even reassess your life and reconnect with those who meant something to you before."

Frank was trying to turn Pete back to Oskar, and he hoped he wasn't being too obvious about it. There would be no way for Pete to know that Frank knew much now of what had happened to cause the bad blood between him and Sven, on the one side, and Oskar on the other.

"I know you're right," Pete had said. "But not in Sven's house. Not yet. I can't turn to another man, even you, that soon in Sven's house. What we did the other night . . ."

No problem, Frank thought, the house was about to fall down around Pete's ears anyway. And this was even better than Frank had anticipated.

"Would you come to me at the Buckhead Ranch?"

"Yes."

"Will you come on Friday evening?"

Pete had agreed, and, so, on Friday evening, when he arrived, Skinner gave Frank a conspiratorial look and said, "Take room one; it's ready and it's our best."

Pete was yielding to Frank immediately in the room, fully committed to the sex. The lights were dim and Pete was on his back, a pillow under his pelvis, and Frank on top of him, between his thighs, slow pumping him in the missionary position when the door opened, and someone else slipped into the room.

Frank knew there was someone else there—he had given Oskar a later time than he'd given Pete but on the same day—and Skinner, who knew all that Frank was trying to do, had sent Oskar up to room one.

Pete was so lost in the fuck, though, that he only knew there was another man when Frank lurched and gave a deep

60

groan as Oskar mounted him from behind and started sliding his cock inside. Frank was fucking Pete and Oskar was fucking Frank, and Frank was doing what he could to control the fuck—keeping it slow until the other two men were fully committed and then picking up the pace so that they reached a frenzy where it didn't matter who was involved in the fucking because it was going to go to jacking off regardless.

When Oskar's chin hooked onto Frank's shoulder and Pete came up to engage in a deep kiss with Oskar, Frank knew that the other two were fully committed. There had been a brief hiccup when each had realized the other was in the threesome, but, as Frank had hoped, both Oskar and Pete quickly recovered and got past the years they had been parted and the neighbors had feuded.

When he knew this either would work from here or not, Frank, maneuvered his way from between the two and left Oskar fucking Pete even thicker and deeper than Frank could and Pete laying back and moaning, with his tongue hanging out. Frank picked up his clothes and silently left the room.

He dressed in the corridor, where another of the male prostitutes and his clients were passing by, and smiled at the mixed gaze of surprise and lust in the eyes of the client. When he was clothed, he went on down to the bar—and to Skinner.

"I didn't hear any gunfire," Skinner said.

"I think it will work. We were almost at the half-hour point. Pete came for me. It shouldn't take long now for Oskar to come with Pete, if they haven't pushed each other away. It's a crucial time. If they go another half hour, it will just be them—and a shoot-off each. I can't see them not being solid again if that works."

"Don't know; we'll see," Skinner said.

"They're perfectly matched, so it needs to work," Frank said. "Pete needs to get out of that cabin; the place is going to fall in on him. Oskar's got a great spread. And Pete can't run a ranch, but he certainly can cook, clean house, and take care of a man. Everything matching Oskar's need."

"I sort of thought you'd land Oskar yourself and escape from Buckland," Skinner said. "You really wag your tail for him, and he can't seem to get enough of you."

"I expect he'll be coming back to me from time to time even if he gets set up with Pete. Maybe we'll do threesomes more seriously. But I'm not in a hurry to escape from here. I like variety and some independence, which you give me. I'm not in a hurry to settle down with anyone. Now, how long has it been?"

"Forty minutes. When it's an hour, I'll stand you a drink."

Frank couldn't help it. He checked the room after an hour. Oskar was on his back and Pete was saddled on and riding Oskar's cock. There was no sign of animosity between the two if one didn't count Pete's cock beating itself up and down on Oskar's belly as they fucked hard.

When Oskar and Pete had been alone with each other in room one for an hour and a half, Skinner got out the good scotch and poured Frank and himself a stiff drink. They clinked glasses and smiled.

"That Pete's gonna have one sore ass and be walkin' funny in the morning," Skinner said.

"Yeah, but both he and Oskar are going to be in seventh heaven," Frank declared.

Body Snatcher

"I agree that it sounds peculiar and there may have been some foul play involved, but I can't understand exactly why you have come to me, Mr. Reardon. Whatever it was, it's over and done with and no ransom was ever demanded—or at least you say none was demanded and paid that you know of. As you say the police told you when you went there, it would be very difficult to establish that a crime has been committed—especially as your son, Robert, won't cooperate."

"I want something done about it. My son hasn't been the same since he came home. He was missing for three days. There were rope burns on his wrists—and who knows what else? And he just drags around the house with a faraway look on his face."

"So, again, what can I do to help?"

"You're a private eye, aren't you, Mr. Gant? And I've been told you are good at it. I want to know what happened—who did something to my boy. He hasn't even shown any interest in returning to college. And he's stopped with his bodybuilding routine. He had been happy in college—and was very active. And bodybuilding was his passion. I want to know what happened. And if someone did this to him—did something to change him in those three days he was missing—I want to know who it was and how I can locate them."

"Yes, I can understand—but to what purpose? If your son won't—?"

"You need not be any part of what happens after that. I will take care of that part."

"I could look into it for you. It would be difficult to have any idea where to start, though, if your son won't help with the enquiry."

"I can give you a couple of places to start. First, you can talk with a family named Connaut. I can give you their address and telephone number. I've already talked to Harry Connaut, and although their son doesn't want to pursue this either and they don't have the money to, I do have the money to, and Harry is willing to help."

"Their son?"

"Yes. Their son and my Robert know each other—they work out at the same gym. And this is one reason I want to track down what's happening. The same thing happened to their son the week before my son went missing. He was at the regional bodybuilding competitions over in Laramie that week—and disappeared after leaving that. Again for three days, and his father says he has completely changed personality as well."

"And what does this young man have to say for himself?"

"Nothing more than my Robert does. He was missing for three days and then he reappeared and wouldn't say anything to account for his missing time. And Harry says his wrists have rope burns on them too. Mr. Gant, we think our sons have been held prisoner somewhere and have been molested."

"Molested?"

"Yes. In quizzing them, we pursued every angle of possibility. And they both closed right down and looked both embarrassed and guilty when we broached the questions of physical molestation."

"Yes, that gives me some place to start. You say they worked out at the same gym. Can you give me the information on that?"

"Yes. And there is another point of similarity. Robert was attending another regional body building competition—over in Rawlins—when he went missing. And I have another name for you. Chet Tarbell, over at police headquarters. He wanted to help, but, as you said, he couldn't put the name of a crime to whatever happened to justify an investigation. But he's the one who gave me your name. And he said that you could contact him."

Chet Tarbell, I thought. I wondered when our paths were going to cross again. He'd been after me for months before I broke off any possibility of getting it on—although I was sorely tempted. He was a real hunk—and I was into handcuffs. But I'd been seeing someone else at the time.

I'd have to telephone him and see what he could add to this to get me started on unraveling what was both strange and intriguing at the same time.

* * * *

"Hello, Chet? It's me, Dale Gant. I understand—"

"Decided to take me on, have you?"

I ignored this. This wasn't about deciding to "take Chet" on, as he said. But I certainly wasn't ready to say "no" to that idea either. I hadn't made up my mind and I didn't want to be rushed into a decision on that.

"This is about the Reardon kid, Robert Reardon. His father said you put him on to me about this possible kidnapping, and he said you'd tell me what the police have on the case."

"Did he tell you that the kid won't cooperate and that we can't officially do anything about it until a claim or some physical evidence of a crime is lodged?"

"Yep. He told me that. But he also told me that you'd be anxious to help."

"Well, I am, but it's not a police matter, so I can't do it on department time. You'll have to meet me after work."

"OK, guess I can do that. You got a favorite bar I can—?"

"How about my place? At 9:00 tonight? You game for that? Maybe you can provide some beer."

I hesitated. Suggesting his place rather than a public spot likely meant that he wanted to help himself as well as help me. But I had to start somewhere on this case. And Chet and I had been waltzing around each other for a couple of months now. I had to start somewhere with Chet too—or just walk away from what he was making clear he wanted.

Chet lived in a trailer out Canyon Road. There were other trailers around his, but what once had been a bustling park was less than half occupied now, and the trailers were set around almost haphazardly among the cacti and sagebrush. His trailer wasn't too close to anyone else's and I would have missed finding it except for the weak-wattage yellow light he had on beside his front door. His Mustang and motorcycle were sitting next to his single wide, and he was standing in the door when I drove up—just in gym shorts and flip-flops. And from the backlighting from the trailer's interior, he was looking really good—all muscled up in chest and arms and a slim waist and tight abs.

I was wearing just jeans and a tight T-shirt and loafers myself, and he whistled at me when I walked between his Mustang and the cycle and into the light from his doorway.

I held up the six pack of Bud I was carrying, and said, with a chuckle, "I assume you're showing approval of the beer."

"That too," he said. Then he withdrew into the trailer and motioned for me to sit across from him in a dining alcove that had a small table surrounded on three sides with benches.

When we sat down, he raised his feet, without the flip-flops, on either side of my thighs, which might have given me a trapped feeling, but instead sent a shiver of sensuality up my spine. His toes were long and fat, which set off my imagination about how other appendages were built.

"About the Reardon case," I opened with, as I handed him a beer and flipped the top off one for myself too. "Do you believe something happened to these young guys?"

"I do. Did Reardon tell you about the Connaut kid too?"

"Yep. Think their experiences are related?"

"I do. These aren't the only similar cases that have been reported. The department is interested, but neither of these young guys will interview, so our own department has nothing going to take on the pursuit."

"But something similar happened before—in another jurisdiction?"

"Yep. Down in Cheyenne. A young guy was snatched during a regional bodybuilding competition there—he was a spectator, not a participant, although he was into bodybuilding."

"Like the two cases here?"

"Yep."

"And he talked?"

"Bingo. He was held for two nights and a day. Bound."

"And?"

"Fucked repeatedly by a masked man in total darkness. He didn't like it much, or so he said. Don't know, though. Sounds a bit kicky. Somethin' that maybe you'd like?"

I just gave him a look and he smiled, shrugged, and continued. "After the second night, he woke up unbound and in a room of a shut-down motel not more than a couple of miles from the competition venue. And he just hobbled out of the motel and headed straight for the police."

"So, what are you thinking about these two guys? That they were snatched from other regional competition events and molested too?"

"Yep. And either enjoyed it or were made too scared to talk—or don't want anyone to know their cherries were popped."

I was breathing a little heavy now. It was partly because of the image of the case that was forming up—and it was partly because Chet now had his feet between my thighs, and I had unconsciously opened to him. One foot was rubbing on my crotch, and my cock was appreciating that—and Chet could feel that it was. He pushed the toes of his other foot under the hem of my T and had the sole of his bare foot on my belly.

"Uh, those are some talented feet you have there, Chet," I said, with it coming out as sort of a croak. I took the top of the foot at my crotch in a hand and massaged his toes and the sole of one foot as his heel continued rubbing on my cock through the material of the worn jeans.

"You haven't seen nothin' yet, unless you stop me. I could take you to the bedroom, bind you and turn out the lights, and fuck you silly. You're not going to stop me, Dale, are you? I haven't read you wrong, have I?"

"About the Reardon case. So, there's nothing official you can do yet, but if I do some stakeout—like at the regional competitions being held where they've gone from here and come up with something you can use, you'd be happy to hear about it?"

"I'm always happy to hear from you, Dale."

And what he heard right then was a moan, because when I'd removed my hand from his foot, he was managing to pop the button of my jeans open. He was massaging my lower belly with his other foot.

"Reardon said, though, that you seemed to be particularly interested in this case." I'd said it as a statement, trying my best not to whimper at what he was doing with his feet, but it was really a question. And Chet took it as such.

"Whoever this guy is, he's crimping my style."

"Crimping your style?"

"Yes. What the guy who would talk had to say was that the guy who fucked him repeatedly was muscle bound, had one monster of a cock, and great stamina. And he was rough."

This wasn't helping me ignore what Chet was doing to me with his feet. "And this crimps your style because—?" I asked.

"It crimps my style because I go to the same body shops these guys getting kidnapped do—and these sweet young things are what I like bringing home and fucking. He's taking my . . . gawd, Dale, you ain't wearin' nothin' underneath."

"No," I whispered. "I'm not."

He knew that because after popping the button open, he'd managed to get the zipper pull between his toes and pulled it down. My cock responded by springing out of the open fly and leaving no doubt that I wanted him.

He also knew something else, although he fished for confirmation.

"You came ready to play, didn't you?"

"If the mood strikes," I answered.

"I'm good at creating the mood," he said with a mischievous smile.

He got the base of my cock between his toes then, and I pushed my jeans down and off my legs. One of my own feet went to his crotch after I was free of my jeans. He pulled off his gym shorts as well, and I handled his nice-sized, engorged cock with my foot as best as I could. I wasn't anywhere as skilled as he was as he was now pulling on my cock at the base—but I didn't have any trouble getting him to engorge.

He leaned over the small table and I leaned in toward him as well. He lifted my T over my head and his hand went under my arms and held me at my side with his thumbs stretched around to thrum on my nipples. Our mouths met across the table.

He moved his face up into my right pit and snuffled and licked me there. When he was working on my left pit, I shot a load onto the top of his foot.

Chet laughed. "Come on into the bedroom with me, and we'll see if I can make you come again. Not with the dexterity of my feet but with the strength of my cock. I've wanted you for some time. I've been told you take cock and that you liked 'em my size. That's not wrong, is it?"

"No, that's not wrong," I said.

As we both stood up and I came around the table, I reached for a pair of handcuffs he had dangling over the chair that made up the fourth side of the table.

"Won't need those," he said. "I'm not really into that bondage shit. A guy's gotta want it when I fuck him—and there's none of this 'he made me' shit when I fuck a guy. You do want it, don't cha?"

"Yes," I said, still in a small voice—a voice that I hoped didn't reveal the disappointment I felt. I like the bondage. I like being taken hard and made to feel it was being forcibly taken from me. I'll happily wrestle a guy and continue to writhe after he'd cuffed me—and then change on a dime and not get enough of him as soon as he got his cock bottomed in me. The guys I fucked always seemed to like that as well. That's why I hung around cops. That's what I thought I'd get from Chet.

I laid back on the bed, my rump at the edge and spread my legs for Chet, as he came in between my thighs and began feeding his cock into my hole as he took my ankles in his fists and opened me even wider to him. He had great technique and worked me well, with me coming a second time before he did his first—and then we managed to come nearly together yet another time after finishing off the six pack. And I knew I'd let him fuck me again if he wanted to—but the full satisfaction just wasn't there, and I knew I wouldn't be pursuing him. He'd fucked me silly, but he hadn't bound me and turned out the lights. When he'd said he'd do that had been the peak of my expectation.

* * * *

I didn't have to drive more than seventy miles to catch up with the next venue of the regionals for the national bodybuilding championships. They were being held in a pretty seedy part of Cheyenne in a boxing gym that must have been in continuous use since the 1930s and not cleaned very often or well since then. It had the heady smell of male musk—and I'll have to admit that it was a smell that aroused me. It had been the smell I was exuding when Chet couldn't get enough of me. He'd said my scent was driving him crazy.

The light was dim, except for a couple of portable spotlights that were hung from the ceiling and trained on a wooden stage, also apparently portable, that ran the length of one narrow side of the room. The boxing ring had been removed, but its footprint was clearly discernible, the square of dark-varnished floorboards under where the ring had stood standing out in stark contrast to the different kind of shine of the gym floor around it, which was stripped of color and polished by decades of male sweat and shuffling bare feet.

The stage was backdropped in black velvet, with large, false gilt frames lining the wall in which the bodybuilders posed for the judges and cameras, and the platform floor was covered in a red runner carpet. Rusty folding chairs must have initially been spaced in rows on the floor of the gym, facing the platform, but by the time I got there, they had been haphazardly pushed to the back and sides.

I quickly could see why. The guys—and a few gals—there to watch the parade of oiled, nearly naked, highly toned muscle preferred to move around the floor, eyeing the meat on display from every angle and forming tight little groups and commenting on whatever it was they liked to comment on at these homoerotic pretenses that the arrangement of muscles "just so" was what this was all about.

They had gotten beyond the bantam weights and were into the light-heavy weights by the time I arrived, and nearly in total, those milling around on the gym floor—most of whom were in some stage of body development to dream of being on stage themselves—were giving their full attention to the guys mugging for the judges. This regional was male only, and I could tell from the stares the guys and gals around me were giving the contestants, the most important muscle to a good many of these gawkers was the one the contestant had between his thighs, which was the only covered part of his body—and even then not too effectively covered.

I didn't give more than a glance to these watchers. What I was watching for was someone in the audience watching the other audience members rather than the stage.

I quickly saw two such guys. One was a young guy with a pretty good body, but with a couple of hard years of effort in front of him to make the competition stage. He was scrutinizing all those around him—and when he saw that I was doing the same, he gave me a hard look and turned his eyes a couple of times toward the shadows at the opposite end of the hall from the stage, where two other young guys were standing and making some effort not to show their faces. Because they obviously didn't want to be seen, I did what I could to see their faces and burn their images into my memory banks.

After running my eyes over the cruising young guy a couple of times, though, I started looking elsewhere. He was too young and trim to fit the bill for what I was looking for.

But then I saw him. Mr. Universe of body. I could tell, even though he was wearing street clothes, that he probably could have been a competitor—in the heavy weights—on the stage if he'd wanted. The only downside was that he was as ugly in the face as an ogre. It looked like someone had taken a hatchet to his face and tried to rearrange the important parts—and for all I knew that might have been what had happened to him.

I first noticed him, because he was looking at the young, trim guy who was looking at the audience members more than at those on stage himself.

And I thought maybe he was about to make a move toward the younger guy. But then he saw me. We played a game of furtive "I see you, but you don't think I do" with each other, but then I saw him break off and slowly move through the crowd—in an indirect path that I could tell was a direct move to the back of the gym. When he got to the back wall, I was startled by the sudden blast of light—coming evidently from a door he'd opened to the street. He turned and gave me a bold look, and I made it known I would follow. If this was my guy, he was getting increasingly bold—which means he was becoming increasingly dangerous.

I followed. When I reached the door, now closed again, I looked around for evidence of someone showing interest in my movements. But I saw nothing out of the ordinary. So, I slowly cracked open the door and slipped out of the gym—and into a back alley. It was a narrow, dirty space lined with trash barrels. I could see normal activity at the head of the alley on a street that would be outside the main entrance to the gym. The other end looked like a dead end in dark shadows, I turned and walked toward the street.

I'd gone no more than ten feet when I both sensed and heard a movement behind me, and had time only to turn half way toward the sound, when strong arms were wrapped around my neck, putting me in a choke hold that had me dead to the world within seconds—and without an opportunity to make a sound.

* * * *

When I came to again, it wasn't to a cheery good morning, or sunlight streaming through the windows as the butler put my morning coffee tray down and pulled the velvet draperies away from the French widows. It was with the pain of a monster cock forcing its way into my channel. And believe me, I knew the difference between the two sensations.

I was in pitch darkness and somehow had been bent belly over a padded saw horse type of contraption, with my wrists bound to my ankles as well as to the legs of the contraption, which had me spread-eagled. The heavy weight of a man was folded over me from behind. I felt hard, full-muscled chest muscles, expanding and contracting with heavy breathing on my shoulder blades, and heavy fingers with jagged nails were digging into my butt cheeks and pulling them apart, as, with much effort—surprising to me as often as I'd been fucked—my assailant was forcing a telephone pole of a cock inside me.

God, it was a glorious fuck. Just the way I liked it.

I felt the strain of my balls being distended toward the floor with heavy weights—at least that's what I guessed they were—not having ever had that done to me before. But it was so arousing and drove me to such distraction, that I was game for the experience.

I also was game for the rapid, deep, and full-stretched fucking this guy—whoever he was—was giving me. He no doubt would not have been as interested in the fuck if I let him know that I was having a ball—that this was the way I liked it and that he was giving it to me beyond my wildest dreams.

Over I don't know how long a period in total darkness, accentuated only by his groans and heavy breathing, and my moans and whimpers, he fucked me in that position three times, each time for what seemed to be forever, and with very little time for his recovery between fucks. I came more often than he did—until I feared that my aching balls would just pop off my body and fall to the floor.

Fat hands went around my neck and I could tell his fingers were searching for just the right position . . . and then I blacked out again.

When I came to, it was still pitch-black dark, but I was on my back on some sort of hard mattress. My arms were extended outward and above my torso and were bound to something at the wrists. My legs were extended up and spread-eagled and bound as well. The Fucking Monster—which is what I had come to name him—was straddling my torso with his knees, facing me. He had the fingers of both hands buried in the hair at the back of my head, and he was pulling my head up, relentlessly, and my mouth onto his cock.

I gagged at the width and length of him, but I gave him what he wanted as I deep throated him, and I sucked him to ejaculation.

Then at least three more times, with little relief between, he was standing between my legs and brutally ramming my ass with his cock in hard, deep fucks that took my breath away.

He released my arms and legs after the third fuck and picked me up bodily. I took what opportunity I had to feel his musculature, and I was sure then that he had been the divinely constructed heavyweight I'd seen eyeing the audience at the gym—and that, from the talkative victim's description, he was the mass molester we were after.

At that moment, the case was solved as far as I could tell of what had happened to the Reardon and Connaut young men and also why the Fucking Monster was doing this. They said nothing, because they couldn't admit that they had reveled in the fucking they got. And the Fucking Monster did it this way because he was so butt ugly in the face, he thought he had to do it in the dark and didn't think any man would take him willingly.

This was nonsense, of course. With the cock he had on him, serious bottoms would stand in line to be fucked—and if darkness was required, they wouldn't see that as a problem. But rationality obviously didn't trump delusion in this case.

Where he carried me next was into a smaller, still-dark room, where he locked me in, unbound. It had a bed and a shower and a toilet. I have no idea how long he let me rest. But in time I heard the turn of a key in the lock and the squeal of a door on its hinges, and he was reaching down for me.

That's when I gave him the surprise of his life. As he leaned over me, I raised one arm and wrapped it around his neck and brought his lips down to mine and gave him a deep kiss. My other hand went to his monster cock, which was already erect, and I moved that between my thighs and to my hole. With a thrust of my hips, I impaled my channel on his cock and wrapped my legs around his waist.

I started the rhythm of the fuck myself, and I felt him trembling on top of me and his chest heaving as if he was about to cry.

I disengaged our lip lock and whispered to him. "If you want to do it in the dark, that's fine. If you want to bind me, that's fine too. If you want to get rough, I'd like that. But I want you to know that I love your fucking and can't get enough of you."

We fucked for hours then, in various bound positions, and a couple of times with my hands free so that I could explore the deep curves of his body with my hands as his cock continued its work inside my ass or mouth, and he gasped and moaned as I'd done for him the day—for surely a day had passed—before.

I spent several hours alone, as before, in the smaller room. And then we fucked again. His fucks were slower now and not so frequent, and we spent more time massaging each other with our hands. I could tell, however, that as new as the experience of a more-than-willing partner this was, his libido—his need to body snatch to fuck—was lessening.

After I was placed in the small room a third time, he didn't come to me again. I tried the door and it opened. The room beyond was empty too, I found out as I found a light switch and brought light into the room—into an empty room. Whatever devices he'd used to restrain and position me in before were gone.

I went over to a window and pulled the heavy drapes aside, not only letting in more sunshine, but also seeing that I was in the building that was immediately adjacent to the gym building I'd gone to for the regional bodybuilding competition. The alley from which I had been snatched was right below me.

I found my clothes neatly folded and stacked by the outer door, and I just put them on and hobbled down to my car—finding three parking violation tickets on the windshield.

I drove home and called no one. But I did look up where and when the next regionals were to be held.

* * * *

At the next event in the regionals, in Green River, I found more than I expected to find. Fucking Monster was there—but so was the young guy who had been scanning the crowd the day I was snatched. I stayed well into the shadows, where neither of them could see me.

On a hunch, in the ensuing days since I'd been let free, I asked to see photos of the Reardon and Connaut sons, and that had panned out. They were the young men I'd seen the guy with the roving eye looking at where they stood in the shadows. I went even farther in my preparation then and asked Chet Tarbell to get me a photo of the guy, Greg Ivey, who had been molested and hadn't appreciated it. This guy at today's event was older and slightly different looking—but not so different that it didn't make me think he was an older brother or cousin of the Ivey guy.

As most of those in attendance watched the bodybuilders on the lit stage, I watched the guys whose eyes were roving the crowd. I caught the moment that Fucking Monster's attention became focused on Greg Ivey's near look-alike—and, at the same moment I saw the look-alike studiously look away from the Fucking Monster. I also caught the movement of the Reardon and Connaut sons to and out of the main door of the venue.

The look-alike slowly headed for a back entrance—slowly enough to be sure he was drawing Fucking Monster in. The look-alike went through the door, evidently to a back alley, and the Fucking Monster went through the same door about a quarter minute later. I was cracking the door and looking out into the alley thirty seconds after that—in time to see Fucking Monster bundling an apparently unconscious look-alike in the back of an old Jeep Cherokee.

As I watched, though, the Reardon and Connaut sons showed up at the scene and sprayed something—probably Mace—in Fucking Monster's face and, when he'd knelt down and gone to his eyes with his fists, handcuffed his hands and, in turn, bundled both FM and look-alike into yet another vehicle—a Chrysler Sebring convertible.

I barely made it to the head of the alley fast enough to catch the license plate number of the Sebring and to jot down the license number of the Jeep—and to jump into my own Mustang—and keep the Sebring in sight as it moved off.

Trying my best to keep sight of the Sebring in the traffic ahead of me, I snapped open my cell phone and punched in Chet Tarbell's number.

"I'd hoped you'd call," he said when he answered. "Ready to go another round?" The tone of his voice told me that he'd thought I'd done just fine when we last met.

"Whenever you call," I answered. "But not right at this minute. I've hit pay dirt, I think, on the Reardon case."

"Oh, yeah? Speak."

"Let's take this progressively," I answered. I wasn't sure why I didn't want to turn this all back to the police at this point. But I didn't. "You check the names and addresses for a couple of licenses for me, and if I still think I have a handle on what's what, I'll tell you more."

"OK, shoot, and I'll call you back as soon as I have something. You on your cell?"

"Yep. You've got the number?"

"Yep. After the other night I put you at the top of my punch list." He laughed at his unintended double entendre.

I clicked out without further comment and concentrated on keeping well back but keeping the Sebring in my sights. It left the town limits and was climbing up onto the mountain overlooking the town, where I could see that people had vacation cabins.

My cell phone buzzed.

"Got your names. The Sebring belongs to Greg Ivey's older brother, Joe. The owner of the jeep is a guy named Sid Bailey. He's got a record that makes me ask if maybe you've fingered him as our body snatcher and molester."

"Yeah, maybe," I answered.

"And if you're pairing him up with Greg Ivey's brother, my guess is that there are going to be some fireworks that require police help."

"Yeah, maybe. Gotta go now, though, or I'll lose them. Just stay by the phone for me, Chet, and maybe I'll have something for you soon—and if you hang in with me on this, I'll have something for you tonight too, if you want."

"Dale. I think it's time—"

"Gotta go, Chet. Just stay by the phone for me—and maybe set up some police response in Green River for me—maybe toward the mountain overlooking it."

"Dale—"

I clicked off and concentrated on following the Sebring, which, a short time later pulled into an almost-hidden dirt drive. I drove several yards above the turnout and turned the Mustang and parked it on the other side of the road, ready for a quick getaway, if that was required. Then I started walking as silently as I was able up the narrow, forest-edged drive.

I got to a clearing, where there was a small log cabin, in time to see Joe Ivey being lifted from the back of the Sebring by three guys and, awake now, but obviously still groggy, being helped up the porch stairs and toward an open door. The Reardon and Connaut sons had now been augmented by Greg Ivey, who must have stayed at the cabin, waiting for them.

The Fucking Monster—I suppose I should now refer to him by his name, Sid Bailey—was nowhere to be seen.

I waited for them to get settled in the cabin and then I worked my way around to the back, where the window ledges came down almost to the ground, as the cabin was set into the slope of the mountainside.

Looking in the window, I could see that the four guys had Bailey stripped naked and spread-eagled on his back on a bed, with his wrists and ankles tied to the four bedposts.

He was being tormented by the four—sexually—and Greg Ivey already had a fat zucchini half stuffed up Bailey's ass. He wasn't enjoying the attention all that much.

I went around to the front and walked boldly inside.

"You guys don't want to do this," I said, hoping I had surprised them enough that they wouldn't just decide to tie me up as well.

"I know who you guys are and why you're doing this. I was hired by your father, Robert, to get to the bottom of this problem. I know who this guy is, and I've already notified the police, who will be coming to get him."

"If you'll press charges, identifying this guy as your assailant, Greg," I said, turning toward Greg Ivey, making sure he knew I knew who he was, "that will get this done. The police are anxious to get it stopped. But there's no need for you four to go down too on the same charges. Clear out now, and there'll be no connection on him being apprehended and the four of you. Believe me, he'll get his in prison where he'll be branded in the most uncomfortable ways for the nature of his crime."

I had spoken fast and with authority before they could get their thoughts organized, but none of them headed for the door.

"You've got about ten minutes to be down the mountain before the police arrive," I then said. "You did good to track him down. Don't make it worse on your parents to have you up on charges too."

"Come on, guys," Joe Ivey, the oldest of the four and probably the brains for what they'd done, said. "He's right."

"How do we know he isn't just a friend of this guy's?" Greg Ivey piped up.

"My dad did hire someone named Gant," the Reardon son interjected.

"He snatched you too, didn't he?" Joe Ivey said, turning back to me. "I saw him do it."

"Yes, he did," I answered, "So, I have as much reason to want him taken down as you four do. His name's Sid Bailey. Here, I'll write his address down, and you can visit him if the law doesn't put him away. There's no reason not to stay out of it, though, if they do put him in prison. And now you have about five minutes to be gone. What's it going to be?"

I stood at the door to the cabin and watched until the Sebring and the other car, a Camaro, that Greg Ivey must have driven to the cabin were out of sight. Then I turned and looked at Bailey, who was looking back at me.

"You acted like you wanted the fuck," he said in a tone that tried to assert authority but had an edge of hysteria to it. "You let me go and I'll fuck you good."

"Oh, I think you'll fuck me good, anyway," I said, as I started stripping off my clothes. That done, I mounted his hips and impaled myself on his cock. I reached back and started twisting the zucchini still stuck in his channel, and he screamed out in frustration and pain as I screwed it further up into him. But he also stayed hard as I rode him to two ejaculations.

It was twilight before I called Chet to tell him where the police could pick Bailey up—and that they should contact Greg Ivey for a start on a formal pressing of charges.

"Oh, and Chet, if your guys ignore the state in which you find Bailey, I'll be extra special nice to you tonight. I'm sure your guys won't mind a bit of revenge having been taken before he was handed over to you. If you think otherwise, I won't tell you where he is."

Chet said he didn't have a problem with that.

I dressed and left Bailey there, the zucchini well up into his channel. As I walked back to the Mustang, I was almost sad that I had to turn him in rather than keep him as a toy.

Desserts

It had been a grueling six-hour drive from their last stop on Sheila Worthington's nostalgic sweep around the region in which she had grown up before leaving for New York, a chorus line, and then a succession of well-heeled husbands, all of whom themselves heeled over and politely and conveniently died during the past parade of decades.

As Dominic maneuvered the Jaguar around the last hairpin turn and turned into the long upward-incline drive up to the resort hotel that wound around the peak of the mountain overlooking a large lake and several lakeshore communities, Sheila sighed and said, "Let's go ahead and eat at the hotel restaurant right after checking in. When I get to the room, I want to sleep the sleep of the dead."

"Sounds good to me," Dominic said, forming a charming smile on his pouting-lipped chiseled face and tossing a black curl out of his eye. And indeed it did sound good to him. He'd felt like he'd been on a tight leash for several days of the trip now. Sheila was OK, and she paid him well to drive her on this trip—and for other driving services—but, boy could the old babe talk. She'd yakked incoherently for the last two hundred miles about people he barely knew—and felt little loss at not knowing well—at the tennis club where she'd picked him up, dazzled him with an overstuffed pocketbook, bedded him, and planted him in her pool house.

When they approached the hostess desk at the restaurant, the host gave them a well-trained gaze and assessed them as money and boy toy hunk. He could see that the woman was nearly spent. She was tall and thin and had been quite a looker twenty years earlier, but now her high-fashion clothes looked a bit rumpled, her heavily applied makeup was beginning to droop, and not every starched hair on her head was behaving. And the hunk, a steamy Latin who looked every bit the nicely muscled tennis pro he really was, looked tight as a stretched rubber band and ready to spring in some direction or other in frustration. He'd also given the host an up-and-down look of speculation that the host had long ago identified as possible sexual interest.

Dominic's eyes met those of the host, while Sheila rattled off somewhat catty—but quite accurate—comments on the over-the-top Western style décor of the restaurant perched high over the lake below, the vistas provided being the establishment's best feature—and the host gave Dominic a knowing look that permitted Dominic the slight escape valve of being able to roll his eyes in a "women, what can you do with them?" fashion.

With a thought not only to the preferences of his fellow workers but also, he thought, to the preferences and needs of this Latin stud standing before him, the host picked up two menus and a wine list and said, "Come with me, please, I have just the table for you."

It was a very nice table by the window overlooking the vista from the resort in Mesa Verde National Park—which Dominic latched his attention on while Sheila talked about the impossibly spoiled frou-frou dog her friend, Maurine, had just acquired. "You'd think that anyone with white rugs and white furniture—all white décor—would think twice about getting a high-strung Pomeranian that—"

Dominic didn't so much see the mountainside tumbling charmingly below him to the edge of the lake as that, looking out of the window, he didn't see Sheila with her mouth flapping as she devoured a hunk of pita bread like a cougar having its last meal. And this, of course, was why he was gazing so intently out of the window.

"Wine, beer, or me?"

"Excuse me?" Dominic said, as he turned. There was his waiter standing beside his chair, talking down just to him and smiling. Sheila was lost in her rambling of all of the cleaning supplies Maurine had tried thus far without success. Sheila wasn't prone to see the hired help anyway, and Dominic had been ordering for her on the cross-country trip.

For the first time Dominic noticed their waiter, who he now remembered as the young man who showed up after the host had said, "Sandy will be your waiter. He'll take good care of you," and then had smiled and wafted off.

Sandy. Yes, Dominic could see where the lad had gotten that name. He was a redhead, although it took Dominic a minute for the "he" to register. The voice had been male, if a bit squeaky, but looking closely at his waiter now, Dominic could see that the rest of it was some sort of question mark. He was small of body and wore black tailored trousers and a tuxedo shirt with a ruffle. And he was standing there, hands on hips and slightly bent at the side that Dominic thought of as a "Bette Davis" stance. All he needed was a long cigarette holder in one hand and he'd slip all the way over into the Tallulah Bankhead pose. His face was made up. It was subtle, but he unmistakably was wearing red lipstick. His hair wasn't long on top, but it was slicked back in an obviously carefully considered "do," and there where long curls over his ears at each side. He was looking at Dominic with an "I just could eat you up" expression in his eyes.

Dominic looked over to Sheila, but she had moved on to rambling about the mistake her friend Dorothy had made in the choice of a tennis outfit or her latest husband. Dominic couldn't gather which it was, and, if both, which was the more serious mistake, and his noncommittal mutterings of ascent seemed to satisfy her and keep her motor running.

Throughout the service, Dominic could tell that the waiter, Sandy, could hardly keep his hands off him and, indeed, he did brush by awfully closely from time to time.

But it wasn't just the waiter, Sandy. Quite frequently, far more frequently than even a famished camel would require, another waiter came by their table, water pitcher in hand, offering to fill Dominic's full glass, with a broad smile or taking away plates one by one when he could have managed all in one trip. This young man was more substantial and a good bit less swishy than Sandy was. He was a tall, well-built black guy, probably a couple of years older than Sandy—and not more than five years younger than Dominic himself.

He was wearing one earring, and his moves were those of a dancer—not nearly as pronounced and given to a fling of the hips as Sandy's were, but in a manner that Dominic knew well—and that he found arousing, having frequented a certain gay club often in relief from the duty his pocketbook required of servicing middle-aged women—and men—at the tennis club.

Dominic could tell just by the way that the young black waiter looked at him that he was interested as well.

And keyed up as Dominic was—all this time on the road with Sheila and no opportunity to pursue the variety of sex he was addicted to—made Dominic go hard and begin to fantasize what he'd like to do with one of these waiters—or both. Maybe at the same time.

At the end of the meal, both Sandy and the black waiter's assistant were standing there, by the table, while Sheila was taking time out from her monologue of society in the town she'd said she wanted to escape for a while, to mull the desserts, finally deciding on the crème brlée.

Sandy turned to Dominic with a smile. "And you, sir? What would strike your fancy? We have a special on strawberry shortcake and also on chocolate cake."

"I'm not sure I can decide," Dominic said, with a winning smile of his own. "They both sound so enticing." Both amused and aroused, Dominic had caught on to the double entendres the waiter named Sandy had been dropping. The black waiter's assistant hadn't said anything during the meal, but Dominic was all the more intrigued by him because of that.

"Oooo, I love your accent," Sandy gushed. "And such a rich, deep, masculine tone. Are you from Mount Olympus?"

"No. I'm Spanish," Dominic answered with a laugh. "We don't have a Mount Olympus. Our people are earthy, not heavenly." He could double entendre too, Dominic mused.

"Oooo, that makes me tingle; it just takes my breath away." Sandy preened, fanning his face with a dessert menu. "Well, if you can't decide, then by all means have both, sir. And after dinner may I recommend our rooftop terrace for an after-dinner delight drink and gazing at the stars in our clear sky here. It's really quite private."

"I'm much too tired for anything after dinner," Sheila said.

All three men turned and stared at her. There had been no warning that Sheila had cut off her monologue and was now paying any level of attention to what they were saying. She had made her statement with a completely innocent face, though, and hadn't followed up with anything but her own preference for sleep rather than any after-dinner activities, so the two waiters dropped back a step and went invisible, leaving it to Dominic to pick up the conversation with her. They had conveyed what they wanted to get across anyway.

"Well, we'll just get you settled in the room then, and I'll bring my laptop back to the library they have here and check my e-mails and do some catching up," Dominic answered with a concerned voice. "You get your rest, Sheila. We have another 250 miles to drive tomorrow afternoon."

Less than twenty minutes later, Chocolate Cake knelt between Dominic's thighs on the rooftop terrace and gave Dominic's nicely proportioned cock expert suck, while Dominic held Strawberry Shortcake at his side, a hand on Sandy's buttocks with fingers snaking into his channel and his other hand stroking Sandy's pert little cock.

Sandy was making little high-pitched babbling sounds, which Dominic stopped by taking the little waiter's lips in his, forcing them open with his tongue, and swabbing Sandy's tonsils.

Strawberry Shortcake panted and whimpered as Chocolate Cake reached over and pulled his trousers and briefs off his legs and then held Dominic's cock erect and steady as Dominic lifted Strawberry Shortcake up and turned him around and swung his leg over Dominic's lap. Together, Dominic and Chocolate Cake settled Strawberry Shortcake on Dominic's cock as Sandy writhed and babbled a range of contradictory short, breathy statements: "Slow, slow, slow, hurry, all of you. I want all of you. Oh god, god, oh god. You'll kill me, I'm stuffed. Yes, yes, yes. Oh, yes, sweetie, give it to me."

Together, Dominic and Chocolate Cake, with Dominic palming and spreading Strawberry Shortcake's butt cheeks and Chocolate Cake holding Sandy at his waist, lifted and lowered him on the full length of Dominic's cock until he stopped writhing and started to moan and beg more insistently for the fuck.

Dominic stood then and walked slowly around the terrace, raising and lowering Strawberry Shortcake on his cock, while the young redhead clung to his midsection and groaned and gasped—and, in short order, fountained his ejaculation.

Then Dominic gently lowered the redhead to the deck of the terrace and turned, strongly erect still, not himself in flow, not yet satisfied, opting now for chocolate cake for dessert.

Chocolate Cake stood and turned fully toward Dominic, smiled, leaned his rump back on a terrace table, and started to unbuckle his belt.

Dominic strode deliberately toward Chocolate, giving him time to drop his trousers. And, that done, he moved faster, grabbed Chocolate roughly—as Chocolate laughed a hearty laugh—turned him belly down on the top of the table, used one hand to establish purchase of his cock head inside Chocolate's gaping hole, and used the other hand to lock one of Chocolate's arms behind his back.

"Yes, yes, Fuck me hard!" Chocolate cried out in a rich baritone—the first thing Dominic had heard him say all evening—as Dominic slammed his cock up inside Chocolate's wide channel. This was the tension reliever Dominic wanted. This was what would unwind him from all those miles on the winding mountain roads today "yes maming" and "no maming" Sheila's inane conversation.

And Chocolate Cake, well muscled and sturdy and robust, cried out that he wanted him rough and deep—and with pneumatic force. Dominic leaned his torso down over Chocolate's back, CC threw his free hand back and laced it around Dominic's neck, and they turned their faces to each other in a deep kiss as Dominic pumped, pumped, pumped.

Strawberry Shortcake moved behind Dominic and grabbed and squeezed his butt cheeks and helped maintain the rhythm of the fuck. Chocolate Cake also was helping, essentially fucking himself on Dominic's cock with long backward thrusts of his hips.

All three cried out as Dominic came. He backed up and plopped down in a chair, while Chocolate Cake turned and lifted Strawberry Shortcake up, laid him down on his back on the table top, slapped the little redhead's legs aside, thrust his own hard cock inside the channel Dominic had so recently reamed for him, and started to fuck him with a frenzy that had the little redhead sliding back and forth on the surface of the table. After a short breather, Dominic approached Chocolate from the rear again, and Dominic fucked Chocolate Cake while Chocolate fucked Strawberry Shortcake, bringing on a triple ejaculation.

Sheila was already asleep when Dominic came into the hotel room and climbed into bed that night. But half way through the night she was rested enough to nudge Dominic onto his back and fondle his cock and balls enough for him to attain an erection in a half-awake state, and then she mounted him. Exhausted, Dominic let Sheila drive.

The next morning, a now-fully alert Sheila, a sleepy and nearly hobbling Dominic in tow, arrived all cheery smiles and gushing accolades in the hotel dining room for breakfast.

Once again a more-than-eager Sandy was their waiter, backed up by a big-smiling black assistant waiter.

As their breakfast was coming to an end and Sheila was babbling about how she wanted to change the curtains in her living room, Sandy leaned down and said sotto voce to Dominic, "Would you have time after breakfast for some dessert, sir? The roof terrace is a great place for dessert and coffee in the morning." Chocolate Cake was standing behind him, looking ever so hopeful.

Dominic raised his eyes, a response on his lips that no doubt would be a classic, but that has been lost to history.

Sheila suddenly stopped running at the mouth, and in a clear, steady, not unfriendly tone, said. "I wouldn't suggest two desserts this morning, dear heart. If you must, I'd suggest just the chocolate cake. It looks more substantial. I was rather hoping we'd indulge in our own dessert of fine old port and cheddar cheese when we returned to the room—and what I was served last night was a little limp from too many sweets beforehand."

Fort Bent

Lieutenant Anderson had just gotten his dick buried inside Lieutenant Hendrick's hole in the shuttered bedroom they shared at one end of the barracks in the Fort Bent stockade when they heard the sentries put up an "Open the gates!" cry.

They were supposed to be taking a siesta, along with every other soldier not on guard duty, to avoid the blazing early-afternoon sun in the southeastern quadrant of the New Mexico territory. Instead, George Anderson and Bob Hendrick had, as they often enjoyed doing during siesta and also at night, wrestled heartily on Bob's bed for ascendance, both knowing that it would be George fucking Bob but wrestling for who would be on top when that was happening. George was crouched over Bob, who was on his knees, his chest flat on the rough-textured khaki woolen army blanket, with his arm pulled painfully across his back and George working his cock inside him.

At the cries from the sentries, though, both sprang off the bed instantly and were pulling on their skivvies so as not to raise questions about what they might be doing other than taking a siesta.

"One of us should be in uniform," Lieutenant Hendrick said. "We shouldn't both go out in our skivvies."

"You go ahead. I'll dress," Lieutenant Anderson said, as his lover popped out the door. The barracks already was nearly cleared of men.

It was a momentous occasion for a sentry to be calling for the opening of the gates. The stockade at Fort Bent had been under virtual siege from warpathing Apaches for over a week. The camp was new, put in place shortly after the Apache massacre at the Mescalero mission twenty miles to the east. The fort was being established to assure the settlers coming into what was territory claimed by the Apaches the they would be safe, but the assurances weren't working. Settlers were either getting scalped or were pulling out in panic. And now the new fort itself was invested.

The Apaches weren't sieging the fort within sight of the walls, but they were out there. And the last two supply trains were long overdue.

As Lieutenant Hendrick headed out into the dusty parade ground, he could only hope that the call for the gates to be opened meant a supply train of wagons from Fort Sumner, where Fort Bent's captain had been trapped, unable to get back to his command, had gotten through.

When the gates were opened just long enough for someone to get through, though, it was just one wagon, and it was a civilian tinker, a single peddler in a wagon, whipping four horses, rather than a supply train. The gates slammed shut again immediately to the sound of the sentries firing from the walls at the top of the palisades. The tinker obviously had gotten here just ahead of an Apache war party.

He pulled the horses to a quick stop, the steeds rearing up, foaming at the mouth, all wild eyed, but obviously fully under the control of the big man now standing in the driver's box of the wagon. He was tall and broad chested, dressed more like the Apaches than like the soldiers of the fort. He wore buckskins and had long, black hair, tied off in a ponytail with a leather band studded with turquoise beads. The buckskin trousers were tight across his thighs, a bulging codpiece laced up with leather strips centered at his crotch. The vest he was wearing was of buckskin as well, with turquoise beading descending both sides, which were laced together over his bare chest with leather strips. The vest didn't come anywhere near to closing over his deeply tanned chest covered with curly black hair.

Despite the long, curly black hair, there was nothing feminine about him. He had a strong face, with piercing blue eyes and a curly black mustache and close-cropped beard. The vest was sleeveless and his biceps, encircled with beaded strips of leather, bulged.

"That was a close thing," he boomed out, in English, but with a French accent. "Good thing someone plopped a fort here." He laughed heartily at his own joke. If the man was at all frightened about just how close it had been for him, he didn't show it. His voice was strong and steady.

Bob Hendrick had made it out onto the parade ground in his skivvies, but as soon as he saw the man in the wagon, which was piled high with trading goods, he stopped dead in his tracks and his jaw dropped.

The tinker's eyes scanned the group of young milling soldiers who had been jerked out of their siesta by the most exciting event to occur here in weeks of virtual siege. When his eyes came to rest on Lieutenant Hendrick, his mouth turned up in a grin.

"Why, hello there, Bob," he said. "You look like you've come dressed for a good fuck."

"Jacques. Jacques Trebec," Lieutenant Hendrick muttered. He saw that the tinker's eyes had shifted down a bit, and he looked down and realized that all he was wearing were his underdrawers—and his cock was still hard from what the sentries' shouts had called him away from. It had all happened in less than a couple of minutes.

Lieutenant Anderson came out of the barracks at that point, dressed in his uniform, but still strapping his sword belt on.

The tinker's eyes shifted to the approaching Anderson. "Speaking of . . . who might your special friend be, Bob?"

"Jacques. What are you doing here?"

"Why I came for you, Bob," the tinker answered. "Don't you remember that I said I would? I came to save you."

* * * *

91

Jacques Trebec joined the two lieutenants in the commandant's office after Bob Hendrick returned to the officer's room and dressed. The other men either resumed their sentry duties or returned to their siestas in the barracks after all had taken the opportunity of sizing up this bigger-than-life character who had dropped in on them.

"Where have you come from?" Anderson asked when the three men had settled down with tin cups of coffee. Hendrick wasn't saying much of anything—and wasn't looking at Trebec too often. Anderson had sized the tinker up, though, and correctly assessed him as competition—even with Hendrick—so he was sticking with business. He had come onto the parade ground early enough to have caught that there must be a history between Trebec and the other lieutenant, and he didn't like it a bit. The man had a sensuality and assurance about him that Anderson, worn down by weeks of worry over the Apaches beyond the gates, didn't feel up to competing with.

"From Fort Sumner," the French Canadian answered.

"Any indication they know what we're facing here?"

"They know two wagon trains didn't come back from supply trips to here or two other small forts. They know there must be trouble with the Apaches. They don't seem to know where exactly the trouble is, though."

"The two wagon trains . . ."

"I saw evidence of both on my way here. Both picked clean. No survivors that I saw."

"But you saw—"

"Yes, I could tell it was Apaches who wiped them out. The arrows were Apache and they had taken scalps. Got them real riled up, you do, bringing in settlers to what was supposed to be open range the army had told them they'd be free on. Their view is that the whole region is theirs."

The three sat there, drinking coffee. Trebec was looking hard at Hendrick. Hendrick knew he was but still wasn't saying anything or looking in Trebec's direction unless he thought the tinker wasn't looking at him. But Trebec's gaze remained on him.

"Have any foodstuffs in that wagon of yours—or ammunition?" Anderson asked, trying to avoid an argument with the tinker over who had the right to be here—he was just a soldier, doing the job he was assigned to do.

"Not much," Trebec answered. "Not enough to extend whatever you have for more than a few days. How many soldiers you got here? I didn't see many comin' out for my arrival."

"Fifteen, including Bob and me," Anderson answered.

"Not many. If the Apaches knew . . ."

"We're doing what we can to keep them from knowing."

They were silent for several minutes, each lost to his own thoughts. Anderson was thinking of their predicament. Hendrick was thinking of the last time he'd been fucked by Trebec. Trebec was thinking of both.

"You're gonna have to try to get word to Sumner," Trebec said at last, in a low voice. "They know there's trouble, but they don't know that it's here. For all they know, you were supplied and the wagon trains ran into trouble farther down the line."

"I know," Anderson said. "I've been thinking we need to try to get word to them for a couple of days now. I'll go pick out a couple of men. I'm senior here. I'll be the one to make the try."

"No, George, you can't," Bob Hendrick said, suddenly coming awake and pulling at Anderson's arm as George stood from the table. "You can't make it. I'm a better horseman. Sorry to have to say it, but I am. I'll go."

"I'm senior, Bob," Anderson said in a quiet, but determined, voice. "I'll be the one going. I'd be called out to give up my bars if I didn't." He stepped away from the table and walked out of the room.

Bob couldn't argue with that. He knew he'd have been expected to do the same if he were senior.

That left Trebec and Hendrick, alone.

"Why are you here, Jacques?" Bob asked.

"I told you. I came for you. I got in here through the Apaches. I can get you out. Only some of them are warpathing.

I supply them. I have a better chance of getting you out of here, hidden under my wares, than you do on a horse in that uniform."

"You know I can't do that. I have responsibilities here."

"Find us someplace private for a hour, and I'll convince you otherwise."

"I can't, Jacques. We can't."

"That other lieutenant's fucking you now, isn't he?"

Bob didn't answer.

"Well, he's getting ready to break out of here. Even if he's successful, it will be nearly a week before he can get back here with relief forces. You'll be here without him. But I'll be here. Have you ever gone a week without a man between your thighs?—since you had your first man?"

"You were my first man, Jacques."

"That doesn't answer my question. When I was fucking you, you couldn't get it often enough."

"We can't. I can't."

"I think you will. But even if you don't, I don't go that long. Either sleep under me while your lieutenant is gone or stand back when I take my choice of the dozen young men who will be left here and who will have me. I saw some of them looking me over. They're sex starved. There are plenty here who will lie under me, I'll wager."

"You wouldn't."

But he did, as Hendrick discovered that night, after Anderson and two young privates had ridden out, saying they'd split up and find separate ways to Sumner, with the hope that at least one of them would get through.

Lieutenant Hendrick was making the rounds of the sentry posts before turning in. He heard them in the guardroom next to the gate as he came to the doorway. Trebec was fucking one of the young privates, standing, against the wall. The private's uniform was on the dirt floor. Trebec was clothed as he had been earlier. Hendrick well knew, though, the utility of that drop-down codpiece in the French Canadian's buckskin trousers. The private's back was to the wall and his naked arms were around Trebec's neck and his naked legs

94

hooked on Trebec's hips. Trebec was fucking him with vigorous strokes while the young private groaned and moaned.

Hendrick was about to intervene, but then he thought, what the hell, the young man was enjoying himself; Trebec wasn't forcing him. Bob knew of the pleasures Trebec gave with that thick, long cock of his. It could be the last pleasure in the young man's life. Besides, the tinker had declared what he'd do if Hendrick didn't lie with him. Bob wanted to, of course, but he just couldn't do that to George while George was out there in peril.

He turned and went back to the officers' room, locked the door behind him, stripped, and lay down on the bed. He went to sleep masturbating himself while thinking of all the things Trebec had done to him when they last were together in St. Louis, and wondering how long he could hold out against Trebec being between his thighs again.

* * * *

Lieutenant Hendrick woke up very late the next morning, roused by the bugle call for breakfast. He rose, pissed in the pot by the bureau, dressed, and opened the door into the barracks.

His view was accosted by two muscular bare legs wrapped around a pair of buttocks clothed in buckskin. Trebec was fucking one of the privates on the end of one of the beds in the barracks. He was standing on the ground, crouched over the youngest of the soldiers, a redhead. The French Canadian was taking the young man in the missionary position in long strokes. He was holding the private's arms over his head and spread, with his fists grasping the young man's wrists. The private's head was turned to the side and he stared at Bob with glazed eyes and a look of rapture on his face as the lieutenant just walked by them and out of the barracks.

Hendrick had caught Anderson fucking the redhead on occasion, so Bob both felt that the young man was getting what he wanted and that Hendrick didn't care to save him from anything. It also was obvious that the private didn't care if Hendrick knew he was being fucked. Discipline was breaking down as the realization built on how hopeless their position here was. Bob remembered that the missionary position was one of Trebec's favorites. He just looked away and marched on, out of the barracks.

Not long after breakfast a shout went up from the palisades over the gate and all ran up the ladders. Those who had rifles at hand carried them with them. The lieutenant was one of the last ones on the wall. Trebec was close behind. The redheaded private, pulling on his skivvies, hobbled out to the porch of the barracks. Seeing him, Bob wasn't surprised to see him hobbling. Few were able to walk a straight line after Jacques had fucked them.

What was to be seen from the wall was a horror. The body of one of the privates who had gone out with Lieutenant Anderson was lying on the ground in front of the gate, his body shafted with several arrows. He had been scalped.

Worse, in the distance they could see Lieutenant Anderson himself, naked, staked out, on his back, on a boulder. His arms and legs were spread and his wrists and ankles were bound to stakes. An arrow shaft protruded from his shoulder, but he still appeared to be alive, if barely. An Apache brave was crouched between his legs and was fucking him. Another one was above his head, taking the first slice of scalping him alive.

With a sob, Hendrick grabbed a rifle out of a shocked private's hands. But Jacques Trebec was faster. A rifle shot rang out and all could see Anderson's head exploded. Hendrick started firing off shots immediately thereafter, but the Apaches had already disappeared on the other side of the boulder.

"You shot him. You shot George," Hendrick cried out as he turned to Trebec.

"He was already a dead man," Jacques answered in a low, calm voice.

"You could have shot one or both of the Apaches."

"It would have only prolonged his agony," Jacques answered "He already was being scalped. It's a shame your shots weren't truer. But I went for the man who needed it most." He stepped forward and embraced, Bob, taking the rifle out of his grip and handing it back to one of the soldiers.

Hendrick was shaking and close to sobbing.

"Come, man. Come with me. You don't want your men to see you break down."

"No," Bob muttered, not himself knowing if he was refusing to go with Jacques or if he was agreeing that the men shouldn't see him break down. Jacques decided for him. He turned Bob and nearly carried him back down the ladder to and then across the parade field, through the barracks, and into the officers' room. Bob meekly allowed himself to be led.

The lieutenant just stood there after the tinker had closed and locked the door and stripped Bob's uniform off him. Bob didn't help him but he didn't try to hinder him either.

Trebec sat Bob on the foot of his bed and then gently pushed on his chest. Bob laid back and just stared up at Jacques, as the French Canadian unlaced his codpiece and let his huge cock flop out. Bob remained watching him as Jacques pushed his thighs apart and moved between them while he was working his cock up.

"Now," the tinker murmured, "like before. Like in St. Louis. You remember, I know."

As he did in St. Louis when Jacques missionary fucked him, Bob raised his ankles to Trebec's shoulders and his arms toward Trebec, for the tinker to grab his wrists and force Bob's arms out and over his head as Trebec lowered his body on him. Bob rolled his pelvis up, helping the man's cock to find his entrance, and he arched his back and drew in his breath, not exhaling again until Trebec had slid deep inside him, where he held, his eyes capturing Bob's.

"Please, we can't," Bob murmured.

"We are. I'm inside you. You think I'm not going to fuck you now? Remember St. Louis. It will be like St. Louis."

"It's been so long," the lieutenant whispered.

"Yes it has," the tinker answered. "You always were the best. Worth savin'."

And then Bob was panting and writhing and babbling who knew what as Jacques began to pump him hard and fast, giving no mercy, knowing that Bob wanted none. Bob's pelvis involuntarily went into motion. He was moving it in answer to Jacques' stroking, and he was making his channel muscles ripple over Jacques' cock as he had learned back in St. Louis that the French Canadian loved—as he did for no one else but Jacques.

Jacques went wild with his cock. Pounding, pounding, pounding. This was nothing like Bob had observed when the tinker was fucking the two privates. This was serious fucking. And panting and groaning, Bob was giving as good as he was getting. This was being fucked. This was more, far more, than George had been giving him. Never, since, St. Louis, had Bob been fucked like this.

Jacques let loose of his wrists, and Bob grabbed the sides of Jacques' massive chest under the vest and crawled up the man's torso, tearing the lacings out of the buckskin vest with his teeth, licking his way up the hair trail of the sternum to bury his lips and teeth in Jacques' nipples and then on up to Trebec's bruising mouth, as the French Canadian lifted him from the bed, went into a crouch with Bob wrapping his legs around the man's waist, and pounded away.

With a cry, Bob lost the hold with his hands and arched back, his shoulder blades resting on the ground, and his arms stretched out, fists digging in the dirt of the flooring. Trebec continued pounding away down into him with his cock.

Bob ejaculated up Jacques' belly, but the tinker just kept pounding away, demanding another round of cum from the soldier.

It was St. Louis all over again. Intense, prolonged, no mercy. Total mastering. Demanding more than one ejaculation from Hendrick.

When the French Canadian was finished, he lifted Bob's body and let it fall back onto the bed, stood up and away from Hendrick, and only then undressed. His deeply tanned body was as magnificent as always. Heavily muscular, the cock and balls massive and hanging low, perhaps a scar or two more than Hendrick had remembered from the previous year in St. Louis.

He avoided disturbing the slick of Hendrick's cum on his belly, leaving the evidence that the soldier had come twice before Jacques was finished.

"Just like St. Louis," Jacques muttered. "You were the best lay then. Still are. Well worth the trip across Apache land."

When he was naked, Jacques stood over Bob, panting until he was fully in control of himself again. He went over and stretched down on his back on George Anderson's bed and Bob heard him breathing deeply, recovering, slow stroking his own cock. After fifteen minutes, during which Bob lay as he was placed on his own bed, Jacques raised his torso, facing Bob, and propped his head up on his elbow. He gave the lieutenant an expectant look. He was in erection again. "Come here."

"No, I can't, not in his bed," Bob whispered, his voice laced with shock.

"Don't tell me you can't. Don't tell me you didn't just give it all to me. Don't try to tell me you don't want my cock. Tell me for true. Has anyone else ever fucked you as good as I can?"

"No," Bob answered meekly. It was the truth. He knew he couldn't hide that truth from Jacques.

Then, more gently, Trebec said, "You have to face it someday. What is done is done. What I did out there today, I had to do. For his sake. If anyone makes it out of this hell hole alive, it should be you."

"So that you can fuck me again?" Bob asked, eyes flashing.

"Oh, I'm going to fuck you again," Trebec said, with a smile. "Now. You are going to show me that you want it by fucking yourself. Look at this cock. You seen anything more ready for you than this? Have you ever wanted a cock more than you want this one?"

Hendrick whimpered, not being able to take his eyes from Trebec's controlling gaze. After a few minutes, he rose from his bed; padded over to the other bed; climbed on top of Trebec, who now lay flat on his back; positioned his hole on Trebec's reengorged cock; and lowered his channel on the shaft. The tinker let Bob fuck himself on the cock for several minutes, and then he lifted his knees, pitching Bob forward into his enclosing embrace, caught Bob's mouth with his lips, placed his feet on the surface of the bed to provide leverage, and began to piston Bob's channel again. Bob couldn't help himself. He set his channel muscles into rippling along the cock again—just as Jacques liked.

Sometime in the night, Bob woke to find that Trebec was gone and the door into the adjoining barracks room was slightly ajar. Assuming that the French Canadian was roaming the fort, finding a young private to debauch again, Bob pulled on his skivvies and went out to the barracks room. Nothing going on there except for men in fitful sleep, the result of exhaustion in spite of growing fear and anticipation of the worst.

He went out onto the parade ground. The sentry in the shed by the gate looked sheepish when he approached, and Bob looked around carefully, assuming that the tinker had been there. But there was no sign of him.

"Where is he?"

The private obviously knew exactly who Bob meant.

"He's out there, Lieutenant."

"Out there? Out where?"

"Beyond the gate. He said that he knew the Apaches and that they were making a point with Lieutenant Anderson and Henry—that there weren't many of them and that they would now go make a point at one of the other forts. He said he thought we'd have time to send out another party, that the Apaches won't be back for a day or two. He said he would check to see if any were there."

"And you let him go?"

"He is very persuasive."

"Did he persuade you before, during, or after he fucked you?"

The sentry lowered his eyes and looked embarrassed. That was all the answer Hendrick needed.

"There's nothing to be helped now. Just be very careful when letting him back in—if he ever returns. I'll send two more men out to you to help guard the gate in case it gets attacked."

"The Apaches don't attack at night, sir. Everyone knows that."

"And everyone knows they shouldn't let a man fuck them while they are on sentry duty too," Hendrick said sharply. Then he turned, returned to the barracks, roused two of his best men from the remaining dozen, and sent them out in the dark. He then went back to bed—but to his own bed, not to George's, and sank into a fitful sleep, knowing that there, indeed, was nothing else to be done.

Jacques was there in the morning, shortly after dawn, announcing his presence by mounting Hendrick's ass in a morning fuck, once more dressed in his buckskins, his lowered codpiece flapping against Bob's butt cheeks as he pumped. When he'd ejaculated, he lay full length on Hendrick's back and whispered in his ear. "I went out of the fort during the night."

"I know you did."

"There are no Apaches out there. There is a window of opportunity for a party to attempt to reach Fort Sumner again."

"Only two of the last party were brought back by the Apaches," Hendrick whispered. "There's a good chance the third made it."

"Not enough chance to rely on. There must be another attempt. You must go yourself. You said you were the best horseman here."

Hendrick didn't answer immediately. The question was whether anyone should attempt it at all, not whether he should be the one to do so. Of course he should. It was his responsibility.

"I don't know about leaving you here with the remaining men. You'd debauch them all."

"And they would enjoy it. And it might be the last pleasure they have. I've only fucked two so far; others have been resistant. Take those two with you."

"So that you can move on to fresh ass?"

"Are you looking for excuses not to go?"

"No, no. You're right. I'll take those two and go."

As soon as he and the two privates could down a breakfast, they were off.

* * * *

101

Jacques had been right. There were no Apache braves warpathing between them and where they met up with the relief troops and supply wagons from Fort Sumner. Bob had been right too, though. The third soldier in the original party had made it to Fort Sumner.

In the end it didn't matter, however. They didn't get back to Fort Bent in time.

When they arrived there, the fort had been burned to the ground. The bodies of six young soldiers were found in the smoldering ruins of the barracks, and only three bodies, riddled with arrows and scalped, were found out in the compound. The fort had been surprised and taken before the soldiers could be mustered out of their beds.

The shock and realization to Lieutenant Hendrick was to note that the body of Jacques Trebec wasn't there. Neither was his wagon and horses. Hendrick said nothing to his captain who had returned with the relief column, but he knew exactly what it meant that Jacques wasn't there.

Jacques had aided the Apaches. He had gotten them into the fort. He had made his views on the settlers being brought into this land quite clear, and those views matched what the Apaches thought about it.

But Jacques could have done that earlier than he did, certainly on the night before Bob had ridden out of the camp. It had been Jacques who had maneuvered Bob to be the one to leave. Jacques had known that Bob wouldn't encounter Apaches, because he had arranged for that. And Jacques had known that Bob wouldn't be in the fort when he handed it over. The man had told Bob he was going to save him. He just hadn't told him how.

Bob wondered what he would do the next time he encountered Jacques—and he knew there would be a next time. Would he try to kill him or would he lay down for him and open his legs? Bob wasn't sure he wanted to know what he'd do. It did anger him that Jacques probably already knew what that would be. And so too, if he was being honest, did Bob.

Hey, Good Buddy

The two had fought each other to exhaustion, each one trying to master the other, until finally they rolled away from each other in the bed of ferns. Joe was the first one to laugh.

"Yeah, but who woulda' known?" Al muttered. "You're such a cute little guy, and you've been eyeing me. I know you have."

"That's because you're such a big hunk—a real bear," Joe answered. "I can admire good muscle definition as well as the next guy." They were both laying on their backs, resting on their elbows, only in their unbuttoned green regulation shirts and their boots. The two were sprawled side by side under the low, protective branches of a tall fir tree. They were far enough off the trail leading up to Lower Mesa Falls that there was little chance of anyone stumbling on them—certainly not a park ranger. Joe and Al were the only two rangers in this section of Yellowstone Park.

"I think I had every reason to believe that this was the muscle you wanted to admire," Al, the big bear, said, as he fisted his still-hard cock with both hands—without overlap. Then he laughed too. Al always laughed at his own jokes. Sometimes others didn't—not just because they weren't as impressed with his jokes as he was, but also because of his intimidating size and the thick matting of black curly hair on his deeply tanned arms and spilling out of the neck of his shirt. He tried to keep the growth down on his chin, but his five-o'clock shadow had been building since 6:00 a.m.

"That's a very nice muscle, yes," Joe answered. "But as we both now know, we both like to be on the plowing end of a 'hide the muscle' game, so this has all been very nice, but—" Joe reached for his gray trousers and started to rise from the ferns.

"Hey, wait. You aren't gonna leave me in this condition, are you?" Al was gesturing at his prodigious hard on.

"What do you propose?"

"Ever done a 69?"

Joe had, and they both therefore managed to come, but it wasn't easy going, and they had to apply more personal attention to their personal equipment than the project probably was worth.

"Kinda tame, wasn't it?"

"Yeah, for you too?" Al answered. "But better than nothing."

"But not better than what's possible," Joe answered after a few minutes as they lay there wishing it had been better.

"Meaning?"

"Maybe a bit of hunting would be rewarded."

"Out here? If you haven't noticed, you and I haven't seen much of anyone but each other for a couple of days—and we've both seen how much good that does. We're both tops. We could just go back to the station and put on a couple of DVDs. I guess I don't need to hide mine now or pretend like I don't know you've got 'em too."

"No, I mean hunting like in for real tail. You know what's down just outside the park near Ashton, don't you?"

"Sage brush and scrub pines?"

"There's a dude ranch down there too."

"Several of them, I think. So?"

"So, one of them—one of the ones closest to the park boundaries—is a gay dude ranch. And those guys come up into the park. I've seen them fucking inside the park."

"I'm not that much into just lookin'."

"Neither am I. I've seen them doing other things too. Interested in a little bit of fishing?"

"Fishing?"

"Fishing for pleasure. Oh, hell, get up and button up and come with me. We'll do a little bit of hunting and fishing."

Al had nothing better to do, so he just grunted, rose up out of the crushed ferns, pulled on his briefs and trousers, adjusted his shirt, and headed out in the direction Joe had already taken.

"Hey, wait up for me. Where we going?"

"Henry's Fork," Joe growled over his shoulder. "Upper branch. You comin' or not?"

* * * *

The two stood there, behind bushes and trees, watching the young guy for quite some time before they made a move. Joe had assured Al that it would only be a matter of time before they could make a move.

"See that pile of beer cans there? He can't last too much longer."

The guy was young, one of those blonds with spiked hair—too blond to naturally be his, although he probably wasn't too far off blond, they discovered when he took his T-shirt off and was just in shorts. The hair on his body was a light, blondish down.

He was thin, what you'd call willowy, with a nice body that was only lightly muscled, but muscled enough to say he wasn't too girlish. His face was sort of girlish, though, more pretty and sultry than manly handsome. His eyes were sort of brooding and his lips sensual and thick. He obviously liked jewelry, because he had multiple piercings with silver rings in them: an eyebrow, an ear, his lip—and when he finally rose up from where he was sitting and stretched and turned half facing Joe and Al, they could see he had a ring in his navel too. His shorts hung low on his slim hips. The curls of pubic hair from his groin peeking out from below his waistband showed light auburn tones.

"There, told you he wasn't a natural blond," Joe whispered.

"Sorta close, though. Looks kinda sissy to me," Al answered with a little snort.

"Out here beggars and choosers and such," Joe whispered back. "Besides, chances are good we won't be stuck with a third top with nowhere to go. I think he's kinda cute. You don't seem to be put off yourself. You've been workin' your yang for several minutes now."

"I'm so keyed up now, I could probably fuck a deer. I got a yin to use my yang."

"Shhh," Joe admonished. "I think we're about to be in business."

The young guy had been sitting beside a stream, where water was racing across rocks in the streambed. He had been sitting next to one of several deeper pools of water, lazily casting into the pool with a fishing line on a bamboo rod and frequently looking away from the pool and taking a swig of beer from the six-pack he'd brought. He looked like he was down to his last can. And he hadn't caught anything, even though the flash of light off of fish scales where the stream raced between the rocks promised that there were, indeed, fish to catch.

The young man stood and stretched. He pulled his pole back from the water and wedged the end of it between two rocks, leaving the line dangling in the water.

The shorts the guy was wearing were cut-off jeans, riding up on his buttocks, with practically no leg to them. A beam of sunlight caught his body as he grasped his fists behind his neck and stretched, working out the kinks, showing off his torso to the best effect. Al gave a little growl.

"Down, boy," Joe whispered. "You're going to get a piece of that."

"You sure?" Al answered. "He's going to get away."

"I don't think so. Wait for it. Just a couple of seconds more."

The young man was gingerly moving out into the stream, moving from one smooth-topped rock to another, being very careful because he was barefoot. His sandals were sitting by the side of the stream next to his T-shirt.

Reaching the middle of the stream, the young man turned toward where the water was rushing from.

Al moaned as the young man unbuttoned his fly, spread the sides of his skimpy denim shorts, and fished out his cock. Holding that in his hand, he arched his back and began to piss in a long, steady, golden arch—into the onrushing waters of the stream.

"Now," Joe growled. Not caring how much noise he was making, he strode out of the tree line and to the bank of the stream. Al stumbled out of the scrub too, in Joe's wake.

"Hey, good buddy. Watcha doin'?" Joe called out in a thunderous voice.

Startled, the young man nearly slipped off the rocks and into the stream. As fast as he could, he jammed his cock back into his shorts, but he left the fly unbuttoned, showing a cascade of curly light-brown hair in the gap.

"Fishing," he answered, although it sounded more like a croak. He could clearly see that he was facing two park rangers. He could also see that the big, scary, bear of the two had one of the biggest and thickest half-hard cocks he'd ever seen protruding out of this fly and being held in his fist. He'd sensed he hadn't mouthed the world "fishing" right and was about to say it again, but he swallowed the word the second time in the realization that he didn't have any sort of license to be fishing in a national park. He'd just slipped away from the dude ranch and come up into the park, following the bank of Henry's Fork. He'd come to the ranch for the fucking, but he'd been more of a sensation there than he had figured. He was fucked out for the moment—or at least had thought he was.

"Sorry, I don't have a license," he sheepishly admitted, not being able to keep his eyes off Al's club of a cock, "But I haven't caught anything. Maybe we can—"

"Fishing's the least of your problems, young man. What were you doing out there in the middle of the stream?"

"Just relieving myself."

"Relieving yourself, you say? Where did you come from? Did you come into the park from that all-men's dude ranch down outside of Ashton?"

"Yes, sir. I'm sorry, but I—"

"How old are you, son?" Joe was doing what he could to put on his official face and tone. It was hard for him to do and not laugh, though, with Al standing beside him and pulling on his meat. The young man was mesmerized by Al's cock. His own staff had come out of the gap in his shorts again and was standing up from his brown bush.

"Twenty."

"Yeah, right."

"I've got ID. There in my wallet, under my T-shirt."

"It's OK, I'll believe you. We can check the ID down at the sheriff's office."

"No, please," the young man moaned. "I didn't catch any fish."

"It isn't about the fish, son," Joe said with a mock sternness in his voice. "It's about that there pissing in the stream. Do you know where that water goes that you just pissed in?"

"Down the mountainside?" the young man answered. He sounded like he wasn't sure. And he sounded like he didn't know where this was going. He was licking his lips and staring at Al's cock, though, which had gone full hard in Al's hand.

"Yeah, down the mountainside. Past that dude ranch you're stayin' in. That water you just polluted is going into the water you'd be drinking in about a half an hour if you were down at that ranch. We take environmental protection very seriously in our national parks. We're gonna have to take you down to the sheriff's office in Ashton."

The young man moaned.

"Unless . . ." Al said.

"Unless what?" the young man whimpered.

"Unless you give it up for Ranger Al here and me. You come from that dude ranch, and I can see that you want it from Al. Promise you won't do no more pissing in the water supply, open your legs for us both, and we'll just overlook that pollution charge—even though we take environmental protection real seriously in this park."

* * * *

Joe and Al stood side by side, arms entwined, on the stream bank as the young man knelt before them and alternately gave each of their cocks attention with his mouth. They groaned almost in unison as he tried to take both cocks together in his mouth at once. Al was particularly pleased when he found that the young man had a ball stud in his tongue— and knew full well what to do with it.

"Hey, lookee here. He's got a ring down here too," Al rang out with glee. The young man was stretched out on his side along a log, with Joe standing behind him, lifting his leg with one hand, and fucking him in a side split. The young man's head was arched over the end of the log and Joe was slow-pumping his throat with his cock. Al had just reached over to pay attention to the young man's cock and found the ring at the base of his penis, where the perineum began, and pulled gently on it.

"Look, it makes the cock bounce," he said.

Joe had claimed firsties, because it was his idea and his setup. Al good-naturedly acquiesced, with the comment, "You'd best go first. After I'd reamed him, he probably couldn't even feel you fuckin' him."

The young man came with Al stroking him and moaned and gagged as Al rubbed his tonsils with his cockhead.

For Al's turn, Al was sitting on the log, and the young man, was sitting in his lap, facing him and fucking himself on Al's staff by leveraging off the soft earth of the stream side with the balls of his feet. He was crouching more than sitting, though, so that he only had to take half of Al inside him. Joe was standing behind the young man, with his hands covering and worrying the young man's nipples. He was nuzzling the young man's neck with his face and trying to tease the young man to turn his face for a kiss. But the young man was more interested in exploring Al's hairy chest with his hands and lips.

"Enough of this shit," Al declared. He grabbed the young man by his waist, lifted his body, and then jammed it down on his cock. The slight blond howled as Al started pumping his ass on his cock, slamming him up and down, burying the monster cock to the quick with each pull.

The young man's torso flopped back toward the ground, and Joe stifled his cries by pushing his cock between the young man's lips and beginning a slow pump.

Afterward the young man lay on his back between the log and the edge of the stream, his arm flung over his face, and moaned quietly.

Joe and Al sat next to each other on the log, both looking satiated and very satisfied with themselves.

"Hey, lookee there," Al sang out, "I think you've got a bite. Better pull in your line."

The young man moaned. He didn't move.

Joe went over and pulled in the line. "Yep. You got one. And it's a beauty. For another fuck, we'll let you take it home, no worries about a license. And no worry about pollution, either. It came from upstream. Your piss is down at the dude ranch now."

The young man moaned. Al leaned over and grabbed him by the waist.

The young man went home with his fish.

* * * *

"Hey, we're close to the stream," Joe said, as the two trudged along in the park the next day. "We might as well check it out."

They didn't bother to approach the spot of the previous day quietly. They just tromped in, laughing and joking with each other. They surely could be heard from a good distance.

As they entered the clearing, Joe and Al stopped in their tracks, both taking on big smiles.

"Hey, good buddies. Watcha doin'?" Joe sang out.

Their young man had brought a friend. The two twinks, each wearing just skimpy denim shorts, with their flies unbuttoned, turned from where they were standing in the middle of Henry's Fork stream, both still pissing in wide arcs into the center of the racing stream, both having broken into broad grins.

The eyes of both of them went to Al's fly, where he already had his monster cock out, ready to give them both a lesson in environmental protection—which Yellowstone Park takes very seriously.

Last Rodeo

Lattimore stopped at corner of the cookhouse as he was crossing from the main house of his ranch outside Laramie, Wyoming, to the corral to train the quarter horse he'd bought on the last cattle drive to Omaha. He leaned on a fence and watched young Kit chopping wood. The young man was stripped to the waist while he chopped.

Bulking up real good, Lattimore thought. Maybe it wasn't such a bad idea to agree to give him a job out of that special school in Rawlins. Kit was slow of thought and Lattimore had been afraid that he'd be more of a hindrance than help around the ranch. But he sure was a looker. And with the two months of manual chores under his belt since he'd gotten to the ranch, he was shaping up to be a hunk of a good looker.

Kit looked up and saw Lattimore looking at him and gave him a shy smile. "Hi there, Mr. Lattimore."

"You pay attention to what you're doin' there, boy," Lattimore said gruffly. "You slice that ax in your leg, and it will be a long, painful ride into the doctor's in Laramie."

The gruffness didn't bother Kit. Gruffness was pretty much all he'd faced in life so far, and he knew Mr. Lattimore didn't mean it. He had reason to believe that Mr. Lattimore liked him—a lot.

"You still taking me with you to the rodeo down in Cheyenne tomorrow, Mr. Lattimore? You said you would. You still taking me?"

Kit had a puppy dog look about him. Lattimore could almost see the tail wagging. And Kit had a very nice tail. Still, Lattimore gritted his teeth. Kit had asked for the same reassurance three times a day for the last week, ever since Lattimore had said he'd take him. He looked around to see if any of the other hands were about. None were. They all were supposed to be off at far corners of the ranch today anyway. He looked back at Kit.

"Well, that depends, Kit. It depends on how nice you can be to me today."

"I can be real nice to you today, Mr. Lattimore. Does this mean you want us to go into the house now?"

"Yes, Kit, this means I want us to go into the house now." The quarter horse could wait, Lattimore thought. His current need couldn't. Kit looked damn good stripped to the waist with his new muscles rippling from chopping that wood.

Kit sucked him about to bursting, kneeling between his knees as he sat on the end of his bed.

"Enough, Kit. Want you to ride it now. Ride it and think about that rodeo in Cheyenne tomorrow."

Kit stood, unbuckled and unbuttoned his trousers, let them drop to the floor, and kicked them away. He stood there, looking shy, waiting for instructions.

"Want you to sit on it right here, Kit. Knees up on the bed."

Kit went up on the bed, crouched over Lattimore's sitting body, and slid his knees past Lattimore's buttocks on either side.

"Sit on it now, boy. Think about the rodeo. Pretend you're on a bucking bull. Bounce on it. Yes . . . yes . . . yes!"

Lattimore grabbed Kit's waist to keep the young man from careening off onto the floor and grunted while Kit groaned at the effort to fuck himself on Lattimore's tool. Lattimore pressed his face between Kit's pecs, sniffed in the scent of honest-work in the youthful sweat, and tongued the young man's pecs and nipples while he waited for his send off.

Later, in the night, Lattimore entered the small lean-to shed built against the side of the barn, where Kit's sleeping pallet was located.

Kit was lying, naked, on his belly, softly snoring. He woke, still drowsy, as Lattimore lowered himself at full stretch on Kit's back, fingers that he'd greased before entering the shed going to Kit's hole. With a groan, Kit automatically spread his legs and moved the top of his feet to lay on top of the backs of Lattimore's ankles. Lattimore had already been here several times since Kit had arrived on the ranch. Kit at first had worried about this special attention Lattimore gave him—but he had settled down to accepting it in exchange for how nice they had been to him on the ranch. A couple of the other ranch hands had been nice to him too—as nice as Lattimore was being.

The fingers were exchanged for something bigger, thicker, and Kit groaned and whispered, "Mr. Lattimore."

"Shush, Kit. Just lie there and take it. Think about the rodeo we're going to tomorrow. Think of yourself as a bull. A big, sexy bull. And I'm the rodeo rider. You can buck your butt like the bull, if you like. Yes, like that. That's nice. That's so nice."

Lattimore leaned over Kit's back, pressing the heels of his hands into Kit's shoulder blades, and raised a bit up on his knees, because, from the power of suggestion, Kit had gotten into the rodeo image Lattimore had woven and was bouncing his pelvis up to Lattimore's groin now, stroking himself on the cock Lattimore had buried in his channel. He was doing most of the work of the fuck.

"Wooeee!" Lattimore exclaimed, as Kit bucked underneath him. "Ride 'em cowboy. Ain't we havin' us a barrel of fun now! We got our own rodeo right here."

* * * *

"Look at that! Look at that, Mr. Lattimore." Kit was grabbing Lattimore's arm and bouncing up and down on the rough board of the stands.

Rodeos were the greatest entertainment you could get all across the West in those days. Those and traveling shows like Wild Bob Hickok's. Kit had never been to one before, and Lattimore turned in his seat and laughed at how much like a child Kit was being in his reaction to the rodeo. He'd lay him over on the seat and fuck him right here if half of southwest Wyoming hadn't come out for this.

They were watching a lithe young cowboy, who the menu card tacked on the nearby post identified as Howling Hank, buck around the ring on a horse that was snorting and rearing to beat the band. Hank was howling too, which Kit thought might have something to do with his name. Kit couldn't quite make out some of the names on the board. They didn't seem to be ones a mother would give a child, but what did he know? This was as far from Rawlins as he'd ever been. In any event, Kit watched the young, blond cowboy with special interest, because he didn't look much older than Kit was himself. Kit could fantasize about that being him. Traveling the world with the rodeo. He couldn't think of anything better.

His eyes really bugged out, though, when the bull riding started with the featured cowboy, Rodeo Bob. The man must have been destined for rodeo fame, Kit thought, from the time his mama had given him his Christian name. Kit could see why he got top billing. He stayed on the bull longer than the other man Kit saw ride a bull that day, and his bull was angrier and bucked more, kept red-hot angry by two clowns teasing and tempting him as he bucked Rodeo Bob around the ring—that and the strap they had bound tightly around bull's nuts.

The bull charged the edge of the ring right where Lattimore and Kit were sitting, and Kit reared back in fear and knocked the beef jerky pack Lattimore was holding out of his hands and down under the open stands.

"Wooeee!" he yelled, both scared and exhilarated, as the bull veered off at the last moment.

Lattimore started to admonish him about losing the beef jerky, but Kit looked so much like an excited child that he couldn't.

The clowns pulled out of the ring after one pulled the strap from around the bull's belly, and the animal quieted down. The audience applauded the skill of Rodeo Bob, giving no credit in the bull's loss of ire to the clowns having stopped harassing it.

Kit turned to Lattimore, eyes wide open and face flushed. "He's the best, ain't he, Mr. Lattimore? He's the fuckin' best."

"Yes, he's good," Lattimore agreed, his mind actually concentrating on how much pleasure he'd get out of fucking Kit that night.

"Oh, look, another bull rider," Kit exclaimed as he turned his attention back to the ring. "But he looks like he's dark brown, Mr. Lattimore. Don't he look dark brown to you? Have you ever seen a man who was dark brown like that?"

"Yes, he's dark brown, Kit," Lattimore said. "Don't see many this far north, but, yes, there's darky cowboys. A slew of them came into the West from the South after the war. Freed but not knowing what to do with themselves. He's too young to be one of those, but probably from a darky daddy and an Indian squaw mammy. No white women would have let a darky from the war touch them."

"He's good too," Kit said, but soon added, "but not as good as Rodeo Bob." He watched the black cowboy, identified as Black Tex on the board, careen off the bull in an arc that put his ass on the ground. The clowns cajoled the bull away from him, as the cowboy scampered up, seemingly unharmed despite the delicious sound of alarm that had gone through the crowd when he went soaring, and hobbled off to the side of the ring.

Lattimore remembered his beef jerky was gone. "Go to the food trailer and get me more jerky, Kit," he commanded.

"Yeah, sure, Mr. Lattimore. Sorry for losing it for you."

When Kit got down from the stands, he got the notion to look for the jerky that had gone under the stands before wasting Mr. Lattimore's money by buying a new pack. He could just wipe them off and save Mr. Lattimore the money. No thought of keeping the money crossed his mind, nor was there any thought that Lattimore might not want jerky that had been in the dirt under the stands along with anything else that had been thrown under there. Such thoughts were a bit complex for Kit to get his mind around.

When he went under the stands, though, he saw two men standing close together. They were kissing and rubbing their hands on each other's bodies. This didn't particularly disturb Kit, of course, because he'd been doing some of that himself with Lattimore and a few of the other ranch hands over the last couple of months. It didn't disturb him when one man pushed the other down on his knees in front of him and started to unbutton his jeans either. He'd had that done to him too.

But it did make him knit his brow when the guy wouldn't go down on his knees but, rather, broke away and walked off along the line of the stands to a break in them and back to the circle of wagons where the ticket and food wagons and a couple of game wagons were.

Kit pulled away from the stands. The man who hadn't gotten what he wanted walked right by Kit and into the circle of wagons. Kit gasped. It was Rodeo Bob. And he looked angry. Rodeo Bob, the biggest attraction at this rodeo wasn't getting what he wanted—what he deserved as the rodeo star. Would he be so angry that he didn't ride anymore? That would be a real shame, Kit thought.

He followed behind the man as Rodeo Bob moved to the second line of wagons. He was opening the door of one when he turned and saw Kit standing there.

"Yes, what the fuck you want?" he growled.

"I saw you under the stands."

"So fuckin' what?"

"I can give you what that man wouldn't."

Rodeo Bob looked Kit over—really looked at him for the first time. He liked what he saw.

"Come into the wagon then."

Kit decided this must be Rodeo Bob's own wagon. Mr. Lattimore said that they put the wagons on flatbed rail cars to move from major city to major city and pulled them with horses from there to the smaller towns. This must be Rodeo Bob's trailer because posters showing him on a bucking horse were plastered all over one inside wall of the wagon.

Rodeo Bob sat on a bed built into one side, his legs spread, with Kit kneeling between his thighs, and groaned as Kit serviced his cock to ejaculation.

"Pretty good, kid," Rodeo Bob said after he was finished and was standing and buttoning up his jeans. "Gotta go get ready for my next ride now, but you were pretty good. Here, here's a free ticket to our next rodeo down in Fort Collins, Colorado. I gotta go now."

"Fort Collins? Ain't never been there. I don't think—"

"It's what I have to give you. That's enough for a blow job. You liked it as much as I did, and you asked for it."

Kit looked somewhat bewildered. He hadn't expected to be given anything for the pleasure of pleasuring the rodeo star, and he didn't know why Rodeo Bob still seemed riled up.

Rodeo Bob left the wagon, leaving Kit holding a ticket to something that was way, way out of his world. The rodeo star had thereby made two mistakes. He'd given that ticket to Kit, and he hadn't specifically told Kit to leave the wagon.

* * * *

Rodeo Bob was on his back on his bed and Howling Hank was saddled on his cock and riding it—and doing a little howling, unrestricted by any thought that anyone could hear them, because the wagon sat on a flatbed railcar riding the rails overnight between Laramie and Fort Collins.

The older man was holding HH by the waist and slamming him up and down on his cock. His head was turned to the side, his eyes focusing on nothing until he saw the slight movement in the door under the counter across from the bed as it opened a crack and then closed and then opened again. It registered in RB's brain that this wasn't natural. Once the door had opened, it should just swing open and move with the lurching movement of the train. It didn't. And what should be in that cabinet—a chamber pot and piss bowl and a stack of towels—were sitting on the floor of the wagon. They were lurching from side to side, with the porcelain bowl in imminent danger of being shattered. The perilous bowl clicked with him first; the opening and closing cabinet door only later. He leaped from the bed, pushing an "ooofing" Hank aside; held the bowl steady with one hand; and opened the cabinet with the other to return it to where it belonged.

"What the fuck?" he and Hank exclaimed almost in unison.

117

Kit was folded up into a tight ball inside the cabinet. It was only with effort that Rodeo Bob managed to haul him out of there. "What the fuck are you doing here?"

"You gave me a ticket to the rodeo in Fort Collins," Kit answered sheepishly. "And I was told this here train was going to Fort Collins."

Rodeo Bob laughed and Hank gave a snort from behind him. The two were horny in an interrupted way, and were frisky to boot.

"Well, you gotta earn your ride to Fort Collins, boy," Rodeo Bob said.

Kit didn't seem to object, although he got in a lot more howling than Hank did.

Rodeo Bob settled on his back on the bed again, and Kit was set down on his cock, facing him. They really started going to town, though, when Howling Hank crouched down behind Kit over Bob's thighs, pushed Kit forward onto Bob's chest and worked his cock in above Rodeo Bob's inside Kit's channel.

They fucked him good and for nearly an hour together as the lurching of the train and monotonous clack, clack, clack of the rails they went over helped with the rhythm of the fuck.

In the morning, as the wagons were being taken off the flatbeds in Fort Collins, Rodeo Bob sat up on the edge of the bed and scratched his balls languidly. Howling Hank was already gone. Curled up on the floor, though, was Kit. Bob nudged him with his foot.

"Gotta get up, kid. We'll put you on a train back to Laramie. Sorry about last night. We got carried away." He didn't sound sorry, though. He sounded quite self-satisfied.

Kit sat up on the floor and rubbed the sleep out of his eyes. "I don't want to go back to Laramie. I want to stay here with you. And you gave me a ticket to the rodeo here."

"How old are you, kid?"

"Nineteen."

"Don't look like it, but I'll take your word for it. No parents looking for you in Laramie?" The young guy looked good naked, even in the daylight streaming through the wagon windows. He'd been a good, willing fuck last night. Weird about doubling him, but he'd gone with it.

"Raised in an orphanage. Can I stay here with you?" Kit was looking up at Rodeo Bob with eyes full of worship.

Bob fucked him again on the bed, with Kit on his back, and Bob laying on him between Kit's spread thighs and Kit rubbing the heels of his feet on Bob's calves. He was as good a fuck one on one as he had been as a double.

"We could see if Stan can find a job for you. But you can't stay in this wagon."

"Why can't I stay with you?"

"Hank sleeps in here with me most nights."

"But there are other times, other nights?"

"Yep, there are."

Stan, who was the manager of the rodeo, was happy to sign on another hand when Kit didn't balk at feeding and cleaning up after horses.

"We always seem to have need for help, especially working with the animals," he said. "Gotta find me a second ringmaster too. It's about to wear me out with all the rest I have to do. You look fit, but I don't want to take on anyone who is going to be more trouble with sickness than help. Go see Doc Pender. Tell him I want him to look you over real good. A job here depends on him saying you're fit."

Kit worried about that on the way to the doctor's wagon. He sure wanted to be fit. He didn't want to go back to Laramie. He wanted to be close to Rodeo Bob. He wanted to be declared fit. And he wanted to use that free ticket to the rodeo here in Fort Collins. No one bothered to tell him that employees of the rodeo got in free.

Doc Pender gave him a complete examination, with Kit stripped down to his birthday suit. So impressed with the young man's physical conditioning was the doctor that his hands were trembling as he felt and probed, and his cock was hard and throbbing. Kit was squatting down on the back edge of the bed in the doctor's wagon, his fists pressed into the bed in front of him, leaning a bit forward. The doctor was standing close behind him, supporting Kit with a hand on his belly and listening to his heart beat through a stethoscope pressed between Kit's shoulder blades.

"Am I OK?" Kit asked for the fourth time. "Gotta have you say I'm fit for me to get this job." This was the sixth time he'd mentioned that.

"Am I embarrassing you, young man?" the doctor asked. "You seem to be tense. You've gotten hard, I see. That's a good sign of health in a young man, though."

"Naw. It's just that Mr. Lattimore, he puts me like this a lot when he fucks me. I'm just anxious that you tell them I'm fit to work here."

Doc Pender took in a gulp of breath at the casual way the young man had talked about being fucked. He dropped his stethoscope, which was on a string around his neck, so it didn't hit the floor, and his hand went to his crotch, where his cock was painfully pushing at the material inside his fly. He unbuttoned the fly and let the cock flop out, fully erect.

"If . . . if you let me pretend to be Mr. Lattimore, I'll tell them you're fit," he whispered into Kit's ear.

"OK, that's good," Kit answered cheerily, happy he could work here—and would get to use his ticket to the rodeo in Fort Collins. "But you don't have to pretend you're Mr. Lattimore. You can fuck me as you; that's OK."

With a little laugh and a sigh, the doctor pushed Kit farther forward, with Kit's fists pressing into the bed farther up toward the head, and started to work his cock into Kit's hole. Kit grunted a bit, but the cock went in without too much difficulty. The kid had fucked often and quite recently too, the doctor realized. He was still open. He was still wet inside. Someone had fucked him right before he came here.

The doctor lost all inhibitions and plowed Kit hard and deep to an ejaculation.

Kit just grunted and groaned and took it. Afterward, with the doctor still embracing him closely and letting his cock go flaccid in his own cum and that of at least one other up in Kit's channel, Kit asked his important and hopeful question again.

"So, you're gonna tell them I'm fit to work here?"

"I'll tell them that if you sleep here in my wagon with me while we're traveling."

Kit gave no consideration to the fact that the doctor had told him yes before, even without that stipulation. He was more happy that the dilemma of where he was going to sleep—although that was really the hiring manager's problem, not his—was so easily solved after Rodeo Bob had said Kit couldn't sleep with him.

"OK," he said, as if the doctor had solved his problems rather than raised other ones. Kit really wanted to be with the rodeo to be close to Rodeo Bob. It didn't occur to him that moving into the doctor's wagon would mark him in the rodeo community as being the property of the doctor.

"You understand what I mean by sleeping in my wagon with me, don't you kit?"

"Yes, I think so. It means you're going to fuck me in your bed but then not make me sleep on the floor."

"Oh, jesuzzz, Mary, and Jehovah," Pender exclaimed.

* * * *

Everything was cooking along just fine for Kit in his estimation down through Colorado and into New Mexico. Rodeo Bob had only had a couple of nights to give to Kit, but what he gave in terms of a fuck left Kit humming like no one else could. Kit wanted nothing more than to be with Rodeo Bob, and although it wasn't happening enough for him, it was happening.

Hank gave him a pretty rough time, but Rodeo Bob was calling the shots, and Hank was getting most of the nights. Kit actually enjoyed working with the horses. They reacted well to him and he'd shoveled shit all his life, both literally and figuratively, and the atmosphere of the rodeo was just too exhilarating for Kit to resent doing it here. Even though Doc fucked him once or twice a night when Kit wasn't with Rodeo Bob, Kit considered it a low price for having a place to sleep, and Doc didn't give him grief about Rodeo Bob doing anything he wanted with him.

Some others, seeing how slow Kit was and how much he put up with while still maintaining a cheery disposition and an aura of innocence, talked among themselves, though, about how much advantage Rodeo Bob and the doctor were taking of him.

Once even, in the wee hours of the morning of the third day in Santa Fe, when Black Tex saw Kit coming out of Rodeo Bob's wagon, while Howling Hank sat across the compound and glared daggers at the wagon door, Tex pulled Kit aside.

"You know he's just using you, don't you?" Tex said. "And Doc too. They're just taking advantage of you."

"I know I'm a bit slow," Kit answered. "But I'm getting what I want. I want to be with the rodeo and I want to be near Rodeo." Kit had gotten on a first-name basis with the rodeo star, but he hadn't grasped that his given name was Bob, not Rodeo. The others sniggered at that, and some mimicked him behind his back, but if Kit noticed, he hadn't said anything or reacted defensively. It was part of the reason Tex had pulled him aside. He was conflicted. The young man was gorgeous and he'd like a piece of him himself, but he was letting people make a dupe of him.

"But they are fucking you—Bob and the doctor—and people are making fun of you for just laying on your back and opening your legs for them. You're better than that. You deserve better than them."

"I like to be fucked," Kit said, as if it was the most natural thing in the world to say. "Rodeo has the greatest cock in the world and Doc P is good to me. I'm doin' what I want to do."

"Others could think they can fuck you too, though. You could wind up giving it to everyone."

"I don't mind. If I like them, I'd let them fuck me. I like to be fucked."

Black Tex couldn't help himself; Kit was just too luscious and open to it. "Do you like me?" he asked in a low-pitched, husky voice.

"Yes. I've been wondering about brown men. I been told they have really big ones."

122

Black Tex fucked Kit against a wall on the dark side of the wagon, pressing Kit's back against the wall, with Kit's arms around Tex's neck and his legs hooked on Tex's hips. Kit found that Black Tex might not be as thick as Rodeo Bob was, but that what they said was true about his length.

Still in position and nuzzling afterward, Black Tex asked Kit if he'd let him do it again sometime.

"Sure, anytime I'm not with Rodeo or Doc P," he answered. And he would have been happy with Tex's long cock inside him again if what happened during the rodeo later that afternoon didn't happen.

Everything was as usual, except that maybe Rodeo Bob had a more recalcitrant bull than usual. The bull sure as hell didn't like to have Rodeo Bob on his back, and he wasn't the least impressed with the antics of the clowns.

When he threw Rodeo Bob off his back to the gasp of the audience and the clowns tried to distract him from the fallen rider, the bull circled around quickly, took a run at Bob, and gored him in the back with one of his horns as Bob was trying to rise. Bob went down again in a heap. The bull backed off, went into a tight circle, and faced Bob again. It pawed the ground, huffed through its nose, and lowered its horns, preparing to charge again.

Men were pouring into the ring to help. Kit was among them. The others went for the bull to try to distract it. Kit went to Bob and covered his body with his own.

The distraction worked, though. The bull turned its head and steamed over toward the edge of the ring—and into the corral set up for the animals and riders to enter and leave the ring.

The manager, Stan; Howling Hank; and Kit were all at the hospital in Santa Fe while they were working on Rodeo Bob.

When the doctor came out of the operating room, he gave the three men a gloomy stare and said, "Mr. Crandell will live. But there was nerve damage. He will be able to stand again—with support—but he won't be able to walk again. And he certainly can't ride. This was Mr. Crandell's last rodeo riding the bulls, I'm afraid."

Hank muttered an, "Oh, shit," which was echoed by the rodeo manager. Kit just looked confused.

"Sorry to hear that about Mr. Crandell," he said, "but how is Rodeo?"

The doctor gave Kit a confused look. Hank uttered, "Fuck," and stood and stomped off. It took a few minutes for Stan to explain the situation to Kit, who then broke down in tears.

Stan and the doctor discussed hospitalization and treatment. The doctor said that Bob needed to have a private nurse for a while—mostly to be there and help keep Bob comfortable—but that the wound would heal quickly. The long-term paralysis in his legs wouldn't. There was no reason why he couldn't be released within a couple of weeks. But Bob would need extra help in the hospital.

Kit lifted his head and said, "I'll stay with him."

"Kit," Stan said. "It'll be tough on anyone who's caring for him. I don't know about paying for an extra nurse, but—"

"I'll stay with him," Kit repeated, his voice laced with determination. "I want to stay with him."

And stay with him, Kit did. Bob was understandably angry and bitter about what had happened to him and how his career—and, to him, his life—were over. Before taking the rodeo on to Albuquerque, Stan assured him that the hospital expenses would be covered and that there would still be a job for him in the rodeo when he could return to it. They still needed that second ringmaster and the doctor had said that, if Bob were braced, he could stand in the ringmaster's box well enough. At all other times, though, he'd have to be in a wheelchair or a bed.

Rodeo Bob wasn't assuaged. He railed and groused at everyone in the hospital, Kit more than others, because it was Kit who was there, with him, all of the time. At some point Kit was doing almost everything for Bob because the hospital staff was tired of putting up with the abuse.

But Kit put up with the abuse—with a smile on his face.

When the two left the hospital, it was Kit who the hospital staffers wished well to and their regrets that he was leaving, not Rodeo Bob.

The moment after Kit lifted Bob's wheelchair up through the door of his wagon when they rejoined the rodeo in El Paso and started to come up the steps himself, Bob turned, backed up the wheelchair, and cried out, "Get the fuck away from me. Just leave me alone. Everyone leave me alone. Just let me die."

Howling Hank seemed quite willing to just leave Rodeo Bob alone. He'd found another rider to shack up with and made no effort to visit Bob.

It was Kit who delivered Bob's meals and took away the chamber pot and who, when he wasn't working with the horses, sat in a chair beside the door to Bob's wagon and waited.

People would pass the wagon by, cluck their tongues, and give Kit a sympathetic look. When they had walked past, though, they more often than not looked at each other and rolled their eyes. "What a dummy," some of them even said.

Kit told Doctor Pender that he'd be staying in Bob's wagon with him when Bob wanted him and he hoped that the doctor understood.

"I understand," Doc Pender said, knowing and valuing the effort Kit was making and acknowledging the deep affection for and loyalty to Bob that this represented, "but it could be a good long time before he realizes he isn't going to die just because he wants to and that he needs the help."

"I can wait," Kit said.

He didn't actually have long to wait. The fifth night in El Paso, Bob fell out of his bed and couldn't get back in again. He lay on the floor for hours, hitting bottom in his anger and frustration. But the only direction he could go from there, because he didn't die there on the floor, was up. Near dawn, he called out, "Kit!" and Kit was there in an instant.

Kit sat Bob up on the side of the bed and cleaned him up with a wet cloth. He sat down beside Bob and held him in his arms.

125

"I'm good for nothing," Bob said in a dull monotone, accompanied by a sob. "I might as well die. Nothing works. I'm good for nothing."

"Not true," Kit whispered. "You still have a job. You'll be a ringmaster. And your legs still work a bit. But the best of you still works and hasn't been exercised in weeks."

"What? What do you mean?"

Kit showed Bob what he meant by moving his hand into the fly of Bob's skivvies and pulling his cock out. He stroked it as Bob began to moan and pant hard.

"It works, doesn't it?" Kit asked. He turned his face to Bob's and they kissed, Bob tentatively as first and then, as he lengthened, thickened, and hardened, hungrily.

Tears were in Bob's eyes. "You're too good to me. You're too good for me now. I can't . . . the others will be after you to . . . and they'll be right."

"Fuck the other's," Kit answered, having no interest in seeing anything complex in this.

"You'll wake up some day. You just don't know . . ."

"Never. Shush now and fuck me."

"How?"

Kit showed him how. He stood up from the bed, lowered his trousers and skivvies, tore off his shirt, and lowered himself on Bob's staff, coming down on the bed with knees on either side of Bob's hips. He wrapped his arms around Bob's head, pulling the man's mouth into his nipples.

Bob let out a sob as Kit began to rise and fall on the cock.

Mascot

Chief had first noticed him when they did the Smithson 4th of July parade. The young man was Hispanic, with a dark complexion and jet black hair and dashing eyes. He exhibited an easy smile and a "gosh-died-and-gone-to-heaven" look as the fire trucks rolled by with the firemen all decked out in their firefighting equipment and hanging off the sides of the hook and ladder truck.

The next day Chief saw him again, standing outside the firehouse, waiting patiently for a call that would bring the trucks out. An hour later, Chief looked again, and the young man was still there, sitting on the curb. Chief was the only one around for the next couple of hours, as the rest of the day crew was off at a practice tower performing an exercise.

The young man looked familiar. It was only after searching his brain that Chief realized he'd seen him out at the Loredo Ranch—a place where men went to meet other men and maybe to get a little action. Most of the guys at the firehouse liked to go out there. They were comfortable with each other—having the same interest bonded the men into a good firefighting team. They were considered the best in the region. They all kept in good shape, and they backed each other well—and you could say they backed each other up real close. But there was no particular need for the other firehouses to know why they jelled as well as they did.

For the life of him, however, Chief couldn't remember in what capacity he'd seen the young Hispanic man at the ranch. Chief certainly hadn't paid for time with the guy there. Although he would have been happy to. He was a real sweet piece of tail. And those doe eyes of his were a real come on. Chief ducked back into the firehouse and continued the inventory he was taking of the equipment—a job he performed every three days to make sure that everything was right there where it might be needed in an emergency.

Chief fantasized about latching his eyes onto those of the young Hispanic's while he was fucking him—watching the change of expression on the guy's face when he realized that he was being mined deeper than usual and that the man riding him had the stamina to fuck him into the ground. Firefighting made a MAN of a man.

An hour later and the guy was still there. Chief thought that showed a remarkable stamina itself, as the day was scorching hot and the Hispanic guy had been out in the sun for hours just from the time Chief had first seen him.

So Chief went out into the drive and approached him.

"I'm just watching," the young man said as Chief came closer. "I make no trouble. I just like to watch."

"No problem," Chief said.

"Really, I stay to sidewalk. I make no trouble."

Again Chief said, "No problem. Really. I'm just afraid you'll fry out here. You want to come in and get a drink of water?"

"Me? Come into the firehouse?" The young man was incredulous.

"Yes, come in and get out of the hot sun for a bit. Do you like firehouses, firefighting equipment? What's your name?"

"They call me Ricky. Ricardo, but Ricky for short is OK to call me."

"I'm Chief," Chief said. "That means I'm in charge here, and if I ask you in for a drink of water, there's no one to tell me I can't."

"You are kind. Yes, please. Thank you."

They started to walk toward the door next to the bay truck windows that were now closed. Chief guided the young man with a hand on his upper arm, and he could feel Ricky trembling at the touch.

"I think I've seen you . . . out at the Loredo Ranch." Chief said it to try to make the young man less skittish, more comfortable. He could feel he was intimidating the young man. Chief was a man and a half himself. All of the firemen were. Most of the time they weren't out on call, they were working out in the gym at the back of the truck bays. They had to be strong and agile to do what they had to do.

But the young man was still trembling. "Maybe. You go to the Loredo Ranch?"

"Yes, we all do here. It's part of keeping our edge—keeping in shape and calming our nerves. It's a tense job you know."

The youth said nothing. But Chief could see he was processing it. And Chief didn't want to withdraw his hand even when they entered the cool interior. Ricky was turning him on. He liked the little guys, and although Ricky was a good half the size of Chief, he was a very nice little piece. And those eyes alone were making Chief go hard.

"You like firehouses, Ricky?" he asked as the Hispanic youth drank first one glass of water and then another and then another.

He hadn't looked like he was sweltering out there, but Chief could see that he was having a lot of trouble quenching his thirst.

"I don't know. Maybe. We don't have them where I come from."

"I saw you at the parade yesterday. You looked like you liked the equipment—the hook and ladder truck and the red water truck."

"Yes, maybe. They were nice."

Chief was perplexed. Ricky had looked like what he was seeing was way beyond just "nice."

"It was the firefighting equipment you came to see, wasn't it, Ricky?"

Ricky hesitated. And then he hung his head low and said, "It was more the men—in their fire suits. If you go to Loredo Ranch, I think you must understand."

129

"You like seeing the men in their uniform?" Chief asked.

"Si." Given a bit reluctantly. And then. "Thank you for the water. I guess today not a good fire day. I hoped to see men racing to fire. My friend Miguel, he tells me men come running out of firehouse still dressing in their uniforms."

Ricky looked up into Chief's eyes, and Chief could see the arousal deep inside the young man.

"You like to see the firemen half dressed, putting their clothes on?" Chief asked.

"Si." Again somewhat reluctantly given.

"And you work at the Loredo Ranch, yes?"

"Si."

"And maybe you like seeing these half-dressed firemen doing something to each other?"

No "si." Just a shrug and a failure to meet Chief's eyes with his.

"You see the building above the truck bays, Ricky? That line of windows up there?"

"Si."

"Do you know what's up there?"

"No."

"That's where the firemen sleep much of the time. And that's where they begin to dress. As chief I have my own room up there."

"Oh." Chief chose to interpret that as a glimmer or more of interest—and maybe understanding. And if Ricky understood, it was a good sign he wasn't backing out of the firehouse right about now.

"If I let you see me dress in my firefighter's gear will you let me see you undressed—and more maybe? If I pay you. You lay with me if I pay you?"

"Me? You want me to lay under you. With you in your fireman's suit?" Ricky asked.

"Or just whatever parts of the fireman's suit you'd like to see me in while I'm fucking you."

Chief could see the interest in Ricky's eyes.

"Come with me, Ricky. The stairs are over here."

The young man was still trembling and Chief was still holding his arm, guiding him, willing him not to back out now. Because now Chief had an aching hard-on.

Chief asked Ricky to undress first—and Chief was delighted with Ricky's nicely formed body—and heartened by the young man's own half hard-on. That was the real gauge of his interest.

Then Chief stripped, giving Ricky a full view of what was waiting for him, and Chief was pleased to hear the intake of the young man's breath when he saw the length and girth of what Chief had and the bulging muscles that went with the demanding job.

And then Chief began to suit up in his firefighting gear. Ricky stammered a request as he was dressing, though, that Chief not put anything on his upper torso other than the suspenders.

"I like chest. And the hair," Ricky simply said. But there was a catch in his voice and his cock was at three-quarter staff now when he said it.

There was a full-length mirror in the room, and Chief looked at himself with just the suspenders and the heavy pants and boots, and he couldn't help thinking, "Damn I look good. This kid knows his fetishes."

"Fireman's hat too?" Ricky asked, almost as if it would be a great favor.

Chief motioned the young Hispanic to him when he'd put the hat on and adjusted the chin strap, and Ricky slowly moved to him. Chief took Ricky's cock in his hand, while Ricky tentatively touched Chief's bulging arm and chest muscles and paused at the fireman's nipples, which were now hard and the size of quarters. The young man gently played his fingers through Chief's chest hair, and Chief took one of Ricky's hands in the one Chief wasn't stroking Ricky's cock with and moved Ricky's hand down the hair trail to Chief's abs and to his belly and then into the opening Chief had left unbuttoned at his crotch.

Ricky gasped at the size Chief had grown to. Now it was Chief's turn to shudder at the feel of Ricky's hand on his protruding cock, and he pushed gently down on Ricky's shoulders, signaling he wanted the young man on his knees.

Ricky gasped and choked on the cock working inside his mouth. He was giving a valiant effort, but Chief knew it wasn't going well.

Pulling the young man back up on his feet, he whispered. "You haven't done this before, have you? What is it you do at the ranch?"

"No, no. I'm sorry. I'm a cook there. A new cook. I must go now?"

"You can go, if you want. But I still want you. I'll still pay you to let me have you. If you still are willing. I won't be rough."

"I stay. I want it."

"Then let's do it right. Come with me." Chief led the naked young man back down the stairs. He hopped up on the running board of the hook and ladder truck and opened the passenger door, which yawned wide outward. He'd gathered a tube of lube and a handful of condoms as they left his room. He handed Ricky up and laid his back on the passenger seat and told him to lift one leg and brace it in the corner of the windshield. Then he moved the other one to reach for the ceiling at the post between the front seat and the back.

Chief spent the next glorious half an hour standing on the running board and rimming Ricky's nice, tight hole and then slowly opening it up with his tongue and lubed fingers so it could take his cock. As Ricky arched his back and moaned, Chief also gave him a good example of a blow job—which ended with Ricky's first ejaculation of the fuck session—and nipped at Ricky's nipples, while Ricky groaned and sighed and clutched at Chief's chest through his matting of hair.

All the time Chief was opening Ricky's channel up for the first time and Ricky was crying out and moaning and grunting and groaning and hanging onto Chief's suspenders for dear life, Chief kept his eyes locked on Ricky's, watching in an experience he'd never forget, the change from pain to ecstasy to exhaustion but full satisfaction at the taking. God, it was great taking a virgin.

"Thank you, Ricky," Chief murmured at the end, when he'd taken Ricky for the second time doggy style from the rear, as both stood on the running board and Ricky's chest was buried in the passenger seat of the hook and ladder truck and Chief's hairy chest was rubbing up and down on Ricky's back in the rhythm of the fuck.

"No, thank *you*," Ricky whispered as he turned his head and Chief took his lips in his. "Sorry I know not what to do."

"You did just fine. You could be our mascot."

"What does mascot job pay?"

"All the dick you can eat for starters. No, no, that was a joke. We'd treat you right."

"You mean other firemen fuck me? Like you did? Dressed like you?"

"Yes, if you liked."

It was just banter, but they were still in a pretty compromising position when the day crew—six burly and boisterous young, virile, in-shape men—returned from the fire tower exercise.

Chief immediately had work to do that took him off to the side. Ricky scampered up the stairs to retrieve his clothing, but not fast enough that two of the guys didn't see him go up the stairs naked. They followed him and cornered him in the room.

"Hey, lookee, Frank. We got a real nice piece of Cuban ass up here with us," said firefighter number one.

"Has Chief been doing you, cutie?" asked firefighter number two.

"He say I could be mascot here," Ricky answered, almost indignantly, not wanting to lose the ground he thought he'd already gained.

"He say what a mascot would do for us?"

"What you want, mascot would do."

Frank and friend immediately started to strip as both reached out for Ricky.

"Only the shirts, please. I like rest of it on, please."

"Whatever you want, cutie."

Chief was busy talking with the men in a group, but it wasn't long until he realized his "group" was down to one and

133

a firefighter in full gear except for a bare muscled upper torso was standing on the stairs and motioning to the only guy still with Chief.

"Oh, my God. Ricky," Chief exclaimed and he headed for the stairs—in time to find the third guy in the second round standing between Ricky's spread legs and feeding his channel deep and vigorously.

"Off him, Clint. He's fresh—or was."

He looked down into Ricky's eyes, glittering now more than ever before, a sloppy grin on his face, and limp as a rag doll.

"God, I'm sorry Ricky. I didn't mean for this—"

"You mad at Ricky?" the young Hispanic asked in a weak voice. "I no good as mascot?"

"You're OK with this?" Chief asked, incredulously. "You want to stay?"

"I want to be mascot," Ricky said in a faraway, but determined voice.

"OK, then. I guess you're up, John," Chief said. As he stepped aside, firefighter number six was already stepping up to the plate and unbuttoning his fly.

"The shirt. Wear everything but shirt. Yes, keep fireman's hat, please," Ricky requested in a small voice.

Night Ride in Old Albuquerque

It arrested my attention as soon as I walked into the room. Bigger than life it was. A mural of four hunky American Indian warriors, three standing on a prairie and the fourth astride one of three saddleless pinto ponies. All of them were decked out in war point, wearing just loincloths and animal-skin boots and with beaded necklaces fashioned like chest armor. They were all looking at the door to the room with belligerent expressions on their faces as if daring anyone to enter.

Since it said on the door that this was the Apache suite, my guess is that they were Apaches. They were rendered in full, vibrant color on a white wall.

I was duly awed and intimidated. It was an unusual touch in the rooms of the Casa de Coronado that I certainly hadn't expected. I hadn't expected to be in this room at all, in a boutique hotel at the corner of Albuquerque's Old Town. It was quite a find—sections of white-painted adobe guest rooms set haphazardly in a lush garden. I might easily have passed it by and ended up in a nondescript chain hotel.

I had come to Albuquerque in search of something special, though. Although what I'd come to find was something entirely different from the Casa de Coronado and its lush setting and huge murals on the guest room walls.

This had been Pete's idea. We had been living together for nearly six months now, starting off as a casual setup of sharing the same studio apartment in Dallas that each of us used only part time, as both of us were in jobs that put us in Dallas less than a third of our time. We had met through a mutual friend who had thought we would hit it off, but both of us had gone into the arrangement purely from a cost-efficient expectation and with the hope that we'd never actually overlap in our need to use the apartment.

But we did overlap and it was a small place with just one, double bed. I was to find that Pete was gay and aggressively so. I hadn't even thought of this as a possibility of a choice. I guess I was more taken with myself—narcissistic—than with anyone else, male or female. I'd slept with women before, but more because it was expected of a rising young advertising executive than because I particularly enjoyed the encounters. Relieving sexual stress was OK, but the woman all seemed to expect something from me that I had no inclination to give.

This bothered me, of course, and I grew to believe there was something cold as ice inside me, something that held me back and made it impossible for me to completely let loose, something that made sex unfulfilling for me and my partner both.

The same thing—the cold as ice thing—happened with Pete.

The first night we both found ourselves at the studio apartment with just the one double bed after a full day's work in the separate jobs that brought us to Dallas—Pete was an urban architect—Pete seduced me. Pete never seemed to find this difficult to do, and I was a pushover. He certainly had me compromised before I fully realized what was happening to me. He was a gorgeous hunk with a healthy ego and an overpowering libido. And I was as naïve as they come—my weakness helped by a good wine buzz and a highly successful day in the workplace.

Pete had me naked and on the bed, with him stretched alongside me, his mouth on mine, and his hand stroking my dick in a progression of seemingly natural and innocuous stages of seduction that raised no flags of doubt and resistance—well, few. I did rather think it was getting out of hand, but he was so charming and we were trying to adjust to being roommates, and I didn't want to be impolite—until he had my dick in his fist. And then he was giving me so much pleasure that I didn't want it to stop. I didn't want it to stop when he was also swabbing the inside of my mouth with his tongue. And I didn't want him to stop when his lips descended my torso, giving special attention to my nipples and armpits and navel—and cock and balls. And I didn't want him to stop when he was showing me what his tongue and fingers could do in my asshole.

I did freeze up and want him to stop, though, when he had his knees between my thighs and was rolling a condom on his cock.

I froze solid then. I didn't try to throw him out of bed—we slept in each other's arms in the single double bed that night and every subsequent night we found ourselves in Dallas together. I even soon learned to give him suck to ejaculation too. But each time he tried to mount me, I froze and cut off the progression of the coupling.

It wasn't that I didn't want it—I most certainly did. I just froze. I couldn't take that next step.

Pete was good about it and patient with me, but I could tell that it wasn't satisfactory for him, that he wanted and needed to go all the way.

I told him I didn't mind if this was as far as we went and that he got his fulfillment in other ways—and even brought them back to the studio apartment while I was there to fuck them. And he did bring a nice young man to the apartment one night—a yielding, dark-haired handsome youth who was quite willing to do a threesome with Pete and me. We lay in triple embrace on the bed and I kissed the youth as Pete fucked him. And I was aroused by this and Pete had his bulb pressing on my opening before I clutched up and just couldn't go through with it. The youth volunteered to hold me in an arm lock for Pete to force me beyond the threshold, but Pete wouldn't do it. I don't know what I would have done if he had forced me. It might have been enough to rid me of my inhibitions, but I'm glad Pete didn't chance it. I have a feeling it would have ended the relationship right there.

I'm not sure why my failure to do it all didn't end the relationship. But Pete told me that he had fallen in love with me—that he was willing to take me the way I was and for us to go no farther than we did. I believed he meant what he said—intellectually. But I was equally sure that he could never accept a limited relationship like that emotionally.

I told him I was willing to adjust my life to his—but only if and when we got over that hurdle.

That's when Pete suggested Gentleman Jim's ranch outside of Albuquerque.

"It's essentially a male brothel," Pete said. "I can arrange for you to go there and be conditioned, if you like. If it doesn't work, it would not be me that you had the bad experience with and we could at least continue on the same level we now have."

"I want to be with you fully, I really do," I had assured him.

"I know you do. But I obviously can't take you that extra step. When you have been initiated, I'm sure we can fuck like rabbits and both enjoy it immensely. But I am not going to force you."

"You say conditioned."

"Yes. If you go there and we pay ahead and you sign a contract, they will take you over the threshold one way or the other."

"One way or the other?"

"Yes. If necessary, they will force you—not roughly but inescapably—and then they follow up. If after the third or fourth time, you aren't conditioned to it—don't want to do it—they will stop. You will have signed a contract to absolve them of all guilt and responsibility, though."

I shuddered at the thought. But I agreed to it. I truly did want to be able to go all of the way with Pete. If this didn't work, we'd be no worse off than we were. Or so I told myself.

Arrangements were made and on the Tuesday in a week I'd taken off for vacation time, I drove from Dallas to Albuquerque, arriving early on Wednesday. I drove straight to Gentleman Jim's ranch.

I was quaking in my boots when the jovial fatherly man met me at the ranch house door and guided me into a central, two-story room with a log-beam ceiling and set up like a Wild West saloon bar.

"Here are your gentlemen of the afternoon," he said. "Zack and Mex." Zack was a big-boned, strikingly handsome cowpoke type with great muscle tone, sandy hair, and a warm smile. Mex was an even bigger and hunkier Mexican of swarthy, slightly mean-looking demeanor.

"Two?" I said in a decidedly choked-up voice.

"Yes. Your contract calls for completion of the service, regardless of the wishes you express in the bedroom, and then conditioning. You are booked for two nights here. Zack and Mex will accommodate you until tomorrow morning and then you will be assigned to another two for tomorrow afternoon and night. We service such contracts with two of our gentlemen at once to assure that the contract will be fulfilled. Only one will be servicing you at a time, of course."

Well, thanks for that "of course," I thought. I swallowed hard on that. I had no doubts that either of these hulks could have me if they wanted—that I wasn't strong enough to hold off either one of them.

"Once you walk through that door with Zack and Mex, you are going to be provided what is in the contract. If you cannot agree to that, don't walk through that door." The man was still smiling affably and he had spoken softly, but I could feel the panic rising inside me.

"Uh. Thanks. But not today, I don't think. I need to think about this longer. Can I reschedule?"

"Yes, of course—for a 10 percent penalty, because you have taken a time slot that cannot be filled by another. You've already paid and if you wish to reschedule we can charge that card for the balance. But you really needn't come back this far again unless you are prepared to go through with the contract. We don't really have time to keep making and putting off appointments. Of course what you've paid is nonrefundable."

"I understand," I said. But I didn't really understand. It wasn't the arrangement I didn't understand. What I couldn't understand was what kept me on the edge, not being able to go in one direction or the other. It would have been different if I had rejected the notion of having Pete's churning cock in my channel—but, intellectually, I didn't reject it. I welcomed it and ached for it. I was even ready emotionally for it, I thought. But I . . . just . . . couldn't go over that edge.

I retreated as far as Albuquerque to think this through. I needed a night or two in solitary to either build up to it or prepare myself to say good-bye to Pete and go looking for some other apartment arrangements in Dallas. It wouldn't be fair to Pete if I couldn't make this work.

This is what led me to stopping at the Casa de Coronado almost by whim. I had decided to drive all of the way to the Rio Grande beyond the Old Town, eyeing the possible motels on the way, and then coming back to the one that had seemed the most attractive. The most attractive, though, had been at the end of my run—just a golf course separated the hotel grounds from the banks of the Rio Grande. I was sure they wouldn't have a room available. But they did. They said they had a signature suite unoccupied, the Apache Suite. And I said I'd take it.

The room was more than adequate. It was large, although the overpowering mural—especially the menacingly expressions on the hulking Apache warriors—made it look smaller. There was a sofa and tub chair under the window wall beside the entry door and an enormous bureau in the corner of the other side. It must have been eight feet tall. The insets of the doors of the armoire were lined with white cowhide with brown splotches—matching the coloring of the pinto ponies in the mural. The base of the bureau held drawers and the top a large TV. The bed was a high king-sized one with sturdy logs as the frame. The mural was on the wall at the left of the door, with the bureau holding down the end nearest to the door, a desk at the base of the mural, and an adobe Southwestern-style fireplace in the far corner.

The room was more than adequate for the one night I would stay here.

At twilight I walked into the Old Town. They were having some sort of concert and Mexican dancing on the square, which had caused crowds to gather, but I walked beyond that and turned right into an alley of shops leading toward the art museum, which was already closed at this hour. I found a small French restaurant tucked back into a corner.

The waiter was very attentive—and quite cute. He guided me through the menu at leisure like I was the only patron in the place, which wasn't true. It obviously was a popular eating place. It had been one of the ones the attendant at the front desk of the hotel had recommended me to. There weren't too many recommendations once you got past Mexican food, which didn't often appeal to me.

The waiter, who said his name was Emile, and who could really have been French for all I knew—his accent sounded authentic enough in my limited knowledge of the language; I'd taken German in college—was impressed at my wine choice. Frenchmen I knew little of; French wines I was conversant in. I should have had a companion for dinner or thought less of the wine. My head was fairly spinning when I left the restaurant.

The waiter had asked about whether I had a companion and clearly was making suggestions that I could have one if I wanted, but if I wasn't going to open my legs for Pete, I didn't see doing it for a French waiter in Albuquerque.

The entertainment was still going full blast when I walked by the plaza en route to the Casa de Coronado. And it made me feel sad and isolated. And mad at myself for not loosening up. I had wasted a perfectly good French waiter with my barriers and my unwanted prudishness.

When I opened the door of the Apache Suite and entered my room, I scowled back at the Apache warriors and fished a book out of my bag to read. I started a fire in the fireplace—it was there so I might as well use it—and settled in the tub chair.

The fire from the fireplace, though, cast dancing light onto the mural and made the Apache warriors look even more menacing and determined to be doing something more than just being plastered in place on the wall.

I couldn't concentrate on the book and I was in a haze of good wine. So, I stripped my clothes off, took a shower, turned off the light, and nestled under the covers of the king-sized bed. As far as I could determine, I went immediately into a deep sleep.

I woke to the sensation of a body lowering itself next to mine. Imagining myself back in the studio apartment with Pete, I sighed and turned on my back, awaiting his overture into a lovemaking that would go no further than a sixty-nine suck but that would be sufficient for me if not for Pete.

I did, indeed, feel a hand on my cock, and I moaned and began to move my hips in slow motion to the grip on the cock. But this didn't feel like the type of approach Pete made.

I opened my eyes to shock. The first thing I saw was that now there were only three Apache warriors on the wall mural, which was highlighted in a eerie, uneven light coming from the dying fire in the fireplace. All three of the Apaches had their faces turned to me now. And their facial expressions were filled with lust.

I started to cry out when I turned my head to see that the fourth warrior's body was stretched along mine. A strong hand covered my mouth, though, muffling my cry, and the other two warriors not sitting on a pony in the mural came off the wall and on the bed, joining the first in manhandling me. A scarf that had been hanging on the loincloth belt of one of the warriors—no doubt a souvenir of some raid on a wagon train—was being used as a gag to stifle my cries.

Two of the warriors held me down, while another one worked my body over with his lips and teeth, concluding the journey at my asshole, where he opened my channel with his lips and tongue, while I panted heavily and bit into the scarf. Then I was carried by the three of them, squirming but without effect, back to the wall. They carried me through the wall and out onto the prairie.

The warrior on the pinto pony was scooting back onto the rump of the horse, taking off his loincloth, and smiling lasciviously at me, while the three other warriors lifted me onto the horse's back, in front of the seated warrior, with my back running up the horse's neck. The horse snorted and set its legs, but it held fast. The seated warrior's cock was in full erection.

The three standing warriors held me in place, imprisoning my arms and spreading my legs, while, as I

142

screamed through the scarf and tensed up and arched my back in fear and pain, the seated warrior put the bulb of his cock to my opening, revolved it around at the rim, and then literally screwed it into me. He stopped a few inches inside me for me to adjust to him. Free hands stroked my body and lips went to my nipples and cock.

Pete's words when he came close to taking me flowed into my mind. "Relax, just relax, and let the tension flow out of your body. It will be easier. The pleasure will enter sooner. You'll be able to take the cock. You'll see."

I closed my eyes and willed my body to relax, which, slowly it did. And as I relaxed, my channel yielded to the warrior's cock and he slowly filled me with his warm, throbbing shaft, moving ever farther up into me. The pain subsided and I felt filled, possessed. And then the cock began to slow pump me and all of my senses focused on my channel. I was moaning and my hips began involuntarily to roll with the fuck. My own hard cock was inside a warm, moist, sucking mouth and I could feel my juices rising. And I gave in completely to the experience, not thinking of the strange, exotic circumstances, but going with the fuck, enjoying it, not wanting it to stop.

This couldn't be a dream, I reasoned. I felt every sensation of the experience—the pain followed by the ecstasy of pleasure. I ejaculated, but the pumping inside me continued and the warm mouth held my cock as it softened.

I felt the ejaculation of the warrior inside me and heard his war cry of release. And then I was being pulled off him by the three warriors. They didn't release me, though.

One warrior, the tallest and most muscular of those who had been standing by the ponies, stood behind me, wrapped an arm around my belly, and bent me over in half. My feet didn't touch the ground. Then his cock was pushing inside me and he fucked me by swinging me forward and back on his cock until he, too, came. This was just a dream fuck, I knew, because there was no pain when he penetrated me—only waves of pleasure. I knew that, at least initially, there would be pain. So, this wasn't real. What it was, though, was a promise of the pleasure beyond the pain.

Exhausted, my eyes swimming in cum, I was carried to the bed then and the other two warriors, one after the other, fucked me as well. Or, rather, I fucked the fourth warrior, pushing him onto his back and straddling his hips, positioning his cock bulb at my hole myself, and impaling myself on his shaft and doing all of the pumping to his first and my second ejaculation. Again, there was no pain from the penetration, only a filling pleasure.

I woke in the morning, woozy from the wine, feeling like I had slept little, and with a strange pain in my loins that I hadn't felt during the dream. But I was purring. I was laying on my side and when my eyes focused they saw the beads of an elaborate Indian necklace on the nightstand. I couldn't remember that having been there last night. I turned my eyes to the mural. All was in order there—or so I initially thought. One of the standing warriors wasn't wearing a beaded necklace and all of the others were. I could have sworn that they all were painted wearing the chest decorations.

And now that I looked harder, their expressions were no longer scowling and menacing. Now they all had a slight, self-satisfied smile on their faces.

I took up the beads and dropped them into my suitcase en route to hobbling to the bathroom. I was hobbling because there was a pain in my ass now—and I briefly thought I might as well have eaten at a Mexican restaurant last night if my ass was going to be on fire in the morning anyway.

I showered and then when I came out of the bathroom, I made a call to Gentleman Jim's ranch. It may have all been my imagination—it probably was. But I felt I was across the barrier now. To make sure, I'd keep that date at Gentleman Jim's before I returned to Pete. I felt no inhibitions now about being topped. Now I couldn't wait for the next time. And besides, Pete and I had already paid a big sum for the contract.

Zack had a piston for a cock, fucking me forever until I had come twice. And Mex had a cock that stretched me to the limit and reached for my tonsils. I thoroughly enjoyed them both—and the two guys from the next day almost as much. None of the four could imagine why I'd come to them with any inhibitions about being cocked at all. But I paid them all

144

well, so none of them got into the particulars on what had loosened me up between the afternoon I'd withdrawn from them, a shaking mess, and the day Zack and I fucked on the floor because I couldn't wait for it to get to the bed.

It was late afternoon when I left Gentleman Jim's ranch, so I decided to stop in Albuquerque overnight again before driving back to Dallas. I didn't intend on checking back into the Casa de Coronado. I didn't need that anymore. I planned to just find one of the chain hotels. But I stopped first at the little French restaurant I had eaten in before. The waiter was still there, but it turned out he wasn't just a waiter. He also owned the French bistro and his rooms were just upstairs. So, I didn't need a hotel room that night and I proved to myself once again that I had no trouble with having my ass pinned to a mattress by a man's churning cock.

All the way home to Dallas in the car the following day, I was wondering if the Indian beads would still be in my bag when I opened it.

Porn War

The song "Kisses Sweeter than Wine" sprang to my mind, because that was what his kisses were. As far as I could tell in the dimly lit Blue Moon resort hotel room in Las Vegas, he was a young hunk, no older than I was. Most of the men in the room were older, a few probably twice or more my age. None were complete throwaways, but he was prime among them. And he had latched on to me as soon as I'd entered the room, probably the last to arrive of eight or nine or twelve. It was that murky in the room. The rest of them already naked. Most of them already humping.

We stood, rocking together against each other in instant high heat, and kissing—those sweeter-than-wine kisses—as he pulled my clothes off me. We all wore face masks, which, along with the dimness in the room, supposedly would make it difficult to identify each other during the meetings of the conclave the next day when we were clothed—but surely not impossible.

He certainly couldn't hide his mop of blond hair or his magnificent build or his extra-long cock completely even in clothes in the light of day in a Las Vegas hotel meeting room. And if he touched or kissed me again, I'm sure I would know it was him.

I could recognize Marty Doans without any trouble. Muscle solid, but a bit squat, nearly bald, and bordering on pudgy—and very, very hairy. I could identify him primarily, even with a face mask, because he obviously was holding court.

147

I'd never seen him naked before, and although I'd heard about him having a super-thick cock, I couldn't see this now. He was sitting on the side of a bed, one of two queen-sized beds in the room, with another man kneeling between his knees and servicing his cock. Which is why I couldn't see it. Two men were on the bed behind him, fucking, and Marty had a cigar in one hand and three or four fingers of his other hand up the ass of the man doing the fucking behind him.

Marty was the organizer of the conclave and a big-name publisher of pornographic e-books. You got your books under his gay male imprint and you could quit your day job.

My books were under his imprint, and I'd never had to have a day job.

So, yes, I knew Marty, of all the guys in this room, even with the mask on. And I also knew the squirrelly little guy who came with Marty, Peter Knoles, who, though obviously wanting some of what others were getting, was nervously flitting around the room from coupling to coupling, but pulling back almost immediately because Marty wanted something or Peter was afraid Marty would want something and someone other than Peter would supply it. Last I saw of him on this night, he was standing at the wall trying to adjust the temperature because Marty complained about it being too hot in here.

Of course it was hot in here with a dozen or so guys in high heat.

I didn't know whose room this was. Probably either Marty's or Peter's. The invitation delivered under my door shortly after I checked in earlier that afternoon just said, "If you're really a player, and we're not talking cards, there will be more of this in Room 103 at 11:00 p.m." The invitation had included a fifty-dollar bill.

The sweeter-than-wine hunk had me straddling him on the bed Marty wasn't using himself. The hunk was on his back, my knees were buried in his pits, and I was arched back, grabbing an ankle with one hand and his cock with my fist, while he sucked me and I slowly face-fucked him. He lifted my torso to vertical after a period of good moaning and servicing, raised my hips a bit more, and brought them forward so that his mouth and tongue could get to my asshole. The underside of my cock was thumping on his forehead and he was bringing me to a boil so fast I hoped I wasn't going to be leaving anything sticky in his wavy blond hair.

He'd already asked me if I took cock or gave it, and my answer of "both, but more of the taking," had pleased him immensely. I knew then that I was going to be fucked by a long cock. In truth, from the atmosphere of the room, I knew I was going to be fucked by more than one. By Marty, for sure, if this was his party. He'd asked me for it before, in New York, but I'd never given it. I'd always managed to fend him off with a plausible excuse. I sure was going to be giving it to him tonight.

Didn't matter to me tonight. I was walking along the edge on a vodka high already, and I didn't mind doing research for my books and being gifted with new plotlines.

I went to arch my back again, but couldn't, because I realized that there was a chest behind me, a chest obviously sporting a studded leather harness. And two beefy, hairy arms encircling me, one holding me in place and the other possessing my cock, slick from the attentions of the sweeter-than-wine hunk. The new arrival had leather bands with studs on them on his wrists, and his arms were tattooed. The hard cock at the small of my back wasn't anything to sniff at.

Between the hunk working my ass with his tongue and the leatherman working my cock with his fist, it wasn't long before I gave the hunk a facial. Sorry about the hair, I thought. A protein shampoo. My ejaculation signaled the leatherman to move me back and set me on the hunk's long, curved cock—it took an eternity for me to slide down that pole—and then he moved around to kneel over the hunk's face and receive attention for his own ass and for me to bend down and suck his cock. He didn't take that position for very long, though. He moved back to behind me, embraced me with one arm, and stuck a popper under my nose with his other hand.

"Inhale this good," a growly voice whispered in my ear. "You're gonna want it. We're gonna go for a DP here."

I moaned and inhaled. I kept right on inhaling—and moaning and groaning—as the leatherman slowly worked his cock in on top of the one the hunk already had buried inside me. The hunk held still with his while the leatherman began to slow pump me. They came almost simultaneously inside me.

My world was spinning from the popper, so I didn't much care or feel very much pain. I did do a lot of groaning and grunting, though.

I think I was only semiconscious, but I was awake enough to realize when the leatherman was pulling me off the hunk and carrying me over and setting me in Marty Doan's lap, facing him, and on what I found was a very thick cock indeed. I just let my shoulder blades fall back onto the tops of his feet and my arms dangle on the carpeting beside me, as Marty began pulling me on and off his cock. The leatherman knelt down and gave me another pull on the popper before sliding his cock down my throat.

I woke I have no idea how much later to the flush of a toilet in the bathroom off the hotel room. The lights were off in the room, but a weak glow of sun was coming in from around the edges of the curtains on the windows and the light was on in the bathroom. The bathroom door was open. I saw a naked, fat, hairy rump standing in front of the toilet. I heard a second flush.

No one else was in the room. My arms were pulled above my head, my wrists bound to the headboard with restraints. My legs also were spread and restrained at the ankles, with leather leads running down to the bottom corners of the bed. The leads on the legs weren't pulled tight. There were a couple of pillows under the small of my back, elevating my hips. And I saw a small collection of toys—dildos and beads—laying on the bed beside me. I had no idea if these had already been used or were waiting to be used.

It all seemed familiar. I wondered if I'd written this scene before. My predecessor under my pen name, Brent, certainly had.

As Marty walked out of the bathroom and toward me, he was adjusting a wide, studded leather band around the base of his cock. He also was stroking himself to an erection.

"Hey, what're you doing?" I asked.

"Wrong question," he muttered. "It should be what have we been doing? Good of you to join the party again. There for a while it was like fucking Raggedy Andy. Too bad you weren't more awake. The part of you that was was enjoying it."

Without further ado, he hopped up on the bed, crouched in a half stand between my spread legs, and reached down and grasped my waist in strong hands. He pulled my pelvis up to his, shifting my weight onto my shoulder blades with my torso arcing down to the head of the bed. He thrust his thick, studded cock inside me and began to pump. Feeling no pain or even difficulty in taking his cock with added studs, I realized that my channel had been reamed well open, with no opportunity to tighten up again for however long I'd been in this room.

Whatever.

I turned my cheek to the side and moaned. He was fucking me good. I just wouldn't look directly at the gnome he appeared to be in this stance. He was fucking me really, really good, in fact.

But the restraints and the toys had me a bit worried.

"Um, Mr. Doans . . . Marty . . . just because I write gay male BDSM doesn't mean I practice it."

"You do now," was his response. "Do you want me to stop?"

"No, not particularly."

"You need another shot of the poppers?"

"Depends on what else you're planning on doing."

"I'll take that as a yes. Before I do it, I'll give you another shot or two. You'll want it."

At the front of my mind was the knowledge that Marty Doans could either make or break a gay male porn novelist.

Before he untied me and sent me back to my room, with another $100 in my jeans pocket, to shower, breakfast, and show up at the conclave only an hour late, I discovered that, no, he hadn't used all of those toys already.

* * * *

I felt I needed a real drink before facing the first session of the conclave, an annual meeting of gay male porn writers, held pretty much in secret wherever Marty Doans' Bent Stallions Publications made arrangements. It wasn't that far from noon. I saddled up to the bar of Las Vegas' Blue Moon resort hotel, a gay guy's only place, and asked for a Bloody Mary double. I'd met Marty before, face to face, in his New York offices when my lover, Brent Davenport, the original Jasper of the Jasper rough sex novels fame, died and I had to establish that I had written Brent's last three manuscripts—his highest-return best-sellers—myself. But I'd never been to one of Marty's conclaves, although I'd been invited before.

The main reason I'd never come was that Brent had been in a war of traded barbs with one of Doans' other best-selling authors, the gay male Romance novelist going by the pen name Niles James. The bitterness was such between them that, if they had ever met at a venue like this, the fur would fly.

I had only come to this conclave because I had been asked to come as a paid speaker—and was assured that Niles James would not be attending. Once here, though, I saw his name on the attendees' list. Obviously Marty Doans was up to something—something that would make him richer. Well, I would just have to do my best to avoid James. I had half a notion to take off my "Jasper" name tag and go in as someone else—but I was a paid speaker in that name, so I guess I'd just have to find out who the old codger was—he had to be old if he was a contemporary of Brent's—and stay clear of him.

When I went to put the Bloody Mary on my room tab, the bartender checked his computer and said, "Your account has been linked to the Room 103 account, Mr. Jasper. You may just cite that room for charges from now on."

Marty, I thought. This was looking more and more like a setup, like I was lured here for Marty to use. He'd made clear before that he wanted me, and I'd only barely been able to outrun him—until now, well, until last night, of course. I'd thought that last night would do it for him, but now he was slowly owning me. I downed the Bloody Mary, ordered another one, and, that one in hand, soared into the meeting room.

A panel session on the difference between erotica and porn—an argument I had no time for; what I wrote was what I wrote—was in full cry. I took a seat toward the back and looked around. There were maybe seventy people there. I wasn't a bit surprised to see that well more than half of them were women. Brent had had a major burr under his saddle about the false genre of women writing "just pretend" or "how we'd like to fantasize our man" gay male stories read mostly by other women. I had come to share his disdain for this quite large share of the gay male porn market, but, like him, not too vocally because many women buying and reading that fake stuff were also buying ours, even though we thought of ourselves as writing for the actually actively gay male.

Over half of the men present were well into their fifties and sixties. Although I felt a bit sorry for them writing what most of them weren't actively engaged in now, I respected that most of them—probably all who dared come to a conclave such as this—had once been active and were now writing from memories they wished to remain captured and arousing them for as long as possible.

Only a few of the men present were young, as I was, or not much beyond forty, and probably writing from active experience. Not that I could say that much of what I wrote was from active experience myself—or was before Marty started taking me under his jaded wing the previous night. I had enough gay sex, just not that much that could be classified as BDSM. I now certainly could write BDSM stories better, the specialty Brent had known best and written most—with the knowledge of experience. At least light BDSM. I could thank Marty for that. I was willing to bet that it was from this core group of younger men here that Marty had chosen his invitation list for last evening's party in his hotel room. And I wondered if more active and intimate sessions were in store during the three-day event. I wouldn't be surprised if they were the only reason Marty even held these conclaves.

I scanned the room several times, trying to pick out who Niles James might be. I couldn't very well avoid him if I couldn't identify him. At the next break I asked the older man I'd been sitting beside if he knew who Niles James was and could point him out to me. He did and could and pointed over to where a pudgy cross between Orson Wells and Truman Capote older man was talking with a well-built young blond guy.

"That's him," the man said. "Writes great Romances. The best-selling author in the Bent Stallions stable."

I bristled at that claim, but I remained polite. I had marked James's looks so that I'd remember to stay away from him, but my attention had already gone to the young blond he was talking to. I was sure just from watching him move and assessing his build that he was the sweeter-than-wine lover I had started with last night—and would have been more than pleased to continue with. Now him I would make no effort at all to stay away from.

I turned to ask the man if he knew who the blond was, but he was gone, and Marty was bearing down on me. I was to have the privilege of lunching at his table, at which he had gathered a bevy of twittering women authors of gay male Romance. It was not lost on me that Marty was introducing me to many disparate forms of sadism.

* * * *

The porn war between Jasper—as initiated by Brent Davenport—and Niles James was of the most bitter sort. It was born from a love-hate relationship. Brent and Niles had been lovers. They met as writers, with Brent writing mainstream sci-fi short stories for a pulp magazine and Niles already writing his gay male Romances for another publication of the same pulp magazine conglomerate. This, of course, was light years before the advent of the computer, let alone the e-book, which had caused the porn novel industry to burgeon because a buyer didn't have to worry about what to do with the book after he'd read it—or worry that much while we was reading it. Although Niles wrote Romances, he practiced BDSM and introduced Brent to the practice before Brent ever thought of writing that genre. It was Marty Doans, a young

BDSM adherent of Niles', who both encouraged Brent to switch to writing gay male BDSM for his startup Bent Stallions publishing effort and came between Brent and Niles sexually.

And it was Marty who tore Brent away from Niles in a living arrangement and who egged on the two in competition with each other as writers and who, gleefully, started and nurtured the porn war between the two. He touted and promoted them both as "the" best-seller in his stable and encouraged and exaggerated the professional animosity between the two. It didn't take the two long to buy into the hype themselves.

This manufactured animosity was a palpable source of energy in this conclave, I clearly could see from the first session I attended. Nearly every side conversation I heard concerned the porn war between Marty's two standards and the fact that this was the first time that anyone had seen both Jasper and Niles James on the list of speakers. That neither name was applied yet in the schedule of sessions and the key concluding session time slot was not filled in yet only added fuel to the fire of anticipation.

If this was Marty's doing, I'd have to give him props as a consummate showman. Even I didn't know for sure what session I was to be impaneled on. The invitation to speak had suggested that I talk about the rules of BDSM in writing, which I found to be laughable. There were no definitive rules for BDSM in either doing it or writing about it, I believed, after having picked up writing it upon Brent's demise. There were, of course, clubs of it with rules of their own—and rules they wanted to impose on others—but I had found that there was a whole range of application of the genre in both practice and stories and that a varying readership could be counted on for falling into this range.

My own BDSM writing thus far had been a toned-down version of Brent's and more heavily geared to bondage and milder toys and full enjoyment by all concerned. I would be the first to admit that I had little personal experience in the heavier BDSM arena and would be writing Romance myself—which only added to my resentment of Niles James dominating that aspect of the gay male market—if given the choice. I did enjoy a rough kind of sex, though, and I had been taking Jasper's work more in that direction. The fans of Jasper hadn't seemed to be complaining about that, at least yet—that I knew of.

Brent had not practiced BDSM techniques with me—well, beyond some of the tying up practices. By the time we met, he had softened and was actually quite romantic with me in our lovemaking.

I had accepted the invitation and the topic and had proceeded to put together a talk on the various techniques, equipment, and toys of BDSM in the gay male world and on how they could be—were being in Jasper's writings—applied to pornographic writing. I would just ignore the word "rules" altogether unless it came up in the question period. And if it did, I knew there would be a knock-down-drag-out fight in the room on what the rules were and who controlled them no matter what I said I believed about it.

As we went into the afternoon session, still without a topic for that last session or a mention of either me or Niles James as session speakers, I became increasingly convinced that I had been given a fake topic and wouldn't be speaking on the rules of BDSM at all, but rather would be paired with Niles in some sort of cat fight to conclude the conclave.

In this I was proved to be quite right.

My eyes kept going to the puckered-lipped, obviously self-satisfied pile of blubber who had been identified to me as Niles James and who sat simpering in the front row of the other section of chairs in the meeting room in the middle of a harem of equally simpering female writers. And as my eyes bored into him, I was aware that others were looking at me too, apparently having zeroed in on my "Jasper" nametag and already in delicious anticipation of what Marty obviously was planning.

When I couldn't take any more of this, I rose and slipped out of the room—I had sat as far back as I could find a seat—and went to the hotel reception desk.

"Is there an appropriate bar I can go to around here?" I asked. "Not in this hotel." I already was taking my name tag off as I asked. I wanted to be away from all of this for a while.

"Appropriate in what way?"

"Appropriate as in being able to have a couple of drinks and a casual take-out fuck by a hung hunk who doesn't have issues or want commitment."

"The Men's Paradise bar is just a couple of blocks west on Western Sahara. Kind of a dive, but there's a play area in back, if that's what you're interested in. A little early, though. They just opened at 4:00."

"Sounds fine, thanks," I said. I was thinking of sex in motel somewhere that wasn't this motel, but I wasn't bothered if it was the kind of place that had action in the back. If it was on the rough side, it was close to where I had been in my early days.

* * * *

I saw him as soon as I entered the dimly lit, nearly deserted bar—my sweeter-than-wine blond hunk from the previous night of sex in Marty's room.

I saddled up to the bar beside him, ordered a beer, and turned to him. He was looking down into the bar top rather than at me, although I had seen him glance up when I entered and then look away quickly.

"Hi, my name is Tim," I said. "I think we've already had a bit of sex. Maybe more than a bit."

He looked up at me, his expression a mix of embarrassment, interest, and amusement. His smile was much too glorious to have been partially hidden behind a face mask. He didn't deny we'd had sex.

"For real? Your real name is Tim?"

"Yep. That I cannot deny."

"In that case, I'm Julian. I admit that I've been looking for you today, but didn't see you at the conclave. Both of those sessions were insufferable, though, and not finding what I was looking for, I came out of that gaseous balloon to soak up my disappointment."

"Anyone tell you your kisses are sweeter than wine?" I asked. "Not to mention that you have a terrific body and a great cock."

157

"So that would make us twins?" he asked, with a laugh. "Gotta admit I was thoroughly enjoying you before that leather guy pulled you away. Nothing half that good again before Marty shooed us all out of there to have you alone to himself. You weren't looking all that conscious when I left. I was a little worried for you, especially when I couldn't pick you out in the crowd today."

"No, I slept through most of Marty," I answered. "Sure would like to take up where you and I left off, though. I'm told they have accommodation for that beyond that doorway over there covered with a beaded curtain."

The room was small and pretty grungy, but it had a quite adequate six-foot-square vinyl ottoman in the center of it that the bartender who took Julian's money wiped down when he'd shown us to the room. It was Julian's money, because he insisted on being dominant and calling the shots, which was just peachy with me.

When we'd been left alone, Julian got right to business, and I let him work, as I had enjoyed letting him take the lead the previous night. We did the sweeter-than-wine kiss thing, rocking against each other, as we stood beside the ottoman, stripped off each other's shirts, and unbuckled and unzipped each other. Julian retrieved both of our dicks and worked them against each other, while he slowly arched me back, bending me over the ottoman. I let him do as he wanted, holding his head between my hands, keeping him in the honeyed kiss.

When he'd bent me to where my shoulder blades felt vinyl, he pushed me up onto the ottoman until my head flopped over the end. He moved around to the head of the ottoman, and I found myself opening my throat to the slow stroke of his cock while he leaned over me and ran his hands over my torso as far down as running his fingers into my pubes and tantalizing the root of my cock. I went right hard for him, which was a good sign to me that he was what I wanted and would scratch my itch. He eventually returned his hands to cover my pecs and worry my nipples.

When he felt the time was right, he pulled out of my mouth, turned me onto my belly, my head still flopping over the end of the ottoman and my arms dangling off the sides, and lay full on top of me, moving his body slowly on top of mine, listening to me moaning softly. He took his time. I spread my thighs a bit and his cock fell into the crack and I felt his cock slide down along my entrance. He lifted his hips, sliding back up to my entrance. Then down and then up and repeating until he felt me shudder in his embrace. If I could have trained my rim to catch his bulb as it passed and suck it into me, he'd already be fucking me.

"Yes, yes, fuck me," I murmured, as I raised my hips to him, presenting for him. But he was taking his time. After a bit of pressure work on my rim with the bulb, he started moving down my body, kissing me on the back as he moved. He had an arm around my waist and he pulled my rump up even more into the air than I had raised it, wanting him to enter me.

His tongue and mouth went to my hole, and I groaned my pleasure and need. He pulled my cock and balls through my legs, having nudged my thighs to spread their stance further. He sucked the cock and balls, giving equal time to those and my hole, as I writhed under his attention and whispered the mantra of "fuck me, fuck me, stick it in, please fuck me, now, please."

And then he did just that, going into a crouch over my hips and folding his body over mine, and slowly, but relentlessly, entering and entering and entering me. I shuddered and trembled as I felt him throbbing and moving inside me, fully possessing me. Not terribly thick, but terribly, terribly long—reaching for my tonsils. Fucking deep. Then shallow; then deep again.

His arms were wrapped around my chest and he rose up on his knees, bringing me with him. One of his arms lay diagonally up my chest. The hand of the other one was stroking my cock in rhythm to his stroking inside me, a stroke that paused and then picked up in a different rhythm and speed whenever I felt I had the measure of it, making me gasp and gulp and beg for more, deeper, faster, harder.

He cupped my chin with a hand and turned my face to his for a sweeter-than-wine kiss that went on almost forever . . . until, with a lurch and a muffled cry, I shot out over the vinyl. I felt his encasing arm pull back from me then and I fell forward on my chest on the cum-slickened vinyl. He crouched closer over my hips, grabbed my waist with his hands, and pumped me harder, faster, deeper to his own ejaculation.

We returned to the Blue Moon separately, after paying extra to use the bar's shower, Julian showering before me, me still lying in a pool of cum and moaning when he was finished. The supper had already started before I reached the resort hotel. Marty's table was fully seated—thank god, I thought. But it was somewhat disconcerting to see that Julian was seated there, and looking fresh and somewhat disinterested. Who would have guessed that just a half hour earlier he had his long cock up my ass? Also seated at the table was the pudgy Niles James. A bevy of old maidish women were fawning over him. Understandable, I thought. He did write that insipid Romance. But then I admonished myself. I rather enjoyed his Romances, I'd have to admit, especially the ones of recent years. I never admitted to Brent that I read them, of course.

I didn't realize before I sat down at one of the few empty seats at another table, though, that it put me right next to who quite evidently had been the leatherman who DP'd me the previous night. I wouldn't have known him from Adam— at least until I zeroed in on the studded wrist bands he was wearing and got a peek at the leather harness under his half-open shirt—but he certainly remembered me. I spent half the meal removing his hand from my thigh and even my basket and listening to him whisper in my ear what he wanted to do to my body. Some of that sounded rather enticing, though, and I didn't have much to say when he pointed out that the last time he groped my crotch, I was hard.

Sometime during the meal I discovered that he wrote leather and biker books, which came as no surprise, but also that he read my—or, more correctly, Brent's—BDSM and rough sex books and was dying to take me for a solo ride, test out positions and tie ups Jasper wrote about, and compare research notes. He even told me, in hushed tones, that he had a whip he'd named Jasper.

He followed me back to my room after dinner, which I didn't realize until I already was trapped in a dead-end hall. The only thing that saved me from a research session, which I'll have to admit I was half tempted by, was that I found my pass card wouldn't work on my hotel room door. I turned and breezed by him, with the explanation that the key didn't work, and he was so nonplused by that, only half believing me, I'm sure, that he didn't impede my passage.

"You are no longer in that room," the hotel desk clerk cheerily told me. "You've been moved to Room 103, and your luggage has already been transferred. Just a minute and I'll prepare you a new pass key."

"Marty Doans again," I exclaimed. I said it loud enough that the leather guy, who had followed me in disbelief out to the reception desk, overheard and immediately vanished. I smiled at the thought that he probably was one of Marty's authors too and knew better than to mess with someone Marty was being possessive with.

I seethed through the two evening sessions, paying little attention to what was being said and looking over at the leatherman occasionally and frowning my "I'm not in the mood anymore" warning. Although he continued to eye me, all it took was for me to look annoyed at him, and he turned his eyes elsewhere.

That night I was reminded that the Blue Moon was a full-service gay male resort. When I entered Room 103, I immediately noticed the sling suspended in the middle of the room from four chains attached to a strong hook screwed securely into a ceiling beam. The sling hadn't been there the previous night and the room had been too dimly lit and filled with teeming naked bodies for me to have noticed special amenities like strong ceiling hooks.

I was contemplating the why of the plastic cover—more of a kid's swimming pool effect because of the lip around the sides—that was under the sling, when a naked Marty emerged from the bathroom and had me undressed and in the sling, with my arms and legs running up and bound to the four corner chains, before I could think of a reason why he shouldn't do it. My attention was riveted on the impossible thickness of his cock. Brent's cock had been impossibly thick. I actually liked impossibly thick cocks.

I told him something of this after I'd finished screaming at the tit clamps he applied to my nipples.

"We don't have to do it this way, Marty. You've got a thick cock. That's enough for me to give you a good time in a fuck."

"I'm startin' to get complaints on your writing, Jasper," he said. He always used my pen name. To him, I *was* Jasper. "Buyers are beginning to notice that Jasper doesn't have the BDSM zing he used to have—rough sex, yes, but you need a refresher in some of the finer techniques and toys, I think."

Refresher? I thought. Heavy BDSM was Brent's bag, not mine. There was a reason I wasn't writing heavy BDSM. But then, as Marty, already inside me and pounding to beat the band, started jerking on the leads to the tit clamps and I resumed some minor screaming again. I recognized that I certainly was getting experience in what he wanted me to write. I wouldn't have trouble writing how pinched and pulled nipples felt like from now on—or how, mysteriously enough, they were, in fact, connected to the arousal of my cock and to my enjoyment of a thick dick working my channel.

I spouted for him. And it wasn't long before I learned what the plastic cloth with the rim under the sling was all about either—when he came inside me, pulled out of me, fisted his cock, and lifted it over my belly.

I'd never actually included water sports in anything I'd written before. But I guess the point was that Brent, as Jasper, had. And that Marty wanted this sort of stuff to be included in Jasper's books again.

I got the message.

* * * *

Peter Knoles, Marty Doans' flighty assistant, was hopping from one foot to the other in front of me the next morning as he handed me the final schedule for the day's sessions, the last day of the conclave. As he got me to accept it, he skipped back a few extra paces from me and almost went into a fetal position, as if I was going to swat him like a fly.

After I looked at the schedule, I certainly felt like doing so—but only because Marty wasn't there himself. Just as I feared, the last session was now titled "Porn War," and Jasper and Niles James were the sole listed panelists.

I could have spit bricks and was building up the effort to do so, when I heard a surprised exclamation of "Shit!"

I looked up and into the wide-open eyes of Julian, who had just appeared in front of me. He was staring at the nametag on my shirt.

"You. You're Jasper!?" he both exclaimed and quizzed.

I looked at the nametag on his shirt. It said "Niles James."

"Shit!" I said.

"But . . . but . . . you aren't old enough," he said, being the first to recover.

"Neither are you . . . to be Niles James," I retorted.

"The original Niles died. Marty wanted to keep the franchise going and he liked my Romance writing, so I took over as Niles James."

"And the original Brent died and Marty had me take over Jasper," I said. I didn't reveal that Brent had been my lover as well. When you're shopping for a new lover, you don't necessarily tell the prospects about the earlier ones—beyond telling them enough to know what you could do. Julian definitely already knew what I could do—and what I would do for him, which was anything he wanted me to do.

"Well, you do Romance just as well as you write it," I said, maneuvering from the sticky situation to more amenable ground.

"You know we're supposed to be sworn enemies," Julian said.

"Yeah, I know. That's pretty much what the schedule of this afternoon's session says. So, what do we do? Cut out again? Leave 'em hanging?"

"I can't afford to do that," Julian said. "I need this gig."

"Me too," I answered.

"Then let's give them what Marty wants. Let's tear into each other in the conclave session and then go off and hide and fuck while they think we're in mortal combat somewhere."

"Sounds good to me," I was quick to agree. "But it'll have to be your room. Marty had me moved in with him."

"He's giving a press interview now. Switch your luggage to my room while he's tied up with that. He'll never find you there. Tomorrow we'll duck out when no one's looking and figure out how we can be together more. I live in New York."

"So do I."

"Sweet."

I smiled, thinking of wine and his kisses.

When I got to Marty's room and opened the door, I shuddered at what I found. The sling was gone, but chains with wrist restraints now hung from the hook in the ceiling. And on the bed was a flogging whip. I gave brief thought to whether Marty had named the whip. I loaded my suitcase and got out of there as soon as possible.

But I had to admit that Marty was right. If I was going to continue to be Jasper, I was gonna need more experience in what Jasper wrote about. Marty lived in New York too. Guess I just wouldn't avoid him and his research sessions. It could only make my writing better.

And he did have a very thick cock.

Retreat to Eremenos

The two figures, looking handsome together, stood at the doorway of the rambling adobe house on the heights overlooking old Santa Fe. They were standing close together, silhouetted shadows as seen from inside the house, where, in the great room beyond the foyer, small groups of people gathered in proximity—but not too near—a long trestle table, drinking wine and talking in subdued tones.

The woman, tall and thin, her skin tanned and weather-beaten without distracting in any way from her finely chiseled features, gave the impression of a Native American princess, accentuated by the long, plaited braid cascading down her back and the beaded band around her head. Her tawny-colored, long, form-fitting dress was of some sort of suede that matched the moccasins on her feet. The desert artist Lillian Vain, one of the centers of the Santa Fe art community in the early twentieth century, had gone native, but, in doing so, had set styles for the art community nationwide.

Standing with her, closer to her, and speaking in low, measured tones was the Western novelist, Edward Deal. Lillian was a tall woman, but Edward towered over her, and the bulk of him, distributed perfectly over a well-muscled body, made the spine-of-steel artist of the desert look almost delicate and feminine. Eschewing the effects of the "gone native" artists' community, which Deal only skirted the edges of, as he was a man's man who valued his individuality and isolation, Deal was dressed in an elegant black suit. His salt-and-pepper hair was close cropped and his mustache well trimmed. He came by his muscular physique honestly, as he was a man of the mountains, although wealthy and well-educated enough to dominate in dignified parlors, and one who wrote novels of rugged men overcoming the brutal natural obstacles of the West.

Lying on the trestle table in the great room was a simple wooden casket encasing the remains of Lillian's husband of twenty years, William Ware, sculptor of bronze statues of cowboys on bucking horses that were represented in nearly every major museum in the United States and Europe. Edward, the closet neighbor to Lillian and the artist community gathered about the Wares, albeit his ranch was five miles distant, was just leaving, having come to pay his last respects.

"It was so good of you to come, Ed. And I much appreciate what you have offered to do for Alo. If he agrees to it, so do I. It is very generous of you to offer."

"Where is the lad?"

"Hardly a lad, Ed. I almost didn't recognize him in Chicago. He had grown into a man."

You hardly noticed him throughout his childhood, Ed thought. But what he said was, "Where is he today? I haven't seen him since we all went back to Chicago to see him graduate from that private school and then brought him back here. You're right. He's grown into such a fine-looking young man, Lillian. Has he decided which college he will go to—or what he wants to do in life? An artist like you and Bill? He's so good with his hands. His wood carvings already are first rate."

"Who knows what Alo wants?" Lillian said, with a tone hovering between wistful and distracted—her mind was still on the composition she had been working on early in the morning before William's friends had started to gather for the last viewing. "Alo was distant from Bill and me even before we sent him to school in Chicago. I have no idea what he wants, although he has mentioned writing novels, as you do. But he hasn't come in from his room for the viewing today. I think he took Bill's suicide personally."

How could he not, Edward wondered as he raised Lillian's hand to his lips. Neither Bill nor Lillian had had much room in their artistic lives for the son and only child, who had come to them almost as a surprise. A beautiful boy, always, who they had named Alo, Hopi for "spiritual guide," and who they had promptly turned over to servants and minor artists worshipping at Lillian's and Bill's feet to raise. Only those close to the family called the handsome young man, barely in his majority, Alo now. To most in the world, he was Al, and when they wanted to be formal, they mistakenly called him Allen. The young man seemed to prefer the separation from his parents' inattentive world, so when alone with him Edward called him Allen too.

"Perhaps, Lillian," Edward said gently, "We shouldn't talk too much about Bill's death being a suicide. It's so distressing to the art world, and probably is doubly so to Alo, coming as it did right after our return from Chicago. Alo was all aglow from having graduated and having his summer here with the two of you stretching out before him. The death must have crushed him. That's why I've offered to take him with me on my writing retreat for the summer. This probably isn't a place he should be now."

If this was a veiled rebuke for Lillian, a suggestion that the wife had no need for the son or vice versa in this time of tragedy, Lillian didn't seem to discern it. "Death is what it is, Edward. We have lived our life honestly. Bill would not have taken his life if he wanted to hide his pain. It was his health, you know."

It was not his health, Edward thought. How little you knew of your husband, he mused, although all he did was look sympathetically into those beautiful milky-blue eyes of hers and cluck his regrets.

As he was standing out on the porch and Lillian was still in the doorway, Edward said, "If he would prefer not being here today, please tell him he's welcome to come over to my place through dinner. He can come back tonight after the . . . after Bill has been taken away to the mortuary."

"Thank you, Ed, I'm sure that would relieve us all."

Edward had spoken what he had just now because he was aware that Alo was at an open window farther down the porch line and could hear every word he said. As Edward moved down along the front of the porch in that direction to unhitch his horse from the porch rail, he looked up directly into the young man's eyes, receiving, as he hoped, a look of relief and affection.

An hour later Alo rode up to a wooden ranch house far smaller and less pretentious than his parents' rambling adobe mansion set in a compound with smaller matching artists' adobe houses circling it. Edward was far richer than his parents were, even though they also were wealthy, but Edward carried his "frontier man" rough and simple persona through to his dwelling. The ranch house wasn't small, but, beyond the great room with its soaring cathedral ceiling and varnished oak cross beams openly showing how the house was constructed, there were just two bedrooms; two baths; a large eat-in kitchen, where the housekeeper reigned and left shortly after noon everyday for her own family ranch four miles away; and a large study, where Edward wrote his novels when he was in residence.

Alo walked into the house without knocking, turned right in the great room, and walked down a dark corridor, past the study on one side and the extra bedroom, bath, and storage room on the other side to the door at the end of the corridor leading into the large master bedroom.

Edward was lying on the large bed, his torso propped up by pillows covered in Native American textiles. He was dressed in the black trousers and starched white dress shirt he had worn to the viewing and had a book open on his lap. He looked up at Alo standing in the doorway, took his wire-rimmed spectacles off, laid them on the nightstand on top of the book he was reading, and beckoned to the young man.

"Come to me, Allen. Come as I like to have you."

Alo lay sprawled on top of Edward, facing up, his right leg extended across the bed and his left leg bent over Edward's left arm. Edward's right arm was laced under Alo's right armpit, with Edward's hand cupping Alo's chin and lifting the young man's face up to his in a deep kiss.

The perfectly formed, naked body of the young blond Alo was writhing slowly on Edward's lap as the fingers of Edward's left hand dug into Alo's channel, snaked up to the young man's prostate, and worked him there until Alo's cock had hardened. When it had, and still possessing the young man's mouth with his, Edward grasped Alo's cock and stroked the young man to an ejaculation.

"You are so beautiful," Edward whispered when Alo had come for him. The older man had released Alo's mouth but not his cock, which he continued to stroke slowly.

"I want you to fully possess me. Fuck me now. Please," Alo whispered.

"I've told you. I can't now. Soon, though, if you come with me this summer."

"Come with you? Where?"

"I've talked with your mother. I am going on retreat for the summer to a dude ranch, a special kind of ranch, in the Grand Tetons in Idaho. I wish to take you with me. Take you from here. Make you a man. Your body is beautiful as it is, but you can work with the cowboys and become even more hard-bodied."

"Is that what you want—you want me to be more hard-bodied before you fuck me? Because I will do that. I'll put on more muscle if that's what you want, if that's what it takes. Or don't you think I am serious about wanting you? I've wanted you for years."

"Yes, I think you are serious about it," Edward said with a sigh. "And I want you too."

"Is it because you are such good friends with my parents that you won't fuck me now?"

"No, lad, it isn't. It's because I want my men experienced. I get no joy out of fucking virgins."

"You will give me these hand jobs and you will suck me off—but you haven't let me do that for you yet—and yet I'm not experienced enough for you?"

"Have you let any other man fuck you? Has another man had his cock inside you?"

"No," Alo answered in a small voice, hesitating a bit as if he was weighing what the effect would be to lie and say he'd already been fucked. "It is you I want."

"Well, I will have no man who isn't well-fucked. Don't ask me to explain. Do you want me enough to let other men break you in first?"

Alo hesitated, but then, in a determined voice, he said, "Yes. If that's what it takes, I will do it. But how?"

"Go with me this summer to the Eremenos Ranch in the shadow of the Tetons. It's a ranch solely for men. Men there will prepare you for me. If you want me, that is what you will have to do. We can be lovers in the fullest sense by July. Will you come with me?"

"Yes," Alo whispered.

"And I feel you hard again," Edward said. "Will you come for me again now."

"Yes," Alo whispered as he moaned and lifted his face to Edward's for another deep, lingering kiss as Edward's stroking of his cock increased in intensity.

* * * *

The train ride from Santa Fe to the end of the rails for them was a grueling one as far as Edward and Alo were concerned, entailing boarding the Atchison, Topeka, and Santa Fe line, headed north to Chicago; getting off in Omaha; and picking up the Union Pacific line, aboard the Overland Limited, headed west. The journey by rail took five days in 1915, and the closest rail stop to the Idaho side of the Grand Tetons was Green River, Wyoming, in the south of that new state. Green River had burgeoned in size—but was still not large—with the passage of the railroad through there having been completed in 1868. From Green River it was another five-day ride by stagecoach over rough dirt tracks north to Driggs, Idaho. The Eremenos Ranch, tucked into a finger of the Teton Valley, projecting into the Grand Tetons on their western slope, was another five-hour ride on horseback.

Fully private compartments and carriages were a rarity on the run north and existed on the Union Pacific run west primarily to serve industrial and railroad magnates. So, semiprivate compartments were the best that Edward could obtain.

When he and Alo were the only ones in such a compartment during segments of travel between station stops, though, Edward would lower the curtains to the corridor; turn the lock in the door; pull Alo onto his lap, with the young man's trousers on the floor at his feet; and finger fuck and stroke Alo to an ejaculation. In this way he kept the young man keyed up for him and continuing to beg for a fuck that Edward would not provide.

Edward fully expected to make Alo his. He just felt he had good reason to fully prepare for it. For years he had intended to make Alo his when the lad reached his majority, and everything he had done in relating to Alo as the young man grew up was to prepare for this relationship without scaring the young man away. In this situation, so near to his goal, though, he needed to exercise supreme restraint, no matter how hard that was for him to do. He needed to do it right so as not to ruin it altogether.

On the stagecoach ride north from Green River, there was a driver and relief driver in the driver's box and a young Mexican man to do the hauling chores, who sometimes sat on top of the stage coach, amongst the luggage, and sometimes in the stagecoach, when it was raining. There were two other paying passengers, in addition to Edward and Alo, composed of an elderly missionary couple en route to working on and spreading the gospel to an Indian reservation.

It rained during the first day of travel, and the Mexican, Pedro, rode inside the carriage, sitting beside the missionary couple, with the massively large Edward sitting across from Pedro and Alo sitting beside Edward. During the trip Edward and Pedro exchanged several glances that Alo didn't particularly appreciate, but he wanted Edward so badly that he wouldn't say anything.

That night they camped on the north bank of the Muddy River, which honestly earned its name. They camped near the home compound of a ranch by arrangement. The ranch family provided meals, although the passengers and drivers slept in tents by a campfire.

The second day of the journey took them to the small town of Kemmerer, where, once again, they camped in a small grove of trees at a ranch that provided meals. Edward had been moody the whole day, even though the weather was good. Pedro was riding on top of the stagecoach.

That evening, as the passengers and drivers gathered from walks they had taken after their evening meal to stretch their aching limbs from a full day's ride in a lurching coach with inadequate springs, Alo noticed that Edward and Pedro had not yet returned. First Pedro returned, stumbling and looking distressed, and lurched into the tent he was to share with the drivers. Edward entered the camp soon thereafter, whistling and almost strutting.

Edward and Alo shared a tent. The previous night, Edward had managed to embrace Alo and quietly stroke him to ejaculation. This second night, though, he merely turned over, with his back to Alo, after a furtive kiss on the lips, and drifted off into snoring.

The next morning, as they were loading the stagecoach, Alo noticed there was no Pedro. So did the missionary couple. The husband of the couple asked the driver about this, and the driver gave a scowl and said that Pedro had taken ill in the night and would be left at the hosting ranch to recover. When the missionaries turned away, though, Alo saw the driver's scowl turn toward Edward, who was in good spirits and not paying much attention to the loading at all.

Alo felt tense the entire day of the ride northwest, across the Idaho state line, and to an encampment on the banks of Bear Lake. The tail end of the Tetons now clearly was in sight to the north. Edward continued humming to himself and engaging in discussions with the missionary couple that Alo knew didn't really interest the novelist at all—and weren't providing anything he could use in his writing, which was normally the only topics that could loosen Edward's tongue.

It also seemed to Alo that Edward didn't want to be engaging in discussions with him.

But that evening, after the meal and while the drivers were setting the tents up, Edward asked Alo to take a walk with him along the banks of Bear Lake.

In a hidden little forested ravine leading down to the shore of the lake, Alo disrobed at Edward's request and took a dip in the water. Edward remained dressed, watching Alo from the bank. When Alo came out of the water and had dried off with his shirt, Edward pulled the young man into his lap and finger fucked and stroked him to an ejaculation, while covering his face with kisses.

Alo had tried to be standoffish and certainly was showing Edward he was ticked about something, but Edward ignored this until after he had made the young man come for him—an activity that Alo was lost to as soon as Edward initiated it.

"Tell me what's wrong, Allen," Edward said.

"Pedro. You—"

"Yes, I fucked him. And we might as well establish right now that I will fuck other men during our relationship. But if you wind up living with me, as I hope you will, I will always be coming home to you. That doesn't mean I will tolerate you fucking other men after this summer. That is just the way it will be. Do you understand me?"

"Yes," Alo answered, trying to keep the whine out of his voice. "But, why would you fuck Pedro and not—?"

"I established that Pedro let men fuck him. He was experienced. I needed the relief. You can't imagine how frustrating it is to be near you like I have been on this journey and not to find sexual relief."

"But . . . anytime you wanted me, you could . . . and Pedro, when he returned . . . Oh, Edward. Oh!"

Edward had moved down Alo's body and taken the young man's cock in his mouth and was sucking it. Alo was lost to him. Edward had only rarely done this for him before, and Alo was transported to the clouds overhead, completely lost to any more questions he might have about Pedro.

* * * *

A man introducing himself as Henry—but saying most called him Hal—met Edward and Alo at the stagecoach stop in the town of Driggs, Idaho. The stop was in front of a saloon and the man came out of that wiping the back of his hand across his mouth. He was a big, strapping redhead who Alo

173

thought was maybe five years older than he was. Alo wished that he could go into the saloon too, but civilization had reached this little town in the shadows of the towering Grand Tetons. He wasn't old enough. It didn't matter that his parents had let him drink from the moment he'd said he wanted to try it. Of course, that had worked as they probably wanted it to. Since it wasn't forbidden and he wasn't at all impressed with his first drunken state, he had only drunk in moderation since then.

He started to tell Edward that he might like to have a drop to assuage the dust of the long journey, but he stopped when he saw the assessing look Edward was giving Hal. In any event, in a short time they were on horseback and on their way east, toward the plain at the base of the foothills into the Tetons. Edward, Alo, and Hal were each astride a horse, and two other pack horses carried their luggage. Edward didn't travel light.

While they rode, Alo asked, out of curiosity, "I don't understand why the ranch is named Eremenos. Is that an Indian word?"

"No, it's because of what happens at the ranch," Hal answered. But then, looking like maybe he wasn't supposed to say anything, he clamped his ruggedly square jaw shut.

Edward looked over to the cowboy and said, "Eremenos? You?"

The man laughed. "I'm twenty-five, and, no, that was never me."

Edward sighed and looked away from the man. He turned to Alo and said, "It's not an Indian word. It's a Greek word. As this young man has said, it signals, although doesn't dwell on the actual import of the word, the business of the ranch to those of us who are interested."

"How so?" Alo asked.

"Eremenos is Greek for a young man, a boy really, younger than you by a few years, who accommodates an Erastes, like me. An older man."

"An older man?" Alo asked, still not getting it.

"Older men who fuck boys, young boys, sometimes as young as nine years old, during the ancient Greek period,"

174

Edward said, with an amused look on his face. "To keep it legal in these United States—even in Idaho now—it's younger men rather than boys. So, you won't find any underage boys at the ranch. It's like Alexander the Great and his young lover, Hephaestion. It was quite common and acceptable in Greek times. The gods did it—Zeus fucked the young Ganymede. And the Thebans were said to have three regiments made of seasoned warriors and their young male lovers. The Greeks married, of course, but they also were permitted to have boys to fuck. I guess 'Hephaestion' wouldn't be readily pronounceable for a ranch name, though. Eremenos is pretentious enough. But I'm sure it does the job for advertising what you can get at the ranch—or near enough if you take into account how young the Eremenos can be."

"So a ranch named Eremenos is a place offering young men for older men to fuck?"

"Yes, of course. They have younger men—for guests like me. But they also have their Erastes—for young men like you." He turned to Hal then, who Alo was somewhat embarrassed to realize was listening to the conversation. "And you, Hal. You indicate you aren't Eremenos, and indeed you look too old to be that, although you do look magnificent. But an Erastes? I think not—not yet."

"I am just a hired cowboy, sir," Hal answered. "There are different jobs at the ranch. I train the horses and handle them—like coming into Driggs to pick up guests like you."

"But you look too sexy to be only that," Edward said. Alo looked sharply at him again, disturbed by Edward's open interest in the man. "I'll bet there are guests who want you to handle them too."

"So, you aren't just teasing me," Alo interjected. "You really have brought me here to prepare me for you to want to fuck?"

"Yes, little one. I want you to work with several Erastes here before being handed back to me. But yes, before we leave here, I am going to be fucking you silly."

Hal cleared his throat. They had reached a rise. "There it is," he said. "Eremenos Ranch."

They looked down in a bowl nearly surrounded by higher ground—much higher ground, the foothills of the Tetons, to the east. The ranch complex was a large one, with several buildings radiating out from a central long, low-slung log cabin structure that was the heart of the operation.

"If you need me while you're here, you can usually find me by that corral over there," Hal said, standing up in his saddle and pointing to the edge of the spread. "I train all of the horses here."

"I indeed may need you," Edward said, laying his hand on the rump of Hal's horse, giving Alo the sense in the look Edward gave the cowboy that he'd lay his hand on the cowboy's rump at the first sign of acceptance.

Alo couldn't see the expression on Hal's face, but he was disturbed enough by the expression he saw in Edward's face.

They were met by the ranch manager in the great room of the central building.

"We are honored that you are staying with us for the summer, Mr. Deal," the manager said. "I understand you will be writing a book while you're here and that . . . ah . . . you have special needs. We have a young man for you, Tom, who I'm sure will meet your specifications. And this," he said, turning to Alo, "is the young man you have other needs for?"

"Yes. I believe I set forth the program for him in my letters to you."

"Yes, of course. There won't be a problem. In fact, seeing him, I can say that there will be no problem at all—not for anything or anyone on the staff who he might fancy."

"That's all of the luggage," Hal interjected. He'd just arrived in the great room with the last of the baggage. He turned and gave Alo a big smile. Alo was somewhat comforted that the smile had been given to him and not to Edward, but he was mostly preoccupied with the conversation going on between Edward and the manager.

"Your rooms are down here," the manager said, as he guided them down a corridor off to the left the great room.

"Rooms?" Alo involuntarily spurted out.

"Yes," the manager said. "Mr. Deal will be in this suite here, with the bedroom and a study. You will be in a single room down the hall."

Alo turned his face, showing concern, to his companion. "Edward?"

"I will be in here with . . . I believe the young man's name is Tom," Edward said. "Until you are prepared to come to my bed in full acceptance," he continued. "I've asked for an isolated single room to be provided for you. One with its own door to the outside. They have such here, they advertised . . . for complete privacy of the guests. As I told you, Allen, until I am assured that you are ready to come to me, we will sleep separately, and I will have someone already ready for me in my bed. Your job is to prepare yourself. I want you to accept anyone who takes your fancy here into your bed. And I do want you to select men to fuck you. I have a routine settled for you, but I want you well-seasoned. The sooner you take care of this the better."

Alo was bumped a bit before he could respond and the manager and Edward already had entered the suite, leaving Alo in the corridor.

"Excuse me. If you could tell me which of these cases is yours and which is Mr. Deal's . . ." the man who had bumped Al, the cowboy Hal, said.

Alo couldn't explain why a jolt of electricity went through him when Hal's shoulder touched his, but it did. Turning away from the door to Edward's suite and shivering with second thoughts of having agreed to come here, the young man busied himself with the separation of the luggage.

* * * *

While Edward holed up in his suite with his writing by day, and with the young prostitute, Tom, at night, Alo spent the first three days settling into the ranch and building up to what he knew was coming. In a few days he was scheduled to accompany a hunting trip up into the Tetons. There would be just him and five of the older cowboys on the ranch—ones

Edward made clear to him when they took their dinner together were of the Erastes category.

"You are going to come back from that two-night hunting trip well fucked," Edward said, with a cheery note in his voice.

Alo wasn't left entirely to his own devices. At Edward's instructions he was given odd jobs around the ranch, mostly muscle-building work, as they had agreed. One of the jobs was to carry bags of feed out to the corral where Hal trained the horses.

The two inevitably struck up conversations while Alo filled the feed boxes, and Hal volunteered to show Alo around the ranch buildings. They ate lunch together the first two days.

On the third day, Alo arrived at the corral to find Hal holding a rope and having a horse trot around him in the center of the ring. Hal was shirtless and Alo felt tinglings in his crotch at watching the rippling of the young hunk's muscles as he exercised the horse. Hal correctly gauged the "tongue-hanging-out" look Alo was giving him and walked over to the wooden-slat fence, raised a booted foot to one of the rings, and leaned on the top of the fence on his elbows.

"I will be direct with you, Allen," he said. "I know what you are here for. I know what will happen the day after tomorrow when you are taken up into the mountains. What will be will be there, but is it true you've never been fucked—that you a virgin to a man's cock?"

"Yes," Alo answered in a small voice.

"And are you here willingly for this preparation Mr. Deal speaks of?"

"Yes. I want him to fuck me. I want to be with him. But he says he won't take me without experience."

"But he doesn't tell you why?"

"No, he hasn't. Do you know why?"

Hal didn't answer this. What he said instead was, "I find you arousing. You make me hard. Do you understand what I'm saying?"

"Yes," Alo said shyly.

"I can be gentle and patient with you for your first time. The men who take you up on the mountain won't be. Mr.

Deal has made it clear to them that he just wants it done. It's not up to me to tell you why he wants it done by five men. Do you find me at all arousing?"

"Yes," Alo answered in a small voice.

"When those men take you into the hills, they are going to fuck you hard. Mr. Deal has certain needs. They will make sure they meet those with you. I can make your first time easier and more pleasurable. Will you let me be the first to fuck you?"

"Yes."

"Now?"

"Here? In my room?"

"No. I know a place up in the hills where you will like it better for your first time. Do I saddle a couple of horses for us?"

"Yes."

"One thing," Hal said when it was really too late to stop. Alo was lying on a bed of ferns next to a waterfall on a stream in a glen up in the foothills above the ranch. The horses were hobbled and grazing nearby. They both were naked, and Alo had melted at the muscular body of the cowboy, who was seven years older than he was and enjoyed the best of a lingering youth along with the powerful body of an older man. Hal had already embraced Alo and run his hands and his tongue all over the younger man's body. He'd sucked Alo to an ejaculation and guided Alo to stroke his cock and even to tentatively taste it. And, with the help of much spit and his probing fingers, he had Alo's passage well open.

"What? Please. Please fuck me," Alo whined between pants. His pelvis was already moving against the palm of Hal's hand cupping his balls, a thumb in Alo's ass.

"You have said nothing about the size of my cock. How big it is compared to many other men. Are you sure, for your first time?"

"I have no knowledge of men's cocks. I just know I can't take it anymore. I want to be fucked by a cock. I need a cock. Now!"

"Perhaps, considering, it is best. But I will be gentle as possible."

179

He rolled over on top of Alo, pushing the young man's legs apart with his knees. He had already selected the place of laying, where the ground had a natural fall of several inches where he had positioned Alo's buttocks. Alo's knees were bent, his bare feet flat on the trampled ferns underneath. Crouched between Alo's knees, Hal positioned his cock so that the bulb pressed into Alo's entrance. The young man already was moaning and panting hard.

"Please, please," Alo murmured. Hal didn't know if it was a plea for getting on with it or pulling back, but it now was too late for pulling back. He had an arm around Alo's neck and lifted his other hand up to cup Alo's chin. He pressed his lips to Alo's, and the young man's mouth opened to take in Hal's tongue. Alo had gone this far with Edward many times.

Hal pushed his cock in two inches, bringing the rim of his cock head to the rim of the entrance. Alo groaned and began to writhe. He made an effort to pull his mouth away from Hal's so he could cry out the violation of his channel, but Hal was holding him fast and pressed into two more inches.

He held there, waiting for Alo to adjust and calm down, which the young man did. Then he released Alo's mouth but continued to hold his head in place.

"Oh, god, oh god," Alo muttered with a gasp.

"You want me to stop or go slower? Are you in pain?"

"Yes, it hurts, but do it. Do it now. Fuck me."

Hal placed his forehead on Alo's so that their eyes were locked. Alo showed both pain and determination in his eyes as Hal gave him six inches of the cock. Alo was panting and breathing heavily. He cried out as Hal began to pump.

Crying out "fuck me, fuck me, fuck me!" Hal gave him the last two inches and set up a steady stroke, which Alo began to meet with the movement of his hips.

When Hal ejaculated deep inside Alo's channel, Alo had already come again and he was laying back in the grass playing with his own nipples. At the point of ejaculation, Hal lowered his lips to Alo's nipples and nipped at one of them, while Alo arched his back and cried out, "Yes! Yes! Yes!"

* * * *

Hal came to Alo's room, through the door to the outside both of the next nights, and fucked him on the single bed. Such was their need to merge into each other's bodies that neither felt restricted by the narrowness of the bed. Hal slept with Alo after they'd fucked but was gone before dawn.

"Are you awake?" Hal asked late into the second night.

"Yes."

"We will fuck again now."

Alo moaned. He loved Hal's cocking but he was exhausted. "We've done it twice already."

"You need to be ready," Hal whispered, he was already moving Alo to his back, insinuating his knees between Alo's thighs, and was pushing fingers into Alo's channel. First one, then two. Alo arched his back and moaned deeply as the third went in. He groaned as the fingers parted, spreading his channel open. He gave a little cry as the cock entered him between the fingers.

"Hal! Hal! God, you're already big!"

"This is for you," Hal muttered, pressing the cock further in without extracting the fingers. When he was in deep, though, and ready to pump, he pulled the fingers out. He grabbed Alo's bent knees and began to work the legs back and forth in the rhythm of the stroking of his cock. Pushing the knees out with each thrust; pulling the knees in with each withdrawal. Alo panted hard, arched his back, and moaned deeply. Hal stroked harder and deeper. Alo panted harder and reached for Hal's nipples and twisted. Hal lowered his face to Alo's, took the younger man's lips in his, and bit the lower lip as, once again, he ejaculated.

They both lay heaving, struggling for breath.

"Hal. I think enough for tonight."

"You'll thank me for this one day," Hal answered with a drowsy voice that denoted that, yes, this was enough for tonight.

The following day and the day after that, Alo got an inkling why Hal had worked so hard to prepare him for the hunting party ride up into the mountains.

The collection of men he rode with were quite varied, but all where large-bodied, grizzled, and muscular hunks in their own way.

By day they did serious hunting of deer, elk, antelope, and bears in the mountains. By evening and night, they did hard fucking. All of Alo. The five of them fucked him in succession, and when the fifth was finished, the first was ready to go again. And from the very first of them, they fucked him hard, although none had a cock the size of Hal's. If he hadn't had the preparation that Hal gave him, from the well-prepared first fuck that was gentle until both lost control of themselves in the frenzy of the cocking, the first fuck from these five would have pushed him at least to, if not beyond, the point of endurance.

And Edward had made clear that this was the schedule he'd set up. He hadn't ordered the initiation of more pleasure than pain. He'd wanted Alo fucked to the edge of endurance.

The men slept in a few tents, but on both nights, nights that were mercifully warm, dry, and full-mooned, Alo had been kept outside beside the campfire as a succession of men fucked him, only occasionally giving him time to cool down or stumble off to piss and to defecate streams of cum. they fucked him over a saddle on the ground, sometimes with him bent over the saddle on his belly, with his buttocks waving in the air, and sometimes with his shoulder blades flat on the ground and the small of his back running up the side of the saddle and his feet either planted on the ground on the other side or wrapped around the thick waist of the bruiser who was fucking him.

Because of Hal's preparation, Alo endured it, but he came down from the mountain bow-legged and loaded for bear in more ways than going on a hunting trip.

As soon as he got back to the ranch, he burst into Edward's suite and into a scene in Edward's bedroom of Edward fucking the young man, Tom, who had been assigned to him.

They were stretched on their sides on the double bed, facing the door, with Edward stretched out behind Tom. Edward had one arm under Tom's chest and snaked back up to where Edward could cover a nipple. Edward's other hand was holding Tom's upper leg almost straight up into the air. Tom was a slender, dark-haired, not terribly handsome, youth the same age as Alo, if not a bit older. He'd had an arm stretched up and around Edward's neck, which stretched out the young man's hairless, only lightly muscled chest. His mouth was hanging open in a grimace and his eyes were nearly popping out of his head.

It was clear that Edward had his cock inside the young man's channel, and they continued moving slightly as they became aware that Alo was standing in the door, indicating that Edward was stroking his cock inside the young man.

Alo gasped and turned to leave.

"No wait," Edward called out. "You might as well stay and watch. You might as well know. Sit in that chair over there."

Alo stumbled to a chair by the doorway he'd been standing in, a chair that still gave him a full view of what was happening. When he'd collapsed into the chair, Edward pushed Tom's raised leg over onto the bed, which made Tom's hips roll toward the door and revealed the cock in the hole.

Alo gasped again. He knew now why a particular young man needed to be assigned to Edward. Tom's body was on the slight side, but his hole was wide enough to take a mature tree trunk. And still it was being taxed. Edward's cock was thicker than a mature tree trunk. There was no telling how much of the cock he had managed to stuff inside the young man, but there was a good four inches of the root on the outside at the end of the thrust of the cock and nearly six inches at the draw back.

Edward continued to stroke as he spoke next. "I want you to sit right there and watch until I'm finished."

Alo wouldn't have had the energy to move even if he'd wanted to.

Edward pushed Tom over on his belly, rolled with him without disengaging his cock, and hovered over Tom's body with his palms on the young man's shoulder blades, his knees between Tom's spread thighs, and his cock continuing to pound the ass. Tom was moaning and groaning and writhing under Edward until Edward jerked, held still, jerked again, and then grunted. He pulled out of the ass, and Alo gasped again at not only the thickness of the cock but also the length of it.

Edward rolled over and sat up. Tom hadn't moved. Edward slapped his ass and said, "Leave us."

With a groan, Tom rolled off the bed and unto his feet, not able to move too steadily. He stooped and picked up a shirt and a pair of jeans from the floor, gave Alo a somewhat embarrassed look, and stumbled out of the room, not able to hold his legs together. Alo could see Edward's cum dribbling down the young man's thigh.

"Strip off your clothes and come over to me," Edward said.

"Are you going to fuck me now—after what you let them do to me on the mountain?"

"This all is necessary. Don't you see that now? Look at this." he held his cock up, still half hard. Not as big as it had been when it was inside Tom's ass, but still bigger than that of any other man Alo had ever seen. Bigger than Hal's. Now it was clear to Alo what Hal had been trying to do for him. Hal must have known—or have heard—how monstrously large Edward's cock was.

"Can you see now why I wanted you to be prepared before I took you? Do you think you could take this cock now? We can check, but I don't think so. I said strip and come over here."

Alo didn't move.

"Do you want to be with me or don't you? This is all necessary if you do. If you don't, get out, tell Tom to come back, and pack your bags."

Feeling numb in his limbs but churning inside and feeling himself harden up, Alo stood up from the chair, stripped, and moved over to the bed. Edward pulled him into the familiar embrace of Alo on his lap. The difference now was that Alo clearly could feel the strength of the massive cock in the small of his back.

Edward pushed him over so that his chest was on the surface of the bed and his buttocks were still on Edward's lap, sideways. Alo gasped as he felt Edward rub the huge cock around on his buttocks. Both were breathing hard as he slapped the cock on the buttocks a couple of times, pushed the underside of it up and down between Alo's buttocks and on the crack, and pressed the bulb at the hole.

Alo gulped in air and gasped. "Oh, fuck. Are you . . . are we . . .?" He was trembling almost uncontrollably. He couldn't get the size of the cock out of his mind. He managed to take Hal, but only with a lot of preparation. Edward's cock was so much bigger.

"I think not, not yet," Edward said, a tinge of regret in his voice. "Someday. Someday soon. I see that you've been stretched." Alo gasped as he felt the invasion of his channel. But it was fingers, not the cock. "You're coming along, but not quite yet."

Edward took up rubbing the cock on Alo's buttocks and thighs. His breathing was getting heavier. "But you've seen it now. Now you know what you have to take."

"Pedro? The guy on the stagecoach?" Alo murmured.

"Yes. He boasted that he could take it. He couldn't— but he did. We'd started and I was so frustrated over not having you. I couldn't stop. He screamed like a stuck pig, but I couldn't stop. I may have ruined him. If I had given in to what you begged me for, I most certainly would have ruined you. But now you know. And now that you've seen it, you can help me by stroking it."

"Do you want me to suck it?"

"I think it would break your jaw. No, for now, stroking it would help."

Edward lifted Alo's body, easily, with hands on his waist, and sat the trembling young man down beside him on the bed. He pulled Alo's chin around to his face with a hand and they kissed, as Alo moved a hand to Edward's cock. He couldn't get his hand around it, but he could—and did—stroke it.

After a few minutes, Edward commanded in a raspy voice, "Get on all fours."

"But you said—"

"Get on all fours, dammit!"

Trying to suppress a whimper of fear, Alo went on his hands and knees on the bed and Edward crouched over his hips. Alo trembled in fear as he felt the bulb of the cock on his thigh, but then he let out a long gasp as the cock pushed between his thighs and, instead of trying to pierce his hole, slid under the perineum and pressed up under his balls.

"Keep your thighs clenched, dammit. This is how I have to take most men. But it's not how I'm eventually going to take you. And it's not how I took Bill." Edward began stroking the cock between Alo's thighs. He reached around Alo's waist with a hand and began to stroke Alo's cock in rhythm with the slide between the thighs.

So shocked was Alo with all of it that he didn't think he'd heard all Edward said clearly—but in the back of his mind he did. For now, though, he was concentrated on this unusual fuck. It was arousing and he could only think on how it would feel with the cock inside him—and thank Hal over and over and over again in his mind for putting him on the road to being prepared for it.

They came almost simultaneously and, with a sigh, Edward pushed Alo over on his side and came down behind him and embraced him. His cock, flaccid now, but still huge, snaked up Alo's back, an ever present reminder of what Alo would have to be able to take.

"Now you know," Edward whispered. "But I must have you."

That snapped back in Alo's mind what he thought he'd heard Edward say.

"Bill. You said Bill. My father, Bill?"

"Yes. And I promised him I would not take you without full preparation. It had been rough for him, but we were young and neither of us could wait."

"I don't understand. You fucked my father?"

"Yes. We were lovers for nearly your full life. Lillian didn't take to either pregnancy or motherhood. After having you, she didn't let your father near her again. He came to me for solace and for—"

"You fucked my father," Alo said again, louder, as he sat up on the bed and looked down at Edward, who had the balls to give him an amused smile.

"Yes, I said so. He eventually was able to take the dick, but it took a long time for him to do so without pain. It's a tribute to what we had that he endured so much for so long to be with me. When he said I could have you too, he made me promise to fully prepare you first. Nothing has ever been harder for me than to keep my hands off you. And now, in just a short time . . . you're stretching nicely . . . maybe the next mountain outing . . ."

"My father said you could fuck me too? He gave me to you?"

"Well, not quite like that." The smile was a little crooked now. "I told him I was going to fuck you too and we argued a bit, but then he just made me promise not to take you like I took him."

"When did you two have this conversation?"

"While we were coming to get you in Chicago after your graduation."

"And he committed suicide when we got back to Santa Fe."

"Yes. Your father always was a bit unstable. It's unfortunate. But in some ways, it's for the best. Fucking you both at the same time would be a little awkward."

"A little awkward? A little awkward?" Alo cried out. "You . . . you . . . bastard!"

Alo struggled to get off the bed, but Edward grabbed for him and pulled him back into his arms.

"Calm down. This is all going to work out. It was meant to be. You want me. God, you are so sexy struggling like this . . . shit . . . I think . . ."

Alo was writhing and sobbing, but Edward was too strong for him. He pulled him down off the bed at the foot of the bed. He bent him over the bed, covered him close, and held him there, rocking him back and forth, with Alo trying to lash about underneath him. Edward's reengorged cock was at his hole, the bulb pressing at the rim. Alo's writhing was only helping it to lodge inside the rim, stretching him to the limit with just the bulb inside him.

They were panting hard again.

187

"Relax, relax. Maybe," Edward was murmuring. "Oh, god, I've got to have you."

Alo screamed and he collapsed on the bed. Two inches of the cock were inside him. Edward raised his chest off the young man's back and held himself over Alo's torso with the heels of his hands buried in the sheets on either side of Alo's chest.

It was only two inches and Alo's mouth was yawning open in a silent scream and his eyes were bugging out—exactly as he remembered Tom looking with seven or more inches inside him.

Only two inches but Edward was moving it in and out.

"Stretch for me, dammit," he cried out. "Relax. Take it. You want it. I want this." His head dipped down to Alo's shoulder and his lips latched onto the hollow of the young man's neck and he gathered up a fold of skin and sucked hard. Just as with Pedro, Edward had reached a point of no longer being able to hold himself in check.

"Yes, I want it," Alo sobbed. His hands were bunching up gobs of sheeting as his arms stretched out in a sacrificial pose. Yes, by damn, he wanted it. Regardless of anything else, he wanted it.

Three inches, with a slow stroke. And then four, all the time Alo's mouth open wide in a silent scream, waiting for his channel walls to split. But then the effort got the best of Edward. His cock spouted cum up into Alo's channel. He collapsed on Alo's back and, deflated, Alo withdrew into himself too, with a sob.

After a minute or two, Edward stood up from Alo, slapped him on the buttocks, whispered, "Maybe next time. Ten inches. Your father took it all. So will you," and padded off toward the other room. At the door, he turned. "I guess that's progress. I've fucked you now and gotten off. It's just not like I'm going to fuck you later. You're off to the mountains tomorrow again for something special. I expect you to be able to take more when you get back. We'll not stop next time until you've taken eight inches at least and you've taken my cum again."

"Bastard," Alo murmured.

Edward laughed. "But I'm your bastard, aren't I? Tell me you don't want it."

Alo opened his mouth, but nothing came out.

"I didn't think so. Go ask Tom. When you're fully conditioned, we'll fuck twice a day. And you'll love every fucking inch of it."

He turned and moved into the room, sat down at his desk, and didn't even look up, when, still sobbing, and dressed again, Alo walked past him and to the door of the suite.

"Send Tom back in, please," he heard Edward say as he moved out of the door.

He found Tom in the passage, dressed just in his jeans, and crouched on the floor, his back against the wall. He looked up at Alo with an expression of foreboding in his face.

"He wants you again," Alo said, his voice dull. "If I were you, I would leave, though. If he asks, I'll tell him I didn't find you."

Using the strength of his legs, Tom pushed his body slowly up the wall to a standing position. Alo could see him shudder as he pushed away from the wall. Rather than walk away, though, he passed by Alo toward the door to Edward's suite, or started to. Alo grabbed him by the arm, though, and whispered, "Why? You could say you left. He didn't tell you to stay around."

Tom looked at him, his eyes blazing. "Because he is Edward Deal. Because I want to know I can take a cock that big. Because you will do the same. Because when he's fucking you, I'll ache that it isn't me."

It was Alo's turn to shudder, as Tom pulled his arm away and entered Edward's suite.

That night when Hal silently came to Alo's room, Alo embraced him, initiated the kissing, pushed Hal down on his back on the bed, and rode his cock. He was still sobbing. Hal just held him and kissed him after they'd fucked and didn't, then, force him to say what was wrong.

As he drifted off, Alo heard himself moaning and panting. He felt his channel filled to bursting. Opening his eyes, he found himself arched back onto the bed, the weight of his torso on his shoulder blades. His arms were spread wide, his hands bunching up sheeting. Standing at the foot of the bed, Edward, an arm under Alo's waist, with Alo's legs stretched up Edward's torso, his ankles hooked on Edward's shoulders, gazed down into Alo's eyes, a wicked smile on his face.

"It's in. You have it all. Last chance. Tell me you don't want me. If you don't, I am going to fuck the shit out of you. Twice a day. Ask Tom how it feels. Tell me you don't want me."

"I want you."

In long strokes, Edward started the pumping, as Alo opened his mouth to scream.

"Allen, Allen," Hal's voice cut through Alo's dream. "What's wrong? You were crying out. A nightmare." He was laying between Alo's legs, his cock four inches inside Alo's channel. He was embracing Alo, holding his torso off the surface of the bed. He kissed Alo on the eyes and the throat; a hand was stroking Alo's sweat-streaked hair off his forehead. "What's wrong, baby? Is it Edward Deal?"

"Yes," Alo whispered.

"You don't have to stay with him. You have options."

"I'm scared. But I want him."

"He's too big for you, baby. Walk away from him. Walk away from the hunting trip tomorrow. You don't know. You just don't know."

"I want it too."

"It?"

"His cock. I want it too. All of it."

"Oh, Allen. No, baby. He's too much for you. You have options. Feel me. Feel me inside you." He sank his cock deep inside Alo. Alo gasped and wrapped his legs around the small of Hal's back. Hall began to slow stroke him, deep. "I'm big enough for you. We're a perfect fit. Stay with me. I'll take you away. I . . . love you."

Alo sighed and put his hips in motion, going with the rhythm of fuck. He reached for his own cock and started to stroke.

Feeling him tense, Hal whispered, "Stay with me, baby. Let's come together. Then you'll know. Then you'll know who you want."

Even their heavy breathing fell into rhythm as they both fought hard to find the other, fought hard to come together. And though they did, it was "Edward!" that Alo cried out as he ejaculated.

At dawn, Alo woke again, alone in the bed.

* * * *

In the morning, Alo walked out to the corral, where the hunting party was forming. It was only to be him and two of the men from the earlier hunt, two of the younger, more muscular men, Charlie and Joe.

Hal was there, bringing out the horses. He was avoiding making eye contact with Alo. First out was a horse for Alo. Their hands touched as Hal turned over the reins, and a chill went up Alo's spine, but still Hal didn't look into his eyes.

Next out were horses for Charlie and Joe. Then two pack horse. And finally, as the men were mounting, out came Hal, with a horse for him and another pack horse.

"What are you doing?" Charlie asked.

"I'm going too. Boss' orders," Hal answered. He didn't meet the eyes of any of the three, though. Alo knew he was lying about that.

As they moved up into the mountains and Charlie and Joe began to concentrate on the hunting, Hal rode close to Alo and whispered, "Any time on this trip you want to cut and run, just come to me. I won't be far off. I won't intervene as long as you want what is happening. But you still have choices. We can be over the Tetons and on our way up to Montana before anyone knows the wiser."

Alo didn't answer, but something inside him fluttered, and he began to work his brain. It was not until now that he really focused on what Hal had said last night—that he loved him. That if it was a big cock he wanted, Hal had one too. One that wouldn't split him apart.

Why was he dwelling on the size of the cock, though? When he knew he had wanted Edward, he had no idea what size his cock was. He wanted him and Edward only wasn't taking advantage of his vulnerability in this because he did have a killer cock and knew that virginal Alo couldn't accommodate it. So Edward cared for him. But Edward had never said he loved him. He only said he wanted to fuck him. And Edward had been fucking his father—and probably caused his father's suicide.

Alo didn't have time to think further on that, though, as Charlie and Joe called out that they had a track on an elk, and all four men were riding off in search of the sport of the kill.

That evening, by the campfire, Alo found out who else was meant to provide sport.

As with the previous outing, Alo was on his back on the ground, the small of his back running up the side of a saddle on the ground, his right leg running up Charlie's beefy naked torso and Charlie holding his left leg spread out from his body. Charlie was crouched over him, fucking him in long strokes.

When it seemed that Charlie was about to come, though, he pulled out of Alo, with a laugh, and rose to his feet. He had an arm under Alo's waist and pulled him up as well. He carried Alo to the other side of the campfire, where Joe was stretched out, on his back, naked, with his head propped up on another saddle on the ground. Joe lifted and spread his arms, as Charlie lowered Alo on top of him. Joe embraced Alo's chest as Alo was lowered on top of him, facing up. Joe also moved his thighs between Alo's and spread them, spreading and raising Alo's legs. Charlie reached in and helped Joe's cock find and then enter, deep, Alo's channel.

Charlie crouched between Alo's raised and spread legs, and as Alo exclaimed in surprise and began to pant heavily, Charlie forced his cock into his channel above Joe's already-embedded cock.

Alo began to writhe but found that that only made the feel of the two cocks inside him feel even tighter, so he did what he could to relax.

"Easy, guy," Charlie muttered. "Such a sweet ass. This is to help you. Boss' orders. You have to take the cock of that writer guy, Deal. Have you seen his cock? Our two don't equal it. But we'll help you take him. Two nights, three times a night should help open you more for him."

Joe started to pump his cock while Charlie just worked to hold steady inside. When Joe had ejaculated, Charlie started pumping to his own ejaculation.

Alo felt full, but he was able to take them—so he knew Charlie was right. That Edward's cock was bigger yet than the two of them.

He looked over in the shadows, where Hal was standing, his own oversized cock out and being stroked. The way he was standing and looking hard at Alo gave Alo the impression that he wasn't doing it to get off on what Charlie and Joe were doing to him but that he was trying to connect with Alo, showing him again the option he had for Alo.

Keeping his eyes on Hal, Alo reached for and encased his own cock, and when he came, it was for Hal.

Later, the two took Alo standing, Alo sandwiched between them, his legs hooked on Joe's hips as, crouching, Charlie fucked him from behind and Joe fucked him from in front. Again, off in the shadows, Hal was standing, ready to intervene at any moment Alo wanted, connecting with him as closely as he could.

The two men were big, but together they weren't as big as Edward. And the two cocks were stretching him, wearing him out. He wasn't sure he could take this a third time in a day. Even twice was a chore. Edward was bigger, quite a bit bigger. And he'd fuck Alo twice a day—mercilessly. He said so. He'd even driven Alo's father to suicide.

The next morning, When Charlie and Joe stumbled out of their tent, expecting Hal to have boiled the morning coffee, the campfire was out, barely smoking, and both Alo and Hal were gone, already far up into the Tetons about to drop down on the eastern side of the mountains and then to travel north into Montana.

Ride 'Em Cowboy

Since the 1930s my extended family has had a remote ranch in a hidden Colorado Rockies valley abutting Medicine Bow National Park south from Laramie, Wyoming. The mountain fasts there—almost alpine in environment—are majestic, but they can be raw and cruel as well.

Our family raised cattle there and took timber off the mountainsides in a planned "thinning" harvest pattern that supported a construction business down in Denver without denuding the forested hillsides. We weren't year-round ranchers, though, eschewing the forbidding winters by centering our lives elsewhere and only using the oft-expanded rambling stone and log ranch house for periodic vacations. Anyone in the family corporation could show up at the ranch after merely checking to see how many others would be in temporary residence. The rest of the year the ranch was taken care of by a long-term foreman and a succession of young—and not so young—wranglers holding fast to the dream of the wild and independent American West cowboy.

These cowboys were a sturdy, if somewhat rough and self-absorbed, lot, many of whom had accommodated to the life of isolation in a wild and remote wilderness by taking whatever opportunities came their way.

Thus it was that, having called ahead to report that I was on home leave from a European tour and planned to take a Colorado rest and recuperation by riding the range and fishing the cold mountain trout streams, I found Big Bill, a handsome if wind-chiseled-featured rangy cowboy of almost indeterminate age hunched over the railing of the stable fence, waiting for me to arrive. He was leaning his lithe and sinewy hard-worked body over the fence with one booted foot on the lower rail and spinning a stalk of oats in his mouth when I caught sight of him. A big grin spread across his creased weather-beaten face when I drove up in a Jeep Cherokee in a cloud of dust and came to a sliding stop beside the covered log veranda extending across the wide face of the ranch house. A hunky hulk of a young blond I'd never seen before was keeping him company at the rail.

"Heard yer were comin' into the valley, Mr. H.," Big Bill called out to me. I walked over toward him, and he stood up straighter as I did and set his creased and oily cowboy hat back on his head so that I could see the glint of welcome in his eyes.

"Yep," I replied. "Got a little tired of being targeted by all those bombs on my forays into the Middle East," I said, with a grin. "Thought I'd come back here for a spell and check out whether there are any missiles here as threatening as those I encountered in Lebanon."

"I reckon we can find a few here if that's what you want," Big Bill responded, with a hearty laugh. "Come for another ride, did you? Wantin' to go up into the hills again like we did last summer?"

"Yeah, that's exactly what I want," I answered. "I need some tension release. I figure a good ride and then several hours in the trout stream will help a lot."

"Doesn't look like you brought the family," Big Bill said.

"Nope. The wife couldn't get away. She's still back in the Mediterranean."

"So, it's just you, is it?" Bill asked.

"Yep. Any of the rest of the family in residence?"

"Not for another week or so. Most of the Colorado family will come in when the leaves have hit their peak of fall color. That shouldn't be for another week or two."

"So, it's just us, is it?"

"Yep, most of the workers have the week off to set up for the long fall run of family in the house. I'm yer cook and general handyman, I'm afraid."

"Suits me just fine," I said.

"So, do you still want to take that ride up in the hills rather than just staying down here?"

"Yes, and the sooner the better. Can you get the horses and all that we'll need together in the next hour or two? And supplies for sleeping out under the stars? I've been looking forward to this for months."

"I sure can," Big Bill responded. "But, uh, where are my manners? Jawing away like this, and not even introducing you to the new hand. Mr. H., this is Long Jack; Long Jack, Mr. H."

As we shook hands, my mind worked over what the "Long Jack" could mean. None of the cowboys went by their real names—in truth, most cowboys out here were escaping something or someone and had no intention of bandying their real names about. I'd found out where the "Big Bill" had come from last summer. I wondered what "Long Jack's" story was. Whatever it was, he was one muscled, blond hunk of a man. Probably Scandinavian in background; maybe over from Minnesota. And handsome. The sun and wind hadn't had time to etch his features yet. He beamed at me, obviously a very friendly fellow.

"And, do you mind of Long Jack comes along, Mr. H.? I think he'd like a ride too, if that's OK with you."

"Yeah, of course," I replied, all smiles. "I'd like that."

"I kinda thought you would," Big Bill said with a big grin.

Less than two hours later, we were in the saddle on three stallions and riding up the ridgeline of a spur rising up from the ranch house into the foothills of the Rockies to the west of the Medicine Bow parkland. This was gorgeous scenery, visited rarely by man. The trees were beginning to change color, but we were in a very warm spell—so warm that we all stripped off our shirts. Although both hard bodied, Big Bill and Long Jack were a contrast in fine manhood. The older wrangler, black haired and on the edge of hirsute, was sinewy and on the thin side, with swarthy, leathery skin beaten by the cruel elements. His arms and chest were ropy with veins standing out on top of hard muscle. In contrast, the younger wrangler obviously hadn't been in the elements out here all that long. He was blond, fair, smooth skinned, and bulky without an apparent ounce of fat on him. He had a deep chest tapering down to a thin waist and biceps as thick as some men's waists. He probably could have broken me in two.

Traveling west toward the Rockies as our horses climbed into the hills, we reached a high meadow, where the air was so clear and clean and the distant snow-capped Mount Zirkel appeared so close that it gave the illusion we could reach out and touch it. Big Bill called a halt at a grassy spot beside a burbling creek, and I was still drinking in the majestic scenery when both Big Bill and Long Jack came down off their horses and approached mine from either side. Big Bill encircled my waist with his sinewy arms from one side of the horse and Long Jack placed his big hands on my belly and the small of my back; both men were smiling at me.

"You've kept yourself in mighty fine shape, Mr. H.," Big Bill said. "Is what you've got there in your pants as nice a piece as it was last summer?"

"Check it out for yourself," I answered.

"Don't mind if I do."

As Big Bill was unzipping my jeans and fishing out my half-hard cock, Long Jack moved his hands up to my sternum and between my shoulder blades and pulled me flat across the back and rump of the horse. He kissed me deeply on the lips and played with my nipples, as Big Bill sucked my cock. The stallion held still, but it was trembling underneath me. Long Jack's mouth left mine and his lips traveled down to my nipples and then down across my navel, and he was joining Big Bill in mouthing my cock and balls. I laid there full length on the back of the horse, sighing and moaning and watching the snow-patterned ragged rocks of Mount Zirkel as the two wranglers shared my cock.

But then Big Bill got serious at sucking my tool and I looked around and saw that Long Jack had busied himself stripping the saddles off of the other two horses and laying them out in the middle of the grass clearing. Then he slowly stripped off his clothes, revealing a beautiful body-builder's physique. I could now see at least how he had gotten the "Long" part of his nickname. He came back and played my mouth and upper torso with his lips and hands again while Big Bill brought me to a groaning and moaning ejaculation with his insistent mouth.

When he was done, Big Bill's lips replaced those of Long Jack's on my lips. Then he whispered in my ear, "Are you ready for that ride now, Mr. H.?"

"Oh God yes," I replied. "I've been waiting for this for so long."

Big Bill pulled me off the horse and carried me over to one of the saddles resting in the center of the clearing. He stripped all of my clothes off except for my boots and the red bandana around my neck—and then he put my chaps on again, which left me bare at the pelvis fore and aft. Then he laid me across the dip in the saddle on my belly and tied my wrists to the stirrups of the saddle at each side with leather strips. After that, he stood where I could see him as he stripped down. His dong wasn't as long as Long Jack's, but it was much thicker, in keeping with his nickname. I moaned at the sight of it in remembrance of how he had plowed me the previous summer when I had visited these mountains.

He went over to the saddle bags on the other saddle and came back with a thick length of leather, a small riding crop, and several packets of condoms. Big Bill hunched down over me on the small of my back, his thick cock laying up between my shoulder blades. He brought the thick leather strap over my head and forced it into my mouth like a bit. Then he held the two ends of it like reins and pulled my head and back up to him in an arch and reached back with his other hand and started slapping me lightly on the buttocks as he rode my back, his cock rubbing up and down between my shoulder blades and mine rubbing up and down on the supple leather of the saddle seat. I could feel my back slicking up from the precum his cock was oozing as he stroked me. He rode me like a bucking horse like that for a while, eventually exchanging his hand slapping with flickings of the ride crop on my tender butt

199

cheeks. He was making shouts and gestures like you'd hear at a rodeo as he rode me. At length he reduced his gyrations to those of a trot, rubbing his cock up and down between my shoulder blades more deliberately; he stopped spanking and flicking my buttocks as I felt my butt cheeks being pulled apart and Long Jack tonguing and then fingering, with lubricant, my asshole.

Leaving Long Jack to prepare my ass for him, Big Bill stood beside me, and I watched him tear open a condom packet and sheath his monster cock with some difficulty. Then he was on my back again, rubbing the sheathed cock between my shoulder blades.

Long Jack's tongue and fingers disappeared and Big Bill slowly pulled his thick, now fully engorged cock back down along my spine until it dropped down into the crack between my butt cheeks and then was at my asshole. I arched my back against the reins and howled to the sky as he entered me with that huge cock and slowly plowed up my ass canal. When he was in to the root, he dropped the reins and I collapsed my head and chest onto the grass on the other side of the saddle and panted heavily at the filling and stretching of my canal.

"Oh God, oh God, you're splitting me," I cried.

"Do you want me to get off you?" Big Bill asked in a bit of confusion and concern. I was from the family; I could end his billet at the ranch with a snap of my fingers.

"Oh no, fuck me," I cried back at him. "I've been thinking of this for months. Fuck me hard."

And then I felt hands on my ankles; Long Jack was pulling my legs up and wishboning them, handling me like a wheelbarrow and opening me wider to Big Bill's tool and the older wrangler was riding my ass hard, just as I wanted him too. After a long, wild ride, he gave a little cry, quickly pulled out of me and pulled the sheath off and fired off across the small of my back. He rubbed the cum into my skin in strokings across my back with his still half-hard tool.

Long Jack was quickly untying my hands then, but not to free me. He pulled me up and turned me so that the small of my back was rising up the side of the saddle, my shoulder blades were flat on the grass, and my butt was suspended resting on the seat of the saddle and pointed toward the sky. Big Bill retied my wrists to the saddle stirrups while I watched Long Jack sheath his cock with a condom and then Big Bill and hunched over my chest, presenting his cock—moist from his man juice—for me to suck. I felt my legs being spread and Long Jack was snaking that long cock up into me and took his turn riding me long and vigorously while I bucked my pelvis up against his, meeting him stroke for stroke.

When Long Jack pulled out of me, ripped off his condom, and started to spout his semen all over my belly and the insides of my thighs, giving little cries of ecstasy all the while, I got the real point of his name—his ejaculation was unbelievably long and full. Big Bill freed me and we all ran down and splashed ourselves clean in cold mountain creek. As I was coming up out the water, though, Big Bill pushed me down onto my hands and knees in the grass and meadow flowers at the edge of the water and fucked me hard again doggie style. After he was done, I splashed back into the water and turned and watched Long Jack fuck Big Bill. They coupled like they did this regularly, which, no doubt, they did.

Big Bill cooked a meal over an open fire and we ate, stretched out against the saddles in the nude, as the warm late afternoon moved into a cooler twilight and the brilliant stars out in this mountain wilderness began to spread across the sky. The wranglers opened the sleeping bags then and spread them out, it being too warm to wrap ourselves in them considering the warmth we generated as Big Bill and Long Jack took turns riding me the whole night long out under a full moon glistening off the snowy Mount Zirkel peak.

The two wranglers managed to catch catnaps between fuckings, but they kept me awake all night. I didn't mind. I had been waiting for this for nearly a year—and that's when I thought I'd just have Big Bill to couple with. The blond stud was a real bonus.

Road Romeo

He was half on, half off the short bunk, with one foot leveraged high to one side on a grab handle in the top center of the back wall of the cab, his back arched on two hard pillows, his hands open wide over the driver's naked buttocks, fingers digging into flesh, moaning in long, building moans matching the long slides of the hard ramrod inside him. The driver, clad only in cowboy hat, red bandana neck scarf, tooled-leather boots, and a broad grin, was crouched over the bunk between the young man's legs, giving him what the young guy had been begging for all the way from Lusk, where the Wyoming landscape had gotten so monotonous that the young man could only think about why he'd bummed this ride and had started moaning for them to stop and get into the back.

The young man started to quiver and writhe, and the driver laughed and stepped up his thrusting, quicker, deeper, all the way out, and then the long slide back in and holding there, as the young man gasped and murmured his surrender. The driver only had to wrap his fist around the young man's cock and pump slowly three times and put his thumb over the piss slit of the angry red bulb before white, slick cum was flowing around his thumb and down the young man's engorged dick.

With a little cry and a long moan, all of the tension flowed out of the young man. But the driver drove on. Still deep, rotating his hips, making the young man rise to him, encircle him with his arms, holding him close, burying his face into the driver's hard chest, asking him now for it never to end.

* * * *

"See, wha'd I tell you? Lookee over there."

"Where?" Dwayne asked, moving his eyes to where Stan was motioning, out beyond the dirty glass in the front wall of the truck stop café in the complex where all the guys stopped to gas and feed up when they were driving through Cheyenne, Wyoming, on a long haul.

"Him? He's the guy with that fancy rig out there?" Dwayne asked, his voice incredulous. And his judgment not all that suspect. Walking toward them from the big, shiny burgundy rig with the extra-deep sleeper behind the cab was a rangy-looking cowboy. And not a new one either—probably no younger than his early forties. He wasn't too tall and certainly wasn't too fat. In fact he looked a little gaunt, all angles, and leathery tan, and wrinkles. Much like most of the rig drivers up here in the badlands of the upper West—well-worn jeans, a faded plaid flannel shirt, tooled-leather boots, a weather-beaten black ten-gallon hat and a red bandana around his neck. But he walked tall, and his step was jaunty.

"Yep, him," Stan answered.

"And you say you can always tell when he's goin' through?" Dwayne continued.

"Yep. It's them young guys over there, just as a told you."

Dwayne and Stan swiveled to take in the three young guys sitting together at a table set down not far from the doorway, between the café and convenience store section. Definitely out of place here. Not truckers by any means. Too young and preppy and "from money" looking. College guys just pulling over for a cup of coffee, Dwayne had surmised. But then he'd agreed with Stan that this wasn't the place that three college guys would pull over to on this stretch of road. There were fast food joints nearby—not to mention a Starbucks nearly across the road.

"Them guys?" Dwayne repeated.

"Yep. I've noticed it before. This is the third time this year," Stan said, turning away from the boys and watching the rig driver approach the café. "He don't come in here that often—I see him maybe once a month, maybe not as often. But I do short hauls, so I'm in here more than I'm not. But I noticed the last three times. Two, three guys like that come in here and order coffee and watch the door, and not long after, his rig drives up and here he comes just a struttin' in the door, pretty as you please."

"Gotta be drugs," Dwayne said.

"Yep, that's what I figure too," Stan said, very pleased with himself—and with Dwayne too.

The rig driver had reached the door, entered the café, and, after taking one long look at the young guys at the front table, turned and brushed past Stan and Dwayne's table on the way to one nearer the back.

"Afternoon, Stan," he muttered as he passed the table. He dipped his hat, although he didn't actually look straight at either Stan or Dwayne, and he didn't slow down his walk. There was no hint he was going to ask if they wanted him to sit at their table.

"Same ta yer, Ralph," Stan answered.

Dwayne started to say something, but Stan shushed him, waiting for the rig driver to get to another table and settle. When he looked up, he was looking at the young men up front—and they were looking at him. Another young man, moving slowly and a little bowlegged, a sloppy grin on his face, entered the café, looked around, and moved to the table where the other three young guys were already sitting. They put their heads together and were whispering across their table.

"You know him?" Dwayne asked in a lowered voice. "You called him Ralph."

"Yep, we've met in passing," Stan said. "I'd heard some other truckers snigger and refer to him as the Road Romeo once, and I didn't know what that meant. So I asked him. He said they must have been makin' a joke about his love for truckin', but then he told me his name was Ralph."

"Anything else? Did you find out anything else about him?"

"Not much. Just that he does the Cheyenne to Billings to Rapid City route, but only now and again, when he gets the

205

hankering. He didn't say—others have—but he didn't say either way that it's more of a hobby with him. That he's got a spread of his own down near Denver and does right well out of it. I did ask him why he trucks, and he just said there were some nice perks involved. I don't know what to think."

"The Cheyenne to Billings to Rapid City route," Dwayne asked. And then he snorted. "That's got to be the most monotonous route on God's brown earth."

"Yeah, but someone's gotta do it," Stan said. "Them folks need things trucked in too. God knows they don't have much of anything worthwhile just lying around to pick off a tree."

"Yeah, but look at the rig out there," Dwayne said. "That's the goddamnest nicest rig I've ever seen. What do you suppose that set him back?"

"More than a dozen roundtrips from Cheyenne to Billings and Rapid City a year, that's for sure," Stan said. "A man could drive that route for a lifetime and not pay for a nice rig like that. Look at the sleeper cab. You ever seen one that big?"

"Nope, I haven't."

Their discussion at that point was arrested by noticing not only that the last young guy to enter the café was now gone, but also that one of the other guys got up and left right after he did. And then one of the two guys who were left was moving toward the back of the café, like he was going to the men's room or something. But when he got to Ralph the trucker's table, he abruptly sat down and started whispering to the trucker. The trucker was smiling and nodding his head from time to time and answering in monosyllables.

"Drugs. Gotta be drugs," Dwayne turned to Stan and whispered.

"That's how I got it pegged," Stan whispered back.

The young man was standing up from Ralph the trucker's table now and as he moved back toward the front, the other young guy, smaller than the first, with sandy-blond hair was walking to the trucker's table and sat down and started whispering, just like the first one had.

"But you say he maybe has a big spread down near Denver of his own? Like maybe he's rollin' in money and just does this as a hobby?" Dwayne sounded more than a little dubious when he was saying this. They both sat there, finishing up their coffee, each already projecting out to where they were going next—Stan to deliver a washer over on Elm and Dwayne to haul ass down to Denver with a load of hogs.

There was movement at Ralph's table again, and Dwayne and Stan looked up. Both Ralph the trucker and the sandy-blond young guy were standing now. Ralph had one hand on the arm of the young guy and he was pointing to him with the hand of the other. They were both looking to the front. The other young guy sitting up there, stood, looking disappointed, and turned and walked out of the café. Then Ralph and the young guy sat back down at the table.

"Drugs, gotta be drugs," Dwayne muttered.

"That's what I think," Stan agreed.

Having now finished their own coffee and big-gulp breakfasts, Stan stood up and moved to the cash register over in the convenience store area and Dwayne went back to the men's room.

When they returned, Ralph, the sandy-blond young man—and Ralph's fancy burgundy rig with the really big sleeper behind the cab were gone.

* * * *

The big burgundy rig was parked at the back of the lot at the truck rest area off Interstate 80 near Rock Springs, Wyoming. The sleeper behind the cab was much too big and stable to be rocking back and forth, but if you walked up real close to the door to the sleeper, you would have heard the noise. The sandy-blond college kid, who had come all of the way from Fort Collins for this opportunity, was a real screamer.

The young man was kneeling on the side of the short bunk, thighs held out wide, fists bunching up folds of the spread on the bunk, and crying out his love for the long, thick cock churning inside his channel—at least he was very vocal until Ralph, the Road Romeo, who was crouched over his back from behind, pulled the young man's face around to the side with a hand under his chin and took full possession of the sandy-blond's lips with his own.

Ralph, the Road Romeo, wearing only a black, weather-beaten cowboy hat, a red bandana, and tooled-leather boots, was taking long, slow slides inside the youth's channel, making him feel every inch of the talented monster cock that young men gathered from all over the region to enjoy and schemed and networked to be in the right place at the right time to petition to get the fucks of their lives.

The young man jerked his face away from the Road Romeo and arched his back and yodeled to the low ceiling of the sleeper cab as he came on the bedspread in a prodigious ejaculation such as he had never experienced before.

And then he started whimpering and panting and groaning as the Road Romeo laughed and just continued his slow pumping deep inside the youth, knowing that the combination of the youth's recuperation powers and his own stamina meant the sandy-blond young man from Fort Collins wasn't yet even half way through the fuck he'd come so far to get.

* * * *

"How long did you say you've been driving this route?"

"Twelve years," answered Ralph. He blew into his coffee to stir up the steam to cool it down, but he was hunched over the table and palming the cup in both of his hands to try to stay warm.

"Twelve years," the other trucker said, and then he whistled.

They both sat there for a few minutes, looking through the glass window of the truck stop café outside Billings, Montana, at the ground frost that wouldn't burn off for another hour or two, certainly not until after the sun had come up.

"Nice rig," the trucker said, nodding his chin toward Ralph's shiny, burgundy rig with the extra large sleeper behind the cab that was strung out on the other side of the concrete pad beyond the line of gas pumps.

"Thanks. I like it," Ralph answered.

"But, man, twelve years on the Cheyenne to Billings to Rapid City route," the other trucker said. "How can you take it? Some of the most monotonous miles on earth, and lonely. God, is it lonely out there on the road."

"Well, I have company sometimes on the road," Ralph answered. "And then there's the perks; they make it worthwhile. And I only get on the road when I get a hankering to get off the ranch. Looking for something different."

"Perks?" the other trucker said. He just shook his head when Ralph didn't answer.

Ralph was busy eying the door. A young man, his breath still misting in front of his face as he came in from the cold, had entered the truck stop café and stood there a minute, surveying the room. His eyes lit on Ralph and he smiled. And Ralph smiled back.

"Speaking of perks," the other trucker continued. "I heard you called the Road Romeo the other day. You know of some nice chickies around these parts? Always seemed so dry and dull around here to me."

Ralph just smiled. But he wasn't smiling at the other trucker; he was smiling at one of his perks.

Roswell's Frontier Motel

Manuel held my hips steady as I shot off up into his face for a fourth rapid time, at last relieving that almost perpetual dull pain in my testicles, spent and no longer suffering, if at least for a few hours.

"Man, that's what I love about you," Manuel said, with a sly grin, as he licked my dick clean. "You come in buckets. It must be nice to be able to do that."

He turned me over on the bed in his El Paso apartment, straddled me, like a cowboy on his horse, and began stroking his luscious brown cock in and out of my ass.

"And this is what I love," I said between gasps. "But it's not fun, coming like that. I've got a condition—extra heavy cum production. I've got to have constant relief, or my balls drive me crazy with the pain. My girl at night, you most afternoons, and I've still got to go to the doctor every couple of weeks to be milked. In between its constant pounding my own meat. I can't wait to outgrow this."

"Well, let me see about that," Manuel said, pulling me up on my knees while he continued to fuck into me hard. his hand came around and wrapped itself around my cock and milked me in rhythm with the stroking of his cock. In short order, I was gushing for him again.

"Ah, I see," he said. "You seem to be right."

Later, as we were engaging in postcoital fondling and kissing, he leaned over, opened the drawer to his bed stand, and took out a business card.

"Here," he said. "Try this place. Ask for the north wing."

I turned the card over and over in my hand, focusing on what was printed on it. It was for the Frontier Motel in Roswell, New Mexico, not all that far away from where I was temporarily working, in El Paso. I could get there on a Saturday and still be back at the defense lab by Monday morning.

"What happens there that would help my problem?" I asked.

"You'll have to go and see," Manuel said with a grin. "I've had others with your problem. I guess you could say I naturally sniff them out. And I've heard going to this place helps."

"Roswell, New Mexico," I pondered out loud. "Isn't that where they had those UFO sightings in the late 1940s that everyone talked and wrote so much about?"

"Yep," Manuel said. "The trip is worth it just for the tourism value."

Two weekends later, midafternoon on a Saturday, I checked into the Frontier Motel in Roswell. The guy at the desk, who looked sort of creepy, gave me a sharp look when I asked for the north wing, but he didn't hesitate in fishing out a key and getting me registered. A studly looking black guy, all muscle and white teeth, had checked in right before I did, and when I pulled my car around to the somewhat isolated north wing, I saw that his Jeep Wrangler was parked near the door to the room I was given.

The north wing was sort of strange in appearance. There probably was only one hill of any height in Roswell, but the north wing of the Frontier Motel, a low, rambling series of wings around a swimming pool in the center court that obviously had been built in the fifties or earlier, was built right up against that hill, its back wall digging into the hillside here and there.

I hit the swimming pool right after I'd checked out the room. And the black guy, who apparently was on my wavelength, had done the same and was just settling on a lounger when I entered the pool area.

212

He said hi to me in a pleasant enough way, but he had the same pained expression on his face that I got a couple of times a day. I quickly surmised that he had the same semen buildup problem I did, and I assumed that this was the secret of the motel's north wing. It was a place where guys with the same problem could come and engage in near-constant sex, and therefore help each other out. It seemed like not much of an answer to the problem, but it also probably was better than nothing.

He could tell just by my walk and how I was delicately moving—and probably by that familiar expression on my face—that we shared this problem, and it wasn't long before we were back in my room and fucking each other furiously.

He had a beautifully built chocolate body and a big black dick to die for. His balls were rock hard and ready to explode.

But he took care of me first. I was laying back on the bed, my legs dangling off the side, and his mouth was playing my cock like it was a raspberry Popsicle. He had one hand pulling at my nipples and the fingers of the other one, heavily lubricated, were working my ass, preparing me for his own release.

He sucked me hard and relentlessly, and it wasn't long before my hands were bunching up wads of bedspread and my head was thrown back with my mouth open wide and howling at the ceiling as I came and came and came in big spoutings down his soft throat.

He swallowed me off in big gulps and then stood between my spread legs, gave me a grin and a chuckle, and just lifted my hips off the bed and pulled my ass onto his engorged cock. My torso was balanced on my shoulders and rising to meet his beefy midsection. I managed to get my legs up and running up his torso on either side of his head and held close to him by his ropy-muscled arms. He was pounding in me hard and deep, jabbering up a storm of appreciation at the tight ass I was entertaining him with and rocking my shoulders back and forth on the bed. I was talking back at him because I was equally impressed with the size and talent of his piece.

He came in floods of cum that confirmed that he had the same problem that I did and then pushed my body completely up on the bed, turned me on my stomach, and covered me with his body close. We explored each other where our hands could reach for a bit, but within fifteen minutes, I could feel both of us getting hard again, and my balls were telling me that I, at least, had another big load to give.

The black stud thrust his cock into my ass and pumped himself to another quick ejaculation and I gave the load I had to give to the bedspread my cock was being rubbed against in the rhythm of the black buck's fucking.

He came up off me then and we set a time to meet shortly after dinner to get our rocks off again—which is obviously what we both were there to do—and then he left me and I went into the shower.

I could have sworn as I was taking a piss before turning on the shower that I could hear soft, rather eerie music and the sounds of gentle moans coming from beyond the shower stall wall. This didn't really cut through my mellow feeling from the great fuck I'd gotten from the black stud at first. This was a motel, and the walls were bound to be thin, and there very well could just be a couple in the next room making whoopee to the radio. But the shower was against the back wall, and that's where the sounds seemed to be coming from—and the back wall was against the hillside. There couldn't be another bank of rooms on that side of this wing.

Mellow I was, though, so I didn't give it much thought as I turned on the shower. And once the shower was on, I couldn't hear the noise at all.

I was soaped up real well and was rinsing off when the strangest things began happening. The water was getting thick and oily. It wasn't unpleasant, that oily feeling, cascading down my naked body and my tensing muscles and my still half-hard piece and my once-again heavy and hard—and beginning to pain me—balls. But it wasn't water, that was for sure. And there was a sensation of motion. My first thought was that we were having an earthquake. We were having an earthquake in the wilds of New Mexico, and here I was buck naked and oily in a shower stall.

But it was the shower stall that was moving. Just the shower stall. Nothing else in the bathroom was moving. The shower stall was turning. And as it turned, an opening was revealed in the back wall.

I tensed and started screaming at what I saw beyond the opening. A large, dimly lit cavern. Moist walls, dripping water, a sense of a pulsating, dim light of changing colors, and soft music. But it was what was moving slowly around in the cavern that made me scream. Spider-like things. Living, moving spider-like things. Big ones. Each twice as tall as a man and four times as bulky. And, as my eyes adjusted to the light, I could see that there were men suspended under some of them, young, muscular naked men, loosely held close to the bellies of the spider-like creatures with strands of webbings. That was the moaning I had heard. The men were moaning.

I shrank back into the shower stall and turned to escape. But there was no escape. When the stall had turned, the back wall had cut off access to the bathroom—to the world that made sense and wasn't terrifying. The only opening now was into the cavern. Still, I shrank back as far as I could against the wall. But I was oily now and slid down into a fetal position on the floor of the stall.

Tentacle like things—a giant spider-like being's appendages—were coming into the stall and wrapping themselves around me. I screamed again as they drew me out and brought me under the belly of one of the beings, turning me so I was stretched out and my chest was turned toward what must be the chest of the being. I looked down, between my legs, as the appendages pulled my legs up to its sides and tucked my feet and calves into some sort of pocket sack on either of its side, holding them there close and opening my legs wide, letting me feel that there was something beating away inside that spider-like thorax, a heart of some sort. When I looked down, I saw that there was a long, thick thing looking very much like an elephant-hung cock hanging between the being's last set of appendages. The cock-like thing was all nubbly and it had a mushroom cap with a whip-like device hanging out of its head. Looking up, I saw another cock-like proboscis hanging out of the being's round little head—and from its belly at the level of my navel was a smaller cock-like proboscis and at chest level two smaller appendages with small suction cup-like hands on them.

Spent from screaming and completely terrorized, I was moaning now. But it wasn't moaning like the other imprisoned men around me were doing. Their moaning was that of passion and satisfied lust.

Why were my feeling different? Why weren't they as terrified as I was?

The spider-like being was lowering his head at me. All I could focus on, though, was that black cock-like thing swinging down from where its nose should be. The tip of it was at my lips, and I compressed them, trying to keep the invader out. But it was forcing my lips open and entering me. It was swabbing the inside of my cheeks with its mushroom cap and secreting a not-unpleasant oily substance into my mouth. A substance that had a calming influence on me as it trickled down my throat. The probe was also moving around in my mouth, caressing my inner cheeks and making small rhythmic movements toward the back of my throat.

I was being face fucked by the spider's head proboscis, but increasingly I didn't care. The soft, eerie music was building and flowing into my senses, and the moaning from those other men around me—moaning punctuated occasionally with a cry of overflowing passion—was becoming more prominent and was beckoning to me.

The two suction cup-like hands were sucking on my nipples, and I felt the bulbous mushroom cap of the spider's other cock, the long, thick, dangling one, caressing the rim of my oiled asshole.

I lurched and tried to turn from it as it slowly rotated and screwed into me, reaching a depth that no human man had explored. But the spider had a firm hold on me with its various appendages, webbing, and the sheathing of my feet and calves at its sides. Suction cup-crowned appendages I hadn't seen before applied themselves to my balls and worked them, teasing testicles into semen production that needed no teasing. Something inside the spider enveloped my toes and began sucking them sensuously. The muscles of my feet and calves were being massaged. Appendages were massaging my butt cheeks and spreading them wider, as the spider's cock probe dug deeper up my ass channel and thickened. The cock probe's nobby sides were undulating along my tender passage walls and stroking my prostate and that whip-like device on the head giving tingles of sensations on walls not yet being discovered, stretched, and massaged.

My cock was going to full attention and I managed to cast my gaze down the length of my torso just well enough to see the spider's probe at my navel level whirring and emitting a thin hollow tube about a third of an inch. The probe moved around until it felt the cap of my erect and throbbing cock. Then as I watched in what should have been horror, but, thanks to the calming mouth swabbing, was more curiosity, leathery prongs sprang out from the side of the probe and attached themselves to the cap of my cock, holding it in place as more of the tube glided out of the spider's probe and into my piss slit. It retracted a bit and then expanded, retracted and expanded, sending shivers down my spine. The it expanded and widened as it ran down into my urethra channel, and I moaned to this entirely new kind of fucking.

I held very still now, know how sensitive this invasion was, as the tube ran down a good distance into the channel.

I could see as I looked closer that there was a line running out of the base of this probe and up toward the ceiling of the cavern, where there was a transparent container of some sort, into which whitish fluid was running in spurts from other lines running up from the bellies of the other spiders that were slowly sliding around the room.

This also was when I saw the black stud. He was under the belly of the nearest spider to me. And he was as attached as I was. And he was moaning for the spider in a way he hadn't moaned for me.

We were all being milked. It was all being collected in that container up there. For what purpose I could only surmise.

But I wasn't much interested in surmising just now. The probes invading my body were working in unison. They were gently moving in and out of me, coming close to the entrance of their assigned orifice and then invading a bit deeper with each reentry. I was being fucked three ways at once and having my nipples and testicles worked to boot. And it was like no other sensation I'd ever had before. The being had left my hands free, and I wrapped them around my cock and gently pumped myself in counter movement to the stroking of the tube running inside my tool, helping to bring myself to an orgasm like I'd never known.

I, of course, came almost immediately—and prodigiously and with a great cry of release—and I watched a stream of whitish fluid run up through the tubing coming out of my piss slit and on up the lines toward the container above.

The spider gave a little sigh, and its heart beat a bit faster as I ejaculated, and I could almost imagine that the fuck was as good for it as it had been for me. The soft music and the moaning around me increased its volume in my brain as the various appendages on the spider caressed my body, encouraging me to reload. And reload I did, and soon the sensuous moaning I heard was my own, and I was making another flooding deposit in the large jar at the ceiling.

A third time, a sixth time, a tenth time. I had never felt as pleasantly spent and thankfully drained before. More coaxing and a twelfth time. The spider was trembling with pleasure. I was a star producer.

And then I woke . . . naked . . . under the running water of the shower stall in the north wing room of the Frontier Motel in Roswell, New Mexico. It was daylight.

I didn't for a second think that this had been a dream. I felt great. My balls didn't ache. There was no semen buildup. At daylight there always had been semen buildup and jacking off had always been my first chore of the day.

I dried and dressed and went to the motel's reception desk.

"Was there something wrong with your room?" the creepy desk clerk asked. And he looked like he was prepared for some weird song and dance.

"Not at all," I answered. "In fact, if the room's available, I want to book it for tonight too."

That afternoon, I saw the big black stud at the pool again. And although we were pleasant to each other and exchanged knowing smiles, there was no offer of a relief fuck from either of us today. We were both saving ourselves for that night.

Shark

"Pretty hot work."

"You can say that again, sir. And that's a pretty hot car you got there."

"Thanks. I'm addicted to Corvettes."

"What year?"

"This year. I usually trade up every other year."

"Shit, man. That's beyond my imagination. Oh, sorry for the 'shit.' We were told not to curse around the motorists."

"No problem. It's a fuckin' good set of wheels."

"Yes, it fuckin' is." The young flagman flashed a broad smile, made comfortable by the man's congeniality, and stepped a couple of steps closer in toward the windshield of the metallic blue Corvette convertible. He was minimally dressed, in keeping with the high heat of summer in western Kansas. He had the requisite fluorescent green safety vest, but no shirt, showing a set of very serious biceps, a tattoo of a sunburst on one. He was blond, with a long ponytail trailing out of the back of his safety helmet, but he'd been tanned deeply by the realities of his job. "Saw the license plate. Shark. That your name or something?"

"No, you could say more that that's what I do," the dark-haired—with gray streaks—dusky-complexioned, goateed middle-aged man behind the Corvette's wheel said, with a laugh. "Hard job standing out here changing a sign from 'slow' to 'stop' hour on end."

"Yeah, gets pretty hot and dry out here—and monotonous, 'cept when someone tools up in a flash car like this one. We've been working this stretch of highway 50 ten miles short of Cimarron for nearly a year now—with nearly a year to go. Pretty much unforgivable desert out here. But it's a job. Don't know what I'll do when the road's done."

"I've got some beer on ice in the chest behind my seat. Could I entice you with one?"

"No, sorry, sir. Can't drink on the job. Sounds wonderful, though."

"I've got bottled water too—ice cold. You allowed to accept that?"

"Yes, thanks, sir."

"Don't need to call me that," the man said as he reached into the cooler and came up with a bottle of designer water. "You can call me Beel, if you've got a name to exchange."

The young man smiled as he reached over and accepted the water. "Zeke. They call me Zeke. Thanks for the water, Bill. I'm sorry you got stuck in line just at the changeover. It shouldn't be more than a couple of more minutes. You might want to put the top up on the Vette, though. It's really hot out here."

"I'm used to heat, Zeke. And it's Beel, not Bill. It's short for something—but I'm sure you don't want to get into that now. It's Friday. You got to do this on Saturday and Sunday too?"

"Naw, we've got the weekend off. And today's pay day. We'll be hitting Wyatt's hard."

"Wyatt's?"

"The local pool and poker hall in Cimarron. We cool off in there Friday nights—trying to double our pay and slaking our thirst from a week of dust out here on the unfinished road."

"So, you're a local, Zeke?"

"Yeah. Cimarron born and raised—which isn't half exciting as it might sound. This town's heyday was back in the Wild West days. Nothin' exciting' has happened here in decades."

"Maybe someone should change that," the Corvette driver said, with a smile. "Any good motels in Cimarron?"

"Well, there's the Cimarron Hotel and the Blue Jay Inn. But notice I didn't answer the 'any good?' question."

"One more private than the other one?"

"Guess that would be the Blue Jay Inn. Here comes the pilot car now, so I gotta step back in the slot and you'll be on your way in no time now. Thanks for the water . . . Beel."

"And thanks for the conversation and view, Zeke. See you around."

Zeke returned to his position, ready to turn his sign from 'stop' to 'slow' without another thought to the man in the Corvette—although he watched the tail of the car drive off with appreciation and envy.

* * * *

"So, you allowed to accept that beer now?"

"What? Oh, the man with the Vette. Bill, was it?"

"No, it's Beel. And I'd really like to buy you that beer—for leading me to Wyatt's. This does look like it's where it's happening."

"Not that anything's happening much around here," Zeke said with a snort.

"I think we'll manage," Beel said in a quiet voice, a little knowing smile on his face.

Out of the automobile, the man—Beel—looked more commanding to Zeke than how he'd remembered him when looking down into the driver's seat of the convertible. He was tall and barrel-chested. Looked like he worked out still, even at his age—which also didn't look as old as before when the gray streaks in his hair and goatee were more prominent. He was wearing an expensive-looking gray tweed Western-cut jacket, matching well-pressed trousers, and finely tooled leather cowboy boots—which gave him the look of a wealthy Texas oilman or cattle rancher. As far as Zeke could tell, that was probably what he was.

For his part, Zeke cleaned up real good too—after he'd showered off the dust of the road construction out on route 50 and shampooed his hair, which now showed its golden highlights. He was wearing faded, but clean, tight blue jeans and a tight red T-shirt, exhibiting bulging thighs and a chest tapering down to a flat belly and small waist. All together the package showed that working road construction earned muscles honestly.

"You play poker or pool?" Zeke asked after he accepted the beer.

"You could say that—both. You think you could get me into a poker game with your construction buddies?"

Zeke could, but he began to regret doing so more and more as the evening wore on. His buddies were losing badly. He was losing too—but then managed to recoup most of what he was losing. So, unlike his increasingly glowering buddies who watched their week's pay slide across the table to sit in front of the quiet, smiling, dark stranger with the strange name, Zeke almost didn't notice that his pile was beginning to diminish too.

"You play pool?" Beel asked Zeke, as the poker players began drifting away, unhappy and pockets nearly empty.

"Yeah. I'm said to be pretty good at it," Zeke answered, eyeing Beel's newly won stack of bills. Zeke, in fact, knew he was better than "pretty good" at it, and he figured on getting what he'd lost and some of what his construction friends had donated as well.

He wasn't as good as Beel was, and it soon became apparent that Beel could show him a thing or two about holding the stick and picking his shots. As Zeke's weekly pay slowly moved from his pocket to Beel's, Beel started showing signs of taking pity on him. From time to time he'd stop Zeke as he was ready to make a shot and stand close behind him, showing him how to hold the cue and line up shots. When he did this, Zeke felt an electric current flow through him, but he was concentrating more on his depleting funds and, after the first demonstration, he could see that what Beel was showing him was helpful and was stemming his loses—sort of.

But there came a time when Zeke had lost far more than he could afford to do. He begged off another break of the balls and moved toward the table where the poker players who had been fleeced were drowning their sorrows in beer and commiserating over their loses, but the glares they all gave him showed that it would be at least a couple of hours before they would forgive him for bringing that card shark into their midst.

He veered off and collapsed into a chair at another table. He didn't see Beel sit down beside him, but he felt that electric current course through his body when Beel put a reassuring hand on his shoulder.

Beel leaned into him and said. "I bet taking a ride in my Vette will help you feel a little bit better. And maybe there's something I can help you with in getting some of your money back."

"A ride in your Corvette?" Zeke asked through a snuffle. He'd wanted to cry, but there was no way that he was going to let any of the construction workers—or Beel—see him do that. "Shit man, I've never ridden in a Vette."

"Now's your chance. It needs letting the lead out of its engine. With all that construction on 50, it was stop and go all afternoon. You can maybe show me where there's some straightaway at night where I can let it blow its engine clean and we'll have a ball."

They sped out on a dirt road north from Cimarron into desolate ranch land, eventually running out of road at the entrance of a homestead marked by log poles with a log cross bar making an arch over the road into a square bordered by a small group of deteriorating buildings with no lights showing.

"What's in there?" Beel asked.

"It's the old Anderson place. They're all dead and gone now, and no one's been able to track down any heirs yet—not that there's anything in there worth handing over."

Beel turned the Vette and drove in under the crossbar and into the courtyard all of the buildings faced. Then he turned off the motor and turned to Zeke. "I told you that maybe there was a way you could get some of that money back."

"Yeah, how's that?" Zeke asked. "I'm not offing your wife or anything." He laughed nervously.

"I don't have a wife, Zeke. I like men."

That took a moment to sink in, but then Zeke shrank as close to the passenger door of the tight-fitting Corvette as he could. "Hey, man. I'm not into any of that shit."

"Then you don't know what you're missing, do you?" Beel asked. "It's not a hard way to earn cash. Certainly not as hard as standing out on a dusty road turning a sign around every half hour."

"I ain't done nothin' like that, man. There's some things money don't buy."

"Oh, well, I guess we'll go back to town then," Beel said, as he turned the ignition key and the Corvette revved up in a rumble. "I've got a roof over my head tonight. How much longer can you cover that department?"

"Wait, man, let me think," Zeke said, the panic in his voice palpable.

"Sure, you think about it," Beel said, as he switched the engine off. His hand moved from the key to Zeke's thigh, and Zeke groaned at the electric touch of him, feeling himself harden up at the mere thought of what was being proposed— and the touch of Beel's long, electric fingers on his thigh. It wasn't as if Zeke hadn't thought about doing it before.

"What sort of money are we talking about?"

"I jack you off and you get fifty back. Seventy-five if you blow me. Two hundred back for each fuck."

"Each? Oh, shit, man." There was a moment of silence then, as Zeke fought off hyperventilation—and watched in horror and fascination as Beel moved his hand to Zeke's basket. Zeke knew Beel could feel him hard—and he knew that weakened any denial or negotiating position he had. He needed some of that money back. He also was aroused; he couldn't kid himself about that. He certainly understood that Beel's hand on his cock understood he was aroused. "I'd fuck you?"

"No, that's not the way it would work, Zeke. I'd fuck you."

"Oh, man. I . . . don't know."

"I like you. I want you, Zeke. So, I'll tell you what. I'll double the offer." Beel was speaking with confidence, and this was being driven home, because he already was pulling Zeke's zipper down. And Zeke wasn't stopping him.

All Zeke could manage was a weak-voiced whimper, "I won't do any blowjob."

"We'll manage," Beel said. And then he laughed, a deep-throated laugh, as he pulled Zeke's nearly hard cock out of his opened fly. He didn't take it in hand right away. He stopped long enough to pull Zeke's T-shirt over his head. Then he turned toward the young blond in the seat and, with one hand, grabbed Zeke's pony tail at the base and pulled his head back tight with the headrest, while his other hand took Zeke's cock and began to stroke.

Zeke groaned at the electric touch of Beel's hand on his cock. He gave a little yip when Beel leaned over and took a nipple in his teeth. He moaned as Beel's mouth moved up to the hollow of his neck and sucked him hard there. All of the time, the motion on Zeke's cock was progressively becoming more rapid. Zeke turned his face toward Beel's and opened his mouth to him as Beel moved his lips up Zeke's cheek.

Then Zeke was gasping and writhing and bouncing his hips off the bucket seat of the Corvette and his cock was being pumped with inhuman strength and pistoning motion.

Beel's tongue and lips freed Zeke's mouth and almost immediately the young man was crying out in surprise and ecstasy, as Beel's mouth sheathed his cock and a hand moved to Zeke's balls, squeezing and rolling them hard and pulling them away from his body. The vibration and suction of Beel's mouth was driving Zeke crazy—but only for seconds.

It was all over in a few brief moments, leaving Zeke exhausted and slack jawed.

"I have you now," Beel muttered, with a half laugh. "Step out of the car, Zeke."

"I . . . I don't think I can."

"Now, Zeke. It's time to earn back big money."

Zeke had never imagined it could be like this. The initial invasion of his virgin ass was a few seconds of excruciating pain, but after that no sensation of pain could have made Zeke forego the experience of Beel's cock working inside him.

Zeke was bent over the hood of the Corvette, his cheek to the warm metal, and Beel was palming his belly, pulling

Zeke's midsection off the car surface and into Beel's pelvis with one hand and arching his back with a fist at the root of his pony tail, as Beel's cock filled and drilled him, sending flashes of electricity through Zeke's body. Beel's cock was vibrating and pulsing and forcing itself deep, deep inside Zeke's channel, stretching him, sending the mind-blowing pleasure of it through his body. Zeke's legs were jelly, but Beel was holding him up and pulling him higher, onto his toes and then letting him down on his heels with the strength of his buried and pumping cock.

It went on for more than an hour, and Zeke came twice more, before Beel gave a deep-throated, lusty laugh and flooded Zeke's insides with four strong, separate spoutings of ejaculate, which gave Zeke hot flashes that raced out to the ends of his extremities.

When Beel pulled out of him and released his belly and pony tail, Zeke slid to the earth beside the wheel of the Corvette.

Beel sat on the hood of the Corvette and looked down at Zeke. Zeke looked up at him and saw that Beel was still in monstrous erection.

"Again," Zeke murmured. It came out as a prayerful request.

"I think not," Beel answered. "It was nice, but I'm not sure it was worth $400."

"No, no. Again, please. I never knew . . . again, please. Not for money."

Beel laughed and stood down from the Corvette hood where he'd been perched. He leaned down and pulled Zeke up and lowered the young blond's back on the Corvette hood, spread his legs with fists encasing ankles, and thrust inside him strongly. Zeke cried out in surprise and shock and his eyes rolled up in his head, but he immediately started moaning and panting and working his hips in the ever-faster rhythm of the fuck that Beel was establishing and extending for endless time.

"I don't want to sleep alone," Beel said as they were cruising back into Cimarron. "I presume that even in a town this size you know of some presentable young man who will keep me warm tonight for a hundred bucks."

"I'll do it," Zeke shot back without hesitation. "Please."

Beel laughed. "I've had you already. I want variety."

"For free. I'll do it for free," Zeke whined.

But Beel ignored that and continued speaking. "An Hispanic maybe. Small and not too stale. But willing. You get me one and I'll sweeten your take by $200."

His name was Manuel. Barely legal, and just starting doing it for money. He was small boned, and a bit delicate—and maybe just a little more swishy than Beel would have liked if he'd had a lineup to pick from. And when he saw Beel's cock, he cried out and headed for the door in the Blue Jay Inn motel. But Beel was too fast for him, and covered his mouth with one hand as he pulled the frightened Hispanic down into his lap and proved that the Hispanic could—with considerable effort and grunting—take all of him, although it was seemingly magic that was required to get all of Beel inside him and the small Hispanic was gasping and working his mouth in a wide-gaped yawn as if he expected the head of the cock to appear on top of his tongue.

As Manuel felt the searching vibration and pulsing and electric current over his channel walls, he began to moan and melt into the lap fuck. Somehow Beel maneuvered his torso around so that his mouth sheathed Manuel's own cock, and they were working in consort as one pleasure-producing machine, as, like with Zeke, Manuel blew and rebuilt and blew again before Beel bathed his insides with his own ejaculate.

After that Manuel couldn't get enough of Beel throughout the night—and Beel demonstrated that there was no limit to what he had to give.

It was nearly dawn before they both slept. And it wasn't more than an hour later before the telephone in the room rang—on the side of the bed Manuel was facing, on his side, Beel's still-half-hard cock deep inside his channel.

Manuel picked up the receiver.

"It's Zeke Candrell," Manuel said sleepily. Then he went back to the telephone and what Zeke had to tell him put him on immediate alert. "He says the construction workers you took all of the money from last night are on their way here.

229

They beat out of Zeke where you were. They've decided you cheated them, and they want their money back."

"Time to move on, then," Beel said in an almost jovial tone as he pulled out of the Hispanic youth and sat on the side of the bed and reached for his elegantly stenciled boots.

"Zeke says he'll meet you out at the edge of town. He wants to go with you."

"Tell him that's impossible. I ride alone—and I have his soul now, what further need do I have of his body."

Manuel disappeared as Beel was finishing dressing— but he reappeared in the passenger seat of the Corvette the older man had parked around on the side of the motel, shielded from view from the street, when Beel came out of the motel room.

Beel laughed and picked him up and carried him back into the motel room. He threw him in the motel room's closet and pulled the bed in front of the door—which is where the construction workers found Manuel five minutes later when they arrived at the motel room, its door gaping open.

* * * *

Three hours later, west of Dodge City, on route 50, young, golden-blond, honestly muscled Jim Steele was standing at his family's mail box at the end of a long dusty dirt road back to the house and outbuildings of their cattle spread. He was on edge and a little piqued because he'd walked all this way down from the barn, where, stripped down to his jeans, he'd been putting the feed out for the horses, only to find there was no mail in the box.

The previous night hadn't been good for him. His steady, Gail, had let him feel her up, but she'd stopped his hand as his trembling finger was about to enter the wet darkness of her. He'd been keyed up and ready to blow ever since. He was feeling sorry for himself and wondering if he'd get anything before he turned old and gray.

He looked north, east, and west, away from the farm, at the slightly rolling, wholly monotonous countryside, wishing he was anywhere but here.

He heard the car approach just as he was walking back to the farm and then turned and looked back at the road when it didn't pass. He rubbed his eyes in disbelief and walked closer. What was a gorgeous new metallic-blue top-down Corvette convertible doing out here on route 50 between nowhere and nowhere else at 7:00 a.m. in the morning?

The driver, the lone passenger in the car, a dusky-complexioned man with an interesting, almost Asian face and black, gray-streaked hair and an unusual goatee smiled at him. Jim smiled back, hospitality being a hallmark of good, honest rancher farmers in the Kansas badlands.

"Hey, you sure look like you're in the need of a cooling drink," the stranger said. "Can I offer you a cold beer? Got them back here just in the cooler?"

"Too early for a beer, mister. But . . . thanks anyway."

"How about water then? You look like you've been standing out here forever waiting for something to happen."

"I feel like it . . . thanks for the water." Beel had already had the bottle out of the cooler and was holding it out toward Jim, across the seats of the Corvette. Out of politeness, Jim accepted it, which brought him to the side of the car. Just putting a hand on the passenger window well sent shudders of pleasure up Jim's spine. Nobody around here owned anything like this.

"There's nothin' gonna happen around here, I'm afraid. But standin' and lookin' at the horizon is a common activity in Kansas. Shit, this is a beautiful piece of equipment—uh, sorry for the cuss word."

"No problem. Yes, it's a fuckin' beautiful piece of heaven. You got a name?"

"Uh, yes, Jim. Jim Steele," Jim answered with a warm smile, disarmed by the stranger's comfort with cussing. "And you?" It was all natural pleasantries, the exchange of names being a long-practiced customs of friendliness and willingness to trust in the ranching and farming environment where everyone helps everyone else.

"I'm called Beel."

"Glad to meet cha', Bill."

"No, it's Beel. It's short for a much more complicated name, but we needn't go into that now. Say, if you're just at loose ends now and wishing there was some excitement in your life, how would you like to take a ride in a new Corvette?"

"Oh, man, would I ever!"

"Hop in. And you sure it's not too early for a beer or two."

"Well, if you twist my arm," Jim said happily as he opened the door to the Corvette and folded his hunky bulk into the passenger seat.

"It may come to that," Beel muttered under his breath, too quietly for Jim to hear, as he looked both east and west down the deserted route 50 and pulled back onto the road and turned around, headed for the deserted Anderson spread.

Snowy, Snowy Nights

In most senses Bran had been invisible at the Hayden saloon the couple of months he'd been there. But as he came out of the back room into the main saloon hall, carrying the bucket of water Levi Yost, the saloon keeper, had told him to use to freshen the bowls in the rooms upstairs, he looked at the tall Christmas tree in the corner. Sadie, Katie, and Faye were busy happily decorating the tree with colorful bows from their own drawers. The tree had been his idea.

At first Levi had given him the fish eye when he'd suggested that a tree would liven up the room and make more men come into the saloon. The saloon and brothel manager had been skeptical.

"We don't need no reason to entice the men to come in here; they show up on their own and fill the place every night. And I just don't know. A live fir tree indoors? I've heard of it, of course, but that's more for those hoity-toity sissies back East."

It was a Christmas tradition that had come from back East, for sure, Bran knew. His family back in Pennsylvania had always had a Christmas tree, bringing the tradition with them from Germany. It was one of the few family memories Bran still had. He'd lost his family to an Arapaho war party when coming over the Rockies below Hahn's Peak in a wagon train. Somehow Bran had been overlooked in the slaughter and had been taken in, here in Hayden, Colorado, on the Yampa River, by the family that owned the livery stable.

Bran had lived with them for a few years, being treated more like a slave that the Union not long ago had fought a war to get rid of. But when old man Toliver had found Bran laying under his son, Quin, on a haystack in the back corner of the livery one night, Bran had found himself working at the Hayden saloon the next day and living in a shed out back.

"That's the place for you," Toliver had said, "and you keep away from my son, you hear?"

And since old man Toliver was holding a shotgun when he'd said that and was looking real mean, Bran had agreed to stay away from Quin—although it had been Quin, of course, who had accosted him.

Bran hadn't been told his duties at the saloon would involve lying under men, although Bran had no illusions that it would come to that. The saloon did have a male prostitute for men who swung that way, the life of a cowboy on the range helping to make a man settle for another man—Sadie, Katie, and Faye, being the girls for the regular customers—and Bran was small, blue eyed, with curly blond hair and had a body that was perfectly formed, and thus ripe for the job. But Bran hoped that he'd have found a way to move on—or back to Pennsylvania to find family—before it came to that. Yost had him carrying water, cleaning up the rooms upstairs between uses, keeping fires going in the fireplaces now that winter was setting in across the valleys of the Rocky Mountains, and doing general fetch and carry duties.

As it turned out, Yost was pleased with the Christmas tree idea, not least because the girls were enjoying decorating it so much that they were bouncy and flirty with the customers, which seemed to be increasing the saloon's revenues.

Bran had worked through the women's rooms on the west side of the second floor and was moving over to the east side, when he became aware that the "best" room on the front east corner was in use. The women had a "best" room at the front on the west corner to entertain the more important and high-spending men too, but this one was the "best" room for Sam, the male prostitute. Behind that room on the east was Sam's room for regular customers, which, of course, wasn't near as grand, and then Sam's own bedroom was behind that, at the back, which wasn't grand at all. It was grander than the shed Bran was sleeping in, though.

From the sound, Bran knew there was quite a session going on in the "best" room. He hadn't realized that any of the rooms were in use this early in the afternoon, but Levi had told him to change the water and towels in all of the rooms, so Bran knew he'd have to slide into the front-east "best" room as unobtrusively as possible and get on with his business.

It was groans and heavy breathing that he was hearing, but it wasn't Sam. Sam was off in Kansas visiting his sick mother. The guy who was moaning was Caleb, Sam's temporary substitute from up Slater Creek valley. Business had picked up with him here. He was younger, fresher, and, some of the clients said, better looking and with a better body than Sam. Levi was making noises about maybe Sam just not coming back, but Bran had talked with Caleb. He just wanted to have money to rebuild a barn for his foster father up in the valley. He wasn't looking for this to be permanent.

Caleb was making more noise than he usually did. Bran decided this meant his customer was extra demanding. He clicked the door open and moved around the side of the room to the water bowl on a bureau. There was a pail beside the bureau. He'd have to empty the old water in that, put fresh water in the bowl, exchange the towels, and creep back out of the room with the dirty towel and pail of dirty water.

It was a big room and fancier than the regular rooms. Both of the "best" rooms were just that, outfitted more like fancy parlors, with red-velvet coverings on the walls and heavy drapes at the windows, upholstered chairs at the fireplace, a braided rug on the floor, and a copper bathtub in the center of the room.

In the "best" rooms, the clients were treated to a bath before the sex. The women and Sam liked using these rooms the best, of course, because they got the men clean for probably the only time in a month—and before if not during sex. The sex usually started when the men were still in the tub, and Bran saw that there was no difference here. Water was sloshed out of the tub and onto the floor like there had been some sort of wrestling match going in the tub—which probably was true. Bran hadn't been called on to fill the tub with water heated up down in the back room of the saloon— one or both of the serving girls must have done that—but he knew he'd be the one to have to clean up after Caleb and this man were done.

The man was tall, broad shouldered, and barrel and hairy chested. Probably in his forties, but a hands-on worker, because he was heavily muscled. His waist wasn't thin, but his abs were laid out in plates like the illustrations of Roman soldiers Bran had seen in picture books.

From what Bran could see of the root of the man's cock as he fucked Caleb at the foot of the four-poster bed, the man was big in that department too. His balls certainly were big. They were flapping on Caleb's buttocks as the man worked on Caleb's hole. Caleb was on his back, running along the foot of the bed, one leg extended to the floor and the other one running up the man's torso. The man was standing on the floor with one leg and had the other one bent on the bed. There were pillows under the small of Caleb's back that turned his pelvis up to give the customer a deep angle.

Caleb was naked and the man was naked too other than that he was still wearing his boots. Bran wondered how they had managed that—whatever had gone on in the tub before this—with the man still wearing his boots. Keeping one's boots on wasn't that unusual, though. One of the things the prostitutes were careful to do was to make sure the man's spurs weren't still on the boots. The prostitutes only made that mistake once. Bran had seen customers in these rooms who didn't even take off their hats—just opened their flies and bent Sam or Caleb over the bed.

Caleb's eyes followed Bran as he moved through and back out of the room. They seemed almost to be pleading with him for some sort of help, and he was groaning and moaning to beat the band. Bran needed no more evidence than that to know that the man was huge in the cock department. But there was no help to give Caleb. He was doing what he was here to do—what he was being paid to give.

Bran trotted downstairs with the dirty towels and pail full of dirty water with mixed feelings. The man's body was powerful looking and it was arousing to think of accommodating a huge cock like the man must have—Quin's cock hadn't been oversized. Neither had been Mr. Toliver's, whose problem with Quin fucking Bran had probably been more one of jealousy than propriety.

The light was dim in the back room when Bran got down there. He threw the dirty towels on the pile beside the washtub and went out into the backyard and dumped the bucket of dirty water, leaving the door to the outside open when he'd returned and pumped clean water into the pail from the pump at the sink.

He didn't know whether Toliver had been in the room all the time or had come in through the open door, but he suddenly found himself in the embracing arms of a strong man behind him, a man who was panting heavily, a man who held a calloused palm over Bran's mouth and pulled his head back, arching his back to the man's chest. Bran's britches were being jerked down from behind and fingers were forcing themselves in his channel. And then a man's cock. Bran knew it was Mr. Toliver because of the crook to the right of the cock. Quin's cock crooked to the left.

Toliver was in high fuck, and Bran was just standing there, taking it, half in relief, because it had been a while since Quin had last fucked him and Bran had left the "best" room upstairs in arousal, when Levi Yost walked in on them.

If Bran expected Yost to intervene, he was mistaken.

"If you do it in the saloon, you pay for it, Cale," was what he said. "You want to take that outside?"

"I'll pay," Toliver growled, not missing a beat in his pumping.

"Best if you come through the front and make it all proper the next time then," he said. And after standing there a minute to watch the stroking, he left the room.

Afterward, as Bran was sweeping out the saloon's bar room and taking sidelong looks at Faye finishing up with ribbons on the tree, Yost called Bran over to the bar.

"You'll be taking up the slack during busy times for Caleb and for Sam when's he's back now, Bran. I wasn't sure whether Cale was shitting me before—whether you took cock—but now that I know you do, you might as well be making the saloon more money. You got a problem with that? If so, you'd best be finding someplace else to work and sleep."

"No, Mr. Yost," Bran answered, his eyes looking down at the floor. "I don't have a problem with that."

"Well, you say yes and we invest in getting you set up here, you are contracted to us. Understand?"

"Yes, Mr. Yost."

It just meant that now more than ever Bran wanted to be able to move on from here.

* * * *

Jeremiah Carlin rode out of Hayden and turned up toward the south end of the Slater Creek valley, which dropped down between ranges of the Rockies from Wyoming territory into the new state of Colorado. He was headed due north rather than northwest to his cattle ranch on the Elkhead River. He'd spend another Christmas and New Year's up at his mountain cabin near Antelope Gap pass on the western range. The ranch hands thought that was where he headed off to from the ranch, but he still had needs, so he'd come down to Hayden first.

Two years. Time for him to be alone up at the cabin. The hands could take care of the ranch. He wouldn't be fit to be around until early January. This would be the third Christmas since he'd lost Seth—at Christmas. One of those freak accidents that is easy to have on a cattle ranch. Jeremiah had been completely unprepared for it. He was twenty years older than Seth. He should have been set for life. He was the one who should have gone first.

And he couldn't even mourn properly at the ranch. He couldn't have owned up to what Seth meant to him. Some of the ranch hands—the cook, Clyde, certainly—had known. But it wasn't something that anyone could talk about in the open. Many of the men did it; they just didn't talk about it. He couldn't mourn Seth in the open.

It had been Clyde's suggestion that first Christmas—spoken softly and with great care—that Jeremiah go on up to the cabin for the rest of the season. He could let loose there, or withdraw into himself. Anything. Anything that came naturally to him. He usually only used the cabin in the spring and fall— to hunt from. It too easily could get snowed in in the winter. And in the summer he was busy with the cattle drive up into Nebraska, to the stockyards in Omaha.

But snowed in was maybe a good thing the way he was feeling. Clyde had been right. He needed to be alone in that season. And withdrawal, just laying under blankets and watching the fire—and putting away the liquor. Hoping it put away the ache as well. That's what had worked, as well as anything could, these last two years.

The horse snorted, bringing him back into the present as they approached the narrow southern passage into Slater Creek valley. He sniffed the breeze. Snow. It would be snowing up in the mountains soon. Down here too, probably. Good.

He got to the cabin as twilight was licking its way down the eastern slope of the western range. He could still see up into Antelope Gap, but there were snow clouds hovering over the western side of that. It would snow before morning here at the cabin.

He put Becky in her stall in the small barn and made sure she had enough to eat and drink to last for days. When they had a big snowfall up here, it would get real serious. There would be days he couldn't make it as far as the barn.

Opening up the cabin then, he left the interior shutters closed on the two windows and started up a fire in the fireplace before unbundling. It was just the one room, with a fireplace at one end, a window and door on the front, with a porch along the front of the cabin. A window on the opposite end from the fireplace. A door off the back. That just led down a narrow corridor to the outhouse. After that first winter up here, Jeremiah had learned the hard way that he needed a clear path to the outhouse. So, he could say that his cabin was fancier than most up here.

Cupboards along the back wall. Two overstuffed chairs at the fireplace, Seth's untouched in the last two years. A small, rectangular table, with four straight-back mismatched chairs, in the middle of the room, between the doors on the front and back, and the double bed at the end opposite the fireplace. There was a grizzly bear rug in front of the fireplace between the two chairs there and a braided rug between the table and the bed. He'd once had a single bed. When he had found Seth, one of the first things he'd done here and at the ranch was put in double beds. It had only been here, though, that they could be free to fuck without restraint. Seth had been a yeller when fucking with abandon. And Jeremiah had a cock that made him want to yell.

With the fire going good, Jeremiah stripped off a couple of layers of clothing and cooked beans and a slab of fatback over the fire, with a coffee pot sitting directly in the fire. He ate alone, hunched over the table, trying not to think any thoughts at all, but with Seth—and his times with Seth, here, sitting by the fire, and over there on the bed—drifting in and out of his mind. That wasn't a reason not to be here, though. It would be the same down at the ranch. But down there, it would be the men being in the Christmas spirit—or trying to. Jeremiah wasn't so selfish as to be down there, all glum and mournful, and keeping the men from getting into the spirit.

He hadn't unshuttered the windows on purpose. It wasn't just to keep the heat in. It also was to keep the world out. Being alone, in the silence, that was all he could take in this season. He did, though, hear the wind and a shushing noise through the chinks in the log cabin walls. He went over and opened the door. It had started to snow, but was still in a tentative state of getting that done.

Good, he thought. He closed the door, went over to the bed, crawled in, still dressed—he'd had a bath down in Hayden that would hold him over for several days—turned his face to the wall, pulled the comforter over him, and laid there for an hour before sleeping, thinking of the good times he and Seth had had in this bed.

* * * *

It had snowed in the night, but not too badly. When Jeremiah left the cabin to check on Becky, though, he could see the clouds were still ominous looking over the western range. From experience, when it looked like this, they were in for a lot of snow, and even if you could get up to the top of Antelope Gap from here, the snow would be so deep on the western slope that you couldn't get down into the Yampa valley.

He heard whinnying as he approached the barn, and it sounded like more than just Becky, so he was somewhat prepared when he entered the barn to find a painted pony stalled next to Becky—the two of them having a friendly conversation—and a young, blond-haired man bundled up in a blanket and lying on strewn hay in the third stall. He kicked the young man's boots, and Bran sat up and rubbed his eyes.

"Had a good sleep in my barn, did ya?" Jeremiah asked gruffly.

"Uh, sorry," Bran answered at the end of a big yawn. "Really sorry. I thought the place was deserted until I saw the horse stalled in here. But I needed someplace to get out of the wind and snow. Really tired. Sorry. Thought I'd be up and gone before whoever owned this horse showed up. Lots of feed and water here. Thought she was being left alone during a hunt or something. The cabin looked all boarded up."

"And you didn't see smoke risin' out of the chimney? City boy, are you? Can't hunt in weather like this. Well, won't begrudge you the shelter, but you need to be up and . . . say, do I recognize you from somewhere?"

"No, I don't think so. Yeah, and sorry about not knowing better. I've come from Pennsylvania." Bran, in fact, did recognize Jeremiah. He was the big-dicked customer working Caleb over in the "best" room just a few days ago.

"Headed where?" Jeremiah asked.

"To California. Just passing through here. Sorry, I'll be up and on my way."

"Not for a while, you won't, I reckon, unless you go south from here into Hayden and then west through the wider gap in the Rockies."

"Uh, I was told there was a pass up this way."

"There is. Antelope Gap. But it's surely snowed in on the western side already, and it will only get worse for the next couple of days. You'll need to lay up somewhere and wait for it to reopen, unless you hurry and go south to Hayden."

"Uh, I don't really want . . ." No way he wanted to be going back toward Hayden. He hadn't asked anyone's permission when he'd left, and he had no idea what being contracted to Levi Yost meant.

"Suit yourself. I guess you can hole up here, if you've got your own grub. I won't begrudge you feed for the horse. Becky will like havin' the company. But you'll have to stay out here."

"Stayin' out here is fine with me, thank you kindly. I have enough hardtack to last until I can get across the mountains."

"Well, just so you keep quiet like. I came up here for the peace and quiet—and to be alone. That's why the cabin looks boarded up."

It was well after his dinner of beans, fatback, and coffee that it hit Jeremiah where he'd seen Bran before—in Hayden's saloon. In the room where he'd fucked that sweet young piece substituting for Sam. If the guy was in that room . . . He surely was a sweet young piece himself. In some ways he reminded Jeremiah of Seth.

He went to bed and tossed and turned. The longer he thought about Seth and the young man out in the barn, the more aroused he got.

It was snowing harder in the night as he left the cabin and walked toward the barn.

The young man was bundled up in the third stall, shaking a bit because it was cold out here without the benefit of a fire. He wasn't asleep though. Jeremiah kicked his boots.

"I *have* seen you before, haven't I? In the Hayden saloon."

"Maybe yes," Bran answered in a small voice. "I've been working there." He didn't think it would go well with him to lie about that. He too hadn't slept, more because of being aroused by what he'd seen this man doing to Caleb than because of the cold.

"You one of Levi Yost's boys?"

Bran hesitated, but yes, over the past couple of days he had definitely become one of Levi Yost's boys—and a favorite of the customers, who were always pleased with fresh meat and who were showing up at the saloon in droves now, probably at least partly because of the Christmas spirit Bran had introduced by suggesting they put up a tree.

"Yes, I was. Not anymore, though," he said.

"Well, we can work out your sheltering and some grub for breakfast in a barter exchange unless you're not willing."

Bran was willing.

"Oh shit, oh fuck. You're so fuckin' big," Bran cried out as Jeremiah started to stuff his cock in. The older man was crouched between Bran's legs. Both of them were fully dressed except for Bran missing the britches Jeremiah had pulled off him. Jeremiah had an arm under Bran's waist, lifting his pelvis up to the cock, while Bran had his arms thrown over his head, clutching at the rough boards of the stall, trying to hold steady at what became the thrusts of a huge battering ram.

"God, I've never had it this big!"

"I can—"

"No, no. I seen you doin' Caleb. I knew it would be big. Do it. Ram it in me!"

Soon, Bran was reduced to sobs and moans and groans as he clutched at Jeremiah's neck with his hands, fighting to bring the older man's lips down to his, and eventually succeeding, even though Jeremiah hadn't wanted this to have any intimacy at all. He just wanted the meeting of his animal need, to fuck someone hard to forget, in only briefly, Seth.

* * * *

Bran once again was awakened by a kick to his boots. It wasn't day yet, but there was a good five inches of snow on the ground, which was reflecting light from the attempt of the sunrise to peek over the Hahn Peak ridge to the east, across the Slater Creek valley.

"Figured you could use some hot breakfast," a gruff voice said. Bran opened his eyes to see Jeremiah standing over him, a plate of porridge in one hand and two mugs of steaming coffee in the other, his fingers laced through the handles. Bran was sore, but he didn't regret the previous night at all. Jeremiah was, indeed, the biggest man he'd ever taken. And he would be OK to be taken by him again.

He sat up and accepted the plate and one of the mugs. Jeremiah crouched down on his haunches and held the other mug of coffee in both hands, letting the warmth penetrate his hands.

"It snowed again last night."

"I could tell," Bran answered.

"Definitely no going over Antelope Gap today."

"Oh . . . well."

"How did you come by that painted pony there, son? You didn't steal it, did you?"

"It's from Toliver's livery down in Hayden," Bran answered. "I did work for the Tolivers. They didn't pay me."

"But they didn't give you the horse, did they?"

"No, not exactly."

"Being as you are coming direct from Pennsylvania . . ." he said it so both knew he didn't believe that one, ". . . then you probably don't know that men get strung up around here for stealing horses. No trials necessary."

"Oh."

"I should turn you in. Take you down to Hayden and turn you over to Cale Toliver—and maybe even to Levi Yost. I doubt Levi gave you leave to go either. Bet you have some sort of contract there. Place is owned by Warren Savage, owner of the Big O ranch. Mean son of a bitch. Bet you didn't know that either. He's not likely to let an investment run away."

"I . . . just . . . want to be movin' on," Bran said in a small voice. "So . . ." He gave Jeremiah a plaintive look.

"So, I'd say, seein' as how the snow is only slowly gettin' here from over the mountain, that I'd best take that painted pony back down to Hayden and leave it where it will be found but folks will think it broke out of the livery by itself."

"Oh. You'd do that for—?"

"I should be overnight doin' it and I'd best get to doin' it. Eat up on that breakfast and then come into the cabin. You can stay there while I'm gone. I'll show you what's what there."

There wasn't much to show, and Bran stood by the door to the corridor to the outhouse, trying to keep out of the way, while Jeremiah rummaged around for what he needed to take with him.

"It's mighty nice of you to do this for me," Bran said.

Jeremiah answered with a grunt.

"I wish there was something I could do to show how grateful—"

Jeremiah looked up at him. Bran could see it in the man's eyes. There was certainly something Bran could do.

They fucked on the braided rug, Bran on all fours and Jeremiah crouched over him, fucking him like a dog. Bran had moved toward the bed when they'd both realized what they were going to do, but Jeremiah had pushed him down on the rug, saying in a rough voice, "No, not on the bed. Not there. The floor's good enough."

Once Jeremiah was gone, Bran looked around the cabin. He needed to do something else to show his gratefulness. The cabin was so drab. It wasn't long until he was out in the forest, picking out a tree and chopping it down with an ax he'd found in a stump in the yard. He brought that in and got it stood up in a corner on the fireplace wall. He went out and chopped wood and brought it in and stacked it on the other side of the fireplace.

He looked critically at the tree. It needed something else to make the cabin look Christmassy. He went out in the barn and scrounged around, finding an old stirrup here and some tops of tin cans there, and bits and pieces of metal elsewhere. The tree looked better with those stuck in its branches, but it still didn't look very Christmassy.

He threw open the shutters inside the two windows and let the light in. That did it. The light shining off the metal ornaments really brought in the spirit. Candlelight and light from the fireplace would do it at night.

Having brought in the light, though, he saw how dusty and dingy it was in the cabin. He used most of the time

Jeremiah was gone cleaning out the cabin. Then he went back into the woods and brought in branches of holly, with a profusion of red berries. Putting those here and about in the cabin really brought in the season.

He didn't know why Jeremiah didn't want him to use the bed to fuck him, but he respected that he didn't—and he thought the aversion might extend to him being on the bed at all—so he slept on the braided rug the night he was alone. With the fire going, it was much better than trying to sleep in the barn had been.

It snowed again that night, bringing the depth outside to more than six inches. Bran went to sleep thinking of Jeremiah's big cock—and what he'd done with it—and masturbating himself to sleep.

* * * *

Bran sensed more than heard Jeremiah return in the late afternoon of the second day. The falling of the snow made a sound, which surprised him. Only being on the silent mountainside as he now was brought home to him that snow—in conjunction to the whistling of the wind—could make a distinctive sound. But so too did the clop of the horses and the jangle of their straps and bridles and of Jeremiah's spurs.

The horses. More than one.

Bran went out on the porch of the cabin to welcome Jeremiah and saw that he had an extra horse. It wasn't the painted pony, however.

"Another horse?" he asked as Jeremiah dismounted.

"I came back by way of my ranch. The horse is packing extra food supplies. And you'll need a horse if you're going across the mountain."

"But I have no way of paying."

"Yes you do," Jeremiah said, giving Bran an intense look, a bit of a smile on his lips.

Ah, yes, I guess I do, Bran thought—on my back, with my legs open. There's always that. Jeremiah led the horses into the barn, which was not easy—there now was more than eight inches of snow on the ground. While he was doing this, Bran went back into the cabin and walked over and sat down by the fireplace. He felt a little deflated that he'd still be thought of as just a hole to relieve Jeremiah's needs. He'd been euphoric when they'd fucked in the cabin—even if it had been on the floor. It's like he was being let into the man's world. It's what had led him to do all of the decorating and . . .

Jeremiah had moved into the cabin and just stood there, his jaw dropped and his eyes wide open.

Bran smiled, waiting for Jeremiah to compliment him on what he'd done to brighten the place up and make it feel more Christmassy.

But Jeremiah's reaction came in a bombastic explosion. "What the fuck? What's all this for? And, you, get out of that chair. That's Seth's chair."

Confused and wounded, Bran sprang from the chair. "What's wrong?" He also wanted to yell, "Who the fuck's Seth," but he didn't.

"What the fuck have you been doing while I was gone? Moving in on me? Trying to be Seth? Well, you're not Seth, dammit. Get the fuck out of here."

"No, I'm not Seth. I'm not trying to be anybody but me. I'm Bran. Bran." It hit him then that they had never, even in their most intimate moments, referred to each other by name. He didn't know this man's name, and this man had never asked him for his name. "My name is Bran. I'm a person. I'm not just a fuck toy. My name is Bran. Not Seth, whoever the hell that is."

"What the fuck? Get that tree out of here. Get out now. NOW!"

Close to sobs, Bran grabbed for the tree and pulled it out of the cabin, past Jeremiah. He dragged it through the snow, to the barn, and propped it up in a corner there. He collapsed into a sitting position leaning up against the side of the stall not occupied by a horse, and cried and rocked himself back and forth, staring at the tree, trying his damnedest to try to pull some sense of Christmas out of it.

He heard the shutters in the house slam shut and went to the barn door. The holly branches had been tossed out into the snow as well. He went back into a fetal position, facing the tree, and rocked back and forth, back and forth. Well after dark he pulled some hardtack out of his saddlebag and made a dinner of that. He went to the door and scooped up some snow to quench his thirst. The cabin was dark, buttoned up tight. But there was smoke coming out of the chimney. He hadn't thought to look up there before, but he did so now.

At least the *man* had some warmth.

It was cold in the barn, and it was still snowing. It must have been more than a foot deep out there by now. Even with the snow falling, the moon was peeking through from somewhere and reflecting off the snow. The landscape was ethereal even if Bran had no reason to appreciate that.

Then he calculated. It was Christmas Eve. He went back into the barn and sat, cross-legged, in front of the Christmas tree, his teeth nearly chattering from the cold despite the blanket he'd wrapped around himself.

"Silent night, holy night." He found he was humming the tune. Then he started to sing it to himself, in low, hesitant Pennsylvania Dutch, almost the original German, phrases, his Omar—his grandmother—had taught him, the notes coming between slight sobs.

He felt so alone, so utterly alone. And rejected. He had no idea what he'd done wrong. And now what? What was he supposed to do? What did the man want him to do? He could saddle that horse and leave now, tonight. But how far would he get in this snow? And in what direction? And would the man come after him as a horse thief? He hadn't earned the horse yet. The man had made clear he had to earn it on his back. Was what he had already let the man do enough? Probably not. He could go out on foot. He wouldn't make it far in this snow. But did it really matter anymore? Was there anyone who cared?

At length he drifted off into a fitful sleep, resolved from moment to moment to rise and trudge out into the snow, but much too cold to start doing it.

* * * *

"I'm so sorry. So very sorry."

Bran wasn't awakened by a boot nudging him this time, but by the man scooping him up off the ground in the barn, moving his cramped and aching limbs out of the fetal position, kissing him on the cheeks and mouth, tears streaming down the man's face.

"I'm sorry. Forgive me . . . Bran, was it?. My name's Jeremiah."

Something had happened to the man in the night, something had worked on his heart in the snowy, snowy night and had turned him completely around. Bran didn't ask him what. He was just thankful—considered it a Christmas present and miracle—that it had happened.

Jeremiah carried Bran into the cabin and over to beside the fireplace, where he had a roaring fire going. He rubbed Bran's hands and feet and limbs as he pulled frozen clothes off the young man, stopping only long enough to get a good slug of brandy down Bran's throat before he was sitting in his chair by the fire, Bran in his lap, facing away from him, with one leg draped over a chair arm, and commencing to rub other areas of Bran's body—his lips, his thighs, his belly, his pecs and nipples, his cock, and, finally, the inside of his channel with a pumping cock as he gripped Bran's waist and raised and lowered the young man's channel on the cock.

He was repeatedly whispering, "Your name is Bran; your name is Bran."

Jeremiah fucked Bran in the chair and on the bearskin rug in front of the fireplace, with Bran on his belly and Jeremiah closely covering his back and, with Bran slightly raising his hips, Jeremiah stroking slow and deep inside him.

And, at last, Jeremiah took Bran to the bed, covered them both with the quilt and side split the young man while turning Bran's face to his by cupping his chin and holding his lips in a deep kiss. An arm was wrapped around Bran's back and a thumb was thrumming his nipple.

Bran gently turned the older man on his back, licked his way down through the hair on his chest, while Jeremiah moaned—and then grunted and groaned as Bran's mouth opened over his cock. After riding the cock to a mutual ejaculation, Bran collapsed onto Jeremiah's chest and the two men drifted off to sleep.

When Bran woke in the morning, the cabin was flooded with light. The shutters on the windows were open. He could only see glittering white beyond the panes of glass. The tree was back in the cabin, standing, not particularly straight, but standing in the corner. The holly branches were back in the cabin, if haphazardly scattered about. Jeremiah, bare-chested and in skivvies, was kneeling by the fire, frying a mess of eggs and bacon. He was humming. The smell that permeated the cabin was of fresh-roasted coffee.

He turned and saw, Bran, still naked, sit up in the bed. The quilt dropped to his waist.

"It's Christmas morning," Jeremiah said.

"Yes," Bran answered, wondering if anything, anything at all was going to be said about the previous day and night.

Evidently not. "There must be at least a foot and a half of snow out there." Jeremiah said it like it was the best possible news he could have to convey on a Christmas morning.

"Is there?" Bran asked.

"It's stopped now. But it will be days, a week or more probably, before Antelope Gap will be passable." Again, he made that sound like it was a present. And Bran took it that way. But a present for which one of them? Or maybe both.

Jeremiah stood up from the fireplace and turned, the frying pan in one hand and a spatula in the other. His skivvies were pulled down in front by the weight of his heavy cock and balls so that Bran could see a line of curly pubic hair along the line of the man's lower belly. The tenting promised that he was in erection. His body was magnificent. A heavily muscled mature man at his peak.

"Three eggs or four?" he asked.

"Three, but for now I want a cock. Just one, but it's got to be big. Inside me. Now." Bran was tossing away the quilt, turning toward the side of the bed, grabbing his ankles, and lifting and spreading his legs.

The eggs were stone cold by the time they ate them. Neither of them complained.

* * * *

It was eight days later. Eight nights of Bran being in Jeremiah's bed, but rarely sleeping there at night. Catching naps in the afternoon as Jeremiah chopped wood and cared for the horses, so that he would be awake and aware of everything Jeremiah was doing with him—to him, inside him—in the night.

The snow was almost completely melted outside the cabin now, and when Bran looked up the mountainside toward Antelope Gap, he could see more rock than snow—and blue skies overhead. But each time he looked up there, Jeremiah would come up beside him, put an arm around him, and say, "Not yet, I don't think. Not safe up there yet." And more often than not, he then would pick Bran up in his arms and carry him back into the cabin and fuck him—in Jeremiah's chair or on the bearskin rug, or bent over the table, or on all fours on the braided rug. Rarely on the bed during the day. But always on the bed, repeatedly—in the dark—in the night. Repeatedly because Jeremiah almost always apologized for the size of what Bran had to accommodate after the first fucking and Bran would respond by demanding a second one.

The afternoon of the eighth day Bran was laying a fire in the fireplace and Jeremiah was standing at the window at the front of the house. The windows had been unshuttered, except in the dead of night, since Christmas day.

"You need to take a crap," Jeremiah said in a soft voice. "And you need to stay back there and quiet until I come and get you."

"I don't—"

"You need to go on back there now," Jeremiah said, giving him a hard look and standing at the front door.

As Bran was moving in the connecting corridor behind the cabin to the outhouse, he heard the front door open and Jeremiah go out onto the porch.

He crept back into the cabin and took a peek out of the window to the front porch. Four riders were strung out across the front of the cabin, one more forward to the other. Bran scurried back to the outhouse.

"Hello, Warren," Jeremiah called out. "What brings you up into the mountains in the winter? I ain't seen no stray cows—yours or anyone else's."

"Strange that you'd be up here in the winter too, Jeremiah," Warren Savage, owner of both the Big O ranch and the Hayden saloon, said. His voice was a friendly one. The two men were both cattle ranchers. Such men normally held together, sharing interests against the increasing encroachment in the region of sheepherders and farmers.

"Christmas. I like to celebrate it alone in beautiful surroundings. Have done it for years," Jeremiah answered. "Even have a tree, which I understand are real popular in the East now. Want to come in and see it?"

Bran started to creep back to the corridor to the outhouse in panic, but Savage's answer stopped him and he returned to standing beside the window and straining to hear.

"No, thanks. They put up a tree in the saloon this year too. Good for business. I guess we'll continue doing that for Christmas."

"So, what brings you and your boys up this way?"

"Looking for a missing man. A city boy from down in Hayden. Been missing since before Christmas. His name's Branton Niederman. Goes by Bran. You ain't seen anyone like that up here, have you? Short, but in good shape. Blond. Looks young, but isn't a child no more."

"Old enough to make his own decisions, is he?" Jeremiah asked.

"Left some obligations in Hayden. But mostly we're worried about him. His folks want him back real bad."

"His folks?"

"Yep. You seen anyone like that up here from before Christmas?"

A fifth man was nosing over toward them. Jeremiah could see that he'd been in the barn.

"Two horses in the barn," the newly appearing cowboy said to Savage as he approached.

"Both with brands from my ranch on them, did you see?" Jeremiah quickly said. "Needed an extra one to carry supplies up here. I'll be staying a spell." He then turned to

252

Savage. "Just me up here, Warren. If I see a man answering that description, I'll surely let you know. But until then, a Merry Christmas to you."

"And to you too, Jeremiah. Quite a snow we had up here. You look like you took the brunt of the storm right here."

"Yep. Almost two feet before it stopped. But it's meltin' off pretty good now."

"It seems to be, yes. Don't know if you heard, but for the first time in years, it didn't bury Antelope Gap on the west side. Folks over there said that, despite the snow, the pass never got shut down. Ain't that something?"

"Yep, that sure is. You take care now. And I hope you meet up with your man. But if he walked up this way into the storm, I doubt you'll be finding evidence of him before spring—and maybe not even then. Bears have gotta eat too."

Savage tipped his hat and the five riders turned and rode off.

Jeremiah waited until they were well out of sight before he gave Bran the signal that he could come out of the outhouse, where he had scurried to before Jeremiah could find out he'd been by the window.

But Jeremiah somehow had known Bran was there. "You heard?"

"Yeah, I heard everything real good," Bran said. "But I don't owe them anything down in Hayden and I'm of age. He didn't say anything about the painted pony, did he?"

"No, he didn't say anything about the painted pony. So, it looks like we fixed that up. But I meant whether you heard what he said about Antelope Gap. He's saying it's safe to go over that pass now—in fact, always was."

"But . . . if they're out there looking for me . . ."

"Maybe it's not that safe," Jeremiah quickly said. "But at night, of course." Jeremiah obviously wasn't looking for an excuse to see Bran off.

"Yeah, there's nighttime," Bran answered. They both looked at each other like they were thinking that the purpose of the night for them was something far different from riding over a mountain.

"Guess you have two choices then," Jeremiah said.

"Two choices?" Bran's heart began to beat fast.

"Yes. You can go over the mountain tonight—or you could wait and go down to my ranch with me in a couple of weeks. I've got enough food up here for two for a couple of weeks. And I got plenty of room down in the ranch house if you're interested in going in that direction rather than over the mountain. So, what are you thinking?"

"I think you know what I'm thinking," Bran said, a smile taking over his face. "But what are you thinking?"

"I'm thinking of what we could use to darken your hair. Just for a while. Just until Warren Savage stops lookin' for you."

The Photograph: John

(Excerpt from the habu novel *Raven Possession*)

Why had he left the photograph there, standing right there in a leather frame on the dresser top? More important, why was the photograph here at all? I had gone into his room to put his things together so they could take them down to Hayden along with the body, and there it was.

To some extent the whole success of the Wolf Creek Ranch had hinged on J. Harvey Kincaid's patronage and goodwill. He had been coming to Wolf Creek for as long as I could remember. And where J. Harvey Kincaid went, everyone else of note followed. He was the pied piper of world literature, an icon of unique proportions.

Back almost in pioneer days, my grandmother had taken a large acreage of homesteaded land in a remote Rocky Mountain valley dipping down into northern Colorado from dusty Wyoming that few others could find, let alone want. And she turned it into a dude ranch for celebrities—writers, movie stars, and politicians mostly—who either wanted to retreat from the pursuing world for a short time or wanted to hunt animals and bag them in privacy.

J. Harvey Kincaid had been one of the latter. He was already a writer of legendary status when he started coming to the ranch in search of the majestic elk in the high, snowy regions of the Rockies bordering on the Medicine Bow National Forrest. He said he identified with the elk, and indeed he had every reason to do so. He wrote celebrated men's novels of male bonding in challenging and dangerous circumstances, themes, and situations that bring out the grit and nobility of strong and bold men. His writing brought him fame and international awards. And his books invariably inspired noble and strong and bold movies that won international awards on their own merits despite the fact that they missed casting the ideal protagonist—J. Harvey Kincaid himself. He was the epitome of the rugged, handsome, square-jawed, determined man battling the elements, whatever they were—and winning and possessing what and how he pleased.

He had come to our ranch three or four times a year from the time I was a child, and my father took him up into the upper slopes of the Rockies, no matter the weather, and they stayed out there for three or four days at a time or for as long as it took to bring back an elk. I always held him in awe; everyone did. He had a rich, deep, expressive voice befitting his stature, both physical and intellectual, and he could tell a story as overpoweringly as he could write one. For years I would sit under the dining room table as he dominated and enriched the dinner conversation no matter what other celebrities were in residence.

As I said, my father was always the one to take him into the mountains. That is, until Kincaid came to the ranch while Dad was gone. That had never happened before; Kincaid had always come only when Dad was here, because it was Dad who took him hunting. Kincaid knew Dad wouldn't be here at this time. He had checked and been told Dad would be down in Durango, looking for cattle to buy. But Kincaid came and he insisted on going hunting, and there was only me to take him. So I did.

I had little idea how to track elk—that had been my father's specialty—but J. Harvey Kincaid was a patient man, a very patient man. We rode across the isolated ridges for days, searching near the tree lines, where Kincaid said my father often took him. By the third day our horses were worn out, and Kincaid suggested that we just lay by in a stand of cottonwood trees next to a fast-running stream in a sheltering ravine he remembered from previous trips.

We ate that night over an open fire, leaning against the saddles we had slung on the ground between the bank of the stream and the line of cottonwoods. J. Harvey Kincaid was his charming best, weaving stores of male bonding and the raw challenge of man against nature in that rich baritone voice of his, in words that were strong and raw but also mesmerizing in their poetry.

The air was crisp and slightly chilly, and Kincaid called me over to sit beside him as he leaned against his saddle so that we could share the blanket. He said we would be so much more comfortable making maximum use of our shared body heat. And I believed him. I had always believed him.

We sat there, against each other, as J. Harvey Kincaid continued weaving the magic of his stories. He asked me questions about what I thought of male bonding, of how close one man could be to another, how much support they could give each other in struggling against the elements. And he helped me provide the answers. He asked me about my connections with my father, and I started to cry. My father and I had never gotten along too well, even though I worshipped him. He wasn't mean to me; he just was remote and always just so sad. Kincaid had talked to me about how rich the bonding could be between men, and I grieved for what my dad and I had missed having. And the more I thought about it, the sadder I got. And I began to cry from the frustration of it all.

Kincaid hugged me and kissed my tears away. And he kissed my cheeks. And he kissed my lips. He told me not to cry, in that mesmerizing poetic baritone voice of his. He told me he loved me, and no one had told me that before, not even my father.

He asked me if I trusted him and if I loved him too. And then, at that moment, I surely did. He was a connection to my father—at this point, a substitution for my father. He was the savior of our ranch. He cared for me and comforted me. He unbuttoned my shirt and comforted the hollow of my neck with his lips, and then he comforted my nipples and my belly with his hands and his tongue.

He was unbuttoning my jeans and slowly unbuttoning my fly, all the time telling me that he loved me and wanted to take care of me. And asking me if I loved him and trusted him. And I did and I told him so. And he told me again of the joys and comfort of male bonding and said he wanted to bond with me. And he asked if I loved him enough to bond with him. And I did. I yearned for male bonding. And I told him so.

He told me it would hurt at first but that it would become glorious and that it would be a connection unlike any other. That it would wash my grief away. He told me that a man fought through the pain for what was important, and asked if I was ready to give myself to him. To trust him to take care of me. He was handling me, stroking me through the open fly of my jeans, and it was a new, pleasant sensation.

He asked me again if we could bond, out here in the crisp mountain air, in the beauty of nature in front of a crackling fire. And I said, "Yes, oh yes."

And I'm sure I meant it.

He was kissing my penis now and urging me to follow his lead. He had his member freed from his jeans and it was thick and long and hard. I tried to do as he was doing—but I gagged and he didn't. He tasted salty and his tool was hot and hard and throbbing and was pushing at me. Between my lips, the unsheathed tip pushing against my inner cheeks and depressing my tongue, pushing deeper inside. I gagged again, but then got the knack of handling him.

He was murmuring at me, giving me encouragement and guidance. Telling me how beautiful my body and my penis were, asking me how his attentions felt. And when I told him I was embarrassed at how I was filling out but that I was feeling pleasures I never had felt before, he told me that I was doing the same for him. That we were bonding beautifully, that I was pleasing him very much—but that we could bond even closer.

Did I want to bond even more fully?

Yes, oh yes.

It would hurt at first, but only at first, he was saying. There, could I feel that?

Ohhh, yes I could. I'd never had anything going in there, only coming out. But, maybe . . . Oh, yes.

He parted my lips with two of his fingers and told me to suck on them. And while I did so, I felt a finger of his other hand moving underneath me, circling the rim of my hole, before moving a bit inside again. And rotating around. Urging me to stretch out.

He stopped this, but only for a moment, as he stripped off my clothes and then his, and we were both naked, skin sizzling on skin underneath the encasing woolen blanket. He had my butt cheeks at an angle against one of his hips. He was holding my side close to his with an encircling arm and the two fingers I had been sucking on were now at the rim of my hole. He put his chin on my shoulder and kissed me in the hollow of my neck. I lurched in a slight, sharp sense of pain as the two moistened fingers slowly pushed into my passage, deeper and thicker than the previous exploration.

I was trembling and whimpering now, and he started speaking to me in low, melodic tones again. Telling me the story of a mountain man and his best friend, out alone for months in the mountains, in a camp not unlike this one. Of how much they depended on each other and how grieved they were at the death of a mutual friend. How they needed to comfort each other. How they need to bond. To bond closely. To become one so that they could face the elements together. To express their love. To do so in natural ways, the ways of time immemorial. Of how wonderful they felt when they had bonded. How there was pain at first, but quickly great joy and release of all their grief and fears.

One of my legs had been coaxed to lay astride his thighs, and I could feel the insistence of his manhood laying hot against my own thigh. I was trying to listen to him, but my attention was increasingly going to what those fingers were doing inside me. Moving deeper. Moving in, separating, spreading me inside, and then coming back out. And then moving in deeper than before. The pad of one had found a very sensitive point, and what it was doing to me made me tense up—and I felt like I had to piss and to jack off all at the same time. I was groaning and moaning, trying to let J. Harvey know that something was happening that he might want to stop if we didn't want to be embarrassed.

But then I jacked off. I tried covering myself with my hands, ashamed, hoping he hadn't noticed. But he just laughed and cooed at me and told me that this was exactly what I needed to do. That this was all merely a stop, a necessary milestone, toward ultimate male bonding. A good reaction. A very good reaction.

To show he wasn't angry or upset, he lowered his mouth to my penis and licked me clean from what I had shot off there. All the time he was telling me this was exactly what was supposed to happen. That this is what happened to those men in the mountains as they moved toward perfect bonding that ended their grieving.

Could I feel as those men did, he asked.

Yes, yes I could.

Was I man enough to pass through the pain of the initiation into the bonding?

Yes. I was as much a man as either of those he was talking about. I was my father's son.

Yes, yes you are, he said. Did I trust him? Did I love him? Did I want to get beyond the grieving and would I let him help me do that? Was I ready to move into the bonding?

Yes. Please. Now.

While still encircling my chest with one arm, he lifted my pelvis with the strong hand of the other arm and centered my hips over his and slowly lowered my passage on his throbbing tool. I cried out as he impaled me, as he slowly pulled me into his lap. I was grunting and moaning and whimpering, and he was sighing and whispering encouragements to me and telling me how good I was doing and how well we were bonding and how nice and tight I was—and sweet—oh, how sweet. And how much he loved me for bonding with him. For being the first to bond with me. That this was very special for him.

I was settled completely down in his lap now, and he was encircling my chest tightly with one arm and holding my belly hard against him with the hand of the other, holding me in place while the impossible invasion and stretching of his hot cock was slowly being accommodated by my virgin passage.

About the time I thought I had managed the pain and we had totally bonded, however, the movement started. He had his hand wrapped around my waist now and he was lifting and pulling me down on that throbbing tool of his. I was crying out for him to stop or at least to slow down, and he was telling me that just a bit more and we'd be beyond the pain and into heaven. And then we were, and I was crying out for him to do it forever. There was still pain, but now I was feeling the passion, the wonder of this bonding thing he'd been telling me about.

He was stroking me up and down on his pole faster and going deeper inside me with each stroke. He was trembling as much as I was now and making animal sounds and using that beautiful voice of his to make love to me with his words just as much as he was by making us one, a single pistoning machine, moving toward release, his cock stroking up into my channel.

I was arching my back against his heaving chest, trying to make us one. My head was flung back and he was kissing me deeply on the lips and swabbing the insides of my mouth with his tongue when he lurched and I felt the flow of him burbling deep inside me.

We sat there entwined for many minutes, as we both worked to bring our ragged breathing under control and he let his hands glide all over my body and his tongue coat me with honey-toned words of how well we had bonded.

Then he told me that we could only really keep the depth of that feeling through frequent bonding, especially at first, and would I give myself to him a different way? Would I show my trust and love by putting myself entirely in his power?

Shortly thereafter, I was bent, completely naked over the seat of a saddle, my belly against the leather, my butt in the air. The saddle had been placed between and a little in front of two cottonwood trees, with the leather straps ending in metal stirrups angled off toward the trees—one toward the tree on the left of the saddle and one toward the right. J. Harvey Kincaid had tied one end of a rope to each of the stirrups, run it around a cottonwood tree, and tied the other end around each of my wrists so that I was held there on the saddle, not going anywhere, denied the use of my hands. Open to him. All of my trust in him.

And then a towering, naked J. Harvey Kincaid crouched down behind and above me, his thighs encasing mine, and he thrust his cock into my puckered, tilted-up hole, and rode me hard to a second ultimate bonding. The second time was not as painful for me, as I was well lubed from his first ejaculation inside me.

And I thoroughly enjoyed the third time, when he had turned me on my back so that my hips were raised up onto the saddle. I particularly felt the bond of this third merging of our bodies, because I could see his eyes. I thought I could see how much he loved me in his eyes. I thought I could see the honesty of all that he wrote and believed about the ultimate goodness of male bonding.

I can't describe the look on my father's face when he came back to the ranch from Durango and found out that Kincaid had been to the ranch and I had taken him hunting. I never wanted to see that expression again. But then, maybe I could have endured it more than what actually happened. Three weeks later my father was dead, having tried to drive over the Rabbit Ears Pass from Denver in a blinding snow storm, where he'd gone to see my grandmother but found she wasn't there. I have no idea why he'd gone to Denver, nor do I know why he tried to drive over the mountain in the snow—everyone knew the foolishness of that. I only know that I'd lost my father—without ever having the chance to have a full relationship with my father at all.

Kincaid became my substitute father. And the feeling of the male bonding that he told me of and demonstrated with me held for a good three years of his visits to the ranch three and four times a year. Each time I took him hunting into the mountains and each time he bonded me deeply and repeatedly. For those three years, I did believe that he was making love to me—that he loved me. But I grew up. For the eighteen years after that, to today, I came to know that he was just fucking me.

But his patronage continued to help the ranch survive and prosper.

For twenty-one years I took him into the mountains to bag his elk—and me. I even began to identify with the elk.

Each time he came to the ranch, he'd call ahead to make sure that I would be there and free to hunt with him.

But not this time. Not for this visit. He had called, yes. My son, home from college for the summer to continue learning to take over the management of the ranch, had answered the telephone and told J. Harvey Kincaid that I wouldn't be here for the week he wanted to visit. I would be up in Laramie at a rodeo. I didn't necessarily need to go to the rodeo in Laramie, but we had reached the stage in my son's training that he needed to face whatever problems came up in the ranch operations on his own without me there to guide and save him from any bad decisions. I wouldn't be around forever. He needed to stand on his own.

He and I hadn't gotten along all that well for several years. We had been inseparable when he was younger, but then something happened—something I'd never learned the reason for—that had cooled him toward me. But this ranch was our family income. He knew that, and he was willingly trying to learn the business from me—even while holding me at arms' length. He seemed particularly upset the day that J. Harvey called to set up his next visit.

And J. Harvey had gone ahead and come, even when I wasn't going to be here. He'd never done that before.

When I returned from Laramie, my son was nowhere to be seen.

"Where's Jamie?" I asked the first ranch hand I ran up against. "Charlene's at reception; Jamie should be there."

"He's up in the hills with that writer guy, Mr. Raven," the cowboy told me.

"That writer guy?" I asked, totally confused. Why had Jamie left his responsibilities here to go off with some dude?

"Yeah, that one you always hunt with, Mr. Raven. Jamie was in kind of a fix because the guy showed up and wanted to go huntin' and you weren't here. Jamie said he had to make a choice; he couldn't be in two places at once, but he knew how you were always saying how important this Kincaid guy was to the ranch. So he went on up into the hills with him to hunt elk, like you always do. Left Charlene in charge. She seems to be doing OK, if you ask me."

I wasn't asking him. I was confused. Kincaid. J. Harvey had come ahead even knowing I wouldn't be here.

That was two days ago. Now Kincaid was dead. Brought down slung over a horse. The cowhands said Jamie told them it was a hunting accident. But I hadn't seen Jamie. I'd been too busy calling Hayden and making the arrangements. The sheriff down there would be up in a couple of hours and he'd be the one to be asking questions.

But here, in my hand, was the source of a question I hadn't really wanted answered. The photograph. It was an old photograph. Two men standing by a makeshift sling between poles holding the carcass of an elk. A photograph at least three decades old. Two hunters. Kincaid on the left and my father on the right. And the way Kincaid had his arm wrapped around my father, I knew. I suddenly knew. I wasn't the first Raven Kincaid had bonded with. And whatever happened up in those mountains two days ago, Kincaid had meant me to see this photograph.

My son. Jamie. It hit me then, and I lurched out of Kincaid's room, stopping briefly at the fireplace in the main room to throw the photograph into the flames, and then out into the dusty courtyard. In search of my son. Before the sheriff arrived.

The Photograph: Jamie

(Excerpt from habu's novel *Raven Possession*)

I saw that photograph. I saw it that first evening, when I went in to turn the bed down because Charlene was busy out in reception. I had already figured he had been doing my dad all these years, and it's something that had come between me and my dad. Not that Dad knew what I knew—or at least strongly suspected. But our connection just couldn't be the same anymore because of it. But seeing that famous author guy, Kincaid, in that old photograph he'd put on his dresser—that just set me off. I could have killed him then and there. Putting that photograph there was like he was flaunting it, flaunting his control and his power.

The photograph showed that big elk he'd bagged up in the mountains here. But that's not all it showed. In the photograph, he had his arm possessively around the waist of my grandfather, who had taken the famous author on that hunt when he was staying at our family's dude ranch, Wolf Creek. And it showed to anyone who might have half suspected it that the elk hadn't been the only animal Kincaid had bagged up in the mountains.

I tried to be angry at my dad for also putting up with Kincaid's attentions all of these years, but I knew he'd done it to keep the family business going. It's what paid for my college down in Boulder; it's what was setting me and the rest of the family up for our lives. And J. Harvey Kincaid, the famous author of those men's novels on male bonding and "man against the elements," was the main patron and pull for our celebrity dude ranch—and had been for decades.

Dad had left me to manage the ranch for a couple of weeks this summer while I was home for college. He'd gone up to a rodeo in Laramie specifically so that he wouldn't be around to bail me out of tough decisions at the ranch. And Kincaid's showing up at the ranch was the toughest decision I was faced with.

He came three or four times a year. But he always came when my dad was going to be there and could take him up into the mountains, up near Medicine Bow National Forrest, to hunt elk—or so they said. Kincaid had called ahead this summer and I told him on the phone that my dad would be gone then. But here he was anyway. And he wanted to go up into the mountains to hunt elk. And he was the patron of the family business.

Of course I took him on up. I couldn't be in two places at one time, though. So, I left my sister, Charlene, in charge at the ranch and picked out the most steady of the ranch hands and paid them extra to do what they could to help her out and keep a protective eye on things while I was gone. And Kincaid and I saddled up two horses and headed up into the hills, toward the still-snowcapped reaches of Hahn's Peak.

I went with the intention of staying my distance, of being polite but standoffish. I didn't want Kincaid for a friend, and I was afraid that if I could get within striking distance, I'd kill the man for what he'd done to our family. Not just what he did to my grandfather and father but how dependent we'd become on his patronage. I couldn't see the point of his fame. I'd read the books and seen the movies done from them, and, yes, he was an engaging, persuasive writer. But that macho male friendship and combining strengths and resolves to take on all comers, whether the scenario was the American West or the battlefields of Vietnam, got old pretty fast, I thought.

But the longer I was riding around with him up in those deserted hills of magnificent wild beauty, just the two us, with him weaving stories for me in a rich baritone voice that lulled and stroked me to the very quick, the more I could see how he worked on a person. He must have been over seventy by now, but he was still quite a man, the virile, solid, handsome man of power and decisiveness that he wrote about, and for which he had received international accolades for four decades.

The third day we had struck camp in a cottonwood grove next to a racing stream running down an isolated, sheltering ravine and then we'd ridden on up toward the snow line in search of elk.

We found a mud slide instead. Neither one of us got hurt—and the horses weren't any worse the wear for the slide either. But we were filthy. With a hearty laugh, Kincaid challenged me to a horse race down to the crystal clear little lake the stream in our ravine fed into, and off he roared with another laugh.

It wasn't his horse, so he flew with reckless abandon and was already off his steed and in the lake before I got there. When I arrived, I somewhat dumbly said I couldn't come right in because I hadn't brought a swim suit and wasn't wearing anything under my jeans for that matter, and he just rose out of the water and threw wide his arms and said there was no need for such modesty out here in the wilderness. He was buck naked and showed off exceptionally well for a man his age. He tossed out a "Real men don't need swim suits" at me in that macho voice of his and, challenged to the quick, I stripped down and dove into the cold, clear water.

We paddled around a good ten or fifteen feet away from each other, cleaning the mud off ourselves, as he wove another one of his male bonding stories for me—a story of young men starting off in life and those with experience of the world doing so much better than those of limited horizons and narrow views. He told of the story of a young architect, taken under the wing of an older, established one. And how their lives merged and how much their bonding developed the lives and works of both in enriching ways that could never have happened if they'd lived in isolation. I couldn't help but listen to his story in fascination. I aspired to being a writer—I'd shyly told him that several summers ago—and I could see parallels. And I fancied I was drawing those parallels on my own.

He suggested a race, a race across the lake. I didn't think that quite fair, an author in his seventies and a nineteen-year-old athlete who had been ranch handing for the last two months. But this was his hunting trip. He was calling the shots. So, I laughed and asked him what we were wagering on. He said if I won he'd both clean and cook the fish for dinner and if he won I'd have to give him a shoulder rub right there in the lake and listen to another story he was trying to work out before he wrote it. He said all of the riding had made his body sore.

He, of course, won. I surely didn't like either cleaning or cooking fish, but Kincaid had much more at stake than I did. Or did from his perspective, at least.

So, there I was, that ten or fifteen feet no longer between us. I was standing behind him in water up to our nipples and massaging his back and shoulder muscles deeply. The water was rippling around us and moving us in waves, moving his butt from time to time back against my groin. And I have to admit this was having its effect on me.

Meanwhile, he was unfolding his idea for a story. About a young man who wanted to write about life but who hadn't really experienced life deeply and fully enough for anyone to take notice of what he put in writing. But then he was taken under the wing of an older, more experienced, far more successful writer. The young man won a scholarship to study with the older man for a year, and the two went off to a tropical island country to work on developing the young man's writing in private, without distractions. But for months he could think of nothing to write. There was no experience to draw from, no passion from which to write. The tropical island went into chaos. A revolution was erupting around them, and they had to hide out in interior rooms of the house they had let. They went through travails of protecting each other from the threats around them, and they became closer and closer. And they bonded, becoming one. And the young man was writing now. Writing from a wellspring of experience and passion. And after the revolution, when they emerged from hiding, he wrote a Pulitzer-winning novel. A novel enriched by deep experience and passion.

Sometime during the weaving of this mesmerizing tale, the waves were no longer moving us together. Kincaid had his butt plastered into my groin now and had my now half-hard cock encased between his thighs. And I hadn't even noticed this was happening until he took one of my hands in his strong fingers and wrapped it around his very hard cock, his hand on top of mine.

He was murmuring to me in that sing song baritone voice of his, "I know you want to be a writer, Jamie," he was saying. "But do you really think you have the experience and passion for it?"

"Yes, of course," I quickly answered, trying to take my hand away from his cock, but being held there firmly in his grip. And then, with more thought. "No . . . No. Probably not. I do find it hard to decide what to write about. And when I do, it often comes out so naive."

"You know what all of the successful men writers have that you're lacking?" Kincaid whispered.

I remained silent, afraid of the answer. And my mind focused on my cock being held closely between Kincaid's thighs and my hand on his throbbing cock.

"Bonding," he continued. "That's the success of my writing, Jaime. I write of the most important things—men bonding and taking on the elements together. I live on passion. I need passion for my writing. I can't imagine that you are different. And I'm eternally grateful for all of the inspiration I get from bonding. And I am a giver. I help those who feed my needs."

He let that sink in, as his thighs began massaging my cock, making it harden out, and his own tool lengthening and thickening between my fingers.

I was confused. And frightened. And aroused. I remembered that I had come out here with some sort of resolve, but I couldn't quite focus on what I had resolved. His voice. His strong body. His very presence. His slow persistence. I was melting.

"Have you ever experienced someone's lips on your manhood, Jamie? Have you ever experienced the passion of that? I have, and it has inspired my writing."

"Uhhh . . . yes," I had to admit. "Sure, there have been girls—"

"And no men, Jamie? No men? The level of passion and inspiration is entirely different, I assure you. No men?"

"No, of course . . . well, there was a fraternity party once last spring—"

"And the passion of it? The comparison of the girl and the boy?"

"Well, I was more than half drunk at the time. But as I recall—"

"Oh, no. You have to be fully there, Jamie. Fully there to make full use of the experience, of the inspiration. Here, let me show you."

"I don't know . . ." But before I could go further, Kincaid had turned me around in the water, facing him. He had crouched down in the water and my legs were hooked on his shoulders as he pulled my torso into his face. He was supporting me with hands on the small of my back and my shoulders and the back of my head were floating in the salt water of the lake while he gave me a cock teasing and deep-throating blow job like I'd never experienced before, not that I'd experienced much of anything like that before at all, of course.

He was right. I had known nothing like the feel of his lips and warm, moist mouth on my cock. I'd had no experience until this moment worth inspiring writing anything worthwhile. I had no passion. This was more passion than I'd ever felt before. Who was I kidding? Kincaid was the real writer. You had to go through what Kincaid had gone through to be a real writer.

I howled with passion and experience as I shot off all over his face, globs of my passion peppering his face. He laughed and deep-throated me and cleaned me off. And then he was standing in shallower water and forcing my head down to his cock and I gathered a whole new experience and a whole new sense of passion. He was mine, centered on me. Giving himself to me. The famous novelist. The man who could be my mentor. Having passion for me. Moaning and sighing because of what I was doing. Stroking himself inside my mouth, ever deeper, ever more vigorously. Crying his own passion as he spouted off down my throat. Centering himself entirely on me. Giving me his all.

He was crouched in the water then, drawing me into his lap, whispering to me of male bonding of wanting to be my mentor, to help give me the experience and the passion I needed to become a first-class writer. He had his bulbous mushroom cap at my rim, and I was grunting and groaning, letting him know I didn't do this sort of thing, that I'd never done this before, that it hurt.

"Experience is pain," he was whispering in that persuasive voice of his. "Passion is pain. The only good writing comes from pain." If I wanted him to be my mentor, we simply had to bond. We had to become as one, to move as one, to share experience and passion. Is that what I wanted?

"Yes, oh yes."

Beyond pain was paradise. Passion and paradise and inspiration. Did I want that?

"Yes."

Did I want to seize it like a man or work slowly into it, taking the risk of being denied the prize by not seizing the moment, not taking the risk? Did I trust him, love him? Or did I want to second guess my actions every step of the way? Grasp the golden ring or take my lesser chances of relative safety and uncertainty?

"I want it all. Now," I cried in my own world of ecstasy. Grab for that golden ring. Fame, fortune.

"More pain at first but then more pleasure, deeper passion, richer inspiration," he was breathing in my ear.

"Richer inspiration," I cried.

And his cock centered on my hole now, he thrust up violently, strongly as he forced my hips down hard. I screamed and writhed and cursed and cried. He started pumping immediately, fast and furiously. My cries of pain and frustration were turning to passion and new heights of ecstasy. He was laughing and yelling out his joy, his victory. The slushing of the lake water inside my passage was operating as a lubricant and increasing the wave sensation of the fuck. He was making animal sounds, groaning and grunting and moaning and speaking rapidly, telling me of the deepness of male bonding in this way, of his love and passion for me. Forever and ever, till the end of time, as if there was no tomorrow.

I arched my back to him and presented my face so that he could take my lips in his and tongue-fuck my mouth. I was lost in love for him. His now for whatever else he wanted to do—as he flowed inside me in three great bursts of virility.

As we rode back up to the camp, he was telling me of plateaus in male bonding and that he couldn't be sure of my commitment without my showing complete trust in him, my willingness to follow his every lead as he worked on developing my writing. To show that I was willing to be dominated by his will, by his knowing what was best for me.

To prove myself fully his to form, I let him strip me and turn me on my belly on the leather seat of a saddle laid out between and in front of the cottonwood trees. Leather straps ending in metal stirrups were strung out on either side toward a cottonwood tree, and lengths of ropes were tied on each of the stirrups and then wound round a tree and tied at the other end around each of my wrists so that I was held there on the saddle, not going anywhere, denied the use of my hands. Open to him. All of my trust in him.

And then a towering, naked mentor crouched down behind and above me, his thighs encasing mine, and he thrust his cock into my puckered, tilted-up hole and rode me hard to a second ultimate bonding experience. Then he turned me on my back so that my hips were raised up onto the saddle. I particularly felt the bond of this third merging of our bodies, because I could see his eyes. I could see how much he loved me in his eyes. I could see the honesty of all that he wrote and believed about the ultimate goodness of male bonding.

That night I slept in his arms, on a blanket, under the stars, and he side-split me from behind once, twice, three times during that long darkness while I listened to the racing of the water in the stream and the wind whistling through the tops of the cottonwood, suddenly full of experience, inspiration, and passion I'd never even imagined before. His manhooded domination was complete. His cock a veritable battering ram, plowing me hard, caressing the inner walls of my passage, shooting off again and again, slathering me in buckets of his virile juices. J. Harvey Kincaid. My mentor. The man who would bring me to the age of mature, experienced, passion-filled writing. The secret of male bonding. Repeated, deep male bonding.

I woke to the sound of the gunshot in the darkness. The fire had gone out long ago. I was alone on the blanket. I stumbled around until I found him, lying beside the racing stream, a smile on his face. The mentor gone, the experience not to be undone. the passion in question. Inspiration surely there, but perhaps never dared to be inked on paper.

I don't know why but a deep suspicion, almost a realization, hit me at that very moment, as I looked down at Kincaid's face, smiling a very self-pleased smile in death. The relevance not very clear but also crystal clear. When my grandfather had died, everyone said it was an accident. In fact, they said it was a accident so often and so distinctly and so loudly that just the saying of it contained the seed of doubting it. He knew the Colorado mountains. He knew you didn't try to drive over Rabbit Ears pass in January in a snowstorm. He knew. But that's what he had tried. Right after Kincaid had taken my father, not my grandfather, on a hunting trip up into these mountains. The Raven men. All of the Raven men . . . including, now, me.

I was careful in handing the shotgun. There were going to be suspicions enough in any event. Motive just below the surface, begging to be set free, hidden, but there in plain sight for any damn fool with half a brain to see.

When I had reached the ranch, the deflated body of Kincaid, devoid now of all of its mesmerizing presence and power—its malicious soul—slung unceremoniously over his horse, I heard immediately that my dad had returned from Laramie and also that the sheriff had been called up from Hayden. I didn't want to face my dad; I was much more willing to face the sheriff. So I hid until I saw the police jeep nose through the log gate up the road. In the end, I was saved any suspicion. While the sheriff was driving down from Hayden, he'd gotten a call that Kincaid had left a suicide note at his home in Jackson. He had terminal cancer and considered a slow death unmanly.

That left my dad. I knew he'd ask what happened between me and Kincaid up in the mountains, and I was fully prepared to tell him that nothing had happened, that Kincaid had been withdrawn into himself the entire time and hardly spoke to me at all the whole three days. There was no one to dispute me, and I saw no reason to indulge Kincaid's last, intentional, I was sure, little victory over the Raven family.

Now there only remained the damning photograph. But I couldn't find it. When I went to Kincaid's room to search for and destroy it, all of his things had been cleared out already and sent down to Hayden with his body.

Western Tail

It had been a hot and dusty ride from Kansas into Colorado en route to my new posting as the postal agent and sutler at Fort Hayden. I'd ridden all day with the Rocky Mountains tantalizingly near without having reached the river they told me was still more than a day's ride out from the fort. I now saw the river ahead, cool and inviting, but I knew I wasn't going to make Fort Hayden today. So, I rode down the side of the river for a couple of hours, thinking about one more night on the trail and about how hot, dusty, and smelly I'd gotten.

The Yampa river beckoned to me—clean and clear and shallow enough to be safe. At last I gave in, deciding to camp out for the night at a place where the land gently slanted down to a quiet section of the river well away from the central current. There was a small grove of cottonwood trees to one side and smooth rock outcroppings to another side, where I could lay my clothes out to dry.

I tied my horse to a tree in the cottonwood grove and laid out some food and water for him. I set up camp at the edge of the grove and laid my rifle up against a tree there. My saddle had gotten pretty smelly, so I scrubbed that down good and dropped it in the sun between the rocks and the grove to dry. Next I stripped off all my clothes, scrubbed them real well, and stretched them out on the rock cropping to dry. After that, it was my turn. I dove into the river and luxuriated in the cool, clean water rolling over my body. I splashed around a good bit and did some hoopin and hollarin out here in the world all by myself and eventually stood and walked up out of the water until it just reached my knees. It was time to get serious. I took up the bar of lye soap I'd used on the clothes and then soaped myself up real well. I felt so good when I got to my cock and balls that I did some extra soaping there and pulled on my rod for a few minutes, enjoying the moment of freedom after weeks in the saddle as well as surfacing fond memories of my romp in the sack with that cowboy in Abilene that night not long ago.

I heard an unfamiliar horse whinnying, and I froze solid. There, fanned out before me between the rocks and the cottonwood grove was a small band of Indians riding fine-looking horses bareback. I have no idea how long they'd been watching me, but they'd had the drop on me for some time.

There were five of them, all young bucks—any one of them with enough muscle to easily handle me. Besides that, the one who evidently was the leader, a particularly impressive looking bronzed specimen, was holding a bead on me with a rifle. The other four strapping bucks had bows and arrows at various stages of readiness.

They weren't wearing paint, so at least they didn't appear to be on the warpath about anything. In fact, they weren't wearing much of anything beyond loincloths, moccasins, and thin beaded bands with leather fringe at the top of their bulging biceps and calves. The apparent leader, though, was also wearing a breastplate made of feathers and turquoise beads held together with silver wire. My immediate assessment was that they were a hunting party that had been attracted by my foolish cavorting in the river. That didn't mean that they weren't hunting for me. I'd been told to be on the lookout for small bands of renegade Indians in these parts ready to pick off the lone white man. And there couldn't be a more lone and naked white man around than me at this moment.

I held my arms out wide in supplication (which may have been a mistake considering what happened soon thereafter) and slowly walked up the shore, sidling a bit toward the cottonwood grove and my rifle.

The leader of the tribe raised his rifle a bit and gave me a look that told me in no uncertain terms that it wouldn't be a good idea to go for my gun. I was a little surprised that he was grinning at me, but then so were the other four. I soon found out why they were doing that.

The leader slipped off his horse and halved the distance between him and me in long, deliberate strides. One of the others in the band rode up close to him, and the leader handed off his rifle. Then he pulled strings at the hips of his loin cloth and the scanty covering fell to the ground. Oh God, was my first thought. It had just been my luck to have run across a band of Indians that swung in my direction. My second thought was that this Indian, at least, swung real well. He had a cock and set of balls that equaled or surpassed his other collection of well-tone muscles. And my third thought was that he must have really enjoyed my unintentioned performance with the soap, because his horse-hung cock was standing straight out.

Unfortunately for me he was such a fine specimen of manflesh that my cock reacted in similar fashion to the situation.

Before I could have a fourth thought, the tribe leader was at me like a pouncing cat. While he moved, the other four Indians came off their horses and gathered around fairly close to us in a semicircle. The Indian leader wrapped a hand around my neck and brought my face to his in a lip lock that showed me he did a lot of this. The other hand went to vice-like grip around my balls and the base of my cock that brought tears to my eyes and me to my knees in front of him just as soon as his lips and tongue released mine. This put me at a convenient level for him to stuff his hard cock between my lips, which he proceeded to do.

He was face-fucking me real well, when I managed to look around and notice that the four others had paired off and were fingering each other in shared excitement. This meant no one had the drop on me with anything but a hard and pumping penis at the moment, and I realized I might have reached the closest point to escape and survival that I ever was going to get. I knew I couldn't get to my own rifle or horse in time, but the Indian leader's horse, a gorgeous big golden palomino stallion, was standing unattended within striking distance.

So, I seized the moment and made a break for the stallion. Miraculously, I was on the horse's back and getting him to start into a trot before the Indians recovered. But then my luck ended. The Indian leader merely whistled, and the horse stopped in its tracks. I thought I was dead now, that they'd just pull me off the horse and rip me to shreds. But the Indian leader did something completely unexpected. He leaped up on the horse behind me, yelled something the horse understood, and we were off, two naked men on the back of a quivering horse, thundering across the plain beside the river. The Indian was wedged behind me. He grabbed my wrists and forced my hands into the flowing mane of the horse, where I wrapped my fingers in the white mane and held on for dear life. The Indian's beaded breastplate was digging into my shoulder blades, and his raging hard was rubbing up and down the small of my back as we were tossed and turned in the charge across the rolling countryside.

I was scared, but that rubbing dick of his and the whole wildness of the situation was turning me on, too. We hadn't ridden far before he made his move. His thighs had been just behind mine, with both of us hanging on to the horse as best we could with them. But in one swift, dexterous move, he took those powerful thighs of his and lifted them around and in front of mine and flipped me forward onto the neck of the horse. This tilted my pelvis up as well, and I screamed in fear and then in surprise and pain as I felt his cock head slide down the small of my back. It held briefly at my asshole as a much too-large a peg came into a much too small a hole. And then the rough rolling of the horse's gait solved the Indian's problem, and with one excruciatingly painful lunge, he had breached my asshole and split me in two with his ramrod, which just kept on screwing up into me as the motion of the horse's gallop naturally stroked his cock and my ass canal together.

I screamed into the wind and struggled against the powerful embrace of the Indian chieftain as we thundered on.

With the aid of the motion, he was pumping me deep with the natural interaction of our bodies.

I realized not only that I was aiding the wild fuck myself with my struggling but also, after the shock of being taken started to wear off, that I now was enjoying this incredible invasion of my body. In addition, I realized and that, once fucked, there wasn't much else for me to do but make the best of the situation. The trembling of my body started to decrease, I slowly stopped struggling against what was happening to me, and I started going with the motion of the horse's gait and the rhythm of fuck it created.

This submission to the inevitable—and suddenly quite pleasurable—must have been what the bronze hunk had been waiting for, because as I quieted down and my body started to go with the rhythm, the horse started to slow down, until we finally were standing still, beside the river, not that far from where we'd started. The Indian's body was covering mine closely from behind, and the pattern and depth of my breathing was beginning to come into synch with his. His cock was still buried deep inside me, but he slowly decreased the thrusting of his hips so that he wasn't pumping me anymore. He still held my wrists in his steeling grasp, and I still had my fingers wrapped in the white hair of the golden palomino stallion's mane. The horse was breathing hard from the wildness of the gallop, but it responded instantaneously to the Indian's indecipherable verbal commands. It now stood very still, it's strong legs rigid, and it remained so until the bronze stud commanded it to move again.

It dawned on me then and this was what this ride had been all about. The Indian chieftain was training me the same way he had trained his horse. He rode me until I got tired and acknowledged that he was in command. I wondered what was next, still afraid for my life, but I decided that my only chance was to calm down and go with his wishes and wants. I had to pretend that I enjoyed being fucked by him. I had to admit to myself, though, that I did enjoy being fucked by him, so it wasn't a case really of pretending. Not only did he have a fat, long cock, but he had a strong, virile thrust to his stroking, and there was nothing more exotic than being fucked by a hunky bronze savage. It was more a case of showing and convincing him that I had been successfully broken to his will.

His lips were in the hollow of my neck, and I turned my head and sought them out with my own lips. He smiled and looked very satisfied as he pushed my lips open with his and put his tongue to work. I responded fully.

I heard him give a sigh and then a grunt of approval, and he released my wrists and, quick as a cat, with the horse holding still and solid, he had changed his position on the horse in relationship to me. He now was in front of me, between me and the horse's neck, and had pushed my shoulders down onto the withers of the horse. We were pelvis to pelvis and dick to dick. He took my hands and had me wrap them around both dicks and stroke them together. I complied, fully cooperating with him. He massaged my chest and pinched and gently twisted my nipples into full erection as I stroked us both. He was thicker and long than I was, but we were both engorging further in response to my stroking.

When he was satisfied I was fully broken to his will, he pushed my hands away and started stroking me vigorously himself with one hand, while he fingered my asshole with his other one. When I shot my load, he cupped his hand over the head of my cock, capturing my amazingly prodigious production of cum, and I watched as he rubbed the cum over his cock and down into my hole. I found this an unbelievable turn-on, and when he then cupped his strong hands under my butt cheeks, lifted my hips off the horse, and looked at me expectedly, I correctly interpreted his unspoken command and took his cock in my hands and guided it into my asshole.

The ultimate surrender, and with a yell of joy that reverberated in the red-rock cliffs in the near distance, he crushed my hips into his pelvis, sending his cock deep inside me, and vigorously pumped my hips against him with his strong hands, fucking me deep and wildly. The horse held perfectly still, trembling ever so slightly under us, as I lifted my legs to the Indian hunk's shoulders and lowered my arms to the horse's side, holding them close against the warm silky hair of the horse's hindquarters, holding myself as still and steady as possible.

The Indian's heavy spouting at the center of me was accompanied by another one of his healthy-lungs yells, which no doubt told the rest of his tribe nearby both that he had had his way with me and that we'd soon return to them.

And, indeed, soon thereafter, we were riding back into my impromptu camp, the bronze stud once again riding close behind me, his dong well up into my ass canal, making sure I wasn't planning yet another escape attempt.

He needn't have worried, because his vigorous fuck had worn me out, psychologically as well as physically. I still feared what the Indians were ultimately going to do with me, but I was so broken in now that, whatever it was, I hoped they'd do it soon and get it over with.

The four remaining tribesmen had been entertaining themselves with each other while we were gone, and they were in quite a fucking frenzy. If I'd entertained any thought that I was going to be reserved goods for chieftain, I was quickly disabused of that notion. When we reached the encampment, I simply was pushed off the horse into the waiting arms of the tribesman who seemed to be the second in command. He was older than the youthful tribal chief, and thinner and more sinewy. But his cock was longer than that of the chief, which meant it was quite long indeed. He simply grabbed me by my upper arms and pushed me back against the slow-rising rock formation where my now-dry clothes were stretched out to dry. He grabbed me by the neck and banged my head down on the rock, the blow being cushioned by my dried shirt, but taking any fight I might have give out of me just the same. His other hand folded one of my legs up against my body between my chest and his. He then positioned his cock, which he just slid up into me to the end and fucked me vigorously to his ejaculation.

I was then handed off to the youngest and bulkiest of the tribesmen, who had the thickest cock of all. He pulled me off the rock and twirled me around to the area between the rocks and the grove. He pushed me down into the sand right beside and across my saddle. My pelvis was elevated on the saddle, with my cock rubbing into the leather. My butt was pointed at the sky. The young hulk then crouched down

281

behind and above me, forced his thick dick into my hole, and fucked me in fast, hard downward strokes. I screamed for him, although I was feeling strangely quite fine to be stretched and pumped in this way, and the Indian chieftain put a stop to the noise by working his knees under my chest and pushing his cock back between my lips and deepthroating me.

The young Indian was quite virile, because he loaded right up again after his first round of coming inside me and fucked me a second time, this time rotating his rod inside me with his hand to stretch me even wider the second time around.

The remaining two of the tribe were allowed to take me together. One laid flat on the ground and the second pushed my asshole down onto his rod, which, thankfully, was a normal size. Then the Indian chief stood and watched with a big grin on his face, while two braves got on each side of me, each with a grip on one of my wrists and ankles and spread-eagled me. The remaining tribesman, who also thankfully didn't have a monster cock, then rolled my hips up and entered me, his cock running in along the top of the rod of the brave skewering me from below. The two of them didn't even bother to coordinate their rhythm of the double fucking them were giving me, but they both were so excited about the exoticness of the scenario that they both came rather quickly.

When the tribe was finished with me, the Indian chief sat close to me astride his magnificent stallion and pointed his rifle at my bruised and collapsed body, as the rest of the tribe members milled around my meager goods, looking, quite unsuccessfully for any souvenir of their adventure that might interest them.

Very quickly, though, the chieftain issued a stern command and the braves donned their loincloths and jumped onto their horses.

I knew we were at the moment of decision. The rifle lowered, looking to my eyes, to be centering more on me. I closed my eyes and something hit me in the chest. But, when I opened my eyes, the tribe was galloping into the distance and I didn't think I had any bullet holes in me. I looked down and saw that the Indian leader had gifted me with his feather- and turquoise-beaded breastplate, which I'm sure was about the only thing he owned in the world other than his horse. I had been gang banged, but I couldn't say I hadn't enjoyed it. And the bronze hunk had obviously enjoyed me too. I had to admit that this was a welcome to the West that I hadn't exactly anticipated.

Who's Jeff?

(Excerpt from the habu novel *Journey to Mirage*)

The cook had fed us with steak and cleaned up and left, leaving the two of us alone. My Santa Fe host put some soft music on and lit the fire. The wine had been excellent and I was feeling it in my head. The white bear-skin rug in front of the fire looked so inviting, and I wanted my head to stop spinning, so I laid down on that on my belly, facing the fire, staring into it and becoming quite mellow. My host left me there for a short time, letting the fire and the music and the soft rug and the buzz from the wine float me away.

He was back, in a short cotton robe. He must have been at least in his late forties or early fifties, but he'd aged well. His leg muscles were firm and I thought that he must have been an athlete at one time—and probably still worked out. As he leaned down to me, the front of the cotton robe opened and I saw a well-developed chest with a matting of salt-and-pepper curly hair running from his chest down in a thin line to where the lapels of the robe met.

"Some port or Cognac?" he asked in a rich baritone. His face was distinguished. A lawyer or a banker or corporate CEO. Even after two weeks, I didn't know. He spoke little about himself, showing more concern for me. So kind. If he hadn't found me at the side of the desert highway, brought me to this big house on the ridge above Santa Fe, and had a doctor in to look at me after what the beating and the hours on the sand by the highway had done to me . . .

The steel gray hair was expertly cut, a perfect-teeth smile. A slight scar under his left eye—his eyes were hazel and so alive—only served to emphasize how handsome his chiseled features were. Model handsome. A healthy Santa Fe tan smoothed out the laugh-line wrinkles.

"No thanks, Mr. Grimes. Another drop of alcohol and I'd go right to sleep."

"We couldn't have that, now, could we?" he answered, the low laugh conveying his mood. "And I've told you, it's Bill."

"I have trouble with that . . . Bill. You've been so kind, and there's such a divide between us."

"We must see what we can do about that too. Here, take a look at these. I work with photography. I'd like to know what you think."

He was handing a folder to me. I opened the cover to find a set of loose photographs. The ones on top were art shots—nudes—of a young, handsome youth. A bit younger than me. About nineteen, I'd guess. The photos were expertly done, although it wasn't the artistry of them that took my attention. Toward the bottom of the pile, the photographs were more explicit—much more explicit, I saw, as I leafed through to the bottom of the stack. And the youth wasn't alone. Grimes too was in these photos. I turned my head toward the sofa to see the cotton robe fall onto it in folds.

I shuddered and stiffened as his body came down on top of me, covering me full length. My torso was raised on my elbows, as I was fanning through the photographs. His hands laced in underneath me and he was unbuttoning my shirt and then pulling it off my arms.

"Relax," he whispered in my ears. "Just concentrate on the photos and let your body drift with me."

I did what I could to let the tension in my body flow away. "Mr. Grimes. Bill," I whispered.

"Sure you don't want to try the Cognac? I still have the taste of it in my mouth," he whispered back at me. He cupped my chin and turned my face toward his, and I tasted the rich, full-bodied nectar of the liquor in his kiss.

His hips were moving against my butt, and I felt the hardness of him through the material of my jeans and briefs.

I felt the palm of a hand on my belly and fingers working at the buttons of my jeans. Instinctively, without conscious control, I lifted my butt into his crotch as the zipper of my jeans was being pulled down. I wanted him to know there would be no struggle, no indecision, no holding back for whatever he wanted. He had paid for this in full. All of the hardness went out of my jaw and I opened my mouth totally to him.

The moaning I heard was almost detached, but I recognized it as mine.

He wouldn't release the hold of his lips on mine and in the wake of the taste of the Cognac, his tongue had invaded my mouth cavity. I could hardly breathe. But I didn't care if I couldn't. He was still possessing my mouth as he was pulling my jeans and briefs below my hips.

Skin on skin now below the belly. A hard dick inside my butt crack, stroking up and down on the rim of my hole. I shuddered and groaned and he released my mouth and gave a low, comfortable laugh.

"The photos. Concentrate on the photos," he said.

I returned my attention to the photographs, pushing through the ones of the handsome youth solo, down to the ones of the youth with Grimes. He was moving down the line of my back now. Kissing and licking my shoulder blades, while one hand pulled my jeans and briefs down and off my legs and the other one worked my nipples and then came down to palm my belly as his lips reached the mounds of my butt cheeks.

His teeth nipped at the sensitive skin of my rump and I groaned as I heard the low, appreciative laugh again. I felt a light slap on each cheek and they were being squeezed and nipped again. A hand went between my thighs and pulled my cock and balls through. I tried to widen my stance, but he moved his forearms to trap my thighs close together, tightly against my dick. A hand possessed my cock and slowly stroked down.

"Bill, Bill," I whispered.

"Ah the divide narrows, doesn't it? Surely there will be no trouble with first names now," he answered back. And then that arousing laugh again. He clearly was enjoying this.

"Do you like the photos?" he asked. "Don't the two of us make the smashing pair?"

"Yes." It was a whisper.

"Does the lad look happy? Am I fucking him well?"

"Yes." It was a whimper, followed with a moan.

He had taken both hands and was spreading and squeezing my butt cheeks with them. When he blew across my hole, I shivered and groaned.

"So nice. Such a rosy bud. And already opening."

"Bill," I whispered. "Bill." And then "Bill!" as he kissed the hole and his tongue started working into me. I writhed under him for countless minutes as he tongued my hole and worked my cock with his hand. Intermittently he moved his mouth down to my cock and balls and gave suck, and during these intervals his fingers invaded my channel and found my prostate.

"Bill, Bill! I'm gonna come. You're gonna make me—"

"Oh, I hope so, Rick, he muttered. I certainly hope so." And then he laughed again.

And I came.

He covered my back fully with his body again and his cock was rubbing inside my cheeks once more. I raised my pelvis to him. Presenting to him. Wanting him. Wanting him to know I wanted him. "Bill," I whined.

"Ah, are you ready? Do you want me inside you? Permission to fuck? Jeff wants his Bill?"

"Yes," I whimpered, all of my senses focused on the shaft rubbing across my hole, not even fully catching the reference to a Jeff.

He went up on his knees, reaching over to the sofa. I heard the slight rustle of the condom packet as he opened it, and then I felt the coldness of the lubricant he poured liberally between my cheeks and worked into my opening with probing fingers. My chest was flat on the floor, my cheek against the photos of Grimes fucking the young man, my arms splayed out at my side. I was up on my knees, though, with my quivering butt raised to him, my legs spread.

Fuck me, fuck me now, was what I was trying to convey.

He crouched over me, pulling my chest up, me now on all fours. The cock was rubbing inside my crack again, sending electric impulses as it stroked again and again against my hole.

"Please. Bill, Please!" I begged.

He laughed. And then I felt the bulb presented at my hole and he was slowly pushing into me. I gasped and my eyes started to water and both my elbows and my knees began to quiver and to give way. But Bill, crouched over my midsection and continuing to enter me, held me up with strong arms wrapped under my rib cage. I felt his lips at my cheeks, and I turned my face to him, letting him possess my mouth again— masking my groans and moans.

Who would have known he was so thick and hard— and that it would take so much length of my channel for him to bottom?

Coming out of the kiss, my face was suspended over the photographs. The one on top was of Grimes crouched over the hips of the young man, who was on all fours—on a white bear-skin rug in front of a fireplace; this fireplace. The expression on the young man's face was one of ecstasy. Bill was looking into the camera with an expression that almost conveyed, "At last; in at last."

Only half hidden below that was a photo of the young man on his back on the same furry rug and Grimes kneeling between his thighs, knees under and raising the young man's buttocks, Grimes fisting the youth's slim ankles and holding his legs up and out, wide. I could see a good two inches of the root of a thick cock at the young man's channel opening. And again, that "gone to paradise" expression on the young man's face.

A third photo was of Grimes completely sheathed, the youth's legs running up Grimes's torso now, his hands reaching around Grime's thick waist and clutching the older man's thin butt cheeks close to him with fingers digging into the flesh, obviously trying to take in every centimeter of the cock. Eyes wild, mouth gaping open, and tongue hanging out. I trembled in anticipation.

He stroked me so long and hard that my elbows and knees did give out and, with a laugh, he rode me to the rug and kept on riding. He was babbling as he fucked me, and I occasionally heard the name "Jeff" spoken. But never the name "Rick."

Fucking me at such depth, and so filling. My channel walls undulating across the shaft as it mastered me. Throbbing, hot, relentless. Strong hands pulling my thighs in tight. Oh, god, the tightness. The almost despair as he pulls back. Oh, no, don't leave me! Oh, shit, yes! at the long hard plunge back to the depths. Yes! Again. Oh, yes! And again. Oh Shit! And AGAIN. Paradise. Faster now—stroke, stroke, hold, stroke—making me pant and writhe against his strong hands and moan—and beg for it to go on and on.

I felt him tighten and take in a long breath and then—with my channel trying, unsuccessfully, to close on his cock and keep him inside me—he pulled out of me, and I groaned at the loss of him and heard the condom being ripped away and then felt the flow of him on the small of my back.

He covered my back with his torso again and continued moving on top of me, stroking the small of my back with his cock through his cum. He hands glided along my arms and took my wrists. I turned my lips to him again. His prisoner for as long as he wanted.

"I'm sorry if you weren't expecting that this evening," he whispered in my ear when he once more let loose of my lips.

"I don't know what took you so long," I answered, with a sigh.

"I thought perhaps I assumed so much. But you are so beautiful and sexy. I couldn't help myself. Hardly a good host."

"You saved my life," I whispered back. "And . . . and the perfect host. Almost too polite, I was beginning to think."

He turned me on my back, my head resting in the pile of his photographs. He covered my body with his, his cock lying against my own between our still-heaving bellies. I looked down the line of his body. His barrel chest with the matting of salt-and-pepper gray standing out in moist curls and below that a still-flat, hard belly—even at his age. I wanted to run my hands through the matting on his chest, to search out the taut nipples I saw hiding there between the curls of the hair. But he had his fists wrapped around my wrists and they were trapped on either side of my shoulders. So, instead, I dipped and raised my face into his chest. I found a nipple almost immediately and sucked it in hard as he gasped and then I nipped at it, which produced a yelp from his mouth and an engorging surge in his cock.

Releasing one of my wrists, his hand grabbed my head under the chin and forced it back into the pile of photographs and his mouth was hungrily attacking mine, his tongue invading, every bit as filling and probing as his cock had been. I gasped and nearly gagged.

I wrapped my legs around his, my heels rubbing up and down his hard calves. His free hand snaked between our bellies before I could completely push in as close as I could to every inch of him. The hand wrapped our two cocks together. And he stroked our shafts and worked my mouth with his until, with a lurch and a shudder, I came again.

He released my mouth and cock then. I could feel he was fully hard again. Amazing for his age. Not so much, though, considering the strength and power of his fuck. He raised his torso off mine a bit and looked down into my eyes. He was smiling that melting smile of his—the one I saw in the photographs when it was clear that he had mastered the young man to exhaustion.

"That's not fair," he said in a tone of false pout. "You've gone twice and I only once. Would you mind terribly if—?"

"I hoped you would," I whispered breathlessly, my mind possessed by what I'd seen in the photographs, as he knelt between my legs, pulled my buttocks up on top of his thighs, and reached over on the sofa for another condom packet. I lifted one of my legs up his torso to hook an ankle on his right shoulder while I watched him roll the condom on his cock and prepared to raise the other to his left shoulder when he was crowned, positioning myself to roll up my rump to receive the deepest thrusts I could eke out of him. I spied three more condom packets on the sofa and shivered in anticipation. I had seen other photos of other fuck positions the young man obviously had enjoyed.

But who, I was wondering, who the fuck was Jeff?

~

About the Author

Habu is one of the pen names of a former supersonic spy jet pilot, intelligence agent, male model, movie actor, and diplomat. A wild youth in South East Asia was spent enjoying whatever sexual opportunities came his way, and much of his gay male writing is about recalling incidents from those days and inventing ones he'd perhaps have liked to experience. He now leads a very quiet and ordinary happily married family life.

An American, he is a published mainstream novelist and short story writer under another name and in another dimension of his life. He has written or cowritten (with Sabb) approaching 1,000 published short stories and over 100 published erotica e-books, primarily of gay fiction but also memoir, straight fiction and ménage fiction.

His hand and creative writing can be seen in stories and books by habu, sr71plt, Dirk Hessian, Shabbu, and Stephen Kessel—among unrevealed others that might surprise readers.

The fictionalized GM memoir *Flying High, Diving Deep* is loosely based on his life experiences. He can be found at the adults only gay male site www.BarbarianSpy.com, which he shares with Sabb.

Our authors always like to receive feedback, and appreciate it when readers post reviews at Goodreads and other sites.

BarbarianSpy
FOR LITERARY HEAT

Not all books listed below may currently be on release.
* indicates the book is available in paperback and e-book.

BOOKS BY DIRK HESSIAN
Xtreme Erotica
The King's Men
Shores of Tripoli
Prophecy of Noto
Pretender's Fate

General Erotica/Romance
Fire Down the Valley
Constantinople*
The Beautiful Way*
Blue and Gray
Colonel's Treasure
Beginning of Time
Labyrinth

BOOKS BY HABU
Gay Erotica
Memoir Faction
Flying High, Diving Deep*
Xtreme Erotica
Apyko: The Greek Pimp
Visits of the Schlange
Second Coming: Emile La Cour Unleashed
Vortex: Sacrificed by Curiosity*
Dark Angel Sounding *(in e-book & included in
Sounding:Ultimate Control Paperback)**
Sounding: Ultimate Control (*Print Only*)*
Sounding Five *(in e-book & included in
Sounding:Ultimate Control paperback)*
General Erotica
Romance
Snowy, Snowy Nights (Christmas Romance)

Four Coins
Lower Than the Heart
Brambleton
Gotta Keep Trying
Finding Amnad
Platres Conclave
Other Novels/Novellas
Cruising Gigolo
Prepared in Cape Verdi
Gilded Cage
House on Park
Anything for Ambition
Dance of the Ravishers
Hard Knocks U*
My Neighbor's Spa*
Man's Man: Tales of a High Priced Gay Hooker*
Trip Money
Clint Folsom Mysteries Compendium Volume 1*
Death to Blonds - Stolen Judgment (Clint Folsom Mystery)
Clint Folsom Mysteries Compendium Volume 2*
The Indian Doctor
Sailorboy
Home to Fire Island
Choke Hold
Gay Erotica Anthologies
Doubled*
Doubled Again*
Tails in the Tropics*
Tails in the Med*
Tails in the West*
Rough Riders*
Grab Bag 1*
Grab Bag 2*
Grab Bag 3*
Grab Bag 4*
Grab Bag 5*
Beyond the Beaded Curtain*

Habu's Christmas Balls
The Sporting Life*
Fetish Galore!*
Literary Gay Erotica
Cairo Surrender*
The Handyman*
Homeward Bound
Journey to Mirage*
Menage Erotica
Cruising Gigolo
13 Ways for Halloween
Luther*
The Indian Prince
Literary GLBT Fiction
Summer of Denial
BOOKS BY SHABBU
Finding Jason
Dirty Pool
Operation Black Jade
Cigars!*
Angel in the Barn
Gayly Complicated*
Despoiling David
The Tree of Idleness*
I Met a Man
The Interview
Rough Road to Happiness
BOOKS BY SABB
Hiring in Hollywood
The Legend of Holleystone Grange
Surprise Encounters
She is He
Wrong Man
Loyal to his King
Barbarian Tales - Book One - Traveler's Tales*
Barbarian Tales - Book Two - Journeys Begin*
Barbarian Tales - Book Three - The Inheritance*
Barbarian Tales - Book Four - Road to Persepolis*